DAUGHTER OF PERDITION BOOK TWO

THE RISE

Published by Upside Down Red Umbrella
First Edition: May 2020

Cover Art by Upside Down Red Umbrella
Digital Art by C. Cato
Edited by 34 Editing, H. Hooks

GLOSSARY

adelphós — brother
StudyLight.org, s.v. "adelphós," accessed January 25, 2020,
https://www.studylight.org/lexicons/greek/80.html
/ad-el-fos'/
noun

akouó — sense of hearing
StudyLight.org, s.v. "akouó," accessed May 22, 2020,
https://www.studylight.org/lexicons/greek/191.html
/ak-oo'-o/
verb

apoloúō — to wash off or away
StudyLight.org, s.v. "apoloúō," accessed January 25, 2020,
https://www.studylight.org/lexicons/greek/628.html
/ap-ol-oo'-o/
verb

atmis — vapor
Bible Hub, s.v. "atmis," accessed January 25, 2020,
https://biblehub.com/greek/822.htm
/at-mece'/
noun

basílissa — queen
StudyLight.org, s.v. "basílissa," accessed January 25, 2020,
https://www.studylight.org/lexicons/greek/938.html
/bas-il'-is-sah/
*noun: **basílissa**; plural noun: **basílissas***

bibliothēkē — library
/bi-blē-ō-'thē-k/
noun

daimónion — demon
StudyLight.org, s.v. "daimónion," accessed January 25, 2020,
https://www.studylight.org/lexicons/greek/1140.html
/dahee-mon'-ee-on/
*noun: **daimónion**; plural noun: **daimónia***

déchomai — to accept/receive
StudyLight.org, s.v. "déchomai," accessed January 25, 2020,
https://www.studylight.org/lexicons/greek/1209.html
/dekh'-om-ahee/
verb

déō doúlos — bond-slave whom is bound to a queen
/dā-ō doo'-los/
*noun: **déō doúlos**; plural noun: **déō doúloi***
verb: déō; to "bind" or "bind together"
Geoffrey W. Bromiley, "Theological Dictionary of The New
Testament," accessed January 25, 2020,
https://www.scribd.com/document/268809488/THEOLOGICAL-
Dictionary-of-the-New-Testament
noun: doúlos; someone who belongs to another; a bond-slave.
Bible Hub, s.v. "doúlos," accessed January 25, 2020,
https://biblehub.com/greek/1401.htm

geúomai — sense of taste
StudyLight.org, s.v. "geúomai," accessed May 22, 2020,
https://www.studylight.org/lexicons/greek/1089.html
/ghyoo'-om-ahee/
verb

grigori — informal, sometimes derogatory, alternative title for The
Watchers
/grə'-gôr-ē/
*noun: **grigori**; plural noun: **grigors***

haîmaboúlomai — blood desire or "lust"
/hah'ee-mah boo'-lom-ahee/
noun: haîma; blood
StudyLight.org, s.v. "haîma," accessed January 25, 2020,
https://www.studylight.org/lexicons/greek/129.html
verb: boúlomai; to desire
StudyLight.org, s.v. "boúlomai," accessed January 25, 2020,
https://www.studylight.org/lexicons/greek/1014.html

háptomai — sense of touch
StudyLight.org, s.v. "háptomai," accessed May 22, 2020,
https://www.studylight.org/lexicons/greek/680.html
/hap'-tom-ahee/
verb

hélkō — to draw or drag off by inward power, lead, impel
StudyLight.org, s.v. "hélkō," accessed January 25, 2020,
https://www.studylight.org/lexicons/greek/1670.html
/hel'-ko/
Verb

Huiói Géenna — Sons of Perdition (The Fallen)
Bible Hub, s.v. "Géenna," accessed January 25, 2020,
https://biblehub.com/greek/1067.htm
/hwee-oy' gheh'-en-nah/
noun: ***huioí*** *géenna*
huioi; sons of God
géenna; symbolic name for the final place of punishment of the
ungodly

huiós — son (shortened usage for Son of Perdition in this book)
StudyLight.org, s.v. "huiós," accessed January 25, 2020,
https://www.studylight.org/lexicons/greek/5207.html
/hwee-os'/
noun: ***huiós****; plural noun:* ***huiói***
author's note: shortened title for a Son of Perdition

krisis — a sentence of condemnation
StudyLight.org, s.v. "krisis," accessed May 22, 2020,
https://www.studylight.org/lexicons/greek/2920.html
/kree'-sis/
noun

lógos — a word, uttered by a living voice, embodies a conception or
idea
StudyLight.org, s.v. "lógos," accessed January 25, 2020,
https://www.studylight.org/lexicons/greek/3056.html
/log'-os/
noun

mesítēs — mediator
StudyLight.org, s.v. "mesítēs," accessed January 25, 2020,
https://www.studylight.org/lexicons/greek/3316.html
/mes-ee'-tace/
noun: ***mesítēs****; plural noun:* ***undefined***

nýmphē — marriageable maiden
StudyLight.org, s.v. "nýmphē," accessed January 25, 2020,
https://www.studylight.org/lexicons/greek/3565.html
/noom-fay'/
noun: ***nýmphē****; plural noun:* ***nýmphēs***

oikía — family
StudyLight.org, s.v. "oikía," accessed January 25, 2020,
https://www.studylight.org/lexicons/greek/938.html
/oy-kee'-ah/
noun: ***oikía****; plural noun:* ***oikías***

ópsis — sense of sight
StudyLight.org, s.v. "ópsis," accessed May 22, 2020,
https://www.studylight.org/lexicons/greek/3799.html
/op'-sis/
verb

ósphrēsis — sense of smell
StudyLight.org, s.v. "ósphrēsis," accessed May 22, 2020,
https://www.studylight.org/lexicons/greek/3750.html
/os'-fray-sis/
verb

paidagōgós — teacher/guide
StudyLight.org, s.v. "paidagōgós," accessed January 25, 2020,
https://www.studylight.org/lexicons/greek/3807.html
/pahee-dag-o-gos'/
noun: ***paidagōgós****; plural noun:* ***paidagōgói***

parakaló — you're welcome
StudyLight.org, s.v. "parakaló," accessed May 22, 2020,
https://www.studylight.org/lexicons/greek/3870.html
/par-ak-al-o'/
verb

phýrama — paste
StudyLight.org, s.v. "phýrama," accessed January 25, 2020,
https://www.studylight.org/lexicons/greek/5445.html
/foo'-ram-ah /
Noun
author's note: used in the book as a term for leave-in hair-conditioning paste

próskairos — temporary
StudyLight.org, s.v. "próskairos," accessed January 25, 2020,
https://www.studylight.org/lexicons/greek/4340.html
/pros'-kahee-ros/
*adjective: **próskairos**; as a plural noun: **próskairoi***
author's note: adj. but used as a noun

pýlē — a gate access or entrance
StudyLight.org, s.v. "pýlē," accessed January 25, 2020,
https://www.studylight.org/lexicons/greek/4439.html
/poo'-lay/
Noun

rhábdos — staff
StudyLight.org, s.v. "rhábdos," accessed January 25, 2020,
https://www.studylight.org/lexicons/greek/4464.html
/hrab'-dos/
Noun

sas efharistó — I thank you
StudyLight.org, s.v. "sas efharistó," accessed May 22, 2020,
https://www.greekpod101.com/blog/2017/11/27/how-to-say-thank-you-in-greek
/sas' yoo-har-es-to'/
Noun

sikários — assassin
StudyLight.org, s.v. "sikários," accessed January 25, 2020,
https://www.studylight.org/lexicons/greek/4607.htm
/sik-ar'-ee-os/
*noun: **sikários**; plural noun: **sikárioi***

The Watchers — guards
    "In the Book of Enoch, the watchers are angels dispatched to Earth to watch over the humans. They soon begin to lust for human women…. The offspring of these unions are the Nephilim, savage giants who pillage the earth and endanger humanity."
    "Watcher_(angel)," Wikipedia, accessed January 25, 2020, https://en.wikipedia.org/wiki/Watcher_(angel)

CHAPTER ONE

A soft thud stirs me from light sleep, and a soft smile to match creeps up on my lips. Careful not to wake my sleeping giant, I ease off the pallet and tiptoe to the watchtower's open window. After a quick backward glance, I stick my hand out, palm the outside wall, and follow its rigid grooves until the part of Blaze's arrow that is not embedded in the stone grazes my finger tip. Wrapping my hand around the wooden stick, I quietly yank it out, close my eyes, pull some energy from deep in the veins of Ceteris, and pop to a spot outside the watchtower fifty or more feet below.

"Holy fuck," Blaze explicates quietly — well, as quietly as one can when startled. "Every. Fucking. Time," he grumbles. "I know you're coming, but you scare me every time."

"Keep using 'fucking' and 'coming' in nearby sentences like that and something *else* is going to start happening every time." Just to deliver the point more clearly, I let my fingertips drag over his shoulder while returning the arrow to his quiver.

Usually, Blaze doesn't respond to my not-so-subtle teasing. This time, however, he does. Talk about startling.

He turns around and looks me up and down, pausing for a brief moment about midway. "I can't imagine you'll get any rounder than you already are. They'll not continue to make you wait after the baby comes. Then, maybe you'll finally stop pestering *me*."

"See now, I thought you were going to say something much more exciting. Like, 'Bend over, and let me show you how I really spear things,' for instance. Instead, you finally respond and all it serves to do is make me feel more frustrated about my situation."

"Feeling sorry for yourself?" he asks with a smile and a wink, walking off into the night.

Struggling to catch up, I huff out an impatient "Yes."

Only a few astral rounds had passed when Oryn explained that the baby inside me was growing much faster than they do in the mortal realm — based on the visual evidence of my rapidly protruding stomach, of course.

Brax had already been in a constant state of panic ever since Kirian announced — shortly after his partial shift into a daimónion — that there was undoubtedly a being growing inside me. As my first déō doúlos to earn an oikía power, Kirian's heightened hearing made it easy to pick up a heartbeat that wasn't my own. "Fast and strong," he'd explained. When my stomach plumped and rounded bigger and bigger each day, Brax's anxiety ballooned right with it.

No one could convince him that his offspring wouldn't be a monster — that it wouldn't kill me during birth — and the rapid growth did nothing to assuage those fears.

Blaze's chuckling floats to me on a light gust of wind, reminding me of the conversation at hand. My oikía — my bonded family — which officially consists of Kirian, Oryn, and Brax had mutually decided that "rest cure" would be the best course of action. This rest cure, in turn, includes a strict "no-fucking" rule.

Which, in my humble opinion, happened far too soon after I'd only just begun to experience the pleasantries of union in that way.

Not much for rules, Blaze has been one of my few sources of entertainment in the meantime. Even despite him getting in trouble after the little stunt we pulled in order to save Kirian from a soulless and mindless life as a true daimónion. That, or a one-way trip to The Void. In his daimónion form, he kept crossing over the boundary meant to separate those beasts from the village, in turn, provoking the village assassins — the sikárioi, like Blaze — to track him down and kill him.

Gone.

Forever.

In the glint of moonlight, my gaze travels down Blaze's flank and comes to a rest on the deep scar that spans from his hip to the upper portion of his outer thigh. In choosing to help me, not only was he putting a basílissa in danger, but he was also risking the village. Oryn — one of Ceteris's few mediators — set the punishment. The hélkō carried it through.

Still, at least once every few sunsets, Blaze whisks me away into the night for bow lessons.

Tonight, once at his chosen location, he stops and turns to face me. As though he'd been listening to my thoughts throughout the walk, his black eyes meet mine and he steps forward once, takes in a deep breath, opens his mouth to say something but closes it and removes the bow from his shoulder. Holding it out at an arm's distance, he jiggles the bow, indicating for me to take it.

"Your stance is still terrible," he announces.

My previously straightened shoulders curve inward as he pulls out an arrow and hands that to me as well. "If it's not fixed by now, I worry it never will be."

Blaze shrugs and gestures for me to step forward with the curve of two fingers. "Stance is the hardest to perfect. You'll get there," he explains, walking around to press against my back.

As I've done hundreds of times now, I set the arrow and lift the bow. Blaze's hand comes to my waist and moves down over my hip until it's on the side of my upper thigh. He then lightly taps me with his fingers. "Close your legs — just a bit," he instructs, pressing his palm inward.

I bring the bow down to my side with an impatient sigh. "Maybe if my stomach wasn't as round as a hut, I'd be able to close my legs 'just a bit.'" Also, having his hand so close to the part of my body that is lacking the most attention as of late does wild things to my insides.

Blaze chuckles and the warmth of it travels over my shoulder. "Maybe," he whispers, moving his hand back up my side and over my rib cage before rerouting and slipping over my bow hand to remove it from my grip. "Though, I'm certain even if you weren't as round as a hut you'd still not be able to close your legs." He loops the bow string over his shoulder and returns the arrow to the quiver. "Let's do something different tonight."

A zing of excitement zooms through me. "Okay!" I respond with a bit too much enthusiasm.

Blaze rolls his eyes and shakes his head. "Not... *that.*"

Again, I deflate a little. "You know, everything about my body is incredibly heightened right now. My breasts are heavy and sensitive. Between my thighs is warm and tingly. Even my skin prickles at every little touch. It's torture."

"Soon, Basílissa. The baby is coming soon."

"How can you be so sure?"

"Because you can scarcely walk, for one." Blaze scoops my hand in his and leads me through the forest in a direction I'm fairly certain he hasn't taken me before. Our pace is slower than usual, because he's right: I can scarcely walk.

"How is the search going?" I inquire even despite assuming I'll get the same answer I always do. With Kirian being part daimónion, he can now hear the call of the lógos in his mind — stronger and more frequently than I do. In my case, Belíar can usually only penetrate my conscious thoughts when I am weak from a lack of energy.

When Kirian had heard Belíar's voice that astral round of his transformation — and in the astral rounds since — he was convinced the voice wasn't traveling across realms from Tartarus where Belíar supposedly resides. Rather, the lógos was nearby, originating from somewhere here in Ceteris. That same voice, calling to the daimónia. Gathering them.

Occasionally, Blaze's attention darts to the sides or behind us... watchful. That is until a spot, different than its surroundings, comes into sight; an open area, clear and visible due to the lack of tree coverage, reveals itself as a light-blue expanse of land, highlighted under streams of moonlight.

Instead of walking into the bare area, he stops us short, lets go of my hand, and removes his quiver. I watch in silence as he fists all the arrows and pulls them out, then props the quiver against his shins and uses his other hand to dig something out of the very bottom.

Before I can tell what it is, he tucks it under his arm, returns the fist-full of arrows to their rightful spot, and slings the quiver onto his back. From there, he removes the collected item from under his arm and, with a couple quick shakes, a thin cloth opens up, billowing in the breeze.

He spreads it over the ground, walks forward, takes my hand, and guides me to the cloth, helping to ease me down onto it... knowing that with the bigger I've gotten, the more difficult it has become to sit on the ground.

I maneuver so that I'm cross-legged, and he joins me on the cloth, placing the bow beside him but choosing to continue wearing the quiver.

We sit there in silence for too long before impatience gets the better of me. "Wh—"

Blaze clasps my mouth. He lets go and with a lowered voice leans toward my ear and says, "Shhh, you'll frighten her."

Eyes wide, I return my attention to the glade. The only "hers" in Ceteris are basílissas, and I'm not sure how fond I am knowing one is in the forest near my territory.

A four-legged creature, smaller than a daimónion, strolls into the clearing. A small gasp escapes my lips, and I cover my mouth so Blaze doesn't have to again. Dropping my hand, I side-whisper, "She's beautiful." The creature is a tawny brown, her coloring a bit like mine.

"A deer," Blaze returns with a side-whisper of his own. The deer's head turns toward us, and everything except her ears freeze; the tips flick and turn, first straight forward, then to the woods where she'd come from. Like the two of us are interconnected, my own ears pick up a sound, too, and my attention moves to compensate. The deer's attention, on the other hand, still remains riveted straight ahead, her round, brown eyes trained on us.

"She sees us," I breathe.

"Yes," Blaze agrees. "Shhh... watch."

Her tail flicks, displaying white underneath. She looks behind her just in time to keep a careful eye on the much smaller deer now entering the clearing — this one covered in white spots and wobbling a bit as it moves forward.

Reflexively, my hand goes to my stomach. The female deer looks in our direction again and the two of us stare at each other, an understanding passing between mothers. My eyes fog, and I lean my head on Blaze's shoulder. "Blaze..."

"Hm?"

"I'm scared."

When I'd rested against him, Blaze had tensed, but he softens beneath me now and brings his hand to the other side of my head. "Do you think she was scared when the foal was born?" he asks.

I blink through my foggy vision. "Do animals feel fear?"

"Oh yes," Blaze says. "But only when spooked, or something threatens them or their babies. The animals here are living, just like humans in the mortal realm. They feed off the plants and other, smaller animals that are fed by the energy you and the other queens provide the land. To them, birthing their young is a natural part of their existence. Nothing to be scared of." Blaze surprises me by placing his other hand over the one of mine that now rests on my stomach. "If birthing young wasn't a natural part of your existence, you wouldn't be pregnant right now."

Blaze lets go of my head, and I sit up straight again even though I wish he'd let me stay like that just a bit longer.

"The foal was just born... earlier today."

"Already walking?" There's no need for us to continue whispering; the mother and baby seem uncaring of our presence as they graze on the ground's nutrients. "Raener told Oryn that he learned human babies don't walk for many moon-cycles."

"Every species grows and thrives differently," he explains. I don't bother to ask how my child will grow and thrive, because none of us know. Not even the paidagōgói in their ultimate wisdom. "But somehow, in most cases, the mother has a built-in intuition that helps guide her... if she's willing to listen. This mother, for example" — he inclines his head toward the deer — "was alone when she birthed her foal. No one to tell her what to do. Yet, here she is, both baby and mother healthy and strong."

"Thank you," I whisper, turning to face him. His eyes meet mine for a fleeting moment, until the baby moves and a large lump rolls beneath the surface of my skin. Blaze jerks his hand away, and I laugh. "The baby is thankful for the pep talk, too, I suppose."

Blaze bows his head. "My pleasure."

The mother deer and foal bound away. Blaze is on his feet, both bow and arrow set and aimed toward the clearing in an instant. Unable to stand quick enough to protect myself, I choose to stay still instead. Breathing heightened, I watch as Blaze searches the dark of the woods for a time before finally bringing the bow to his side and returning the arrow to his quiver.

"Time to get you back to the tower before Brax wakes up," he states, putting the bow over his shoulder

15

and reaching down toward me with both hands. I take hold of them, and together, the two of us haul me up.

Usually, our parting is a bit more mutual and casual. Something has him on edge right now, though, and in my compromised state, I'm not much for sticking around to find out.

"I can travel from here, if you have something to take care of."

Blaze nods.

Without further ado, I create a travel pýlē.

Unbeknownst to Blaze, however, the tower isn't my next destination.

Not yet.

CHAPTER TWO

Blaze

Tension, no doubt at least the weight of that foal, rolls off my shoulders and back when she leaves, and I twist my neck side-to-side. I hadn't realized we'd been here for so long. Too long.

Doing so becomes easier every time we're together, though. Every time, she gets closer, testing those boundaries.

Every time… I let her.

Even though I know it won't end well.

I continue having her believe she's not yet practiced enough to wield a bow of her own — that she needs more time. But the truth is, she's damn near better at it than I am. As soon as she knows the truth, though, that's when our hidden meetings will end. If not sooner.

As much as I pretend to gripe about having to teach her, I don't want to stop. Not yet. Not ever.

"Losing your touch, Sikários?" Kirian's voice meets my ears. I was so wrapped up in Adrestia that our time together encroached on my meeting with the half-breed daimónion.

"Of course not, there was plenty of touching happening."

Kirian laughs, the sound downright haunting — part huiós, part dark being, part beast. "She's going to be displeased when I'm not at the beach waiting for her."

The two of us have an arrangement: he watches out for Adrestia and me during our training sessions, and I keep an eye on them when she sneaks away to the beach to meet with him afterward.

After all, if we're going to be stupid, might as well be smart about it.

"We'll talk and walk this time, hm?" I suggest. Even still, he'll be late for their meetup, as he usually bounds away and can sprint almost as fast as she can travel. Despite the beach and the forest being on opposite sides of the territory.

Kirian grunts in agreement, and we start our trek through the village. "The heartbeat is strong," he begins.

"She didn't say anything, but I could feel her stomach hardening and softening beneath our hands. The only indicator of this new change was when she'd mentioned being scared. She knows the baby is coming soon, too."

"Yeah, I heard." The daimónion's clawed hand lifts and rubs the back of his neck. "What you did… with the deer… that was great. Thanks. Thanks for helping her in that way."

"When you moved out there, I was afraid you'd started a—"

"Yeah… I'd guessed." The two of us fall silent while we pass the main portion of huts. "My control is getting better, though. Every hunt."

Kirian and I are realms different, but one thing connects us: essence. I like to make it disappear… he, on the other hand, likes to consume it. Didn't take long for him to realize that the land doesn't nourish him like it does the huiói.

Unfortunately, when it comes to his survival here, he got that part from the daimónia rather than the

18

huiói. Daimónia feed on already-consumed energy. Whether by attacking a déō doúlos, via a queen's energy directly, or from a travel pýlē — to which he's been stealing a small amount from Adrestia every time she travels on evenings like this one. Since attacking a déō doúlos is out of the question, and she doesn't travel enough for it to fulfill his needs, he desperately began to seek out alternative measures.

Creatures, much like the deer and her foal. Hogs and other beings of the sort work, too. Unlike how predators feed in the mortal realm, however, all he needs is the energy within their essence. To get it, he discovered he could use his canines to pierce the creature and consume it that way. If he's careful and leaves enough, eventually the creature will recover, reanimated by the land's energy once more.

In the beginning, it wasn't like that, though. Most of his prey did not survive. "Have you fed?" I ask, always on the ready for him to say *no*, leaving me to stop him short of his meetup with Adrestia.

"Of course," he responds.

Generally we leave it at that, but something is weighing on his mind, so I wait patiently for his next comment. "The lógos is reaching out more often lately. Stronger."

I'll admit, I begrudgingly agreed to be Kirian's confidant for selfish purposes at first. The lógos being the primary reason for me to interact with a daimónion in any capacity other than putting an arrow through it.

I never expected to enjoy the companionship.

My body wants to come to a dead stop, turn to him, and listen with rapt attention. Instead, we continue walking, and I give him a casual, "Huh."

Truth is, the sikárioi have been running themselves into the ground trying to find where all the new daimónia are coming from — and, of course, where the lógos is originating, if not from Tartarus where Belíar belongs.

Of course, only a small portion of the sikárioi are taking it seriously. Belíar isn't capable of traveling between realms.

Neither was a mortal. Nor another female.

After an extended silence, I inquire further. The daimónion's hands move to his nub-covered head, and he slaps his skull repeatedly, squeezing his eyes shut. When he opens them, they're the red of his daimónion. I don't move my hand to the bow just yet, but my fingers twitch at my side… ready.

When his eyes turn back, I squeeze my fists tight and loosen them to relieve the built-up tension. Right now, the situation doesn't call for any further poking. Not just before he's about to see Adrestia. Keeping him as calm as possible is preferable.

We'd easily avoided the topic of Adrestia fucking him on the forest floor in front of my team and her forming oikía, but now seems an opportune time to mess with him about it… if for no other reason than to calm the beast.

"So…" I clear my throat. "What's it like fucking a basílissa in the middle of a war zone?"

That snaps him right out of his mental battle in an instant. He coughs and looks down at me. "Other than being terrified I was going to kill her, it was… delicious." His tongue snakes out as if he's reliving the experience.

"Whoa there. Keep that damn thing in your mouth around me."

Kirian laughs, that deep, booming sound I swear I'll never be able to hear without a shiver running down my spine. Obviously, that had been his first taste at what his body would need to survive, so it comes as no surprise the flow of her essence was the part that stood out most to him.

Me, on the other hand. Watching her ride his cock... Belíar, I wanted it to be me—

No. No I did not.

I shake my head and squeeze my eyes shut tight to erase the image from my mind.

When she'd willingly offered up her essence to a daimónion, right there in front of a bunch of essence-hungry sikárioi, little did she know every single one of us had our weapons drawn and aimed right at his head. Ready for the kill shot.

"Why did you help her?" Kirian asks, broaching why I was out there with her in the first place.

"I owed a certain paidagōgós a favor. Alright, Daimónion... I need to go kill something, and I can't do that until I'm done watching your back during your time with Adrestia. Time for us to part ways."

Kirian's eyebrow rises. "That'll only make it worse, you know," he states, not at all misunderstanding my need.

"Not sure what you're getting at, Beast."

He rolls his eyes. "Yeah, okay. Watch us, go kill something... then sleep it off. Since that's all your useless cock can do anyway."

A low growl resonates in my chest — the result of too many years spent in the woods. The Fucking Maker. Gave us desires, but absolutely no way of appeasing them unless a queen does so. That... or time. Time we have plenty of. Maybe.

Problem is... those desires have gotten a lot worse since she planted that damn bond-call and my traitorous body accepted it.

CHAPTER THREE

Adrestia

K irian's deep breathing and solid heartbeat meet my ears before he appears on the sandy hilltop, which isn't at all unusual, especially since he projects his hearing oikía power well before he ever gets near me — as a safety precaution, I suppose. So I can be on guard, knowing his daimónion is coming, too.

Of course, since I'm apparently fearless — to an extent — nothing about Kirian and his daimónion frightens me.

"Something got you worked up?" Kirian makes his presence known with that rugged, gravelly voice I love so much. Before the shift, his voice was already deep; add his daimónion into the mix, and it's like fucking, minus the fucking part. Sound-fucking. And when he laughs… the sensation reverberates along the soles of my feet and between my toes, not unlike the squish of the damp sand caressing them now.

"No, of course not. Why would you think such a thing?" I dismiss his uncanny ability to sense my heightened desires after those secret meetings with Blaze. There's probably nothing more to them than a simple need to orgasm. Certainly not a bond-call.

Of course, when I casually suggested he become a próskairos — *my* próskairos — since he keeps insisting he's not interested in being a déō doúlos, he just laughed and laughed and laughed.

As a result, every night after our time together…
there's a pent-up need balled low and hot inside me.

"Why would I think such a thing?!" Kirian
mocks, aghast. "Well, your heart rate, for one. It's going
a little wild." He sits beside me on the seaside, brushing
his arm against my shoulder before lowering his voice
for the next part, "Just like it always does when you're
desperate for a fuck." His voice returns to normal,
"Which is quite often lately."

"Well, yes, that's because my men keep refusing
me." There's a possibility I'm pouting, but grown
women — queens — probably shouldn't pout, so I
convince myself whatever it is I'm doing is most
certainly not pouting.

"They just want both you and the baby to be
safe."

"Yeah, I know." I sigh and press against him,
seeking as much heat and physical contact he'll allow me
to get away with. Which, of course, only worsens the
matter. What with all his big, bulging part-huiós, part-
beast muscles rubbing against my highly sensitive skin.
"I want that, too. Along with other… things."

He chuckles, and it travels through my body like
a piece of kindling catching flame. Kirian becomes
contemplative for a moment before clearing his throat
and saying, "That baby is coming soon. Very soon."

I remove my head from his shoulder reluctantly.
"Yes. Before the next sunset would be my guess."

Kirian grunts and nods. "That got me thinking…"

"Uh oh."

He scoops a long finger under my chin, scarcely
— but intentionally, no doubt — letting his claw trace
the skin there before turning my head toward him. "This
entire time, they've worried the baby would come too

24

soon because of how fast you and the baby have grown in size." I close my eyes, enjoying the simple touch of his finger beneath my chin; that's about the extent of contact I've been allotted since my belly began to poke out — the lot of my men concerned the baby and I are too fragile, even despite my protests. "Now, the baby is coming no matter what, and... I think you should, too."

My eyes spring open to find Kirian's ocean-blue orbs sparkling down at me, those silver waves of our essence-bond churning within. I want to say "Really?!" with a squeak of excitement, but instead, I narrow a glare at him and state, "Do not tease me."

"Mmm, I am not teasing you... yet." Kirian leans forward, brushing his lips against mine before snaking his tongue out just enough to give me a taste. At that simple touch, my entire body clenches with need and my eyes close as I hum, desperate for more.

At my sides, I dig my fingers into the shore in order to prevent myself from mounting him on the spot. His gaze drops to the clumps of sand now balled in my fists and his lips turn up in an amused grin.

"Before you get too excited—"

"Too late."

Kirian laughs. "I'll forewarn you that my cock will not be involved in this." The pout returns — this one unable to be countered by an attempt to remain regal and queen-like. "But I'll still have you roiling and crashing, just like those waves."

The offer is too hard to refuse. I'd gone long enough. But I trust my men, and that same worry — that same fear for my unborn baby's safety — spikes within me. As much as I pout or complain, I do it in jest mostly. The feeling sorry for myself is a real thing, though. But at the end of each astral round, I know every time the sun goes down, I'll be okay with it all over again the next.

When Kirian gives this tempting offer, I feel the safety of it wrap me in a cocoon. The baby is coming soon no matter what. His or her time for growing healthy and strong is in the past. As a group, we've done everything we could up until this point to make sure the pregnancy environment was as safe and secure as possible — knowing what we know.

Which really isn't much.

But it's enough... hopefully.

"Not complaining about my earned oikía power, but sometimes I sure wish I knew what was going through that mind of yours. Mind-reading powers would be nice."

"Oh, no... that's a terrifying concept." I laugh. "However, if you ever want to know what's on my mind, simply ask, and I'll tell you. I have nothing to hide."

"Mmm," he rumbles, leaning his head down and snaking his tongue out to tease my lips again, just as he'd promised. He doesn't stay there for long before his lips hit my neck and down to my shoulder and beyond. Every inch lower he moves, I lean back just a bit more until the sand is prickling my forearms, knees are bent, and thighs are spread open. Ready.

Kirian wastes no time, knowing we have very little left if I'm to get back before my giant wakes up and goes on a rampage looking for his basílissa.

The daimónion's long, lithe tongue snakes out and slips through my folds, twisting and turning, driving me wild in no time.

When the length dives inside me, my breathing increases and hips lift as I greedily press against his face. His tongue slides out and laps lightly at every delicate area. Unable to keep my hands to myself any longer, I fall to my back in the sand and bring them to the top of his head, my palms cupping over the nubs of his horns and using them as a grip so I can grind against him.

Something sharp nicks me, and my hips jerk, but then the sharp pain quickly morphs into pleasure. Kirian hums, taking a moment to trace his tongue over where he had nicked, going nice and slow in doing so.

When his mouth attaches to the tender spot and he sucks and flicks, a powerful and intense orgasm tosses through me, causing my entire body to tighten and shake intermittently. Having gone so long without, the sensation is almost too much. Every crash of water over the rocks nearby mimics every crash and recede within me. Over and over again until my body is supple and weak.

Breathing is hard to do, but I manage one careful, deep inhale and exhale at a time until the tension in my belly loosens and the rest of my body can enjoy the aftereffects of a much-needed release.

Kirian climbs atop me, resting on his forearms at either side of my head and bringing his nose down to bump against mine, careful to not smush my belly in the process. "You know, I'm fairly certain we've never done that before. Prior to Falling, I mean."

I know exactly what he's talking about. There are brief moments that happen often — when we're holding hands, leaning against each other, or sharing small kisses — where a sense of deja vu comes over us. In a different time and place we'd done those same things together.

What he and his daimónion had just done to me is most certainly not something we'd experienced. "Maybe because where we came from doesn't have daimónia," I offer.

"Hm. Maybe." A big smile lights up his face. "Though… something tells me the Drea from before was much more innocent and fragile than you are now."

That is something else I have felt the truth of more often lately than not. That moral compass which was apparently present stronger before I Fell, heckling me, still challenging the ways of this realm on a regular basis. Still making me question everything I do despite there being no free agency to do such things here. The "right" things.

"Yeah." I tilt my head to the side to avoid his mocking glare.

Kirian sighs and places his hand on my cheek, drawing my attention back toward his face. "We'll figure it out, Drea. But no matter what, I love you. I loved you then, and I love you now. We don't know much, but that is one thing I know better than anything else. Most days, it's the only thing I know."

Everything else is still just one big, confusing question. I mean, sure, we'd come a long way since the day we fell alongside each other. But there is still so much uncertainty. Too much.

"Maybe we're overthinking it," I mention. "Brion said that we all fell from Elysium. Perhaps that's all there is to it. You and I fell. The visions I've had are of that moment. Nothing more."

"Maybe," Kirian answers, pushing off the ground and reaching out both hands. With quite a bit of effort on both our parts, he helps me stand.

I've had quite a lot of time to contemplate. To meditate on The Fall. To try anything and everything I could in order to tap into those still-lost memories. Because I know they're significant. But beyond what little visions I had received, the veil is just as shrouded for me as it is for any of the Fallen huiói. Every being here — aside from The Watchers who Fell under different circumstances and whose punishment was, in part, keeping their memories — has no memory of The Fall. All they have is faith in what they've learned from the codices and scrolls written by the trusted paidagōgói themselves.

After dusting off the sand from my butt and arms, I smile up at him. "Thank you for... doing that thing... with your tongue. Pretty sure that's something that has changed since before, too."

"As has everything about my body that is more daimónion than huiós." A cautionary groan leaves my lips. "Ah, still up for more, hm?" he asks.

"Always, I fear. Dare I say, my being in a constant state of horniness is worse than the ever-present hélkō."

"Horniness?" Kirian laughs at the irony of that comment. Because... horn nubs and such.

"Yeah, a mortal term. Oryn said it derives from the way a working male's cock sticks out much like a beast's horn." My eyes flick to the top of his head and down to his cock. Which is, indeed, sticking out.

"If I didn't know better, I'd say you like my horns."

"I do. Very much so."

Kirian smiles, but it doesn't quite reach his eyes. "You'd better get back," he whispers, leaning down and giving me a soft, quick kiss.

CHAPTER FOUR

The leaves, dirt, rock, and every grain of sand my feet touch on the forest floor is an exacerbated sensation. The sting, pleasant. The cool air whizzes over my face and dries my eyes. The scent of... fear... is tantalizing. The scent of essence, even better. The heady mix of both propels me forward.

But when I look down at my feet, they're different — longer, wider, and tipped with claws that dig into the gritty soil.

Hunger consumes me. Agonizingly, my stomach twists and churns — an ache so strong my body launches ahead, desperate to feed.

My target location comes into view, and I screech to a halt. A clearing. The clearing Blaze had taken me to. Running no more, my survival instincts kick in and I drop low to the ground on all fours, watching as my next meal strolls across the sandy ground in search of a meal of her own. Red haze coats my vision as the beast inside takes over, heightening my ability to see the pulsing energy that swarms through the essence in her veins.

Again my stomach churns, and I curve inward on myself grasping at the ache. But when I look down, my claw-tipped hands are covered in essence, and the ache blossoms outward along with the growing stain of essence coating my stomach.

Movement ahead catches my eye, and my gaze flicks up toward my prey. Beside her, another creature. Much smaller. Much more innocent.

So much more energy.
Enough to heal.
To satiate.
I dive forward.
"No!" Both my voice and the voice of my beast
howls.

* * *

MY THROAT IS RAW, muscles and tendons are tight, and my body shakes relentlessly.

"Adrestia!" A voice different than the beast's howl penetrates my mind. "Adrestia!" it yells again, and the sound is paired with an aggressive jerk of my upper body. Air fills my lungs and my eyes fly open.

Brax's large body is hovering over me, his massive hands gripped around my upper arms as he engages in another shake.

"Brax... Brax, stop," I gasp out around heaving breaths. It's one thing to wake up from a nightmare, it's another to wake up from a nightmare with another nightmare looming in giant form above you.

Not that Brax is a nightmare. So far from it... But being woken by an upset grigori is nothing less than terrifying. If this were the first time, perhaps it'd have been more shocking, but it has happened before. More often lately.

"I'm okay," I whisper, cupping his face with my hands. "Shh... I'm back. I'm okay."

"No, Basílissa... you are not," he says. Brax's hands refuse to leave my arms. Refuse to loosen.

"Look at me. Look in my eyes." His transformed clear-blue eyes are wild. Unfocused. Panicked. "Now, it's your turn to come back to me," I coax.

A tightness balls up inside my belly and radiates outward, spreading from my front and around to my lower back. My hands drop from Brax's face to curve around my stomach.

The sensation is so strong — so different than the small pangs from before — that I can't help but look at my hands to make sure they're not covered in essence like in my nightmare. Essence, however, is not what I find. Beneath me, there's wetness… and a lot of it.

"What do I do?!" Brax raises his voice. It takes me a few heartbeats to process everything. To wake up from my nightmare and face my just-as-intimidating reality. In my own panic, I reach for the land's energy. But it doesn't come to me — doesn't respond to my call. My body uses too much of its own energy to counter whatever is happening in my womb.

"Carry me. You need to take me to Rae—Oryn. Take me to Oryn. I… I think the baby is coming."

Brax's hands finally loosen.

They drop like lead.

He stumbles backward.

My giant falls out, inanimate, sinking like a rock to the depths of the sea right before my very eyes. "Brax!" I scream. He passed out. He fucking passed out, and I'm about to give birth to his offspring.

With a deep inhale, I push off the pallet, step over my giant, and leave the room. Just outside the door, my eyes travel into the darkness leading down the tower's steep, winding steps.

If he doesn't expire from shock… I swear to Belíar, I'm going to expire him myself.

One excruciating step at a time, I descend the tower, occasionally yelling out Kirian's name with the hope that my déō doúlos with the auditory oikía power will hear me. But I'd been told time and time again that the watchtower is protected. In more ways than one. It's one of the many reasons why this has been my dwelling during this pregnancy. That, and because, although huiói and déō doúloi alike have been working tirelessly, my personal dwelling is still not ready.

Another tight spasm wracks me and I pause, no more than ten steps down, palming the stone wall for support. Once it passes, my journey down the stairs continues.

This goes on and on for what feels like a full astral round. To the point, in fact, that I fear something is actually terribly wrong with Brax. He should have come back to consciousness by now and rushed down the stairs to my aid.

Eventually, the exit appears and I escape the tower, immediately yelling Kirian's name on exit. Out here, no matter where I am, he'll hear me. Not only does his oikía power bind us in that way, but his ability is also heightened on account of him being a half-breed. Part beast, part man.

When he arrives, I'm on my hands and knees rocking back and forth, trying not to scream the pain away. Kirian drops beside me and runs a solid hand from between my shoulder blades down to the base of my back.

Unlike with Brax, I do not have to instruct Kirian. As soon as the wave leaves and I am able to stand again, he scoops me up and rushes to Oryn's hut. When we arrive and find Oryn inside, an immense weepiness overcomes me. Both because he's actually in his hut, but also because now that I'm here, with the very déō doúlos who had helped me plan and prepare for this moment, I know there's no more waiting.

No turning back.

Kirian places me on the pallet, and both he and Oryn step outside. Somehow, the two manage to speak quietly enough that I cannot hear, which means Kirian is utilizing his powers to silence the projection. But, right now, I can't bring myself to care enough to get angry or frustrated. Nor to care enough to be bothered by whatever it is they're talking about.

By the time Oryn steps back through the cloth-covered entrance, I have crawled off the pallet and am kneeling at its edge instead, fingers tearing into the reeds. My grip is so strong, I fear reeds will be embedded in my palms by the time this is over.

Unable to move much, other than to rock and sway, I follow Oryn's motions via sound, instead. In my mind's eye, I envision the steps he takes, the motions he makes, beginning with his trip to the corner of the room. A trickle of water tells me he's wetting a cloth and squeezing out the liquid. This is confirmed when he returns and the cool material hits the clammy, heated skin of my forehead.

For the first time since I shot up out of the nightmare in the throes of labor, my body relaxes. A pent-up breath seeps from my lungs, moving the wild strands of kinky hair that float around my face.

Oryn comes down to my level, sitting beside me on the ground. "Talk to me," he says. "What can I do for you?"

"It hurts," I respond. Seems pain follows me wherever I go, and just when I think I have it figured out — and how to combat its many facades — a new type shows up, proving I don't fully understand it at all.

"Yes," Oryn says, and I narrow a glare at him. He clears his throat. "That's what Raener's research has indicated would happen. Brax's memories also."

"Speaking of Brax," I grind out, "someone needs to go check on him. He passed out when he realized the baby was coming."

Oryn's eyes widen. "How—"

"One step at a time."

"Oh, Adrestia…" Oryn's expression begs for forgiveness… for something he didn't do. Not really, at least. We all know now that my oikía is nontraditional, and their availability to stay by my side even more so.

"No matter. I'm here. We didn't know Brax would pass out because of that. And… he's been getting better about essence." Brax has always been the sensitive type, even despite his size. The sight of essence is particularly trying for him.

"We'll get him down here." Oryn's eyes pierce me with a promise. The two of us give each other a hard time because of how our binding came to be — we both had an agenda having nothing to do with becoming bound. But of all the men, Kirian included, Oryn has grown to somehow know and understand me on a level much deeper than the others.

Oryn knows that I want — no, need — Brax here. He's my protector. The baby's seed-father. But also one of the reasons why I'm so frightened to birth this infant.

I need him.

I've not admitted this to anyone, not even Oryn. But Oryn knows. And knowing he knows, knowing he'll make sure Brax is down here with me, causes more tears to come. All my fears and worries spill in torrents onto the reeds where my head rests.

Oryn's hand pushes my hair out of my face and uses the cloth to wipe those tears. "Not such a fearless and amazing queen, huh?" I push a breath through my lips, making them vibrate.

Oryn smiles, his dark-green eyes glinting in amusement. "Quite the opposite. I believe this makes you an even more fearless and amazing queen."

Another wave of pain takes over, causing my entire body to shake. Oryn had held it together pretty well up until that point, but when it wanes and I open my eyes, he's as white as sun-bleached limestone.

A rustle of fabric precedes the sensation of air brushing over my damp skin. Several presences fill the small space at once, and I turn my attention toward the door. Kallias and Raener have joined now — Raener's face ash-stricken and eyes wide, Kallias's eyes sparkling in delight.

Over the course of my captivity, Kallias had caught me lingering a time or two at the beach after my meetups with Kirian. He'd scold me each time, but would often stick around with me for a while anyway, sharing stories of his experiences as a wanderer and describing resplendent scenes of the different places across Ceteris he found particularly beautiful.

In this moment, I realize only the men who hold an important title are who I have been hiding my moonlit rendezvous from: The Watcher, mesítēs, and paidagōgós.

The former... is still not present. "Has anyone checked on Brax?" I ask, resting back on my heels.

They exchange glances. "I'll go," Raener offers. Which doesn't surprise me at all. He's always still trying to stay as far away from me as possible. Even if it means helping the one being who he dislikes most.

I offer a "thank you" as he swiftly exits the hut.

Kallias squats beside me and his mouth pulls into a huge grin. "Woman, that hair of yahs has seen bettah rounds."

A strained chuckle comes out of me, but the act of doing so triggers another wave of pain.

Unlike the others, Kallias doesn't seem worried. Quite the opposite, in fact. He moves behind me and digs his thumbs hard into the base of my spine, adding more pressure there than the pain itself presents. The action somehow counters the twinge. Not entirely, but enough to make it somewhat bearable.

When the wave passes, I ask, "How… how'd you know to do that?"

He clears his throat. "Uhm… well now… that is a story for anotha time, alrigh'?"

When I don't agree with his request right away, he leans low behind me, meeting my ear, "A story I think ya migh' like, if ya can be patient 'nough t' wait." Until we're alone for another storytime together on the beach I presume.

Kallias finally gets the desired response when I nod. As soon as that's taken care of, he addresses Oryn, "How's her energy? I know when watchin' tha animals give birth while I was in Kainda's territory, tha land had t' feed 'em tha whole time."

Oryn's eyes meet mine before returning to Kallias. "She's… right now she's somehow healing herself. When a contraction comes, her energy levels lower. When it stops, her energy replenishes itself."

I might not know a lot… but I do know that is not at all normal. Especially since I couldn't even pull enough of my own energy earlier to travel out of the watchtower.

CHAPTER FIVE

Raener

Never in a million existences did I think I'd ever watch a grigori lose it. This giant being having a breakdown. Were he still part human, I imagine he'd be crying right now, too. Not that I blame him at all, though; we're all panicked.

"Stop. Please stop pacing," I beg. If there wasn't risk of getting my neck snapped, I'd knock some damn sense into him. "You're driving me fucking crazy."

Fortunately, he heeds my request, plopping onto the ground, leaning against the hut both of us have refused to leave for the entire morning and on into mid-astral round.

Inside, Adrestia whimpers. The whimper turns into a cry. The cry is shortly followed by a wail.

Every time.

Every. Single. Time she does that, my pulse intensifies and stops all at once. Despite that not even being possible. There's no other way to describe the way it stutters, stops, and picks right back up again in quick succession.

Brax groans, his meaty hands clasping behind his neck as he tosses his head back and bounces it against the hut several times.

For the first time since I practically dragged him here kicking and hollering, he finally says something. Something we're both thinking, but neither of us have had the stones to say aloud. "The Nephilim… it's going to kill her, Raener." Muttering those words aloud, the fear he had been trying to contain storms to the surface. For both of us. I've never seen him more scared than in this moment. For a grigori, that's saying something. "They scream... that's what they do when being torn from the inside out." His voice shakes.

The hut's curtain flies open and a disheveled Oryn pops his head through. "She's asking for you."

Again my pulse intensifies... only to stutter and flatline again when Oryn's attention seeks out the equally disheveled grigori instead of me. "Brax!" he raises his voice, attempting to pull the giant out of his panicked trance. "You. Your Basílissa is asking for your attendance."

Brax's face turns a greenish-white. "No." His head shakes emphatically, eyes wide.

Oryn's cheeks turn the brightest shade of red I've ever seen on the mesités, his lips press together, and his nose flares as he takes in a deep breath. "Fine," he grinds out through clenched teeth. "I'll tell her you've refused."

Brax shoots up to his feet, much faster than a giant can normally accomplish. "Mesités... please... no," he begs, using Oryn's official title after having avoided doing so most of his existence. "I will be of no use to her in there. When that abomination comes out, I'm bound to slaughter it... which I fear won't bode well. Do not put me into a situation where I can't control myself."

Oryn's tightly pressed lips loosen a bit, and he lets out the breath he had taken. He looks at me, and I shake my head; I can travel to the mortal realm a billion more times, read a billion more scrolls, and the answers won't be there.

We're now fairly well versed in how to birth this baby, but that's the extent of our knowledge. What the

39

baby will be, and how detrimental the end result, we are unsure.

Adrestia would not, under any circumstances, let us talk her into any alternative measures. In fact, after the first mention, we wouldn't even dare suggest such a thing, lest she unleash her ever-growing, and incredibly hormonally driven, powers on us — or the area — or both.

"One sun-cycle at a time," was her rule. She'd give no other option. "If the baby is born an abomination, I'll do whatever must be done myself. We'll make decisions one sun-cycle at a time."

In this moment of this sun-cycle, she decides to storm through the hut's closure — all belly and glistening, tawny skin. Her hair is frizzed out like a wild animal's mane, similar to when she had first Fallen.

"I tried to stop her!" Kirian bellows, bursting out of the hut.

Adrestia stomps — or rather waddles — over to Brax, places her hands on her hips, and glowers up at him.

I'd thought he was pretty pale just moments ago, until the color in his face at her scrutiny drains more.

"You. Did. This. To. Me." She accuses in between choppy, strained breaths.

Anger flits over Brax's face, but he quickly controls the slip, blinking away his frustration. "Yes, Basílissa, I know."

Adrestia's anger ceases for a time, and her glower softens. But only to be quickly replaced by a grimace as the baby possesses her once more.

Her hands immediately shoot off her hips and land on the top of Brax's thighs as she bends her head down and takes gulping breaths — or so tries.

Kallias is the last to join us, rushing in behind her, placing his hand in the middle of her lower back, and pressing hard.

"What are you doing to her?" Brax rumbles, his fear momentarily transforming into protection and anger.

"More than wha' yah are doin', man." Kallias somehow keeps his tone even, though the words are coated with bitterness.

Adrestia's nails make tiny imprints on Brax's skin, but such a small thing doesn't bother him at all. He stares down at her, arms out awkwardly to the side.

"I have an idea," Kallias says. "Let's take her t' tha beach? She seems t' like it there."

Many mortal women had given birth in or near water — its restorative properties calling to them. Why I didn't think to suggest it myself frustrates me. She had become quite fond of the beach during the few mooncycles of her pregnancy.

Though, part of me wonders — and hopes — those frequent visits have been due to something else entirely. When I had once asked Kallias why she goes down there so often, he'd responded with, "Says she's chasing lightning."

Unfortunately, we hadn't experienced a lightning storm in a long, long while — a near-equivalent example of how long it has been since the night I was able to touch her for the last time.

"I... can't... travel..." she says, followed by a clenched-teeth squeal as the possession nearly brings her to her knees.

"The walk will help encourage the baby to come," I explain, pulling on what knowledge I have regarding the topic.

41

The surprise of hearing my voice, with how little we talk anymore, shocks the possession away, and her attention flits to me. But she doesn't say anything, she just nods and attempts to stand again.

"Are you not worried about The Seven finding out?" Brax finally pipes in.

Adrestia had done a good job keeping the pregnancy a secret from the territory and, most importantly, from the other basílissas. Most of her astral rounds have been spent in the tower with Brax and the daimónion… only traveling to the beach at night. Often even waiting to do that until the weather was inclement and huiói were seeking shelter.

I know, because I often waited for her there — even if she wasn't aware. Kallias would often go to her there, too, after she'd been standing in the rain for a long while, tilting her head back, letting every inch of her skin absorb each individual drop.

As much as it hurt — as much as I wish my millions of nerves could be those millions of rain drops — I still waited and watched.

The next day, Kallias would go to the tower, and the next time she would appear outside, her hair was in a different style. Sometimes braided, sometimes in tight curls around her face.

By now she could take care of it herself, but Kallias never lets her, even despite the effort. He would fix it, the rain would come to ruin his handiwork, and he would fix it again.

"Paidagōgós," Oryn's use of my title snaps me back into the moment. I shake my head and regather my thoughts.

The Seven.

Right.

"This is progressing faster than they'd have time to do something about it, so no. Plus, the baby's arrival in and of itself will likely change the very dynamic of Ceteris. If the infant survives birth, there will come a time soon where keeping the child a secret will be disadvantageous."

Adrestia reaches out to take the daimónion's proffered arm.

Far gone are the moments when Adrestia would still reach out to me, unthinking of the consequence. Still I yearn for it, even though I had to go out of my way to make sure contact wasn't made; just having her reach out was enough to let me know she still cared.

Unfortunately, those moments are past now.

The walk to the beach takes roughly three times longer than usual. The baby possesses her sooner and sooner between times the closer we get to the water.

There's a buzz of excitement between the group, but that excitement is also interwoven with fear. Every time Adrestia stops to squat and sway her hips, riding out the waves of pain, Brax turns away and stares up at the sky, refusing to watch.

At one point his mouth moves, eyes squeezed tight, in an impression of prayer, which is quite possibly the funniest thing I've seen in a long while. Sorry, Big Guy, no one's listening down here.

Once we arrive, the sun now beginning its descent from mid-astral round, Kallias takes her hands and walks her to the edge of the water. Oryn and Kirian follow. Brax and I perch on the nearby rocks.

We had tried to veer off to the top of the hill, to watch from a distance, but Adrestia was quite vocally in disagreement with that idea.

"Want me to hold your hand, Grigori?" I smirk at the still-blanched giant.

Brax snorts, trying to get situated on the rocks. Several rocks, in fact, since he can't fit on just one.

Desperate for distraction while his seed tries to take the love of my existence, I turn to the familiar snark between us. "Through my travels and my studies, I've learned that many men enjoy fucking pregnant women. How's that been going?"

Not that I really want to hear about other men's cocks inside the female I can't be inside, but it makes for entertaining conversation at least.

"Are you dense?" he asks, down right shocking the shit out of me.

"Are you talking to yourself again?" I toss back.

"Wasn't it you who put it in Oryn's head that we shouldn't fuck her while carrying child?" he asks with all seriousness.

"Wha—no. Why the hell would I say that?"

"You mean this entire time I could have been fucking her and *not* getting her pregnant — because she's already pregnant?"

"Yes, I don't see why not."

Brax fires a killer glance at Oryn.

"Is anyone else fucking her?" I ask.

"No," he rumbles. "At least, I don't think so. We've all been worried it would hurt her too badly. Or — Maker forbid — the baby." That last part is delivered with a note of sarcasm.

At that, I can no longer keep my growing mirth contained. A burst of laughter barks out of me. "She's been with child for an entire pregnancy now and hasn't been pleasured? What has been her opinion about that?"

44

Brax glowers at me. "She's constantly trying to climb on my cock. I even woke up to her on top of me one night — almost hurt her trying to throw her off me. Kirian won't touch her like that either."

"Because the baby?"

Brax shrugs. "That and because he can't control his daimónion urges yet."

The fact they're still letting the half-breed daimónion abomination be near her for extended periods of time is a damn surprise. But, then again, there's no *letting* her do anything. That female does what she pleases.

It's a miracle she has not lashed out at being denied the pleasure I imagine she is quite eager for. "Damn good thing her pregnancy wasn't as long as a true mortal's... what did you guys plan on doing should she turn to using the hélkō against you for refusing?"

"Take a lesson out of your book, of course," Brax responds. "Stay away."

"Tartarus hath no fury—"

Adrestia's piercing scream pulls us out of the conversation, and before Brax can think to not look, he reacts, his attention shooting instantly to Adrestia.

Kallias is squatting behind her, his hands on her hips. Oryn is in front, hands cupping her cheeks as he whispers — something sweet and encouraging, knowing him.

The daimónion's shoulder supports one of her hands, while her other hand is pressed into her thigh to help her balance.

When one of Oryn's hands drops and slips under the water to her center, out of the corner of my vision Brax's attention swivels the opposite direction. Unlike him, I am unable to keep looking away, though —

45

riveted on a scene we're not supposed to be watching. Not here in Ceteris.

Adrestia's shoulders move up and down as she takes in short, choppy breaths. Oryn's other hand drops into the water, and my feet carry me off the rocks toward my queen unbidden.

I try to rationalize with myself — to turn away — to join Brax in avoiding this, but it's impossible.

Adrestia senses my presence at once, but she still doesn't reach out to me. I'm instantly grateful, because I'd hate to deny her during such a pinnacle moment. Her glassy gaze does meet mine, though, and the smallest smile appears on her lips before they press together and she bears down, both humming and groaning at the same time.

Seeing for myself that she is okay, I turn to leave, but this time she does reach for me. Not with her hand, but with her voice. "Raener," she pants. "Stay…"

I squat in the water at her side opposite of Kirian, keeping my hands to myself. "Almost there, Basílissa," I whisper in reassurance as her eyes lock on Oryn and she nods.

Kallias pushes the hair off her neck and over her shoulder before scooping some water into his hand and pouring it over her exposed skin. Her hand squeezes the daimónion's. He leans over to give her an encouraging kiss on her cheek.

"I feel the baby's head," Oryn says.

Adrestia's eyes fog with tears and she swallows hard, her breathing accelerating once again.

"When you feel ready, when the urge to bear down consumes you, push hard," I whisper as Kallias's hands drop back down to her hips and he digs his thumbs in deep at the base of her scar.

Adrestia's shoulders draw up high on a deep inhale, and on the exhale she screeches, squeezing her eyes shut tight and pushing with the strength of eight queens combined.

Oryn's eyes drop to between her bent legs, and he gets a proper hold on the baby before lifting its little body from the water.

Adrestia lets go of Kirian, and her hands meet Oryn's as the baby emerges. The first thing I notice is the baby's tawny skin — just like Adrestia.

Adrestia's calm, sweet voice verifies the second thing I notice. "A little girl," she whispers, cocooning the baby in her arms and drawing her against her chest as she sits back on her heels.

Adrestia's chin meets her collarbone as she crooks her head down in a way far enough to continue looking at the babe without pulling her too far away from her bosom.

In my stupefaction, all my knowledge goes to the wayside. But when Adrestia's mouth curves downward, everything comes rushing back; the baby is supposed to cry. Make a noise. Something.

I reach forward and pinch the bottom of her little foot, and she lets out a wail louder than the crash of wave behind us.

Then my body goes flying backward, and I land with a splash near the shore, a rather large male hovering over me, raring his fist back.

I roll quickly to the side and scramble up, thankful that I'm faster than Brax despite his strength.

"What the fuck are you doing?" I yell, trying to gain my footing.

"You hurt the baby."

"I—are you serious right now?! You were threatening to kill it on birth just a few sun-positions ago!"

Brax lunges toward me, but an unseen force has him stopping and doubling over before he can reach me.

"Brax!" Adrestia yells, laughing. "Come meet your daughter."

The hélkō she had used against him is no match for hearing those words come out of his queen's — and lover's — mouth. The giant becomes stock still, blinking like the dunce he is and swallowing over and over again as he tries to move the words in his brain to his mouth. "Daughter," he finally mumbles.

But he still doesn't move. He drops his voice low, looking right at me. "Is she hideous, like me?" he asks, all seriousness.

Belíar, I want to say "yes," but I bite my tongue. Waiting to hear my answer is enough torture on the grigori anyway. "No… in fact, she looks like she could be Kallias's instead."

Brax's eyes widen before turning into a squint as he glares down at me. "Fuck you," he says. Out of spite, he stomps toward Adrestia, forgetting why he didn't want to go over there in the first place.

CHAPTER SIX

Adrestia

B rax practically slings Oryn out of the way. The aggressiveness isn't intended, but even a little push from the grigori is enough to send someone not expecting it flying.

His big, giant form squats down in an attempt to get to my level, but doing so is difficult. Instead, he sits in the water, drawing his knees up to bracket me.

In order for him to fit, all the other guys have to move. But since Brax absolutely refused to join in on the delivery, and this is the first occasion he's approached me since, no one complains.

"What is a Nephilim supposed to look like?" I whisper, removing our little girl from my chest and holding her out toward Brax.

Brax stares down at the tiny thing, his mouth open. The grigori is speechless. He alternates shaking and nodding his head, even adding in a head tilt occasionally and squinting at her.

When he finally does speak, he says, "I've never seen anything so amazing in my existence."

"Well, you did create her, so you have every right to think so," I remind, bringing her back to my chest.

Brax shakes his head emphatically. "No... she's too pretty to be mine. Maybe Raener was right... maybe she belongs to Kallias."

The baby's head bobs like a blind mole trying to find its way through a tunnel until she works her way down to my breast and latches onto my nipple. The suction is way harder than expected, what with my only experience being my males teasing me there.

What's worse, the strong hold makes my body contract painfully again, just like it had before. And again my body heaves to push.

Panicked I call out for Raener and Oryn.

"We are here," Reaner says.

"S-something else is coming out of me," I whine.

Raener hurries to my front, nudging Brax out of the way. His eyes scan my body as he pulls on all his studies.

"The placenta," he decides. "The organ that was holding her inside you. It… it has to come out, too."

Another tightening occurs, and just as he had determined, this "placenta" comes out.

Beside me, a sudden splash sprays upward, and I curve my upper body around the baby, turning my head to see what has happened. Brax is now sitting in the water again, blinking repeatedly and swaying slightly.

Still at my front, Raener chuckles.

To pull Brax out of his near-fainting spell, I return to the topic we had begun talking about before Raener had to take over. "I was under the impression that having sex was required to make a baby." I glower at him with a single eyebrow raised. "That leaves you, Oryn, and Kirian as the only culprits. As my déō doúlos, you know that."

"Oh… right," he says, now staring at her again.

"You never answered my original question," I point out.

"What question?"

"Does she look like a Nephilim?"

"Not at all."

"Well… she's feeding like a human," Raener adds.

"Does that mean we'll need to feed her like one when she gets bigger?" I ask. Raener shrugs. A sudden weakness overcomes me. My limbs begin to turn heavy, my eyelids drooping. "Is... feeding supposed to... drain the mother?" I can no longer lean back on my heels, so I adjust to sit. The water rolls around us, lapping my stomach and the baby's butt.

"Brax," Raener addresses. "Bring her to the rocks for me? The cord isn't pulsing anymore; we need to cut it."

Brax nods and carefully scoops both me, the baby, and her dwelling organ, taking big, splashing steps over to the rocks.

In my periphery, the other birth attendees move along with us.

"Uh... just hold her, if you can," Raener instructs, and Brax finds a stable spot on the rocks to sit, resting me in his lap. So exhausted... so drained... I can scarcely hold my head up now; it falls to a rest on Brax's broad chest.

Still intrigued enough to keep my eyes open, though, I watch as Raener places the placenta on a rock, picks up a small, sharp stone, and strikes the cord several times until it separates.

"Kallias?" Raener snaps his fingers to get his attention. "Do you have one of those strings you use for Adrestia's hair braids sometimes?"

Kallias jogs to the hill, digs inside his pack, and jogs back, string in hand.

Oryn is beside me in an instant, taking one of my hands in his, but addressing all of us. "The baby isn't feeding from her like a normal human," he says. His tone has changed. A warning? "She's consuming energy... in a significant quantity."

Oryn keeps talking, but his voice becomes muffled as I fade in and out. Worried my hazy focus will hurt the baby, a rush of adrenaline enters me, and I slip my finger between her mouth and my nipple to release the suction. Before I pass out and am unable to make a trip with Oryn to the mortal realm, I quickly place her in Raener's arms, climb off Brax, and crawl a good distance away, lest he be at risk of accidentally making a detrimental trip with us and be sent to The Void as a result.

Just as soon as everyone is safe and Oryn is by my side, we clasp hands, and I use my now-accessible remaining energy, combined with some from the land, and send us to the mortal realm.

* * *

WHEN ORYN AND I RETURN, energy reserves replete, my daughter is surrounded by four doting men.

Raener is still holding her, and only then does it dawn on me that he's doing so without getting hurt. My chest constricts at the sight, both swelling and breaking all at once.

I want to run up to him and put my arms around them both, but the laws of this land do not allow such a thing — something that I hope to change very, very soon. I'd spent enough time alone in the watchtower during my pregnancy to plot and plan a number of things, and how to break the rules and make Raener mine was one such thing.

Oryn and I approach the group and Raener's eyes meet mine, gaze filled with a brutal mix of love and longing.

"Have you held her yet?" I ask, turning my attention to Brax.

"No. No, Basílissa; I will break her." Brax backs away from the circle as if the mere mention of holding the babe will make her jump into his arms. "I will wait... until she's bigger... and at that time, I will consider again."

As frustrating as it was that he wouldn't come anywhere near me during her birth, his fear of such a small thing is... humorous.

Raener passes the baby to Kallias instead, walking past Kirian to do so. Kirian's ocean eyes flash red. I approach his side and lean my head on his shoulder. "You want to hold her."

"Very much, yes," Kirian answers.

"You will one day, okay? Let's just make sure your daimónion isn't going to... do anything strange."

Kirian nods, wrapping me into a hug. He smells different now, as a daimónion. My olfactory ability picks up the subtle hint of the ash and tar that still remains in his veins from the partial conversion. With my chin propped on his wide chest, I look up at his face. A lot of him has changed, but he's still Kirian. I trace the scar on his jaw — the first one he got right after we Fell and the hélkō was trying to drag him away.

"They still don't trust me," he rumbles.

"Is that unwarranted?" I ask.

Kirian takes in a deep breath and sighs. "No."

"Well, if it's any consolation... I trust you. With our daughter's existence and mine."

"That was pretty amazing, you know. What you did. Bringing a being into existence. You were so... beautiful."

"Thank you for staying by my side the whole time." In fact, Kirian had seldom left my side hardly at all since being freed from the cage.

53

He kisses the top of my head, and I step away.

As if the guys can sense that I am beginning to miss her against me, Kallias meets me halfway and places her in my arms. "Your dwellin' is still nah done, but... it is ready 'nough t' where ya an' tha baby are welcome t' move in today," he announces.

I had not expected such a thing to happen — not so soon — but I know that he and a number of other huiói from the territory had been hard at work getting it done.

Pleased with this news and overwhelmed with excitement, I beam up at him. "Yes, I would love that."

CHAPTER SEVEN

I am shocked to discover they'd been "constructing" it right under my nose all along. If I would have looked out of the watchtower window and really been paying attention, I would have seen the efforts happening right before my eyes.

But I seldom looked out the window unless the moon was high and Blaze had come to whisk me away. Looking out the window while the sun was out only ever served to frustrate me more — to remind me that I was stuck in there when it was so beautiful and bright outside.

The men and several villagers stand in front of the old sacrificing temple — the same circular compound I'd landed in on my declivity into the village. The same one I was in when I'd called Brax's energy toward me and commanded him to retrieve Kirian from the woods.

Its exterior doesn't look much different, aside from the patching of several old cracks and crevices. The feel is different, though.

Embedded in the stone and into the ground around the compound, a blend of what oikía powers I have earned swirl in the very foundation of the structure. Kirian's, Oryn's, and Brax's — each unique sense-power sparking within, bringing the structure to life.

For a moment, I gape in awe at the invisible current of power, then I turn toward Oryn, eyes wide. "Ho—wh—"

Oryn chuckles and wraps his arm around me. "When a basílissa's dwelling is ordained as such, a natural protection is created. One of those unexplained occurrences, sorta like the cages. The oikía powers combine to form a defensive shield over the dwelling and everything inside."

Again, I turn my attention to the dwelling. There isn't much by way of aesthetics: just a tall, red-stone circular structure. "Does it still have a maze within?" I inquire, remembering the stone maze which separated the interior from the exterior and vice-versa.

Oryn's mouth quirks up to the side. "Glad you asked. It does. That very maze is the reason we decided to use this, as opposed to building something new from the ground up. Well, that, and because building from the ground up would have taken much longer. If you decide you are not pleased with your dwelling, we will change it in any way you see fit. Even if that means starting over. But, the maze..." His smile widens. "These passages are actually designed to catch intruders. Should one somehow get past the oikía protections, that is. There are false openings" — his voice drops menacingly — "and deadly traps."

I bring the baby a little closer to my chest and give her a protective squeeze, eyes wide. "Will the baby and I get trapped in there, too?"

"No, Basílissa. That is not possible. For you will not use the passages to enter." Oryn walks around the structure toward the other side where two Watchers stand guard.

I look up at Brax, who had been quiet by my side, and he gives me an adorable wink. "Don't get any ideas, Basílissa," he says, reminding me of the conversation we had a while back about him sharing me with his regiment.

The two guards take a knee. Brax bends down to my ear. "I told them to do that."

A laugh bubbles out of me. "Thank you, gentlemen. You may stand." The guards stand, all silence and broodiness.

Brax isn't done. Pride oozes out of him just as it had Oryn and he continues, "They are required to participate in the same atmis ritual Oryn once participated in."

Oryn had explained this to me, about how his cock was able to function, despite our nontraditional binding. The first step was discontinuing the atmis apoloúō ritual — a ritual that controls sexual urges so functioning huiói can perform their duties without their cocks getting in the way. This ritual is primarily for mesítēs, because most other huiói's don't work anyway. Since I am apparently part mortal, The Watchers' cocks work around me just fine on account of their backstory.

I press my lips together, desperately trying not to let my amused grin show. "You really thought of everything, didn't you?"

"Yes," he says, straightening and puffing his massive chest out.

"Impressive," I add, fueling his flame of confidence.

Every inch the shadows move along with the sun, my body becomes stronger and stronger. Healing from the arduous process of delivery.

It is now recovered enough — dare I say almost entirely — the pesky spark of need that follows me everywhere, flicks to life when Brax has straightened to his full height and his cock is on display close to my head.

His very-much-working cock.

The one I haven't been able to use.

Oryn had waited patiently for our conversation to end before gesturing for me to walk between the two giants and into an opening.

Baby still nestled quietly in my arms, Brax, Oryn, and I step inside the entry room. "This is the only way you can get inside. From here, you must use a special pýlē to enter the main chamber."

"How will my déō doúloi get to me?" I inquire.

"This pýlē is fed by the oikía powers your dwelling now contains. Déō doúloi will be able to form their own pýlē strictly for the purpose of entering and exiting."

I shoot a glance at Brax, knowing this would have been quite something for him to accomplish. "Have you tested this?" I ask as casually as possible.

"I have." He gives me a toothy grin.

"Oh, that's... amazing!" Sure, I'd tried to be casual about it, but the excitement just beneath the surface of his response is contagious. "Oryn? Can my déō doúlos deliver me inside with their pýlēs?"

"We can, yes," Oryn answers.

I look way up at Brax, my own large grin plastered on my face. "Would you like to do the honors?"

Brax's face blanches. "But... y-th-I..." His panicked gaze darts to our daughter and back up to me.

I turn to Oryn, and we share a look of understanding before I pass her to him for safe keeping. Looking up at Brax, I hold out my arms and say, "Better?"

He swallows hard and nods.

"So, you would risk my safety but not hers? Should I be upset about this?" I ask in a stern voice.

Brax's eyes widen and he shakes his head emphatically.

With an inhale and exhale, I accept that with Brax, it is what it is. Plus the fact that… well… it's endearing, his concern for her.

Before Brax takes my hand, though, Oryn speaks up: "Basílissa? I… um… I don't feel comfortable traveling with her either. So, if you could just hurry back…"

A laugh bursts free. "So, all this planning — every detail strategically figured out — yet there's no other way but through my own pýlē to make sure she is safe in the confines of my dwelling as well?"

Oryn shakes his head, wordless — for once.

Part of me battles with determining whether I should continue being amused… or being irritated at this point. For now, I choose amusement, giving him a chuckle before nodding my agreement.

His entire body seems to drain of tension at my response, which only serves to heighten my amusement.

I turn back to Brax, hold out my hand, and he takes it, blinking rapidly and swallowing hard before clearing his throat and closing his eyes. A turbulent pýlē forms around us — quite a large one at that.

What's even more unexpected is that we pop into the main chamber from about nine feet too high — him no doubt envisioning our landing from his vantage point, which is about three feet higher than mine. Lift my feet that high, and needless to say, I quickly become grateful that he made the call to not carry the baby with us.

I fall on my back from suspension and Brax nearly lands on top of me. The pain rivals that of giving birth; for the first time, I'm convinced something inside me broke. Like, literally. I lie there, struggling to breathe for a moment. The fall for Brax wasn't as bad considering his size; he's quickly on his knees, moments away from picking me up, when I hold my hand up in a halting motion. "Wait."

He freezes.

"Just… give… me… a… moment."

When I pull from my energy to heal whatever is broken, this time — unlike when I was birthing the baby — it does not replenish. For now, the amount used isn't significant enough to where I can't continue for a bit. But if anything else requires the use of my energy reserves, I will surely need to feed. And, honestly, I'd rather just relax and enjoy my daughter for a while first.

Once healed, I open my eyes and meet Brax's concerned clear-blue gaze with a smile. "Maybe you're the one who needs to learn how to fly," I state, repeating what he had said to me during our first travel together.

"Please forgive me, Basílissa," he begs, bowing forward all the way until his nose touches the ground. An act that he has not yet done for me, as it's typically hard for grigori to do.

"Oh, now… that was fun." I chuckle, trying to ease his worry.

His head rises so quickly I fear it'll snap off. It only takes him a moment for that big grin from before this mishap to return and he says, "Yes, it was."

We both stand, and I look up at him. "Good call passing the baby off to Oryn, though."

He takes in a deep, shuddering breath before letting it out and nodding. A few heartbeats pass, and we both burst into laughter. Both at the hilarity of it, but also at the fact that we have a new baby and had a potentially close call. "You're much more cut out for fathering than I am for mothering," I point out.

"All I know is that they can break… very easily."
He pauses. "And, I break things… very easily. The baby
and I are not a good mix."

"That will change," I state with confidence.

Brax shrugs.

With that behind us, I finally get a good look
around me. In many ways, the circle is just as I
remember. At least by way of size and shape. The dirt
and gravel beneath my feet is the same as before, too. No
matter if you're huiós or queen, the floor will always be
terra. With the very land feeding and nourishing us, it's
important that we have near-constant contact with it.
Even in the watchtower the floor is covered with a layer
of dirt.

Other than that, though, it's realms different.
There's a gorgeous reed pallet — huge. Unlike all the
others I have seen, this one is covered in decorative
material. I walk up to it and run my hand over the cloth.
It poofs up in the middle, and I press down, watching in
amazement as it slowly expands again when I let go.

When I steal a glance at Brax, he shrugs; if I have
questions, they'll need to be directed toward one of my
other déō doúlos.

Continuing my exploration, I find a mat on the
ground — much bigger than the ones typically found in
the lesson huts.

Brax stands posted near a doorway. This one in the
form of a door that resembles the ones the watchtower
has rather than the huts' cloth flaps. He extends an arm,
gesturing for me to enter, and as soon as I cross the
threshold, he says, "This one was my idea." Instead of a
proud smile, though, a tremor works through him. I take
a look around and my eyes settle on another reed pallet
like mine, but about a quarter of the size. A circular reed

mat, opposed to the rectangular ones I usually see. Atop it, there's an enlarged set of hubbub; the disks are palm sized and the sticks about the breadth of an arrow but several inches shorter.

I swallow hard and blink repeatedly to clear the overwhelming emotions building.

"For the baby," he explains.

"Wow, Brax... I'm... speechless. This is amazing."

He sits down on her pallet. It lifts a bit on one side — as pallets tend to do when he even so much as touches one — his head falls into his hands, and he rubs them over the short hairs before looking up at me. "I'm sorry I wasn't there for you," he says.

Any anger I'd been withholding disappears, as it tends to do easily where Brax is concerned. I sit beside him, but my weight is still not enough to counter his, so I relax and fall against his side, letting gravity do its thing. "You care. I know you do. My anger or frustration was only external. Promise. In my heart, I know you didn't behave that way to anger me."

His big hand lifts and wraps around the back of my neck, his thumb reaching over my jaw and up my cheek. Naturally, I lift my head to look up at him, and he bends down, kissing me for the first time since I went into rest cure.

"Mmm," he rumbles. "You know, it has been hard to refuse you."

"Sure didn't seem like you were having a hard time with it. You quite easily swatted me away when I tried in the middle of the night."

Brax's eyes nearly cross trying to narrow into a glare at me from so close. "It was hard," he says with that deep, raspy voice.

"Well" — I straddle his large lap and rub against him — "What do you think now?"

A look of utter shock crosses his features. "On our daughter's pallet?"

"Oh" — I look down at the pallet — "right."

"Also, no… we… we need to figure out a better way to make sure this doesn't happen again."

"Make sure what doesn't happen again?"

"Another baby."

"She's not a Nephilim, though."

He blinks at me. "No, she's not, thank The Maker."

Well, those are sure words I don't hear very often down here.

"So, in short, you're saying you still won't fuck me."

"Yes, that's exactly what I'm saying."

One of my eyebrows lifts, and he actually has the audacity to smirk at me. "You" — I point a finger at him — "are difficult!"

His grin widens and his hands slide to my lower back as he guides my hips farther away from his cock, in turn bringing my breasts flush against his chest. His large cock stands at attention just inches behind me even despite his refusal. "Do you believe I enjoy getting hard and not being able to use it?" I shake my head. "No. Waiting makes it better when it does happen, though. So… keep being patient. Kallias has a huiós traveling to collect a special plant that should help make sure you don't get pregnant again."

"Keep being patient? I haven't started being patient."

"You're right, you have not." Brax laughs, taking my head in his hands and kissing me soft and slow. When he pulls away, he lets out a heavy sigh. "Thank you," he says. "For giving me a beautiful daughter." His big blue eyes turn glassy. The beings here in Ceteris don't cry, but I know if they could, my giant would have leaked a few tears in this moment.

"I know you didn't give me her intentionally, but I'm thankful, too," I share. The both of us fall quiet, looking around the room that is now hers. "I guess we should give her a name?"

Brax grunts and smiles. "I have put some thought into this."

"Oh? Have you?"

"Yes. Why do you sound surprised?"

"Because you've been terrified of the concept since its discovery."

"Hmm, you are not wrong. But still, I have. I know how much you love the sea, that's where I got the idea. But when she was born in the water today, I knew the name would be just right. Seala." He looks down at me expectantly.

I love it. Everything about the name, but especially how he pauses for a heartbeat after *Sea* before pronouncing *la*. "Seala. Born of the sea. Perfect."

He takes in another deep breath and lets it out, relieved.

"Speaking of her... I promised Oryn we would hurry back."

Brax quickly stands, slides my body off his, and takes my hand.

"I'll take us there," I say with a grin, not wanting to use any more of my energy to heal broken body parts. He grimaces and shrugs apologetically as I use the compound's built-in oikía energy to pop us back to the entrance.

CHAPTER EIGHT

After retrieving Seala, I immediately take her into the main chamber and through the door that leads to her room. In the meantime, my déō doúloi all create their travel pýlēs and congregate inside.

There's nothing relaxing about the transition. My new dwelling is bustling with activity. Right away, Oryn had requested my permission to go ahead and allow visitors. That a few huiói had been given permission to bring gifts. In order to get inside, though, one of my déō doúloi must personally deliver them. They all chose Kirian as the honorary chauffeur, mostly due to how intimidating it is for a half-breed daimónion to be in charge of using a pýlē. That is another reason why he was chosen.

The honor of such a position made Kirian feel appreciated and helpful. That, in and of itself, made the decision a worthy one in my opinion.

After showing Seala her room, to which she wasn't very vocal about, I situate the two of us on my large pallet, ready to accept visitors.

Oryn sits by my side, acting as both déō doúlos and mesítēs, to make sure everything goes on without a hitch.

"They're visiting a queen," I whisper out of the side of my mouth, "and I am sitting on a pallet. Seems... I don't know... less than regal."

Oryn chuckles and the faint light tilting in from the high cutout in the stone twinkles in his eyes. "You, my queen, can sit wherever you please. Why sit on an uncomfortable decorative stone seat, when you don't even need to get out of the pallet?"

He makes a good point there, not to mention the fact that I'm utterly spent and becoming more so as the sun gets closer to setting and Seala begins to feed more.

"Besides," he adds, "only a few huiói are coming to you directly. The rest will meet Seala at the gathering we're setting up."

"When is this gathering?" I inquire.

"Within the moon-cycle. We want to give you a little bit of time to rest and adjust. Plus, we'd like to continue keeping this as much of a secret as possible for just a little bit longer."

That was another of the several reasons I'd been mostly locked up during my pregnancy. Needless to say, a rounded belly on a basílissa is quite easy to spot. Especially since no basílissa has ever become pregnant.

Because no basílissa other than me is part human female. Yet another secret that we can't keep hidden forever and will soon need to be revealed.

Unlike within my new dwelling, other queens can arrive and depart via pýlēs into the territory whenever they please. That knowledge makes me increasingly grateful for the privacy of my new dwelling, seeing as anytime I'm in the village, our secrets are significantly more visible.

We won't be able to keep her contained for long. She, like me, will need the balm of the sea. The heat of the sun. The light of the moon. I look up toward where the open sky once was — to where I descended from — and study the patterns in the thick cloth material that now covers the compound's open roof area.

"Ready?" Oryn asks.

With a deep sigh, I nod.

The first travel pýlē crackles in front of me and Kirian pops in with... Kallias. Kallias's wide smile lights up the space. "My Basílissa," he says, bowing at the waist with one hand behind his back and the other over his chest. When he straightens, his eyes widen and he looks at Oryn. "How should we address the baby? Nýmphē? Basílissa?"

Brax grunts from his sitting spot near the corner of the room used for pýlē arrivals. "She is not available to be taken to the 'marriage bed' — nor will she ever be — so we are not calling her a Nýmphē."

I press my lips together to refrain from laughing. When I had Fallen, Oryn explained that all Fallen females were first titled Nýmphē due to their... availability... for the males. Only after completing a bond does a female become a Basílissa.

"Is there not a word for an unavailable female?" I inquire. All the men shake their heads. "I think it's perfectly acceptable to call her by her name. Seala."

Kallias bows again, and whispers "Seala," reverently under his breath before standing straight once more and stepping forward to display what he had behind his back. Kallias had fashioned a vessel of sorts, in a material much like the containers he uses to mix the ingredients for the hair phýrama. This one is tall and teardrop shaped, coming to a small opening at the top. The top is closed by a matching teardrop-shaped plug. Kallias sits on the edge of the pallet closest to me, puts his fingers around the plug, and opens the vessel. A beautiful aroma wafts out, the inner tip of the plug visible now and glistening. "It's an oil pressed from a seed," he explains.

"Smells lovely," I take in a deep breath, even though that's not necessary with how sensitive my sense of smell has become since bonding with Brax.

"You can use it in your hair, or on your body. May I?" he requests, holding the dropper near Seala.

"Yes, of course."

Kallias dabs a little on her forehead and uses his thumb to spread it across, his coloring only a bit darker than her earthy skin tone. He leans down and kisses the top of her dark hair before standing and placing the gift on a stone pillar nearby. I press my nose against the top of her head, breathing her distinct scent in along with that of the oil.

"Would you like him to stay?" Oryn asks, preparing for the next visitor.

"Yes, I would." I offer Kallias a small smile. He'd quickly become somewhat of a best friend to me. In the way a male can be when he does funny things to my insides every time we're near each other. Kallias moves toward the stone wall, crosses his arms, and nods with a smile before getting into a protective stance and staying like that.

My heart does this hard thud, and I look at Oryn. Oryn smiles broad and shrugs. "And if I would have said *no*?" I ask, amused.

"I would have tried to convince you otherwise. But… I wasn't worried."

"Of course you weren't." I chuckle.

Seala writhes in my arms, and for the first time since Raener pinched her earlier, she lets out a displeased whine.

Oryn's eyes widen. "Seems she disagrees with the decision to keep you here, Brother," he addresses Kallias.

Before Kallias's smile can drop, I return with: "Impossible. No, she wishes to feed again, I believe."

No one questions my decision. Seala attaches to me easily. The dip in my energy level as a result of her feed is instantaneous. Oryn places his hand on my shoulder. "I will pay close attention to your reserves, but you let me know if we need to prematurely discontinue accepting visitors."

"Let's see who we have next."

Kirian nods and pops away.

"He's already quite good at that," I point out, impressed.

"Seems even your dwelling likes to break the rules a bit." Oryn winks at me. "When he creates a pýlē it gives him a small feed of energy."

"Oh, that's great!" I've known since soon after his shift that there's something different about his feeding practices. But he has been quiet about it, and I don't want to push him too hard or fast. When he's ready, he'll explain it to me.

Kirian returns, two huiói now with him: Xanth and Kohbi. I realize that I've yet to see these two separate, which I find curious.

Brax straightens and peers down his nose at the two males. The look has a mix of wariness but also curiosity. Oryn introduces them, and they both fall to their knees, noses to the ground. Typically, their hands are flat against the ground when they do this, but Xanth has his fingers curled around something resting in his palm.

As for Kohbi — my territory's only próskairos — he does not appear to be carrying a gift.

When the two stand, I use this unique opportunity to tease my men. "Ah, I see you all have given me a próskairos as a gift... I presume to make up for the" — I start counting and ticking off my fingers, soon pointing down at my toes and wiggling them as I do so — "well, look there, I don't have enough fingers and toes to add the number of times you men have refused me in the 'marriage bed' as of late."

Kohbi's eyes widen much larger than I expected them to be able to, considering their shape. Brax glowers at me, but chooses to not respond.

"No, my Basílissa," Kohbi responds, "I cannot be given as a gift. A queen must choose to utilize a próskairos. It's… it's something you must want."

"Oh… I wan—"

"Kohbi an' Xanth traveled t'gether t' Superbia t' get a special herb for ya." Kallias steps forward. "Kohbi was once a próskairos for Amrita, so he knows tha territory an' flora well. Plus, Xanth specializes in herbs an' other plant-related things." Kallias casts a glance at Brax and Brax nods.

The two men step forward and Xanth hands the stone vial to Oryn. "Please forgive us if this is at all offensive my queen. From what I have heard, our gift is not a traditional one, but your men have requested it, and the effort alone to attain it, we hope will please you."

Oryn opens the vial and shows me the contents. Nothing spectacular: a ground brownish-green powder.

Kohbi speaks now. "This is an herb that Kainda would often request from Superbia when there was a need to aid a viviparous animal. When bringing forth young might risk the creature's existence, she would administer this herb so that the creature would not be filled with offspring again."

This is the first I have heard Kohbi speak more than short, quick comments. Like Kallias, he has a unique accent to his voice — though different in a way that leads me to believe he must be from a different territory than where Kallias hailed.

Xanth takes a turn. "You just wet the tip of your finger, dip it into the vial to collect some of the power, then place it under your tongue.

"It is safe for hu—for queens. We are not animals."

"We are as close to animals as we can get. You even more so," Xanth explains.

Kallias adds to the conversation, "Kainda never did or gave anythin' t' her animals without trying it first herself."

I gesture for Kallias to approach. He does so, bending down to my level. When I flick a quick glance at Kohbi and Xanth, they step as far away as they are able to in the chamber.

"Kallias, my body is not like the other queens' — do you feel certain this is safe for me to consume?" I speak the question as quietly as I can so as not to offend the gift-givers.

"Yes, Basílissa, I do. We also had Raener compare it t' human females' responses t' similar contraceptives."

Those are enough answers for me. I gesture for Xanth and Kohbi to return to the base of my pallet. When they do so, I offer my thanks. With a grin, I include, "Though I fear this puts you out of the running to be my próskairos, Kohbi. Because having this powder means I will be able to use my grigori again. He may take up too much of my time now for any need of a próskairos."

"That is okay, Basílissa. I do not intend to go anywhere, should you change your mind."

A new buzz fills the room, but it is quickly snuffed out when Brax stands to his full height, his cock swaying in front of the próskairos. "Do not use your persuasion on my queen. If she should choose to have you as a próskairos, she will do so without your influence."

Kohbi looks way up at my giant and... smiles. "I don't need my influence, grigori. Every queen finds a próskairos useful at some point in their existence. It's only a matter of time," he states confidently.

Kirian steps forward now, taking Kohbi's hand in one and Xanth's in the other, quickly popping them out of my chamber before the entire place is brought down by an irate giant.

I turn to Oryn. "What, you didn't want to ask if I'd like them to stay?"

Oryn laughs. "We can bring them back in. Would you like them to stay, Basílissa?"

Brax rumbles his irritation and plops back down.

"Oh... I suppose not. Might make it quite stuffy in here if they did."

"Yes, I agree," Oryn states.

Brax and I share a look and I raise an eyebrow at him. "I fucking hate próskairoi. Almost as much as I hate paidagōgói."

"Any reason I need to know other than the fact that they fuck queens?"

He stutters for a moment. "They're... slimy."

"Slimy?"

"Yes, like the bottom of the rocks in the sea if you dig them up."

Oryn sighs. "He's right... it's a stereotype but they can be. I know, because I have experience as one. Once becoming a próskairos, we are somehow hardwired to make déō doúloi's existences a living Tartarus. To keep them out of their queen's pallet. Just... for fun."

"Interesting."

"Quite." Oryn winks at me. "Ready for your next visitor?"

I peek down at Seala, as she continues to feed, and take stock of my energy levels. They appear fine for now, albeit much lower. Still not low enough to be concerned or to call off the rest of my visitors, though.

Kirian pops back in shortly and for just long enough to get the go-ahead from Oryn, then pops back out and back in again with Blaze.

Blaze's arrival honestly surprises me. Considering the only time we ever see each other is in the dark of night when he's whisking me away, hiding the activity from my déō doúloi. "Ah, what a pleasure," I say. "I see you were able to carve time out of your busy schedule to see me."

He straightens, and the side of his mouth lifts. "Yes, quite inconvenient really. Never thought in all my existence I would hold the hand of a daimónion," he states, giving a dramatic shiver as he steps forward. The first visitor to not genuflect. Which is also not surprising where Blaze is concerned.

Instead, he sits directly at my side, scooping his hand around my head and kissing my forehead before bending down and running a finger along Seala's plump cheek. Which is awfully close to my breast. His black eyes lift to meet mine. "Fawn," he calls her. "She's colored like a fawn… and beautiful like one," he says.

"Her name is Seala," I chuckle.

"Not around me. I refuse to call her something after the sea, when she so clearly needs a forest name."

In the corner of the room, Brax grumbles.

"Calm your log, giant." Blaze laughs. "It's only a nickname."

Seala takes that moment to pop free from my breast and turn her mouth toward Blaze's finger instead. Blaze's eyes twinkle in amusement — as much as black eyes can twinkle, that is.

"I'm afraid I'll need that back, Little Fawn. I have a gift to give your mother," he says, wiggling the tip of his finger out of her mouth.

Her big eyes watch him as he removes his bow and quiver, placing them between us on the pallet. It is only then that I notice the bow is not the same as the one we use in the woods together — the one I often steal from him in order to practice.

Blaze clears his throat to get my attention. "Your own bow... so you can finally stop using mine."

Eyes wide, I hurriedly pass Seala to Oryn, eager to get my hands on the weapon. Lifting the bow, I twist it right and left to get a good look. This one has decorative, engraved patterns running down each side. "I love it," I whisper.

"I had help," Blazes shares. "Kallias carved the bow. Raener..."

The shock at hearing Raener's name in relation to participating in something has my attention jumping from the bow to Blaze in an instant.

Blaze clears his throat again before pulling out one of the arrows. If the bow was the most beautiful weapon I'd ever seen, the arrow itself rivals it. He twists it between his fingers and places it in his palm, bending his head down while holding his hands out to present it to me. "Raener," he continues, "told me what to carve into the arrows." With a closer look, I see exactly what he's talking about. The arrow appears to have some lettering on it. Lettering different than what I've seen during my travels in the mortal realm. "Each arrow represents one of your déō doúloi, and their matching oikía power. The words are Ancient Greek. This one says *geúomai* — the Greek translation is 'to taste.'"

I glance at Oryn, and he smiles in return.

My attention moves to the quiver and I peer inside. Four arrows remain. I relocate them from the holder to my lap. "Read them to me?" I request of Blaze.

He returns the geúomai arrow to the quiver and nods. I raise the first one and trace my fingers over the gorgeous symbols before displaying it to him. "*Ópsis*," he translates. "Sight."

This gives me pause, since I do not yet have the oikía power of sight. Though I have often wondered, of course, which huiós might become the déō doúlos to share that power — that wonderment often leaning toward the very man sitting before me.

The male that insists he'll never become a déō doúlos.

I brush aside that thought for now and pick up the next arrow, studying the symbols before once more holding the arrow out for Blaze to translate. "*Ósphrēsis* — sense of smell."

I share a quick glance with Brax before studying and lifting up the next. "*Háptomai*," Blaze responds. "Touch." Another of which I do not yet have. Another I thought I knew to which male it would surely belong.

Brushing aside the thought as quickly as possible, so as not to dwell once more on the certain paidagōgós I wish I could have, I lift the final arrow. "*Akouó*," Blaze verbalizes.

"Hearing," I complete, since I know this arrow represents Kirian.

Blaze nods once, and I share a glance and smile with my daimónion.

Kallias speaks up, "He makes it out like we did most of tha work, but we did nah. Nah really." Blaze shrugs, dismissing what Kallias is trying to say. But Kallias continues. "Ya know how much he does nah like t' leave tha forest. An' how much he does nah like talkin' t' others. He had t' travel a bit t' get everythin' needed. An' he had t' approach each of your current déō doúloi t' set tha power into their individual arrows."

I place the arrows all back into the quiver, finding it more difficult than expected to look into Blaze's eyes again. My mind works through what to say, but with my lack of filter from brain to mouth my tongue delivers, "If I didn't know any better, I'd say you actually like me."

"Never said I didn't," he responds with a smirk, leaning over close to deliver the remainder of his comment, too low for any being in the room to hear aside from Kirian. "I simply said I'm not interested in putting my cock in you."

"There are plenty of things you can put in me, Sikários... I've seen quite the collection in your hut," I whisper in return.

Blaze leans back, eyebrow raised and that cocky side-grin still plastered on his face. He chuckles and shakes his head. "Alright, I believe that is my cue to leave."

He stands, but my hand shoots out seemingly on its own, catching his fingers before he steps away. All joking aside, I say, "Thank you for the gift. I'll treasure it for the rest of my existence."

The smirk fades, and he takes in a deep breath. Instead of letting it out right away, he holds onto it, as though there's something else he wants to say. When the breath finally leaves him, all he responds with is a sharp nod before walking over to Kirian and taking his hand as though he can't leave fast enough.

Oryn holds up a finger, halting Kirian from leaving just yet. He turns to me and asks, "Ready for your next visitor?"

My gaze moves toward Blaze, and he's studying the cloth ceiling. With a sigh, I give Oryn a nod of acceptance. Kirian had watched the exchange and also nods at my mesítēs. Then Kirian and Blaze leave, the spark of the travel pýlē scarcely disappearing before Kirian is back with my next visitor.

CHAPTER NINE

Raener's black eyes pierce mine and hold for several heartbeats too long before he blinks, steps forward once, and bows just as Kallias had — one hand over his chest, the other behind his back. "Basílissa," he breathes.

"Paidagōgós," I respond, equally as formally if that's how he wants to play this.

The flash of frustration and hurt that crosses his features, however briefly, does not escape my notice. Perhaps he spots those same emotions flicker across my own expressions. Perhaps he still feels the same pain and heartbreak I do.

Then again... maybe he doesn't.

Raener steps forward, looks around the chamber, and finds whatever it was he'd been searching for. Walking over to a small, raised seat, he drags it beside the pallet, choosing to sit there rather than on the pallet with me. In the meantime, Oryn returns Seala to my arms.

Once situated, Raener displays what he'd been holding behind his back: a rolled scroll, similar to the many I had noticed before in the nooks inside his dwelling. This one, in particular, is a bit brighter and less worn than the others.

Placing it betwixt us, he unrolls the scroll, taking up every bit of space between me and where his knee touches the edge of the pallet. The parchment is filled with markings — words — from top to bottom.

Beside me, Oryn straightens and his previously relaxed posture hardens. My attention leaves the scroll to seek him out, to make sure everything is okay and there isn't some sort of unseen danger.

Worried, my gaze travels from the hard bob of his Adam's apple, to the inward curve of his eyebrows, and finally at the undeterminable emotion swimming through his dark-green eyes. My hand grabs his, and I squeeze gently, hoping he'll return to me and explain what's wrong. His fingers wrap around mine and squeeze back, and he blinks away the emotion. Instead of speaking or explaining, though, he tilts his head toward the parchment in a silent instruction to return my attention back toward Raener's gift.

Before I do so, though, I catch the gazes of Brax and Kallias. Both men have straightened and don similar, unidentifiable reactions. Kirian and I share a look; his confusion mimics my own.

Trusting my men… trusting that whatever has them more attuned to what's going on, but nothing to be concerned about, I finally return my attention to Raener.

His black eyes bore into mine, but with a flick down, I notice his somewhat ragged breathing. With another glance, I notice the way his finger lightly taps the edge of the parchment.

"Are you up for a lesson?" he asks, voice low.

Not too long ago I wanted nothing more than an indefinite amount of lessons from him. "Always," I whisper in response.

His black eyes meet mine before he dips his head down and takes in a deep breath. "I'm aware you are not educated in the ways of the paidagōgói, nor what it is — other than teaching — that we do." I shake my head and

79

blink at him expectantly. "So that's what I'd like to share with you in this lesson."

A thick silence descends between us — a special type of silence. Panic suddenly consuming me, I dart an anxious glance around. Brax holds his hand up and points to his ear. Perplexed, I look back at Raener again.

"You've created a shield of silence around you and me," Raener explains with a breathy chuckle. "Seala, too."

"Should I remove it?" I ask, eyes wide. The first time I created a shield of silence, I had done it unknowingly. The second time, purposefully. Seems the power is more an intuitive one than anything else.

"That is up to you," Raener answers.

I meet the focused attentions of the other men in the room and they all seem accepting of my decision either way. "I am ready," I decide.

Raener nods and continues. "One of the most important jobs of paidagōgói, is to record Ceteris's history. But these aren't just simple play-by-plays of events. We were given the power of revelation. The paidagōgói are the only beings in Ceteris that still have a link to The Maker."

My eyes widen impossibly large, but my tongue remains still, my ears and mind ready to absorb more. All of it.

Raener's eyes travel briefly to Brax, and the two of them share a look, even despite Brax and the others being unable to hear our conversation. "This is the main reason why the grigori and paidagōgói are at such odds with each other. The Watchers were the only beings once upon a long time ago that held this ability. But when they lost The Maker's trust, they lost the ability to receive messages — revelations — and guidance from The

Maker. Those keys were passed on to a new group of beings: the paidagōgói. We did not Fall out of disobedience," he explains. "We Fell to share the knowledge of how Ceteris would serve its purpose in The Maker's plan. And, ultimately, how to best serve that plan."

"You… can speak to The Maker?" I ask, bemused.

"Well, yes and no," he begins to explain. "Revelations from The Maker come more in the form of the spark of an idea. The flame of an intuitive knowledge or belief. A certainty when you would otherwise feel uncertain. The trick lies in our ability to translate the messages. Writing them comes easy enough. Determining what they mean — their significance — is where the challenge lies."

"I can't even imagine," I respond on a breath.

Raener gives me a small smile before clearing his throat, dropping his gaze back to the parchment, and tapping the swirls and lines of lettering. "As I said just a moment ago, we don't record stories. Expositions. But… I wanted to for this occasion. So… I wrote down every detail of Seala's birth from the moment I arrived at Oryn's hut, to the moment—" the words catch, and he clears them free "—to the moment you placed her in my arms and left with Oryn to feed."

Words get stuck in my throat, too, and I swallow hard, willing those tears that are building not to fall. But they do. One drop at a time, they track down my cheeks. There comes a point where I can't see anything through the fog of liquid.

"Adrestia," Raener says, only worsening their declivity. "Please…" he begs. "Please don't cry." But I can't stop; Not only am I crying due to the beautiful gift, the tears pour free also because I can't hug him. I can't do all the things to prove how grateful I am that he was part of the experience. Saying "thank you" isn't enough and it never will be.

He pushes his hand across the parchment, bringing his fingertips as close to my leg as he can without touching me before curling them into a fist and leaning back on the stool. He waits patiently until I calm down.

When I can focus and listen again, he straightens and points to a part at the bottom of the parchment that is separate from the rest. "After I finished, I received a very unexpected revelation in the form of a Name Blessing. This type of blessing is not something paidagōgói usually receive. Rather, they are more often only received by certain mortal messengers. My only guess is that I was able to receive it because you — her mother — are part mortal. Perhaps she is, too, but that has yet to be determined, of course."

I study the scroll, but the writing therein is not something in which I am versed. Raener catches my attempts and raises his eyes to mine again. "May I give her a proper blessing?" he asks. "By reciting this short revelation aloud to her?"

"Yes, I... I would love that." This entire time, the silence shield was restricted to just the three of us, though, and with something so seemingly significant, I want the others involved, too. With a look, I inquire as to whether or not I can allow them to join us in hearing this blessing.

Raener takes a look around the room and gives me an apologetic look. "Yes," he responds, "but only Oryn and Brax. Kallias is not yet bound to you... and Kirian is part daimónion; we aren't sure how intertwined his connection is with Belíar."

With a nod of understanding, I extend the shield to include Brax and Oryn. Whether or not a watchful Kallias and Kirian can tell they haven't been included, I am not sure.

Welcoming each into the conversation, Raener tilts his head toward Oryn "Adelphós" and gives Brax a haughty grin "Grigori."

In brief, he explains to them about the revelation and how he would like to recite it. The two nod, quietly aware.

Raener reaches forward and lifts her tiny hand.

Seala, be steadfast in your growth. Rise to the challenges you will face. Teach, help, and prepare — for deliverance is a future not bestowed to many. Dive deep and fly high.

As soon as Raener is done, we all reflect for a moment. When I finally glance around at my men, Oryn displays a look of stunned reverence, and Brax's eyes are on Raener with more compassion than I've ever seen him deliver toward the paidagōgós.

Brax stands, wraps his arms around Raener's shoulders, and lifts him out of the seat and into the air, squeezing him tight.

When Brax places Raener back onto his feet, the look of utter astonishment in Raener's black eyes is enough to turn my silenced shock into laughter.

Once we're all done enjoying the hilarity of the moment, Oryn clears his throat, bows at Raener, and says, "Adelphós, hearing you recite our daughter's blessing was great honor. One we will not soon forget. Nor ever." He turns toward me. "Basílissa... thank you for allowing us to be part of something so revered and special. Blessings are not a thing of this realm. We are not worthy of spiritual endowments. To be in the presence of a being" — his gaze drops to Seala — "who is worthy of such a gift, is a gift in and of itself. One we are so grateful to have received."

Brax steps forward toward Raener again, but Raener holds out a palm. "Once was enough, giant. Enough to last me an existence, in fact."

Brax clears his throat and lets out a raspy, "*Sas efharistó.*"

"*Parakaló.* It was an honor," Raener responds, giving Brax a small bow.

I place my hand on Oryn's forearm, and he looks down at me. "Sorry to pause the moment, but I need to release this shield before my energy becomes too much lower." I return my attention to Raener and bow my head down for several moments before lifting my gaze to his. "Sas efharistó," I whisper, mimicking what Brax had said, knowing it meant *thank you.*

"Parakaló," he responds with a bow of his own.

When his head lifts and he bends down to roll the scroll back up, our eyes meet. The very tip of Raener's finger grazes my leg, an action that means so much more than words or gifts ever could to me in this moment. He doesn't grimace, doesn't draw attention to the attack of the hélkō. If it weren't for the pain in his eyes that I've become so accustomed to, it would have been hard to tell anything had happened. At my side, my own fingers twitch with a desperate need to return the touch. To respond in wordless kind. Instead, I lift them to Seala's head and trace her hairline, dropping my gaze from Raener, to look at my daughter instead.

Chest heaving with each strained breath. Each tear withheld. Each nerve I mentally cauterize to refrain from seeking out the feel of Raener's skin against mine. The only thing that takes me out of my mental battle is the sound of Oryn's voice, and the warmth of his hand on my shoulder. "Adrestia," he whispers. "Everything okay?"

Raener had been so sneaky with it that even Oryn didn't notice. He did notice, however, my physical responses. "Soon," I respond. "I… I think I need some time to… recover." More fitting words to describe how I feel are lost on me, so that's the best I can do.

Oryn nods, sending a quiet instruction to Kirian. Kirian leaves, taking Raener with him. The rolled scroll remains at my side as the only reminder of his presence. Brax bends down and places a kiss on my forehead followed by doing the same to Seala. He then uses a giant-sized pýlē to leave the chamber on his own. When Kirian pops back in to retrieve Kallias, I stop them short, finding my voice again. "More than anything right now, I'd very much like to wash. I have sand embedded in my hair, and in other areas, too, I imagine." For the next part, I lower my voice trying hard to sound like a queen despite feeling so far from it. "But I don't want to be alone."

That single touch from Raener was enough to fill me with equal parts love and loneliness. An odd combination that hurts on so many different levels.

"Oryn?"

"Yes, Basílissa?"

"Would you be willing to stay here with Seala while Kallias accompanies me to the beach?"

"Of course." Oryn leans down, slips his finger beneath my chin, and lifts my gaze to his. For a moment, I assume he's going to say something. Set parameters. Something to keep me safe. Instead, he brushes his lips against mine before kissing me soft and slow. When he pulls away he whispers, "The gift he wishes he could have given you." He scoops Seala out of my arms and gestures at Kallias to step forward. "Pamper our queen, hm?" he says with a wink and the dimpled grin I so seldom see anymore.

CHAPTER TEN

Rather than use a pýlē to travel to the water, Kallias and I choose to walk instead. Half the enjoyment of our beach excursions is the walk there and back. When our heads dip below the hill that barricades the beach from the rest of my territory, only then does Kallias clear his throat to break the comfortable silence. When I look at him in response, he glances up into the sky and takes in a deep breath.

He slings his pack over his shoulder and removes the several recognizable items often used for washing.

"Is… something on your mind?" I inquire when he closes his mouth instead of letting out whatever it was he had considered saying.

Kallias pauses the preparations. With his back toward me, I am unable to make out his expression. Strangely enough — and quite concerning — he ignores my question. Or, simply chooses not to answer. Which is very much unlike the man who is typically quite open.

With everything gathered, he turns and faces me head-on, his black eyes piercing and tawny, wide chest moving up and down with each carefully controlled breath.

After a few moments, he finally opens his mouth to speak: "Ah, I do nah want t' over step, or pressure ya, Basílissa, but ya need more déō doúloi. Ya an' Oryn can nah continue t' do all tha feeds alone."

Shoulders straight, chin jutted, I place my hands on my hips and look into Kallias's eyes. "That is hardly my fault; I had been instructed not to fuck at all while carrying Seala inside me."

Kallias lets out a sigh followed by one of his hearty chuckles. "Yeah, I know. But ya are nah carryin' her inside ya *anymore*." His eyes travel down to my stomach and back up to my face.

Instead of saying anything more, he jerks his head to the side, gesturing for me to follow him into the water.

"I... can wash myself," I say haughtily.

"Nevah thought ya could nah," he responds. Of all the huiói I interact with, he is also the best at redirecting my attitude. "But ya know I like t' help."

And the truth is, I very much enjoy his help. But more so his companionship. Of which I seldom tire.

Kallias places the items on the edge of the rocks beside us, and with some of the wood ash concoction pre-made, he gathers all my hair into one of his hands and tugs my head back into the water to dampen it. He pours the wood ash mixture next, saturating the locks, and massages it into my hair and scalp with his fingertips.

"Hair first?" I ask, curious. We usually put the clay on and let it dry a bit before entering the water.

He hums in response as he places his hands on my shoulders and leads me deeper. Instead of rinsing my hair right away, as he typically does once we're in this deep, he presses his body flush against mine from behind. His hard, long, and most definitely triggered cock slips between my legs, brushing against every nerve that is more than eager to feel and experience again.

That Kallias can harden is not new knowledge for me, though he does hide it well... usually. During our washes I've felt the occasional brush when the water makes it bob or he accidentally steps too close.

This time, though, it wasn't an accident.

Pulse going wild and untamed in my veins, I rest my sudsy head back against his chest. I had asked him early on if he was interested in me and he'd said *yes*, but he hadn't since shown much proof of carrying that interest over into anything more than what we presently have — a friendship.

"Are ya still interested in me?" he asks, running his hands over my shoulders and down my arms.

"Never stopped being since the moment we met," I whisper back, my voice hitching on a gasp as he purposefully grinds his hips against mine.

"I do nah have tha desire t' do things like most other huiói," he explains. "That is why I have nah accepted your bond-call yet."

It's hard to care about — or be concerned with — anything *different* when he's speaking with that accented baritone and rubbing up against me.

When I remain quiet, Kallias continues, "Damn, I want ya," he licks the edge of my ear with the tip of his tongue. "But there are other things I'd like t' do first... Before fuckin' ya... Leadin' up t' that..." Between each elaboration, he kisses me, starting just below my ear, and ending on the top of my shoulder.

Ahead of us, the sun approaches the horizon, almost ready to put on a show. With the way his words and actions stir up my insides, everything around us seems so vibrant and crisp.

"Mmm," is all the response I can muster, pressing my backside against him.

"Does nah work that way, my queen," he says, chuckling again. "Use yah words."

"Was there a question?" is my breathy reply.

Kallias is quiet for a moment, then without twisting his words, he asks, "Can I tie ya up... before I fuck ya?"

I turn in his arms and gawk up at him in shock. "Tie me up? That's... a thing? Sounds fun! When? Right now? Yes!"

Kallias's wide, beautiful smile shines bright.

Without another word, he pulls my hair into the water, rinses it out, and leads me back to the shore to grab his supplies.

Everything gets placed into his pack, the pack gets slung over his shoulder, and he takes my hand in his, guiding me wordlessly down the shoreline, away from the bowl of rocks that is our usual spot. "I've been waitin' t' show ya this spot. With tha hope our bindin' would be tha reason I take ya here."

We walk to where the hill ends, and he turns to the right, guiding us behind it. I had imagined this area would be more flatland, much like the rest of this territory, but it's not. In fact, the hill doesn't end at all; it opens instead. Water travels a path into the hill's mouth, and the grassy ground morphs into sand and stone.

We wade inside and he directs me toward a protruding rock that bulges to a bumpy peak in the middle of the water.

The two of us climb atop, and he sits, knees up. I follow suit, tilting my knees to the side. Kallias picks up a stick and begins to scratch something into the moss and dirt-covered mound between us. First, a circle. From the circle he draws four scraggly lines, adding in a somewhat misshapen drawing of... a body? More squiggly lines, which appear to be connecting to one of the four previously-drawn lines. The middle line now circles the middle of the crude stick-figure drawing. And the third and fourth lines appear to be attaching to the figure's legs.

"As ya know," he begins, "I once lived in Avaritia for a long, long time. Kainda was nah a terrible queen, but she was a selfish one, of course. Oftentimes, her actions were too self-servin'. An' oftentimes, that negatively impacted her subjects an' tha land she governed. Our partin' was nah dramatic, nor was our personal history. Simply due t' her greed, I could nah be on board with becomin' a déō doúlos. T' make it easier on tha both of us, I left.

"You can do that? Just leave a territory? A queen?"

"Most of tha time, yeah. If we are nah bound, we do nah have t' stay."

A brief sadness fills me at this news. I would not wish for the huiói in this territory to desire to leave.

"Unsure where I wanted t' go — nah yet certain if tha rebel territory was for me — I traveled. From territory to territory. Traveling is nah easy, Basílissa. It's nah for everyone. That's why most do nah leave," he answers, no doubt picking up on my unease, desiring to give me what reassurance he can. "Of the places I traveled," he continues, "Superbia was one of my favorites... Tha territory, not the queen." He gives me a wink and a big grin.

Superbia. A name I learned not too long ago means "pride" and belongs to Amrita, the Basílissa of Pride. Each queen's territory, the more proper name of her sin specialty.

"Their culture, is... intriguin'. One of tha things I learned there is tha act of rope tyin'. Since I like t' do stuff with my hands, I quickly began t' enjoy it. When I got here, before I decided t' interact with tha other huiói, I spent a lot of time in this cave, tyin' knots, makin' patterns... things like that. Amrita likes t' see her men tied up and suspended, though she is never tha one to do it herself. Her déō doúloi or other resident huiói will.

"As intrigued by it as I was, I often helped… eventually got around to doin' it solo, in performance for Amrita."

"You enjoyed it." I smile at him.

"I enjoy many things with my hands, Basílissa." He winks.

I return my attention to the lines in the dirt. "Tell me more about what you've drawn."

Kallias takes in a deep breath and taps at the drawing with the stick. "This is a — terrible — example of tha suspension I'd like t' work on ya."

I mull the words over in my mind. "So, you will tie me and lift me so that I'm hovering in the air? Then what?"

"Yes… and then… whatever you'd like," he says. "I know touchin' ya makes yah skin sing in response. We can start with that," he suggests, referring back to all the many bumps that rise on every inch of my skin whenever he touches me.

"Sounds… fun. How about you explain more to me, while you get started?"

CHAPTER ELEVEN

Kallias nods, making an added effort to tame the growing smile on his face. The man is excited, that much is evident, yet he still tries to keep his composure and the beaming grin to a minimum.

He walks to the edge of the small rock protrusion, leans forward a bit over the water, and hooks his fingers into a crevice in the stone above his head. A hoop-like apparatus drops out, swaying side-to-side, but otherwise stays connected and hooked to a point inside the cleft.

Kallias grips the hoop and hangs off it for a few seconds, displaying its sturdiness. "This is where you'll suspend from, if ya decide yah are comfortable 'nough t' take it that far," he explains as he swings back to the edge of the mound, lets go of the hoop, and returns to my side.

He takes a few bundles of rope out of his pack and sets them each beside us in their own piles before choosing which one to start with, unraveling it, and looping it over my head. "For now, we'll start with a chest binding. See what ya think 'bout that."

Overcome with curiosity, it's not at all difficult for me to relax and simply enjoy the show of Kallias's handiwork. In the front, he criss-crosses the rope above and beneath my breasts. But when he steps behind me, I can no longer watch what is happening. "Does this feel too tight?" he eventually asks.

"Not at all," I reply.

"Would ya like it t' be tighter?" he inquires further.

"I'm okay with having it tighter, but you are more knowledgeable on this topic, so how about you do what makes you happy, and I'll let you know if something displeases me?"

Kallias lets out a quiet chuckle. "Nah sure there's a better answer than that. I might still ask ya questions sometimes, if that's okay?"

"Yes, of course," I respond.

When he's done preparing my chest and upper arms, tying my wrists together at about mid-back, he instructs me to lie on my belly and bring my heels to my butt. Getting into this position is a bit difficult to do — lying with my belly and chest on the ground and my head to the side is a bit awkward — but as soon as he begins to wrap another bundle of rope around the calves and ankle of one leg, the awkwardness of having to hold it in that folded position lessens significantly.

For the other leg, he wraps the calf, ankle and foot, but doesn't fold and bind it to my thigh.

The chest restraint already compromised my ability to defend myself physically, but now that my legs are bound, too, I have little to no control any longer. As a knee-jerk thought, I cycle through my oikía-earned powers for ways to get out, should a need arise.

I'd been practicing my powers, both here on this beach with Kallias or Kirian by my side, but also in the mortal realm during my many feeds over the past couple moon-cycles. Unfortunately, none of those would prove useful for escaping this rope.

Being restrained clearly is my weakness.

My danger zone where control is concerned.

"Ya sure are thinkin' a lot, Basílissa." Kallias breaks the silence. "Tell me what's on yah mind?"

94

With my cheek pressed to the ground, facing his direction, I attempt a smile up at him, but the gravel of the rock scratches my skin. "Just determining how to get free should there be an emergency. Nothing to be concerned with, though."

"Well now, if yah are nah comfortable enough t' trust that yah are safe here durin' this, I would rather wait."

Oh no. No more waiting.

I narrow my eyes at him the best I can in this position, and he chuckles. "No, I quite like what's going on and am looking forward to what's to come," I insist.

Kallias nods, accepting my answers. "The last tie will be in yah hair — if ya are agreeable."

In response, I shrug my shoulders a bit, but they don't move much due to having my biceps tied to my sides.

"Words, Basílissa," Kallias laughs.

"I'm not disagreeable until I experience it firsthand, then I'll have more of an opinion."

"Good answer. Roll t' yah side, and I will help ya up," he instructs.

With a little assistance, I roll to the side of my folded leg and together we adjust me onto my knees. With my center unbound, I am able to straighten or sit back on my heels now. Whichever I prefer.

From this position, though, I can notice something I had not been able to just moments before. Kallias's hard and incredibly erect cock. With him standing, and me kneeling, I begin to wonder...

Curiosity swirling through me, I glance up at his towering form from under my eyelashes as he wraps the long, loose end of the rope that's binding my chest and arms around the palm of his hand.

Everything comes to life around me, my powers wisping outward to play: Water laps like a whisper along the outer walls of rock and against the hill we're mounted on; A light breeze coming through the maw of the cave cools my exposed skin; The ropes seem to emit heat, though, resulting in an extra-sensory experience.

Just beyond the opening of the cave, as if the cave was hand-carved just for the sole purpose of having a sunset view, the sun now dips close to the horizon and shares with us the vivid oranges and pinks of a newly established sunset.

Kallias stills, and his gaze drifts toward me. "Are ya usin' yah powers righ' now?"

"Not really using them, no…" I respond on a whisper, my eyes now riveted once more on his working shaft. "Just… allowing them to breathe."

Astute as he tends to be, Kallias turns to face me and takes the two steps forward that will bring him much closer. With his towering form looming above me, his eyes like dried lava, he reaches down with his non-roped hand and cups my face. His thumb slips down and over my jaw to the part of my neck just below my chin before the rest of his fingers scoop around to the back of my neck.

Kallias doesn't squeeze, but rather continues dragging his thumb slowly down the center of my throat and back up again. Memorized by this cathartic way he touches me, primes me, my body relaxes in the bindings, and I let go, allowing my upper body to sink down so that I am now sitting on my heels rather than kneeling erect.

Without a word, the pad of Kallias's thumb comes to the middle spot just under my chin, and he pushes upward, encouraging my neck to arch back farther.

These males might be subservient most of the time, but it's clear that on most occasions, many — though certainly not all — prefer the opposite role. One of dominance where intimacy is concerned.

It's amazing to me how little Kallias has to do for my body to thrum, vibrate, and ache. Just this small show — trial — of dominance proves to drive me wild. Especially when his hand drops from my neck and he takes a step back. I want nothing more in that instant than to keep him right here to see where else that touch leads.

He walks to the rocky edge, leans forward, and grabs that swinging hoop. Once in his grip, he unravels the rope he'd twisted around his hand and expertly ties it onto the hoop, creating a pulley-type apparatus. When he pulls on the loose part, now, the rope that leads from the loop to my upper back becomes less slack. He clears his throat, and continues his instructions: "We will use yah unfolded leg t' get ya to a temporary standin' position, so I can carry ya into tha water."

"Okay," I respond, remembering he prefers I use words rather than head gestures.

He wraps his arms around my waist and ribs, making sure to provide my upper body as much support as possible, and lifts me until I am able to balance on my unbound leg.

"Ready for me t' pick ya up?"

"Yes," I answer.

He carefully scoops one arm under my thigh, his hand on that arm holding onto and supporting the shin of my bound leg. His other arm remains around my back and over my bound arms.

From there, he carefully wades us into the water. Mere feet past the hill, the underwater terrain changes significantly in depth, and in an instant he is chest deep, holding me against him just high enough that I'm not fully submerged.

With a quick adjustment, he eases my lower body into the water until I'm once again balanced on the one leg, my face the only thing above the surface.

"How are ya, Basílissa?" he asks, keeping one around me for support, since I can't use my own arms to hold myself up against him.

"This is exciting," is my response. "What's next?"

"I'm gonna attach yah leg-thigh bindin' t' tha anchor. After that, I'll alternate tightenin' tha chest and leg pulls until yah are suspended enough for me t' bind yah free leg an' hair t' tha anchor."

"Okay." I give him a big smile. "I'm ready."

"When yah are suspended, it will feel different. The suspension will make tha ropes tighter addin' compression to certain places, while relievin' pressure from others. If you do nah want t' talk, I do nah want t' bother ya with questions. But I will need t' know if ya do nah like somethan."

"I promise to tell you if I'm not enjoying something."

Kallias's wide smile returns, and the hand that still has some rope wrapped around it emerges from the water to cup my cheek. The thick rope separates the warmth of his palm from direct contact with my skin, but his thumb and fingers are still able to drag lightly down my cheek and along my jaw before he leans down and brings his lips close to mine. However, when I try to lengthen my posture, pushing up onto the tips of my toes, he moves just a hairsbreadth farther away to where I cannot connect our mouths.

His smile is replaced by the tug of his bottom lip behind his teeth as his eyes travel down to my mouth. He lingers like this for only a heartbeat longer before instructing me to lean my shoulder against his chest so he can tighten the chest and arm pulley enough to hold me still.

Once I'm situated against his chest, he lets go of my waist and uses his now-free hand to wrap the remaining slack around his rope hand. Once wrapped, he tugs on the rope, going several inches at a time until there's new slack to wrap around his fist. After a few pulls, the tension of the rope that leads to my chest and arm bindings is solid.

"Tha water is what helps t' make this suspension possible," he explains. "When I begin t' pull yah leg up, yah body's natural ability t' float will aid in supportin' the ascension. Tha fact that yah chest bindin' is mostly already set, we'll only need to tweak it a bit to get you to the height we want."

"You... the height you want."

"Ah... righ'. Tha height *I* want." He smiles at me once more before reaching above us and unwrapping a new rope from the hoop dangling above.

The water also serves to help keep me balanced. Should I be on land right now, trying to balance on one foot, I'm certain I would have face planted by now. Even still, when he lets go of me for a brief moment, I find myself wobbling a little.

To counteract the motion, Kallias's hand supports me again, pressing his palm against my chest instead of scooping his arm around my waist. When he moves it down a little I understand why. Should he move his hand down farther, the added weight to my midsection will make me dip forward, submerging my face into the water. Which we certainly don't want.

"Basílissa," he says over the gurgle of liquid receding from the nearby rock.

"Hm?"

"If I let go of ya for a short time, will ya be able t' balance on yah own for long enough for me t' tie this off?"

"Yes, I think so."

"Okay, just in case, trying leanin' your hip against my shoulder if ya need extra support."

"A-against your shoulder?"

Kallias grins wide before his head disappears into the water, his hands using the shape of my body to find his way down to where he needs to be. Which is not where I need him to be, I realize after all this touching and tying and talking.

Just as he had mentioned, I am now able to lean my hip against his shoulder while he wraps and ties the dangling rope to the calf and ankle of my free-standing leg.

When he emerges, he's holding two ropes. The one he'd just attached, and the loose one leftover from my leg and thigh that are bound together.

With a quick hop, he slings both ropes through the hoop in order to create their individual pulleys. "I will pull these at tha same time so that yah bottom half emerges balanced. But I'll need t' tie 'em off securely before letting' go. So for tha next while, I'm gonna be behind ya. I'll watch ya closely, though. Maybe speak t' me until ya don't want t' speak anymore? Just for my own piece of mind?"

"I can do that," I respond a bit breathless, feeling a flutter in my belly and a pounding in my chest for the first time since we started.

Kallias gets started right away, alternating smooth tugs from each rope to ensure balance. First he focuses on lifting my free leg until it's floating directly beside my bound leg. This, of course, causes my upper body to tilt forward and my chin to dip into the water, requiring me to lift my head higher. I relay this information to Kallias, sharing that having my chest suspended higher would be more preferable. He responds immediately by adjusting the chest and arm pulley.

Once that's more ideal, he continues lifting my bottom half until the only thing touching the water is a small portion of my stomach. He quickly ties them off as promised after first making sure the binding around my legs feels okay to me.

Remnants of water drip from the suspended ropes, pinging against my skin with each cool drop.

As soon as my legs are suspended above the water, the compression Kallias had warned about is evident in my chest and upper arm area. About that time, as it constricts my breathing a bit, I fall silent... opting to simply feel rather than speak. We'd ventured down to the beach with my energy levels already pretty low, but not too much that I'd need a feed right away. Enough, though, that it creates this surreal aphasic sensation when mixed with the breathlessness and the different amounts of pressure everywhere the ropes press into my skin.

Everything is a bit uncomfortable... yet not. Mostly, it's a good uncomfortable. Except for my neck, which sort of just dangles unless I lift it. Not realizing I'd closed my eyes, I reopen them and lift my head, deciding that even though I'd prefer to not talk, it would probably be a good idea for me to update Kallias on the unpleasant discomfort I feel in my neck. When my eyes open, Kallias is just coming around to my front.

With the suspension complete, he and I are now almost exactly nose to nose. Lost in the many sensations, I forget for a moment what I needed to express and instead my eyes travel to his lips before drifting back up to his black gaze. I blink once to clear my thoughts and say, "My neck hurts a bit."

Kallias nods, his attention serious but filled with an unbridled heat. "Tha hair bindin' should help with that."

I'd forgotten about him mentioning a hair binding. "Great," I say with a lazy smile. Kallias's fingers push through my hair with ease, and I piece together now why he'd conditioned and rinsed my hair first. Because if he hadn't, there'd be no way he would have been able to work through the tangled strands. Once every bit is gathered in his hands, I feel a twist and a gentle yank, then one of his hands drop and he leans over to grab a smaller rope from the rock's edge. From there, he twists the rope into my hair, and after a few more moments I feel the rope-provided support as he ties this new section to the hoop. This tilts my head up just enough to keep it where I had lifted it naturally.

Once complete, he holds his hands up in front of my face and wiggles his fingers. "How's that?" he asks.

I groan, allowing myself to feel everything for the first time without some small thing hindering my comfort.

Kallias's chuckles and the sound rolls through me. "Words, Basílissa."

"Everything feels wonderful," I share.

His hands come to my cheeks, now both free of rope and the tasks at hand. Those captivating lips finally come close enough to brush against mine. My eyes close, reveling in the feel of his warm breath and the softness of the kiss.

Before, I was able to meet him for the kiss, even if he didn't let me finish the motion. Now, I am bound to his wishes and desires. Should I have any, of course he'd expect me to speak up, but I am more curious to see what he chooses to do. That concept intrigues me more than what I might choose to have him do myself. Plus... the unknowing... the anticipation... already has me in a state of mind that should he give the command for me to orgasm, I very well might do just that. Without a need to even be touched.

His lips brush mine again, feeling in the most simplest of ways — in the gentlest of caresses — and I wonder for a moment how he is able to refrain from doing more. More everything. How he can stay so controlled in such an emotionally and physically intense situation.

"This is torture," I choose to relay. The speech is the only way I can get my mouth to move against his.

"That's exactly tha point." Kallias winks, and as a direct response wetness and a throb of need forms between my thighs.

Our eyes meet, and he drags his thumbs over each of my cheeks. He leans in and fully connects our mouths. First tasting me with the slow tracing of his tongue along the line of my lips. Then devouring me, by dipping his tongue inside and twisting it around mine nice and slow. He continues palming my cheek with one hand while remaining engaged in the kiss. The other hand leaves my cheek and he drags his fingertips down the side of my neck to my exposed shoulder. Every inch of my skin on that shoulder and arm rises in bumps in response to that touch, just as he'd predicted.

Our lips disconnect, and he kisses along the same line he'd traced, making those bumps reemerge in an instant. While his mouth moves back up my neck and to my ear, his fingers take a different path, moving over the rope that binds the top of my chest, until he reaches the exposed skin of my breast. First, he takes it in his palm, cupping me gently, filling his palm and caressing the breast with gentle squeezes. He switches breasts while bringing his mouth back to mine and dipping his tongue between my lips for another anguishing kiss.

By the time that foray ends, his fingers are back to the first breast, toying with the peak of my nipple. Our kiss breaks and he brings the hand that had been cupping my cheek down to pinch and flick the opposite nipple in rhythm with the other.

Kallias gives me the first pain test by pinching the outermost tip harder than he had before. A gasp escapes my lips, followed by a moan. My body responds in kind, covering in those bumps that seem to always speak on my behalf.

Then he does something I'm most certainly not expecting: he slips his hand to my ribcage and nudges me backward just enough to cause the slightest swinging motion. Which, in turn, makes my aching nipples dip into the cool water before emerging again on the upward swing.

The opposing sensations cause my body to tense and relax all at once. To bind in pain and unravel in pleasure. Lost in the sensation, I scarcely register that Kallias had dipped his head down. But when his hot mouth covers one of my nipples, adding a warmth where the cool water had previously been, an unexpected orgasm crashes through me. Kallias quickly moves back up and he crashes his mouth against mine, riding the wave with me through the meld of our kiss.

When my breathing finally calms and I am able to open my eyes again, Kallias is looking straight into my soul. "Mmm," he says simply, licking his bottom lip before drawing it behind his teeth. "Amazing," he includes. "Adrestia, I've never seen anything more beautiful than you."

That's one thing I've always thought about Kallias, too. Everything about him is like a painting. Every line and muscle. His smooth, rich coloring. The way his bright, white smile lights up even the darkest of caves. I want to share the same sentiment, but every part of me is heightened right now. Sensitive. All I can do is close my eyes and… feel.

Again his lips meet mine in a gentle kiss, but this one doesn't last long. One step at a time, he undoes all the hard work he spent getting me to this point. The process is careful and quiet. Lost in every moment of the experience. In every touch, every pain, every pleasure, I'm wholly his right now. And he knows that. He'd been careful when suspending me, but he's even more careful now, allowing me to descend both literally and mentally without effort. There comes a point where the ropes no longer bind me, and I'm in his arms being carried back up to the rock and placed gently on my back.

CHAPTER TWELVE

Only when I am on my back, and he is no longer holding me against him, do my eyes open and meet his once more. Those deep, black eyes have already lightened, unless it's a trick of the sunset. What we set out to do is not yet accomplished; more is needed to complete our bond.

Kallias, however, is done waiting. Every bit of the process for him, every step, an added aphrodisiac. Still wordless and weak, I don't want my happy silence to deter him, so I reach for his face and pull him down to me, lifting myself into a kiss. This time, he lets me take the control, receiving it as my acceptance. Of the tying. Of the suspension. Of the soon-to-be-accomplished binding.

He takes my hips in his hands and adjusts me to be sure there aren't any uncomfortable rocks digging into my back. He'd been in this cave and on this hill enough times to be able to map out each individual bump and groove. My lower half fits perfectly in a shallow dip in the rock's formation. My back rests up and over a curved protrusion.

Kallias's head dips down and he takes one of my nipples between his teeth, giving it a good nip as he situates his knees betwixt my thighs. When his mouth leaves my pert nipple, he's ready. The length and width of him hard and extended.

Before finalizing the bond, his gaze rakes over every inch of my skin where the rope branded and he traces the patterns with a feather-light touch. The markings his actions left behind cause his cock to twitch in appreciation, serving as a reminder of the next task at hand.

As though he has done this part before, he enters me with a smooth confidence. A grunt emits from his throat on the first thrust. His head falls back, eyes close, and his long twists of hair fall off his shoulders as his fingers dig into the flesh of my hips. When he pulls back, slipping out of me just enough to make room for the next thrust, his eyes open and meet mine. The two of us connect on the next stroke, eyes locked onto each other, completely enraptured. Kallias pulls out just enough before slamming back in with the combination between groan and grunt.

The color of his eyes changes right before me, with our gazes locked and consumed in one another. The black fades, but not by much, changing to a mesmerizing golden-brown that mimics the deepest of oranges of the waning sun. They change just in time for me to catch that special moment before the sun disappears fully and we're in absolute blackness.

Again, all my senses heighten in order to compensate for the lack of light. My eyes quickly adjust to the dimness; little specks of green and iridescent blue sparkle inside in the cave, bringing light to the otherwise extremely dark surroundings. A salty flavor coats my lips, coming into the cave on the faintest of breezes. A mixture of that same salt, the chalkiness of red sand, and Kallias's desire hits my heightened sense of smell as we tumble into the darkness and into each other, churning like the building of a wave and crashing at their end.

The energy concocted from our binding provides enough to sustain my reserves so that I no longer need to feed right away and can, instead, stay here in the arms of my newest déō doúlos.

Kallias is careful not to fall on top of me with my body balancing on the rocks the way it is; he sits beside me, scanning my body dutifully to make sure everything is okay as he casually begins collecting everything into a pile. It is in this moment when I realize exactly what his oikía power is. What it has hinted toward being all along. I sit straight up and take in everything around me, realizing I can see inside the cave quite well considering the sun has now disappeared.

A number of thoughts hit me at once: An exceeding gratefulness; Giddiness over our new binding; A rush of adrenaline as our shared oikía power flows between us; But... also, a moroseness settles on my shoulders, heavy and suffocating. Before bonding with Kallias, I hadn't really taken into consideration that, according to Oryn's hypothesis, only two more males would become my déō doúloi. I had wrongfully — and naively — assumed Blaze might be one of those candidates. That he'd be the one to give me the power of sight. That Raener would be "touch."

But now, there's only one more spot, and I realize just how much I'd become so attached to both Blaze and Raener. How much I'd hoped they would somehow, even despite holding titles beyond the huioí meant for bonds with a basílissa, become mine.

From the moment Kallias and I had first seen each other, I wanted him, too — this want, no doubt, heightened on account of his oikía power. Kallias is, indeed, a sight to behold. Getting to know him only served to fortify our budding relationship and bring us to this point.

So, during a moment where I should be celebrating, basking in the moment with my newest déō doúlos I am instead... confused. Upset. Frustrated. Angry. All these misplaced emotions at quite the inopportune time roiling through me.

Fucking Belíar.

"Basílissa? Words?" Kallias whispers, tossing the now-filled pack behind us.

But I can't tell him. Not Kallias.

Kainda was selfish. That's what turned him away from her. I don't want to disappoint him. I want to be everything his former queen wasn't and more.

"I wish I could read tha' beautiful mind of yahs," he says, mimicking the same sentiment my daimónion had shared.

"No... you do not," I whisper.

Kallias nods, not undermining my response. "If nothin' more, I do want ya t' know that it is nah unusual for tha bein' who was tied in a suspension t' experience a wave of emotions before, durin', an' after. I have nah suspended a female before now, but tha male huiói do... so I am sure it migh' be tha same for ya."

My head turns toward him abruptly. "That is... reassuring. Though, I'm afraid these ones won't just go away."

Kallias nods and looks over the rocks and water into the depths of the cave, no doubt testing out his now-obvious oikía power.

Instead of dwelling on what had inconveniently taken me out of this moment with him, my eyes focus into the distance as well. "All these... flickering lights? They're amazing. What are they?"

"Ya know... I am nah sure. I've never been able t' see 'em b'fore. He pushes up with a grunt and reaches to a cleft of rock above us to poke one lightly with his finger. The thing — creature? — flattens, undulates, and changes a rainbow of colors before constricting into its previous small ball again. He returns to my side with a shrug.

"Well, they're beautiful."

Another pesky thought creeps into the crevices of my mind, just like those creatures unseen by the average eye. Suddenly consumed by the thought, I turn to him and ask, "Did you truly want to be my déō doúlos? Or did Oryn put you up to this?"

Kallias is far too quiet for too long. Anxiousness and frustration bubble inside me, festering.

"Both," he responds just before I open my mouth to press further.

The answer is not what I want to hear. My pulse throbs in my temples, causing my vision to pulsate in kind. Only after I've taken several steadying breaths does Kallias continue. He'd known in that moment, I wouldn't have heard him anyway — my temporary, though not entirely gone yet, anger deafening me.

"Oryn does nah have tha ability t' change tha rules of tha only free agency huiói have here in Ceteris. He can nah tamper with tha end result of a bindin'. He can nah plant tha seed. Most of all, he certainly can nah force my dick t' move inside ya. Nor make it work. That, Basílissa, was all tha efforts of both you an' me. Together."

His blunt and honest response does calm me a bit, but I continue to wait for the part about Oryn's involvement.

"Oryn came t' me as a friend and as a mesítēs worried about his queen's safety. I do nah blame him. He was hopin' I would accept yah bond call tha nigh' of tha gatherin'. I did nah… and I am sorry for that. For riskin' yah existence in that way."

So much went on in those short few astral rounds, so much I was dumb to due to my lack of memory and knowledge. One thing I know for certain happened, though… the one thing that did not escape my notice… was why Oryn bonded with me. Because Kallias — nor any other huiós — wouldn't. He did what he had to do, not what he wanted to do.

"Well, it all worked out, hm?" I say nudging him with my shoulder. "You know, as irritated as I want to be with him, I shouldn't be. I used him, too. To save Kirian."

Kallias laughs, catching me off guard. "Ya an' Oryn dance aroun' how ya two became bound as though ya each believe tha other does nah care. Just because Oryn's dick worked beforehand does nah mean tha hélkō would have allowed ya two t' be bound without that deep-rooted mutual agreement. The one both of ya refuse to nourish."

"No, the hélkō allowed it because if he didn't do it, I would have been sent to The Void. He was saving my existence."

"He has been inside ya since. Why did tha hélkō allow it tha next time?" Kallias presses a question I can't refuse to consider.

I replay the time when I had the haímaboúlomai — the blood desire — and took advantage of both him and Raener. With a shrug, I state, "I don't know the parameters of his position well enough. But I imagine if he would have denied me, there would have been… problems. And isn't that what he makes sure doesn't happen? Problems?"

"Yeah. But he can nah prevent 'em all. Believe what ya want t' believe, Basílissa. I choose t' believe Oryn cares about ya above — and separate from — his responsibilities as a mesítēs."

He gives me a long, hard look, those golden-brown eyes penetrating me. "Oryn is nah who was on yah mind, though," he calls me out. "If ya do nah want t' share with me, I understand. But, I am here to serve ya, an' I would like t' be able t' do that."

My eyebrows curve in and I shake my head. "No, I am not yet worthy of your loyal services."

Kallias raises a single eyebrow. "Ya are more than worthy."

After a moment of reflection in those persuasive eyes, I finally deflate and give in, choosing to approach the topic with a single question: "Is the number of déō doúloi permanently set upon the realization of the oikía powers?"

"Ah, I see what ya were thinkin'," he says with a soft smile. "Come, let's wash an' talk about it, hm?" he asks, standing and reaching out to me.

I gladly accept, ready to scrub all the sand and grit off and feel the balm of the water against my skin. Kallias slings his pack over his shoulder and the two of us wade out of the cave until our feet once more hit dry terra. We walk along the shore hand in hand to the bowl-barricade of rocks and he places his pack down.

We continue to where the water meets the terra and both begin to scoop up the red clay, covering every inch of our skin. With my late-night excursions to this very beach, I'd quickly learned that the red clay doesn't dry without the sun, so washing after sunset doesn't quite have the masking and exfoliating properties as does washing when the sun is high in the sky. Nevertheless, it still works wonders with refreshing and rejuvenating.

The two of us step into the water together, muddying it up as the red clay falls into the pool of liquid in clumps and creates a liquid paste.

Kallias is contemplative in the meantime. It isn't until we're done and walking back up the hill that he returns to the topic of my troubled thoughts. "Oikía size is a complex thing, Basílissa," he starts. "Take some of tha other queens'. Since we have spoken a bit about Amrita today, I will use her as an example. Her oikía power grouping is weather related." He pauses, allowing me to contemplate this for a moment.

Which, of course, triggers a question, of which he waits patiently for me to ask. "But, Vanya... the basílissa who helped me into the village. Did she not use the wind? Her oikía, though, has to do with elements, right?"

"That's right." Kallias smiles. "But she did nah use tha wind, she used tha terra, creatin' enough of a force t' make a sandstorm. Tha force itself gave tha impression of wind — because air is all around us — but she did nah use wind directly. The two are nah tha same."

After I nod for him to continue, he does so: "Amrita, on tha other hand, is weather specific — sunny, cloudy, windy, rainy, stormy are tha main ones. But there's more to it. Temperature is a significant player, too. Wind over a warm ocean can create devastation. Without tha warmth, however, she can nah create tha storm."

At the top of the hill now, I choose to walk, rather than create a pýlē, so we can continue the lesson.

"Therefore," he resumes, "She took a temperature-specific déō doúlos, in order t' strengthen her other oikía powers. Because, she can nah actually control tha sun...

113

which made her quite displeased by tha way. Now, she can manipulate tha temperature as long as it goes along with tha other factors that are in play."

"Interesting!"

"Yeah. Kainda... she will probably nevah be done takin' new déō doúloi. Animal orders? They might nah all exist here in Ceteris, but there are many in existence in tha mortal realm. When she began her oikía and surpassed ten déō doúloi, she thought perhaps her oikía would consist of both major and minor phyla — falling in tha range of about thirty."

"Thirty?!" I gasp, unable to wrap my mind around taking that many men into my own oikía.

Kallias laughs. "For our Queen of Greed, even thirty was nah enough. Thankfully — for her — that number easily shot up, takin' into consideration not just phyla, but different classes as well. Over one-hundred. Next came orders. She has nah yet exceeded that number, but that sure would nah surprise me if it happened one day."

"Wow. I... I can't fathom that many."

"An' I did nah want t' be one of that many." He squeezes my hand, stops walking, and turns to face me. "That is why I did nah accept yah bond-call righ' away. I was selfishly waitin' t' see what yah oikía power groupin' would be. Tha size of it."

I blink up at him, appreciating how open and honest he always is. "And I don't want hundreds. At least, I don't think I do." My gaze drops and I take in a deep breath. "But I do want more than five," I add on a quiet sigh.

Kallias dips his head down to catch my eyes and persuade them back upward. "The hélkō can ultimately choose yah oikía, but it can nah choose who ya decide t' love an' want. This… can be a problem for queens sometimes, because they will need t' keep tryin' until their power-grouping is complete. Other times, an oikía ends up being bigger than what tha queen initially expects."

My thoughts return to Kallias's examples of Kainda and Amrita. "Can you think of any way my oikía power grouping might expand beyond the five senses?"

Kallias shakes his head. "No. I can nah."

My shoulders droop and I nod in acceptance of his answer. He cups my face gently in his palms and runs his thumbs across my cheeks. "No matter what happens — what huiói become yah déō doúloi — Raener and Blaze will both serve ya until tha end of their existence. Ya will nah lose them."

"Guess I'm a selfish queen, too," I whisper, tempted to drop my gaze again. I keep it locked on his, though. For support. To steady me.

"Love is nah selfish, Adrestia. Love is tha most selfless act of all. It comes unbidden and stays with us for an eternity. We will do anythin' for that love, even tha most painful things."

I press my cheek deeper into his hand, absorbing the warmth there. "Thank you." I turn my face to kiss the inside of his palm, and he slides his hand down and around to the back of my neck, bending forward to conjoin our mouths instead.

The kiss is soft and sweet. Reassuring and grounding.

"Ready t' return t' yah dwellin'?" he asks, taking a step back.

"Yes," I smile at him, feeling much better now that I have a friend — and lover — helping me to carry the weight of my worries. One point he made, though, stood out amongst the rest. One that will drive me forward and carry me through what it'll take to make Raener mine. "…even the most painful things."

CHAPTER THIRTEEN

:come to me:

No. No. No. No. No.

My own deep and brutish voice echoes through my mind, trying to override the persuasive whisper of the voice that haunts me.

My rough breathing, worsened by the stress of my pace and stride, still isn't enough noise to override the voice.

His voice.

A force — strong and determined — a force I've felt before, hooks into my stomach and yanks me several yards backward. Back in the direction from which I came. Back to the place from where I'm trying to run as far as possible away.

With a growl, I fight against the pull, pushing forward toward an equally invisible wall that prevents me from advancing.

Instead of words, the voice tempts me with mental visions of energy. Young energy. New energy. Delicious, tempting energy.

:feed:

No. No. No. No. No.

Beneath my feet the ground rumbles, energy seeps through the terra's many veins. My entire body shakes with a desperate hunger and I fall to my knees, inhaling the sweet scent. The ground rumbles harder, opening at my fingertips as if I'd ripped it apart. Teetering on the edge of a gaping abyss, I peer into the never-ending depth. Bodies. Hundreds. Thousands. Turn to dots as they disappear into the blackness.

A single feather floats up on a gust of air and I scoop it between my clawed fingers. Such a beautiful thing held by such grotesque claws.

Another gust of wind and the feather slips away. I rush to collect it again before the wind carries it too far.

But it's too late.

* * *

BELÍAR'S VOICE ECHOES in my head as I startle awake:

:come to me:

I hold Seala tighter, visions of daimónia and Fallen angels still lingering in my mind.

I need to feed.

In a sleepy haze, I remember waking up to a squirming baby, quickly attaching her to my breast, and immediately falling asleep again. My hand seeks out Kallias, and he immediately responds to my touch, startling with a snort as he shoots up to a sitting position.

"I am weak," I state.

Kallias nods, stands, and looks around the room. "Who will watch the baby?" he asks with a gruff voice.

None of my other déō doúloi are here. Brax is likely working in the watchtower while Oryn is off taking care of his responsibilities. Kirian... "Where's Kirian?"

Kallias shakes his head, his brows flattening.

I tuck Seala safely against me, approach Kallias, and take his hand, but just as I'm about to pop us out of there, I remember my newly received bow — my official power object — and I drag the three of us over to the corner of the room where it is kept. With Kallias's assistance, we put on the quiver and place the bow over my shoulder.

Then I quickly pop us out of the dwelling. But even that is too much. Before I fall to the ground, scarcely able to stay upright, I hand Seala to him. "Blaze.... Take her to Blaze. He'll either be in his hut, or near his assigned area of the forest."

Kallias gives me a sharp nod and runs off, holding Seala as close to his chest as possible.

Anxiety courses through me. Worry they won't find help. Worry I'll be taken down by the hélkō before he can return.

Leaning against the inner wall of the entrance room, I slide my back down the stone, closing my eyes while still willing what energy remains within me to carry me for just a bit longer.

"Basílissa?" Comes a raspy voice. My eyes snap open to find one of my dwelling's assigned Watchers bent over and peering into the opening. "Should I get Brax?"

I shoot to my feet. "Yes!"

Kallias rounds the corner in an instant, less a baby. "Blaze was in his hut," he explains on a ragged pant. "Wasn't very fond of tha idea, but I left b'fore he could give her back t' me," he adds with a side grin.

A bit of the tension in my muscles drains away. I turn to the guard. "Let Brax know I had to feed and Blaze has Seala, will you?"

The guard nods, straightens to take his post again, but doesn't leave.

Kallias taps his temple. "They communicate differently than we do."

"Oh…" I look up at the giant curiously before returning my attention to Kallias. "Ready?"

Kallias looks down at his cock, which happens to be extended to its full form. I laugh and cup his hand. "That's not what I meant."

"I know… but it does nah know that." Again he peeks down at the swell. He closes his eyes, takes a deep breath, opens them again, and looks back down. No change. "Ah, well… never mind, guess I'll travel into tha mortal realm for tha first time with my dick hard."

* * *

AFTER A NUMBER OF FEEDS with Oryn, I expanded the amount of ground I would cover in the mortal realm based on my attending déō doúlos's power. Which, before now, was only ever Oryn since Brax and Kirian are both out of the running.

Well… technically Kirian can travel to the mortal realm, but the presence of daimónia there is highly frowned upon.

Unfortunately and ironically enough, several daimónia escaped Ceteris by jumping into a special pýlē my binding with Kirian had created. We have yet to hear or see the result of their unwanted transfer.

Only a matter of time, I imagine.

Either way, traveling has everything to do with intention, so I made my primary intention taste-related every time Oryn and I would influence together. That way, I would experience plenty of new mortals with new desires and unique ways to deter them from the path of so-called "righteousness."

For this trip, I focus on sight as my intention, completely uncertain where it'll take me or how that will translate into the potential to influence sin.

Kallias and I arrive at a cafe. The place is relatively dead by way of activity. For a bit, the two of us simply stand there, taking in the scene. Like me when Irisa had delivered me to my first influence, Kallias has never seen the mortal realm. These tables, the mugs filled with hot "drinks" are all new to him. Each item he sees becomes recorded in his mental files instantly. So, really, it's only for a breath that he doesn't know what something is. Because in the next, the knowledge is there, ready to be used and incorporated into a feed.

The two of us make sure the entire scene is acknowledged before getting started.

Kallias's eyes widen. "I did nah know this would be so easy. T' find tha sin, I mean."

"Oh… you've found it already?" I ask, impressed because I've always struggled with this part. Oryn is usually the one to nudge me in the right direction, I suppose since my déō doúloi have the primary powers and I'm the one borrowing them. "Tell me a story, hm?" I encourage, taking the bow from my shoulder and reveling in the feel of the smooth wood beneath the tips of my fingers.

"Tha man there in the corner. Workin'?"

I nod, reaching into my quiver to pull an arrow. When my fingertips graze along one of the feathers, a buzz courses through to my palm. I pluck the arrow free.

"He comes here for tha barista."

Eyebrow raised, I search over the machinery, seeking out this barista Kallias speaks of.

Pretty girl.

Young.

With another nod, I hold out the arrow in front of me, trailing my gaze along the engraved symbols. Kallias's arrow. A huge grin covers my face as I turn to him. "Palm up," I state. Kallias's hand shoots out, I wrap my fingers around his and slice his palm open with the tip of his arrow.

Kallias hisses but otherwise doesn't complain as I close his palm and squeeze the essence onto the letters carved into the wood. The word *ópsis* glows and the energy from his silver essence wraps around the shaft.

When the entire thing dims, indicating the process is done, I eagerly line the arrow up in the bowstring.

"She is cute," I say, bringing our attention back to the barista.

Kallias chuckles. "Mmm, cute isn't exactly what he's thinking."

"No?"

He shakes his head.

Again my eyes seek out the barista. Now she's leaning forward, wiping down the counter, her ample breasts plump and over-filling her top. "Oh..." My attention returns to the man. The bottom of his pen is between his lips as he furiously chews on the tip with his head tilted down just enough to use the top of his laptop screen as a barricade to peer over it at her.

"He is bound," Kallias continues.

My eyes widen. "To a queen?!"

Kallias laughs. "No. To a wife. Similar, though. A wife that does nah wish t' share him."

"Well, I wouldn't want to share my déō doúloi with other queens either," I state matter-of-factly.

"There are some relationships here where the sharing of females is not accepted. Others where it is. Earth does nah work tha way Ceteris does."

"So I've noticed. It's like they have rules... but they don't at the same time. They most certainly don't have anything enforcing those rules. Like the hélkō."

"Free agency. Tha's what gets everyone in trouble here. It's wha keeps 'em out of trouble, too, though."

This place is so confusing, I am unsure I will ever fully understand the way it works. I lift my bow hand and adjust the arrow to aim toward the man. Kallias comes up behind me, placing his hand on my shoulder. A flicker of images, thoughts, and memories transfer into me through the touch. But they are not from Kallias. They belong to the man.

And this man had already fucked the girl once.

I watch as he continues to fuck her again... this time with his eyes. He closes them, leans back in the chair, takes in a deep breath, and his head falls back... mouth moving to speak silent words.

I let the bow and arrow come to my side. "What is he doing?"

"Quick," Kallias says. "Influence him now."

I lift the bow and arrow again as fast as possible, aim, and pierce the man in the shoulder. Kallias walks up to the spot where it landed, picks it up, and returns it to my quiver.

"To answer your question, Basílissa," Kallias continues where we'd left off, "he was praying to The Maker. Seeking help."

"The Maker helps them?"

Kallias shrugs. "I do nah know The Maker," he states. "Whether he helps them or nah, I am unsure. But the act of prayin' itself redirects their thoughts in tha least… and, in turn, sometimes their actions."

The man collects his things, and rushes out of the cafe.

My low energy remains low.

"That's… the first time an influence has not fed me." I stare, stunned, at the now-empty cafe chair. "One way trip," I whisper. "What do we do?"

Kallias looks down at me with a frown. "I'm sorry. Maybe Oryn is better at choosin' tha victims that ya will be able t' influence easier."

I place my hand on his forearm. "I am not upset. I just know that I don't have enough energy to travel back to Ceteris and back to the mortal realm again."

Kallias contemplates for a moment. "Can we leave this building?" I nod, my attention darting toward the door. "He — that man — is still impressionable. I can feel him," Kallias explains. The two of us rush to the door and outside. Kallias points to a nearby vehicle, and we jog up to it. The man sits inside, eyes closed again, head back against the headrest. Again I set the bow and arrow and aim, reciting my own incantation, of sorts, beneath my breath. Speaking to my arrow. Weaving in the influence I don't quite understand but am convinced will work. Kallias's hand steadies me again, pushing the influence through my arm and hand and into the arrow.

"There's another way. Different. Safer," I whisper to both to the man and to my power object. His anguish hits as though he'd started up this vehicle and plowed right into me. When his eyes open, though, energy webs into my veins. When his hand flips the laptop screen open in the passenger seat, that web spreads and thickens. Every step closer he takes, every time he taps into that free agency one small decision at a time, I attain more energy. It's strong and filling... because he was strong at first. He'd tried. Only now does he fail.

As the man powers on his laptop and pulls out several pictures of the same barista — one's taken without her permission — I remember Oryn explaining that the strongest feeds often come from breaking someone who is trying extra hard not to break. They want redemption. Yearn for it. But they also want what they can't have all while still expecting or hoping for this so-called redemption.

The man's hand slips into his pants and he strokes himself, his eyes scanning every inch of the barista's skin he'd captured on image. When he closes his eyes and his head falls back against the headrest, it isn't to seek help from The Maker. He calls to me — to Ceteris's influencers. A moment of unbridled pleasure to ease his pounding need and get him through the day.

CHAPTER FOURTEEN

Kallias

"For several moons in a row, Adrestia has woken up drained. She's havin' nightmares, too." Every bein' in tha room listens t' me intently, from teacher t' giant. Gettin' Adrestia's oikía t'gether was a task. Spread out across tha territory. Never t'gether. It's a wonder how tha hélkō ever agreed t' these bond-calls. Why other queens could nah have taken huiói with titles as déō doúloi makes sense now that I'm experiencin' first-hand tha drawbacks of such.

Plus, there's a damn daimónion.

"Why hasn't she said anything?" Oryn asks.

Careful t' reel in my growin' frustration, I take a deep breath b'fore respondin'. Nostrils flarin', I can nah help but t' grind my teeth along with tha reply: "None of ya are 'round when it happens."

Of everyone in this room, I am now tha only true déō doúlos by way of havin' only been a huiós b'fore our bindin'. I understand that it falls on my shoulders t' make sure she's receivin' tha proper care of a déō doúlos. But I am just one man. Nah only that, but there are two females t' take care of. Adrestia needs a bigger oikía. A proper one. With huiói who have time t' take care of her. Of them. Both of them.

Oryn, Brax, an' Kirian all have their reasons. Commendable ones. An' they do all spend time with her an' Seala. Every day. But bein' both a déō doúlos an'

126

holdin' a title is a new concept t' all of us. They are doin' their best t' balance those responsibilities. But it's nah 'nough.

"She won't take anymore huiói," Raener says.

"Do ya even know why?" I ask, voice raised. His black eyes pierce mine, but he does nah answer. I throw my hands up an' growl. "Because tha men she wants are nah huiói!"

Raener refuses t' humor my comment with a direct response. Instead, he speaks on tha original topic. "Seala is growin' fast, much faster than mortal children. Perhaps the nightmares could be stemming from the amounts of energy Seala pulls from Adrestia while they sleep."

Tha room falls even more silent. With Seala walkin' an' beginnin' t' talk already, tha amount of energy she consumes from Adrestia is substantial. What's worse, she does nah even take tha breast anymore. All she has t' do is rest beside Adrestia or hold her hand. Any type of contact, really. All that growth happenin' in tha matter of a handful of astral rounds. We've all witnessed it — from her first steps, t' her first word.

Oryn hasn't even finalized tha Birth Gatherin' he's been preparin' for. If it does nah happen soon, she'll be a grown female.

With as calm of a voice as I can manage, I state, "I fear for their wellbein' — I am only one male. What happens when she becomes weak from energy loss, an' her oikía are nah available t' help her? I will stay by her side, I will nah falter in my protection, but she needs more than jus' me."

Oryn speaks up, addressin' Raener directly. "Maybe Seala needs to begin traveling to the mortal realm? Influencing to feed? Even though I hate the idea of her going there. The mortal realm is a mess. Horrible place to raise a child."

"So, instead, she stays here, locked up in a dwellin'? Is that much better?" I grind out.

"Yes," they all respond in unison.

Raener runs his hand through his hair. "Maybe you're right. How about we get the Birth Gathering behind us and then we'll talk to Adrestia about giving it a shot."

Tha group of us nod in agreement, but I set up this meetin' with an idea of my own. "I have another suggestion," I begin. They all lean forward. "We encourage her an' Kohbi t' spend more time together. She does nah have t' take him as a déō doúloi, but she can accept him as her próskairos an' we'd at least have someone who can bring her t' a feed if somethan drastic happens an' both Oryn an' I are nah available."

Brax hadn't said a word this entire time, but at this suggestion he grunts an' his fists clench in his lap. Of all of us, he an' Kirian are tha most helpless. Neither able t' travel an' help her feed. They would, if they could. "I don't like it," he says simply.

What we've all failed t' explain t' her 'bout próskairoi, is that once tha basílissa gives him tha position of próskairos within her oikía, they carry a different sort of bond. A connection of tha mind that even her déō doúloi do nah share. This is likely why Brax is tha one t' speak up 'bout it, tha Watchers sharin' somethin' similar between them.

Próskairoi need t' know when a queen is desperate. Where she is, an' why she's drained. They learn all this through their mental connection. They can use their dicks t' transfer enough energy into a queen so that she can travel or simply create a temporary pýlē usin' their own energy t' get tha queen t' tha mortal realm. All as a last resort in dire energy level situations.

However, when a queen takes a próskairos they often tend t' use their workin' dicks for recreational purposes, too. Often.

Oryn, a past próskairos, speaks t' this. "It's not so bad, and the connection only hits after the queen's energy dips to a certain level. Are any of you really bothered by her fucking another male?"

"Me. I am bothered," Brax answers.

Raener laughs. "For as big as your cock is, I'm always so stunned at your lacking confidence."

"I do not lack confidence," Brax rumbles.

Raener's amusement fades, though, an' his features take on a rare compassion for tha giant. "You can not help her in the way Kohbi could; that is enough to take a man down in confidence a notch." Tha two share a look of understandin'. Grigori an' paidagōgós, two lineages that often have nothing in common, now share a common misery.

"Well, the gathering will be held soon," Oryn reveals. "Kohbi will be there. We can make sure he's close by. Maybe that'll be enough for her to interact naturally with him a bit.

We all grunt in agreement, nah botherin' t' say farewells or anythin' of tha sort b'fore headin' out. Just as everyone is leavin', though, Brax's raspy voice stops us short. "Seala is off limits. Kohbi touches her, I'll kill him. No questions asked."

CHAPTER FIFTEEN

Adrestia

"**A**re you sure this is a good idea?" I ask Oryn, feeling a bit unsettled about announcing the secret we've worked so hard to keep. Much less in celebration form.

"She's growing too fast and needs to be quickly assimilated," he states.

"We could just keep her in Adrestia's dwelling for her entire existence," Brax insists from the opposing room.

"No, Da!" Seala squeals.

That's what we all want, but we're well aware that it's not possible. An existence for immortals is quite a long time. Oryn's right, the sooner we get her assimilated, the faster she can learn how to feed and protect herself.

Seala's disagreements are stamped down and quickly change to a burst of chuckles, soon followed by Brax's raspy laughter. Seala zooms out of her conjoined room, squealing in delight as Brax stomps behind her in chase. One of his giant steps versus a couple dozen of hers.

"We'll need the support of the territory huiói. The more Fallen we have backing us, the more protected she'll be," Oryn explains.

"So how is this going to work… I show up with a child on my hip?"

"No," Brax stops beside me, leaving Seala to run rampant through the dwelling. "*I* show up with her on my hip."

My head falls back, eyes reaching for his facial expression. "You'll hold her? On your hip?" I press my lips together to manage a growing smile. Sure, it hasn't been long since he was adamant about not holding her at all, but I suppose I was still not expecting it to happen so soon.

Brax looks down his nose at me, crossing his arms over that massive chest. "If I don't, tomorrow she'll be too big and it'll be… weird. I'm not carrying around my grown woman-child."

At the rate she's growing and changing, I'm sure that assessment is not far from the truth. Laughter floats out of me at the visual. "You've carried me," I state, allowing my smile to break free.

Brax bends and scoops me up into his arms. Seala watches the motion, falling backward onto her butt when her eyes can't quite track that high without her losing balance. She lifts a chubby arm and points up at the two of us, mirth in her green-gold eyes.

Brax puts me down, grinning at his daughter.

"To answer your question, Raener and Kallias have begun spreading the news." Oryn's expression is one of uncertainty. "This will be the first time the villagers have seen Seala; it will not be the first they've heard of her."

We have spoken about this part with each other before, during the rare occurrences that I visited with either Raener or Oryn — mostly Oryn, of course — one of the main topics we'd discussed was that of how and when we were going to make her existence known to the rest of Ceteris.

Of course, at the time, we did not know the baby wouldn't be a Nephilim, nor that she would be female. At that time, everyone's hands were tied. The pregnancy was a big secret. Which is one of the several reasons why my evening excursions were some of my only ones. At one point, we decided that if the baby was... well... a normal baby, considering, Raener and Oryn would begin selectively making announcements. First beginning strictly within our territory.

Traveling is possible between territories, but it is not easy. So, the risk of a huiós leaving to deliver the news abroad is unlikely in a short period of time.

Due to the sensitivity and nature of the topic, Raener had learned that the paidagōgói were bound by some sort of lineage rule that would prevent them from delivering news of her birth to the other queens. When I tried to ask more, he shut me down... as Raener is so inclined to do, as of late.

Well, not entirely. He's bound to answer my questions, I just couldn't figure out the right ones to ask that didn't end in him finding a loophole with the response.

"There will be no formalities today," Oryn continues. "We are not going to sit her in front of a crowd of huiói, nor are we going to draw attention to her. They know the purpose of the gathering is to celebrate. She'll mingle and play, just like you did at your gathering."

Brax snorts. "There is a lot Adrestia did at her gathering that Seala will not be permitted to do."

Seala peers up at her da again before turning her attention toward me. "What did you do?" she asks.

I squat down to her level. "Oh... I danced and played." I drop my voice to a whisper, "And I snuck away from Da!"

"That won't happen today — or any day," Brax takes a knee beside me and points a giant-sized finger at her.

She wraps her hand around it and squeezes. "I will try. If Ma did it, so can I." She smiles up at him.

Brax groans and wiggles his finger in her grip. "There is a lot Ma can do that you will never do, child."

Laughter filling me, I stand and wrap my arms around his neck to press our foreheads together. Brax lowers his voice, bringing his mouth to my ear, "Like take a grigori cock... she'll never do that."

Unable to repress it any longer, a chuckle escapes. "Let's hope she doesn't become a woman too soon, right? Because I imagine something like that will happen one da—"

"Never," he says, swatting my ass.

I lean in and give him a kiss, to which he reciprocates, but only for a couple seconds before his gaze goes sideways to Seala. When he realizes she's watching, he pulls away and clears his throat.

I return to the floor and pull her in close. "Ready to see the forest, and the sun, and the sea?"

Seala nods emphatically. "Yes!"

* * *

THE LINGERING LOOKS and casual recurrence of curious huiói passing by were bound to happen, so we had all prepared ourselves for such things. However, what we didn't prepare for was how... social... Seala would be. With her never having seen the outside since the day we brought her into the dwelling, aside from the occasional trip to Blaze's hut when in need of someone to watch her, we naturally assumed she was going to wander around, taking in all the sights. Kallias — Papa K — had planned a trip for her to the water, Brax to the watchtower, and Raener — now referred to at all times as Rae Rae — to the bibliothēkē. A day full of immersive experiences.

But she's far too distracted by all the huiói. She wants to be near them, listen to their stories, tell stories of her own.

"Come on, child, let's go for a walk," Brax rumbles, catching her in motion as she runs to a congregating group of huiói. The same group who, earlier, were listening to her tell them of a dream she has — one about a realm more beautiful than this one. Of wings and wishes.

Raener had recently insisted on holding story-time with her once per astral round: mini lessons, where he would tell her short stories found in Ceteris's codices. Now, her mind is rife with tales of her own. Behind closed eyes, her imagination runs wild and free.

Much like how she fights against her da to do now.

Brax had disappeared for a time, warning us that if anything happened to her in his absence, someone would pay. When he returned, he held some sort of large cloth — one similar in size and shape to the decorative one on my pallet — wrapped around his massive frame.

Seala effectively turns into a fish when he attempts picking her up, slipping right out of his hands. Becoming quite accustomed to her tactics, though, his second attempt is successful. He strategically places her into the cloth he's wearing, quickly wrapping it around to secure her to his torso.

Eyes wide, I watch a giant attempt to wear his no-longer small child, in ever-increasing amusement. "Looks like you waited a day too long after all," I point out. Though, considering he's a giant, she doesn't look too awkward up there. Now, should one of us attempt wearing her, she's big enough now that... it would certainly be a bit awkward and challenging.

Brax grunts. Wearing his daughter sure brings a whole new dynamic to being a Watcher. That protectiveness, though, does something funny to my insides. Something that had temporarily gone a bit dormant with the hustle and bustle of life filled under the constant watchful eye of a child, copious numbers of trips to the mortal realm for feeds, and... well... sleep. The last moon-cycle or so has been the longest of my existence.

"Where to first?" Brax asks her, looking down his nose to the top of her head.

"The ground," she responds.

"Which ground?" he tags back.

"This one."

"Nice try."

"Rae Rae will listen to my stories," she states. "Take me to him."

Brax stomps off toward the paidagōgói's dwellings, assuming that's where Raener is hiding, having spent the previous astral round, and the early part of this one already speaking to a fair share of huiói.

I press my lips together to repress my reaction to her choosing Raener as her first stop... having chosen that activity, no doubt, because she knows Brax and Raener butt heads. If Brax is bothered by it, though, he keeps his frustration to himself.

Kallias and Oryn fall in line. Up until this point, they'd been intently watching the crowds for any misdeeds, and patiently waiting for Seala to be ready to move on from the center of the village.

Either because of the lull of being held, or the fact she can't move and is now forced to look around, she finally begins to take in her surroundings. Her eyes trail up the watchtower, scan the reed beds as we approach, and peek around Brax's arm to study the forest in the distance. Her young mind is connecting everything we've told her with everything she now sees.

When she started talking, more eloquently now, we realized that she gathers information much like I do on feeds. And that's primarily why everything is happening so quickly. Her interactions with the territory huiói today have been a perfect example. Her speech and ability to speak clearly and in longer sentences having already blossomed just in the matter of a few sun positions.

When we arrive, the five of us enter Raener's courtyard, "Rae Rae," she screeches. "Save me!"

When he doesn't answer, my thoughts get carried away with reasons why. Unlikely ones, but reasons nonetheless. I break away and step down into his personal scriptorium. My eyes naturally land on the pallet first, but he's not there. When I look to the right, to where his reading pillar stands, that's where I find him. Head propped up on his chin, he'd fallen asleep studying a scroll.

I reach my hand out to draw my finger down his arm and wake him up, but catch myself and clear my throat instead. "Raener," I whisper.

He immediately jerks to attention. A black canister of liquid and quill fly off his pillar and splatter onto the floor.

"Holy shit," he breathes.

"Sorry," I respond, rushing to collect a cloth and help clean up the mess.

Still half asleep, he shoves his fingers under his spectacles, and rubs his eyes with a groan before looking down at the scroll he'd been either reading or working on. He quickly rolls it up, steps over the mess, and places the scroll into one of the nooks in his wall.

Now on my knees, doing my best to sop up the ink, I keep my head down. He soon joins, using the tip of his finger to slide the cloth out from beneath my palm without touching me. "There are better reasons than this for a queen to get on her knees," he says, meeting my gaze. The light coming through the opening shines directly on him, highlighting the deep, dark pools gathered under his eyes.

"I shouldn't have startled you," I state.

"I shouldn't have fallen asleep," he returns with a groan, taking over the cleanup. He only pauses for a second before asking, "What are you doing here?"

"That's a better question for Seala; she requested your presence. And… she tends to get what she wants…"

Raener grins. "Of course she did. Just like her ma—"

"Her ma doesn't always get what she wants," I state, pushing off the ground and immediately exiting.

"Fuck," Raener's quiet mutterings follow me out.

I wave a still-Seala-wearing Brax inside. He bends down, somehow managing to duck walk and balance her on his chest at the same time. I follow behind, entering shortly after. Brax stares down at Raener, an amused smirk on his face. "Scrubbing the ground suits you, Paidagōgós," he quips.

Raener doesn't even look up. Not until he's done. When he stands and sees Seala's expression at being worn by Brax, mixed with the actual sight, he bursts into laughter.

Once calm again, he says, "Let that poor girl free so I can give her a hug."

Brax looks down at the wrap, twisting and turning to find the point where it's tied. His panicked eyes meet mine. "How do I undo this thing without dropping her?"

Raener steps up, shaking his head, those black eyes gleaming in delight. Seala whimpers and gives Raener a pleading look. He throws her a wink before instructing Brax to hold her under her butt while Raener unties the cloth and unwraps it.

Brax and Raener work together to get Seala loose, and as soon as she is down, she jumps into Raener's arms, and he spins her around.

Now unencumbered by Seala, Brax removes the cloth from around his body and takes a seat on the bench. As soon as Raener puts her down, Brax insists she step back over to him; as much as she fights her da, she does obey most of the time. This time is no different. Seala approaches and blinks at him expectantly. He takes the large cloth and expertly wraps it around her a couple times, once over the shoulder and around her waist. Watching in amusement, I lean against the open door frame as he covers our daughter from neck to feet, leaving only a single shoulder bare.

"This… this is why mortals clothe themselves. It all must've started with an overprotective parent," I point out.

Raener shoots me a smile, and everything stills for a moment. "Makes things easier, that's for sure. Those of us on Ceteris — grigori notwithstanding — have preordained assurance that we don't touch a female without consent; humans, however, do not. Men and women alike, it's all part of the overall plan to tempt and test them as much as possible."

My thoughts drift to the feed I went on with Kallias, and he and I share a look. The girl in the scene was clothed, but the man went wild with what skin he could see.

Seala stares down at her covered body, wide-eyed and horrified. Kallias steps in, and stoops to her level to adjust Brax's handiwork in a couple places. "Ya look just as beautiful as ya did before. What do ya think, hm?" he asks.

She crosses her arms and glares over Kallias's shoulder at Brax. "It's baggy and uncomfortable," she states.

Brax shrugs, returning an unimpressed look of his own. "Can you still tell stories while wearing it?" he throws back.

"C—well… yes, of course," she responds.

"Great. Should be no bother then," he replies.

Seala takes in a deep breath, drops her hands, and her fists ball at her sides. Very much a Brax response, which only heightens the growing mirth in the room.

Raener takes one of her balled fists and spins her around. "Let's go for a walk. You can tell us all a story on the way. How does that sound?"

Her fists loosen and she scoops her hand into Raener's and nods eagerly.

CHAPTER SIXTEEN

Raener and Seala take a spot ahead en route to the central portion of the village where festivities always take place. Her excitable voice floats back to us, always followed by Raener's deeper responses. Peas in a pod, those two.

The sight fills my heart with both appreciation and disappointment. I would never change her ability to interact with Raener. I just wish I had those same privileges.

Once at the gathering, Raener brings her to one of those same congregating groups as before, allowing her to sit amongst them and engage in chit-chat. He steps back, but only enough to watch and listen from a few feet. One of the men in the group stands, separates from the crowd, and heads toward us.

Kohbi, I soon realize.

He is not with Xanth, though. Xanth had been in the kanab shelter, entertaining the huiói.

Having already experienced a full day, Brax, Oryn, Kallias, and I take a spot near the fire. Kohbi joins us, making a bold move at sitting directly by my side. Brax loops around to sit on the side of the fire opposite us, perched on a log seat, elbows digging into his thighs, fingers templed at his mouth, the flame of fire dancing in his blue eyes as he narrows a glare at my new companion.

A comfortable silence descends on us as we all relax, knowing Seala is under Raener's care. Still, we all sit in a place where she can easily be seen, should we decide to glance up and check on her ourselves.

"Guess we'll need to take her on all those adventures a different day," I say after a time.

"Maybe somewhere new once per day to correlate with Raener's lesson," Oryn suggests.

Brax, Kallias, and I nod in agreement.

Kohbi sits still and quiet, twisting a seemingly freshly plucked reed around his finger. He continues doing this over and over again until a sphere is formed. A number of questions begin to form in my mind about this strange huiós. Primarily why he is here, now, sitting beside me crafting. I lift my gaze to Kallias, whom I know has interacted with Kohbi on more than one occasion.

Kallias gives me a soft, encouraging smile.

The gesture alone speaks loudly.

He is trying to help me with my oikía troubles.

Setting me up with a way to increase my protection, whilst not eliminating the only remaining oikía-power sense.

"Where did you travel from and for which basílissa were you once a próskairos?" I inquire.

Kohbi's gaze rises to meet Brax's from across the fire for a heartbeat before turning to me. "I am from Superbia originally. However, I became a próskairos under Basílissa Vialla of Vanagloria."

Vialla, oikía mother to dark magic. The first of The Seven to fall. An unease settles over me. "And why did you leave her?"

Kohbi scoffs. "Vialla cares for no one. It's a miracle she formed an oikía at all. I became her puppet out of desperation. As soon as she was done with me, she kicked me out of Vanagloria. Told me to leave and never come back."

"And you did nothing to trigger this?"

141

His gaze drops as he twists the reed, building on the previous shape. "She was displeased with my appearance," he states simply.

Here in my territory, the huiói range in appearance and dialect. The stark difference between Kallias, Raener, and Kohbi are a perfect example. Three very, very different men in both appearance and tongue. None of them are unattractive by any means. Just... different.

The Basílissa of Vanity.

"Hm, well... I do not find your appearance off-putting."

"Thank you, Basílissa," he states with a smile. Kohbi extends his hand, palm up, and displays the finished craft he'd been working on. A thumb-sized doll made from twists of reeds.

I accept the gift, running my finger over each little leg and arm.

Just as we're easing back into more quiet reflection, the air charges with the telltale electric spark of a traveling queen. Instead of seeking out the pýlē, my eyes move toward the group where Seala is.

Raener is already on it, though, pulling her from the group. Beside me, Brax has managed to move faster than I've ever seen him, closing the distance between us and Seala in just a few giant-sized strides.

"Stay behind me," he whispers. And the fact that I can hear him tells me my daimónion is present somewhere nearby, too. Having reacted to the buzz of a queen, no doubt. Up until this point, he had been patrolling the forest with Blaze and the other sikárioi.

The beautiful, blue-purple mix of the vortex indicates which queen has joined us before her actual presence does, though. Sitara. Queen of Sloth. Powers of

Emotions. Ruler of the territory Acedia. Previous — and present — shared "owner" of Oryn.

I take a step toward him, slipping my fingers between his. As soon as Sitara is visible through the remnants of her pýlē, her eyes immediately land on where Oryn and I are conjoined before flicking her gaze up to mine.

"Basílissa," she says, tilting her head in a queen's version of a respectable bow as she begins to approach. After a few steps, though, she and her attending déō doúlos stop abruptly. Both their attentions shift to the group Seala was just sitting amongst, and, in turn, to Brax and Raener who stand side-by-side. A sight which is quite unusual for a paidagōgós and Watcher, in and of itself.

Her route immediately changes. She doesn't continue approaching me, but approaches where Seala is being hidden instead.

Oryn drops my hand and rushes to step in front of her. When he cuts Sitara off on her path, she raises an eyebrow before peering around his shoulder to the unusual pair of side-by-side guardians.

I catch up to join Oryn just as he addresses her, standing close enough to him so that I can both block any visual of my daughter as well as state a wordless claim on Oryn.

Sitara's attention moves from Oryn to me and back again. "Basílissa Sitara," he addresses, "what brings you to our territory today?"

Sitara smiles, seemingly unperturbed by the number of oddities piling up. "Well, I have always been inclined to believe that where large numbers of beings are congregating, that's where the most useful information can be found. With fewer steps to attain it, of course."

"We gather here often," I answer.

"Of course. However, there is also a significant loss of energy taking place in all of Ceteris. This territory shows most of the depletion." Her attention once more tries to move beyond Oryn and me. "Something here is stealing energy from the land, and it's making an impact on the entire realm."

Without thinking, my head shakes as my panic begins to build.

Sitara's mouth lifts to the side. "Interesting," she coos. "Now, that is quite a recognizable emotion. One only ever stumbled on in the mortal realm. Love, filled with a desperate and unrequited protective instinct. An all-consuming type that goes well beyond what beings in Ceteris can experience. Funny how love is the most basic of the complex emotions, don't you think? Love controls us, not the other way around."

With every word that comes out of her mouth, my pulse quickens. But hearing the lyrical, "Ma?" come from behind me has the opposite effect, bringing my pulse to a near-stop.

"Ah…" Sitara chuckles. But her eyes are wide… stunned. "I feel you, child. Come here."

After all the protection — the attempts to keep her hidden — all the guys cave under the queen's request. Fear of the hélkō harming our child is more debilitating than the idea of her approaching a basílissa.

But first, Oryn lays some ground rules. These rules said more cautiously than ones before. "If you harm her, the hélkō will send one of your déō doúlos directly to The Void. She is important." Sitara's indigo eyes flash at

Oryn, but once they cool she gives him a nod. "Seala, come meet Sitara, one of Ceteris's queens like your ma."

Seala steps forward, Oryn bends to whisper something in her ear, and Seala tilts her head forward in a small bow before straightening and looking Sitara in the eyes.

Sitara stares down at Seala for an uncomfortable amount of time. Too long. "Seala is not the reason for the draining energy," I explain with desperation. "She feeds directly from me."

Based on Sitara's next expression, however, this news is even more surprising. "Is she mortal?" Sitara finally breaks the silence.

"She feeds on energy from Adrestia, not milk like a mortal would," Raener steps forward and answers. "Adrestia has been doing her part. Fueling the land. Seala feeds from Adrestia's reserves. This, in turn, actually makes Adrestia influence more frequently, thus she's likely providing a higher contribution than most queens."

Sitara shakes her head. "Doubtful. All the queens are influencing twice — triple — as much right now just to keep their territories salubrious. Honestly, it's exhausting. I'm tired of leaving my pallet. Which is why I've decided to look into this myself."

Her attention hesitantly turns away from Seala toward me. "Fix it," she demands as though doing so is simple.

Brax reaches between Oryn and me and pulls Seala back to hide her behind him again.

Sitara's attention trains on Oryn, only flicking toward me for a brief moment before she places her power-object hand on his shoulder. The colorful ring glows. Not well enough versed in using my new bow and arrow, I don't even have it on me to use against her.

Instead, I do the first thing that comes to mind; I place my own hand on Oryn's arm, dipping into our combined oikía powers to counter. It's not enough, though. Nowhere near. Sitara squeezes his shoulder, and I fly backward, losing the connection before anything can be done. In an instant Sitara and her déō doúlos are gone... Oryn, too.

CHAPTER SEVENTEEN

Brightly colored flowers and copious herbs surround us; Sitara had taken me to the central courtyard of her dwelling. The sight is a double-edged sword, serving both as a reminder of my past under her direct rule... and just how lackluster Adrestia's dwelling is in comparison. She deserves so much better than what we've been able to provide.

Flora is not the only thing I am greeted with; a few of Sitara's déō doúloi lounge around... dare I say just as lazy as she is. "Ah... the mesítēs has decided to grace us with his presence," one announces. "How long has it been? A couple thousand years?"

The déō doúlos who had joined Sitara on her visit to Adrestia's territory speaks on the topic: "There has never been a more difficult task than accompanying Sitara to pay him a visit, all the while instructed to not speak my mind in his presence."

Sitara rolls her eyes and walks away, having no time nor patience to deal with their cattiness. Of course, being here means I am stuck... until she chooses to bring me back.

Or I can travel by foot. But the idea of wandering through Ceteris for weeks has me following behind her as though I'd never stopped being her próskairos to begin with.

Of course, Sitara leads me straight into her chamber where the rest of her déō doúloi are, as is typical

147

for an oikía. Their sole purpose is to be available for feeds and fucks. The visual serves as yet another harsh reminder that Adrestia's situation is so far beneath what's normal and expected.

Kallias is right, she needs to expand her oikía. He needs more déō doúlos brothers; ones like him that exist to serve her. Nothing more, nothing less.

Sitara lounges on the largest pallet beside the déō doúlos who specializes in the emotion of happiness. Of all the emotions, she has always been partial to him, simply due to the fact that all the others are often too complicated to engage with on a regular basis.

Since her oikía has been formed for so long, and each have had an incredible amount of visits to the mortal realm to immerse themselves in their given emotional powers, most of the déō doúloi have gained the traits and characteristics of their emotional specialty.

He smiles broadly, and fires a keen glance at Sitara for approval before leaving the pallet. "Oryn! Adelphós!" As soon as Sitara nods, he jumps up and embraces me. "Great to see you," he says, patting me on the shoulder. "What brings you back here? You finally joining us again?"

"Why I am here is a great question. As to your second inquiry… that answer is simple. No." I glare at Sitara over his shoulder.

Sitara's lips curve in a half-smile. "Everyone may leave except for Oryn." She lifts her hand and makes a shooing motion. The room clears. Sitara motions for me to sit… on the pallet beside her.

I take my chances, choosing a different pallet, but am instantly met with punishment from the hélkō — a sensation I don't often experience since it is usually me who sets the command.

Sitara simply reclines, waiting. When I've had enough of the punishment, I cave and sit beside her. Her indigo eyes study me carefully, unblinking. With a sigh, she says, "Your bond with the new basílissa is not... complete. Does she know?"

"No," I answer through clenched teeth.

"Why do you keep secrets from her when you clearly are in love?"

I bite down, grinding my teeth before stating: "Do not analyze me, Sitara."

"I do not have to, Oryn. You've always shown your emotions outwardly." She only pauses for a breath before taking another hit. "Does Raener know?"

"If you can so easily determine my emotions, then why don't you tell me the answers to your questions?"

Sitara shrugs. "You know how my powers work. I can dig... or you can tell me."

My mind considers all the different ways I can explain this without actually explaining it. Something Raener has always been better at than me. Regrettably, she is a queen, and I must answer her unless it poses a danger to another being.

And as a mesítēs — one who has once served for this particular queen — I know she is not a threat. Of all The Seven, she is the good one. The *only* good one. For that reason, my mesítēs privileges will not help me here.

"Raener doesn't know... yet. Adrestia senses the difference, but her lack of knowledge in how things work in Ceteris prevents her from piecing the facts together to form a full understanding."

"Explain." Sitara yawns, stretching. "Because now, I'm not so sure I know either."

I throw my head back and stare at the peaked ceiling. "There is much Raener and I do not understand,"

149

I start, returning my attention to her. "Just when we think we have something figured out, we discover we're wrong." Sitara's raven-colored eyebrow rises. "For instance, my involvement in her transition to queen. Kirian and her held a bond when they Fell. She was already a basílissa, but because he could not accompany her to the mortal realm, she was unable to gain energy. Of that much, we at least got accurate. The events that happened next, we did not. She still exists due to... luck... for lack of a better term."

"Oh, I doubt that. Luck does not exist. This Kirian you speak of? Is that the huiós who was caged when I first met her?"

"Yes," I respond. Sitara nods for me to continue. "She needed a déō doúlos who was not caged. One who could bring her into the mortal realm for a feed. However, she'd not interacted with any huiói. She had no potentials." I continue on to explain the oddity of Brax's working cock and how his attempt gave her enough energy to travel. How it worked and how I was able to deliver her to the mortal realm. As a mesítēs. The last time, I later discovered, I would be a full mesítēs. "From there forward, I've been in an unusual state of limbo."

Sitara's eyes widen. She's come to the same conclusion I eventually came to. "Correct me if I'm wrong... rather than her déō doúlos, you are her próskairos? And the young one's father is the Watcher who was protecting her today?"

There's no need to correct her. Lazy she might be; stupid she is not. Próskairoi can serve more than one queen, though it is quite rare considering each queen can only have one próskairos. Right now, two basílissas own me, but Sitara is well aware that the more "senior" the queen, the more power she holds in situations where ownership is involved.

As if she can read the thought, Sitara's eyes travel downward. To see if my loins react appropriately to our close proximity now that I am no longer taking the atmis. Unfortunately, it does. There's absolutely nothing I can do to thwart my cock's response to my queen. If she commands me to fuck her, I have to... or be taken by the hélkō and sent to The Void.

Which, of course, is a problem. But the worse problem is that now that Kallias — a true déō doúlos — is in her oikía, I am unable to bring her to the mortal realm. Every time since that first night we fucked, since she was a queen but didn't have anyone else to bring her to feeds, my próskairos status allowed me to do so. And every time, I treasured it. Helping her. Guiding her.

That isn't the case anymore. Only an emergency would require my assistance. Fucking, though... we can do that anytime.

Sitara places her hand on my thigh and slips her fingers between my legs. "Sitara," I warn. But it's an empty threat. She knows that. Nonetheless, her hand moves back to the top of my thigh before transferring to my forearm instead. "You've always been one of my favorites, you know?" she whispers, dragging her fingers up over my bicep and to my shoulder. Unable to control my own body under her influence I lean into her touch. My thoughts and words are all mine, though. "Your oikía were not of a like mind. Plus, you only liked me for my cock."

"It's a nice cock." She shrugs. "You're one of the good ones, though. That's why I like you." Her hand wraps around the back of my neck and fingers tangle in the base of my hair.

A buzz zings through my scalp, and I attempt to pull away from the push of power, but she wraps her free hand around the other side of my neck and pulls me toward her. "Be still." Her lips brush lightly against mine, and my cock jumps in response.

I've never felt so powerless in my existence. As a próskairos, I was always powerless, but now my mind and heart battle with the actions of my body. Sitara places the light kiss she had started, and her power explodes inside me. My back arches and every muscle seizes. Then... in an instant... the power is gone. My cock soft.

Sitara's hands slide away from my neck and she scoots back, reclining once more. I stare, wide-eyed at the flaccid appendage.

"You... released me?" I choke, darting my eyes back up to hers.

"Well, not in the way I'd prefer to," she chuckles flicking one more glance at the appendage that used to very much be hers. "No more secrets, Oryn. And when you tell her about this visit, make sure to explain that the kiss was an essential step to cut the próskairos bond between us.

"Damage control takes far more effort than I'm willing to engage in." She pauses for a few heartbeats before continuing, "Before you go, though, tell me more about the child. Is she the mortal the prophecy speaks of?" Sitara swallows hard, her face losing a bit of color.

"No. She is not... Adrestia is," I answer.

"So the prophecy is in effect after all?"

"Yes."

"What role does her daughter play?"

"That, I am afraid, I cannot answer."

"Cannot, or will not?"

"Cannot. We don't know. There is nothing in the codices specifically about a child."

She takes in a deep, shaky breath and blinks a couple times before asking the next question: "How much time do we have?"

"Very little."

CHAPTER EIGHTEEN

Adrestia

The sun goes down, the gathering having been immediately called off as soon as Sitara stole Oryn from the territory. Brax whisks Seala to my dwelling for safe keeping, Raener joins them, appeasing her impatience with lessons and stories for a time.

Kallias stays by my side through every raging attempt to travel to a different territory. But I know too little about Acedia to bring myself to the correct spot in the realm.

Instead, it just weakens and frustrates me to no end. Kallias and I travel to the mortal realm to raise my energy levels more times in half an astral round than I care to admit.

I have never felt more powerless in my short time here on Ceteris than in these moments. All these powers, this revered "title," and an oikía, and I have no control. Not really.

Sitara will bring him back, though; of that much, I can sense. And when she does, I am ready. This time... I have my bow and arrows. This time... she will not abuse her power where I am concerned.

Senior queen or not, I will fight for Oryn.

That's exactly what I do when the Basílissa of Acedia returns, traveling into the center of my village, Oryn in tow.

Faster than I've ever managed in training, my bow is locked and loaded before her pýlē essence clears. Problem is, as soon as I pull back and motion to loose, Oryn steps in front of her, hands up.

So much red consumes me on learning that he is protecting her. I sprint forward, swipe my leg under him, and he drops hard onto the ground. Leaping over him, I tumble into Sitara, disengage her from her déō doúlos, re-nock my bow, plant my foot firmly on her chest, and aim directly between her indigo-colored eyes.

When her déō doúlos bolts upright to his feet and moves to take me down, Sitara holds her hand up, palm out toward him, halting his attempt.

Sitara doesn't move. Her chest scarcely stirs to breathe under my foot. But it is not her that speaks. Oryn does. "Adrestia. Let her go." The following hiss that comes from his lips does not escape my notice. I remember the sound all too well from a moment early on when he'd tried to command me, but the attempt failed. His attempt is no different now. The hélkō punishes him.

Even still, I keep my focus locked on Sitara, pulling the string tighter. With the briefest flick of a glance to the side, I spot Kallias stepping in front of Sitara's attending déō doúlos.

"Adrestia," Oryn addresses me again, placing a hand on my shoulder. The fingers of my arrow hand shake and weaken under the strain of the taut line. My own chest pitches double time, to make up for the stillness of Sitara's.

"Let me go, Oryn," I grind out before adjusting my shaky fingers. Oryn does let go, choosing, instead, to step forward where he can catch my focus that way. Or so try. But I remain true to my task. Again, I adjust my fingers over the feathery base of the arrow, pulling the line to its max.

Another hand meets my shoulder, another voice. "Adrestia, look at me," Raener's voice meets my ear, my name flowing from his tongue. Not Basílissa. Adrestia. That he would touch me, shocks me out of the red haze, and I glance over my shoulder. Raener's there... but it's Blaze whose touch grounds me on Raener's behalf.

"Let's give Oryn enough time to explain what's going on, then you can decide whether or not Basílissa Sitara will be punished for what she has done within the borders of your territory," Raener speaks low. Cautiously.

Meanwhile, Blaze's hand moves down my bicep, to my forearm, and his fingers wrap around mine, taking control of the arrow.

He places the arrow back into my quiver, and I lower my bow arm. When Blaze lets go of me, I step off her chest, bend down until we're nearly nose to nose, and whisper, "Leave."

Sitara promptly stands, her déō doúlos quickly returning to her side at Kallias's behest. In less time it would take to snap my fingers the two of them are gone.

I turn on Oryn. "Choose, Oryn. I'm tired of being a business transaction! Me, Sitara, or your job!" I create a pýlē of my own and leave, unable to control my thoughts, words, and actions without anger and frustration muddling the truth: having him gone terrified me. The thought of another queen claiming him made me feel that fear ten-fold.

I was worried he wouldn't come back. When he did, and he proved his loyalty toward her, well my pride — and my heart — couldn't handle it.

* * *

THE COOLNESS IS a welcome sensation against my arches and between my toes as my feet mold into the damp sand. The crash of waves a welcome sound to drown out the din of rampant thoughts in my mind.

Eyes closed, I step forward into the water, allowing the lick of wetness to cool the heat that consumes me from toes to face. After a few deep breaths and several more steps into the depths, I lean my head way back and open my eyes, wishing for lightning like I always do. Only stars meet my gaze, though.

"Ma?" Seala's voice cuts through the cacophony of waves crashing and I spin around. Arms open wide, Seala rushes toward me. I wade to the shallows and scoop her into my arms while my eyes search the shore to see who brought her.

Oryn sits on the hilltop, moonlight shining down on him like a beacon.

"What are you doing here?" I ask my daughter.

"Rae Rae was needed to help with something. Da was called to the tower because of an intruder."

"And so, Oryn brought you to me?"

She nods emphatically in my arms. "Papa K is here, too."

"Oh? I don't see him."

"He's hiding," she giggles. "Just in case you need to feed."

"They found me too easy," I whisper, taking her hand in mine and walking backward, encouraging her deeper into the water. "Perhaps it is time for me to reconsider where I escape to from now on." I give her a wink.

With all the trust in the universe, she wades in deeper until about chest-deep. I scoop her up, using the water's support to hold her on my hip and carry her the rest of the way.

Once deep enough, I pat her on the thigh and instruct her to straighten her body. "Lift your butt and stretch straight. Let the water hold you." She does exactly as told. With one hand supporting under her back, I direct her arms outward into a T-shape. "I'm going to let you go now. Be calm and still."

"Okay," she whispers, scarcely breathing.

When I let go, she drifts perfectly, her brown curls floating around her head. "Relax and breathe normal," I instruct with a quiet chuckle. She lets out a slow breath, closes her eyes, and inhales. On her next exhale, all the remaining hesitation in her limbs washes away with the next rise and fall of a gentle wave.

For a moment, I stare in wonder, taking all of her in, from the brown curls creating a watery halo around her face and head to her long eyelashes, the smooth and fawn-like color of her skin, and those beautiful freckles that cover her nose. Freckles like I have, according to Oryn.

"My daughter," I whisper, "you are everything pure, wonderful, and perfect."

Her big eyes open, the reflection of the moon catching in the green-gold orbs. "Just like you," she states.

"No... no, baby girl. Nothing like me."

She closes her eyes again and takes in another deep, calming breath. "Ma?"

"Hmm?" I hum, placing my fingers on her ankle, and slowly moving her into a light spin.

"What do you remember about Elysium?"

The question catches me off guard, so I have to think about it for a time. "Well, you know, we are not supposed to remember anything about Elysium. But I do remember falling. Kirian and me."

"In Elysium, souls destined for mortality get to pick their families before going through the veil. Raener taught me that. I remember... I remember choosing you, Ma."

Something funny happens to my heart on hearing these words. Seems love has too many definitions to count, just like pain does. This type of love so strong, in fact, pain is interwoven there. A debilitating, painful, sort of love.

I had a lot of expectations about what mothering would be like but never anticipated wishing there was more time between growth stages. Nor did I anticipate this bond.

As fast as she is growing, as smart as she is becoming, I am exceedingly grateful in this moment that her mind is still ripe with imagination: healthy, creative, and intelligent. She far supersedes anything my imagination could've conjured. "Thank you for choosing me" — I smile down at her, wiping a few stray pieces of frizz from her forehead — "it is an honor to be your mother."

"You're welcome," she says, and I can't help but laugh.

"As your mother, I suppose I should insist that it's time to get some sleep, hm?"

"Oh no... you don't have to do that. I'm not sleepy."

"No?... I am."

"Okay... well, in that case."

Again I laugh. "Thank you for your permission. Now sink your butt down and stand up."

Seala's eyes widen. "But, we're so deep."

"Are we?"

The question has all her balance-concentration lost and she looks to the side, bending at the waist in the same motion. Her butt hits the shallow bottom, and her hands catch her. During our conversation, I'd slowly worked her back up toward the shore, sinking to my knees the more shallow we'd gotten. In her relaxed daze, she hadn't realized I was eventually shallow enough to sit while she continued to float.

After the initial shock, she stands and makes her way out of the water. Kallias waits to intercept her at the hill. Before he walks away, though, he bends to Oryn's ear and says something to which Oryn responds with a simple nod.

Dripping wet, Seala takes Kallias's hand, and the two of them disappear into the night, leaving just Oryn and me. Oryn stands immediately, whether out of respect or to catch me before I travel away, I am unsure.

The water and my time with Seala have certainly calmed me enough to at least begin a conversation with him, though. Whether or not I'll survive it through to the end is yet to be determined.

Gathering all my hair, I squeeze out the sea water that had accumulated in the tips as I approach. Oryn watches from a distance at first, until I get closer, then he steps toward me and holds out a hand to help me sit on the grassy hillside.

I take it, because I feel as though a little groveling on his behalf will do us well. "May I speak freely?" he asks.

"You can try," I respond.

He takes a deep breath. "Sitara released me."

Relief rushes through my veins, but with it comes a number of questions. "Why?" is the basic one I choose to start with for several reasons: Who in their right mind would give Oryn up? What's in it for her? And about a dozen more curiosities.

"In short, The Seven are horrible. Sitara, however, is not. Never has been. My assumption is that this has a lot to do with her oikía powers. Understanding emotions brings a whole new dynamic to humanity, so to speak... considering we're not humans. Understanding emotions, though, gives her the perception of humanity. Which is why, she, like you, doesn't quite fit in with the others." Oryn hardly takes a breath to separate his thoughts. It all comes out in a string of desperation until the end, when he finally does breathe.

A nervous, subordinate Oryn? This is new.

"She took you from me."

"If she'd have asked permission, would you have granted it?"

I open and close my mouth a couple times before answering. "I would like to think I can make rational decisions when presented the opportunity to do so."

"When you were protecting your daughter?"

That shuts me right up for a moment. But when I do find my voice again, I say, "She didn't give me a chance to decide."

"Well, she's accustomed to the other queens. It is all for one here. If a queen asks for permission to do something, that means she's inferior to the queen of whom she requests permission."

Unsure how to respond, I remain quiet, letting him continue in whichever way he deems appropriate.

"Basílissa," he addresses, moving into a bowing position, nose to the ground. Something I haven't seen him do in a while. "Please forgive me. I knew something like this would happen; I should have been around more to at least explain it to you. Prepare you. That's on me."

I place my hand on his, and he looks up. Right now, I'm grateful for my newly earned oikía power of sight, because even in the night I can see his green eyes and the sincerity therein.

"Sorry I over reacted," I respond.

Oryn returns to a normal sitting position. "Don't apologize yet," he whispers on a sigh. "There's something else I need to tell you." He immediately rolls into the next topic: "You and I are not bound completely. Technically" — he draws his knees up and wraps his arms around them loosely — "I am your próskairos. You accepted me — used me — because I was available to do so. This created a certain partnership between us, but not the tie of a déō doúlos."

"But," I interject, "You have an oikía power... and... and your eyes changed. Your essence swirls silver."

"Yes. When a queen and a próskairos start a strong enough bond, the próskairos will often take on a diluted version of the power he would be eligible to receive should he ever convert fully to a déō doúlos. Or an offshoot power of another, similar one, should the basílissa's oikía already be formed. A queen's próskairos-binding can also be strong enough to 'mark' him as hers. Our binding is strong. It's just not... I'm not part of your official oikía."

"If that's the case, how were you able to accompany me on feeds?"

"A próskairos's job is to serve a queen that is in desperate need of assistance. Only when a déō doúlos is not available. In an unusual turn of events—"

"Kirian was my déō doúlos, but he was unavailable." I cut him short, wanting to challenge my ability to comprehend the complex system here.

"Right." Oryn smiles at me.

"What does this mean for us?"

"It means whatever you'd like it to mean, Basílissa. You can keep me as your próskairos, release me, or we can complete the bond and I will become one of your oikía."

"What does this mean for your mesítēs position?"

"I will remain a mesítēs for as long as I am your próskairos, or in the event I am released. If we complete the déō doúlos bond, I will no longer be a mesítēs."

Oryn loves his position.

As if he can read all the thoughts now swirling with this news, Oryn straightens, brings his hand to my cheek, and directs my face toward his. "Like you, I don't do anything I don't want to. That's what landed me in the mesítēs position to begin with," he says. "I don't regret being with you. Helping." His eyes search mine, but what they're looking for I am unsure. "You do not have to make a choice right now."

Oryn's thumb drags across my cheek and his eyes search my face. With every gentle swipe, a ping pulses between my legs. My gaze drops to my lap and back up again. In a moment of realization, my eyes widen. "Y-are you using your próskairos powers to influence me to fuck you right now?"

Oryn's eyes twinkle, rivaling the starlight. "Yeah. Sorry."

"No you're not."

"You're right." He laughs, and I decide I quite like this new, bold Oryn.

"I have a question for my mesítēs," I say. Oryn's hand drops and he nods, listening intently. "I am well aware that my oikía is... lacking. And, on top of that, it is... unique. For my safety" — I drop my voice, turning my attention to the sea — "and our daughter's... do you think it's best you become a déō doúlos or remain my próskairos and mesítēs?" Releasing him, I deduce, is not an option I am willing to agree with.

When I return my gaze back to him, he, too, is looking out into the vast sea. "Well," he starts, "your current oikía, as well as Raener and I, all agree that it wouldn't hurt for you to have a próskairos in case of emergencies. Which, mind you, tend to happen often where you're concerned, Little Rule Breaker." He turns his face toward me again, and that dimple appears when he grins and winks. "That was when I was still pretending to be your déō doúlos. The easiest próskairos option, of course, is Kohbi. If you like him enough... or even if you don't but choose to bind him as your próskairos in an official capacity anyway... the truth is, we all believe you still need more huiói in your oikía."

Oryn stresses the word *huioí*, and I narrow a glare at him. "You know that's not going to happen. So far, Kallias is the only huiós to whom I intend on being bound."

"Basílissa," Oryn presses, "do you understand the consequences of that decision? For both you and Kallias?"

Unable to look him in the eyes and admit that I have a pretty good idea, but apparently am too selfish to do anything about it, I look away. "I do not want to build an oikía out of necessity. I want to select my men because

164

I love them. Want them. And… most importantly… because they feel the same way about me." For the next part, I drop my voice to a defeated whisper. "I already screwed that up once… I don't want to screw it up again."

Again Oryn's fingers come to my face to redirect my attention away from the sea and back toward him. "I know we came together each with our own agendas, but I do care about you. Deeply. I want you, Adrestia. Whether it be as your próskairos, or as your déō doúlos… or even as just a friend should you release me." His Adam's apple bobs over a hard swallow, and those green eyes search mine again. "I did not make a mistake. And I don't think you made one either."

I nestle my cheek into his hand and close my eyes. After a few heartbeats, Oryn's warm breath and soft lips graze against mine. "Give me another chance?" he whispers against my mouth.

My head nods in his palm, but my words are consumed when he connects our mouths, kissing me for the first time because he truly wants to… not because he has to.

165

CHAPTER NINETEEN

Again, when I close my eyes and let sleep take me away, visions of the forest, essence, energy, and fear warp in my mind. Unable to continue sleeping this way, I wake up, grab my bow and quiver, and check on Seala before leaving my dwelling.

With this new setup, sneaking away is practically impossible, though. The only spot I can travel to from directly within the circular walls is the entrance opening — the same one guarded by two of Brax's workmates.

A grunt of disapproval meet my ears when I'm caught attempting to tiptoe by. "Where are you going, Basílissa?" one of the guards inquires.

"To see Blaze. Do you approve?" I ask with the raise of my eyebrow.

"Yes." He gives me a sharp nod.

"Good, because I was going anyway."

He narrows a glare down at me, arms crossed.

I smile up at him, and give the other guard a smile, too, for good measure before stepping far enough away that they aren't near my pýlē when formed.

Only about a quarter of the time Blaze can be found in his hut, but when seeking him out, that is still where I always begin searching when we don't have a planned meeting. Like now.

Tonight, my search ends quickly. Much to Blaze's antipathy, I pop right inside his hut unannounced. He bolts to his feet, weapon somehow at the ready — a small dagger this time, aimed directly at my throat. Right now, though, the piecing together of who his blade is touching takes a moment longer than usual. Something comes over me — a buzz of some sort. Familiar, yet not. I make the smallest of movement toward him, encouraging his blade to indent my skin and draw the barest of essence.

Blaze immediately snaps out of his shocked daze, and he stumbles backward and falls onto his pallet, breathing heavy. "Tempter's bane, Adrestia! I could have fucking killed you!"

A small stream of my silver essence trickles in a line down the edge of his blade and his gaze tracks the movement. He takes in a deep breath, closes his eyes, exhales, then looks up at me with one, slow blink. There's a heaviness in his features that isn't usually present. A weariness.

He stands, approaches me, and brings his hand to my neck. As his palm pushes up the length, his eyes drift from mine and down to my mouth. "You're..." Blaze clears his throat. "There's essence on you," he finishes, swiping his hand down my neck the opposite way before pulling it back and displaying the fluid.

He steps around, moves to a washing basin in the corner of his hut, rinses his hands off, dampens a cloth, and returns to me. Keeping distance, Blaze thrusts the cloth in my direction.

I refuse the proffered cloth, and, instead, tilt my head back and close my eyes. Silence smothers the room. An eternity seems to pass. But the cool, damp, and slightly rough material does eventually meet my heated skin.

When he's done, I straighten my head and open my eyes. Blaze's black gaze meets mine. I step forward until his erect shaft bumps my hip. His eyes widen and he shoots a glance down before swiftly turning around and returning to the basin.

Curious.

I turn and approach him from behind, pressing my body flush against his. "Haímaboúlomai," I whisper. Blaze is experiencing blood desire. Work must've been busy for him tonight. "You know... Oryn said there are five senses. I only have four déō doúloi." Even though Oryn isn't officially a déō doúlos, I still find myself claiming him as such.

Blaze straightens and turns around, meeting me nose to nose. He takes in a deep breath and his gaze drops to my lips. "Exactly," he says. "One more spot. How's that plan for claiming Raener going?" His eyes lift and pierce mine. The words pierce me harder than his eyes do, though, and I retreat backward to escape the judgement.

He steps around me and collects his bow. "Been a while since you've come to me," he states. "Before you gave birth." There's a bite to the words. He clears his throat, walks to the hut exit, and motions toward me. "Come here... I have something to show you."

* * *

HAND IN HAND, Blaze leads me through the woods just as he has done on many occasions. On this trip, however, we go farther than I have ever journeyed into the forest before.

The walk is long and filled with silence until I remember why I sought him out to begin with. In part, because all that talk about growing my oikía made me want to see him. That part I keep to myself, though, since he has expressed many times that he's not interested in

168

being bound. "I've been having nightmares," I reveal after a while. "They're getting more frequent… and frightening. All of them take place in the forest; I am a beast. A daimónion, I guess. Every time, I get hurt or am already hurt when the dream starts."

Blaze's fingers tap the outside of his thigh as he contemplates this revelation. "Have you told anyone else?"

"No… but I suspect Kallias knows, since he sleeps beside me most nights." Blaze nods. "Thing is, it—" The rest of my explanation catches when a large and unusual hill presents itself in our direct path. Blaze stops and squeezes my hand tighter as my eyes scan the odd mound in the faint moonlight. When I take a step forward to get a better look, Blaze counters the motion, pulling me back to his side.

"Daimónia," he says. "Just over twenty by my count, if I was keeping up accurately with every kill. The last couple astral rounds are a bit of a blur, though." Blaze drags his free hand over his face. "These are just my kills. Other sikárioi have similar counts in the various sections of your territory." Blaze's earlier wariness and blood desire make sense now.

Now that I have a better idea of what's in front of us, I am able to easily spot the long fingers, nubs and horns of various shapes and sizes, and the glimpse of frozen expressions amid the pile.

"Why aren't their bodies putrefying?" I ask.

Blaze answers as he stares blankly at the pile. "That only happens when *you* kill them. The first time you killed that daimónion, that was the only time I'd ever seen one putrefy into the terra like that. These will be burned," he explains.

Again, my eyes flit over the pile, stomach twisting into a knot. Hand covering my chest, I turn to him. "Kirian? Where is he?"

Blaze's eyes lock with mine. "In your dwelling, right? I thought he stuck around there most nights?"

"Yes… but he wasn't there when I woke up." My pulse runs wild. "He…" The words trail as Blaze's attention flicks around the pile in a panic, his chest rising and falling, and in turn making mine do the same.

An apparition appears in the darkness beyond the pile and between some trees. With thoughts of Kirian at the forefront, my mind clings to the assumption that the new presence is him.

Blaze isn't of a like mind, however, and an arrow pierces the daimónion between his horns before I even have time to conclude that Kirian wasn't the target. When I move to bound forward, still not reassured — still unconvinced that Kirian isn't buried in that pile — Blaze grabs my wrist. Voice low, he breathes, "Ready your bow; I can sense more."

Eyes wide, I follow his instruction, pulling out an arrow. "What if one of them is Kirian?" I whisper as he moves behind me so we're positioned shoulder to shoulder at an angle to compensate for our quivers.

But there's no time for him to answer. Or rather, if he does, I am unable to acknowledge the response because a daimónion leaps out of a dark hiding spot right toward me. In a matter of a couple quickened heartbeats, I piece together that this daimónion has larger nubs than Kirian and doesn't have hair — a trait only Kirian has, due to his half-breed state. The arrow sails through the blackened woods and pierces its left breast.

In this moment, I'm exceedingly grateful for the oikía power of sight that I'd been gifted by binding with Kallias...

...and for Kirian's shared power of hearing. A *thoomp* meets my ears, followed by a low growl, coming from the direction Blaze is covering. In an attempt to be a good partner, I continue to scan the area within my half-circle of responsibility, now tapping intentionally into my newest oikía power. The shadows lighten, but my heightened sight doesn't reveal anything.

"This side is clear," I inform as my kill turns to ash and is absorbed by the ground.

Blaze's bicep bumps mine as he pivots, and I focus on matching his movements, turning with him. Now, I face the mound of expired daimónia and he faces the way we came. After a moment of silence, the loosening of his shoulder against mine in combination with the slow release of breath, indicates that he has lowered his bow hand. Taking note, I slip my bow over my head and settle it comfortably. Neither of us move otherwise.

A buzz and vibration hums and tingles at every point of contact our skin makes. Blaze's body moves against mine as he inhales deeply. "Kirian is okay," he says on the exhale.

"How do you know?" I ask.

"Um..." he clears his throat. "One of the reasons I can track these beasts so well is because, in addition to my normal tracking skills, I can also... sense them. Kirian's presence translates differently than normal daimónia. When you'd asked, though, I second guessed myself. Thinking back, I feel confident none of the daimónia I took down were him."

That he can sense Kirian and the other daimónia... does come as a surprise. "What about the other sikárioi?

171

You said there were piles like this throughout the territory."

"Kirian doesn't leave this section," he answers with assurance. Since Blaze knows this territory intimately, his answer sets me at ease. "Plus... I sensed him just a moment ago. He's gone now, though."

"When you'd turned to check the portion of the woods we'd come from?" I surmise aloud.

"Yeah." Blaze shifts from one foot to the other, and that buzz between us returns. He doesn't let it linger for long before creating enough distance between us to make it stop. Only then do I turn around, the heat of his body, and sense of security our proximity provided, having kept me pressed firmly against him in the interim.

When I turn around, he steps to the side and passes me en route to the first daimónion. He then bends down, slips his hands under the daimónion's underarms, drags him to the pile, and rolls the body at an angle to balance it on the mound of other carcasses.

To help, I walk to the other daimónion he'd just killed and try to do the same. Unfortunately, strength is not one of my specialties. Even when I lean my entire body into the attempt, the daimónion doesn't budge.

Blaze approaches, eyes gleaming in amusement, and grips the daimónion's ankles — if that's even what they're called on a beast. Together, the two of us hoist the body up and walk it closer to the pile before strategically placing its form on top of another.

Reaching into a small pocket on his quiver, Blaze pulls out a piece of material before taking one of my hands in his and using the cloth to wipe off the black essence that had transferred to my palms.

The light, careful strokes don't at all match the erratic sound of his heart when the thrum floats to my ears. Nor does it match mine, which is behaving similarly. My gaze travels past our hands in search of the proof that often counters his supposed lack of interest.

Proof is precisely what I find, and my lower body responds to the sight of his cock throbbing between us. With a hard swallow, I avert my attention to his face with a slow and cautious upward slide of my gaze. When my eyes meet their mark, his are already locked on a new target. Me.

Both my heart and my body knows it wants Blaze. But as Blaze's fingertips graze my palm, eyes locked on mine, a war wages in my mind. Was he right earlier when he'd so casually reminded me there's a choice to be made? That there may only be room for one more oikía member? That, if Blaze and I bind now, the already slim chance Raener could be mine, too, would be negligent?

Or do I lean toward what Kallias explained about queens challenging their oikía-power parameters… with the hope that somehow there's room for both? Problem is, right now an adrenaline-fueled desire has us both consumed. Our bodies come together on their own until my chest grazes his heated skin and his hand has moved up to lift my chin. All my senses are overwhelmed by the loud, throbbing pulse in my ears as his lips brush against mine. Only to switch to a muted hum the moment he separates us.

Blaze turns his back on me and walks away. "Go to Raener," he says over his shoulder. "He is the one you need. Not me."

A new type of heat consumes me — a dangerously boiling one — combined with both a dash of relief and a heap of regret.

CHAPTER TWENTY

One astral round, when Raener was giving Seala a lesson, he'd explained to her where Ceteris's bibliothēkē was located: atop the tallest mountain, on the outskirts of Superbia, Basílissa Amrita's territory. There, he had explained, the land peaks and valleys in waves of terra instead of water.

Kallias had also been in Superbia during his wanderings. While twisting or braiding my hair each night, he would describe these lands in grandeur, vivid ways.

Having heard earlier that Raener would be at the bibliothēkē instead of his dwelling — which would've been more preferable since most of the paidagōgói's dwellings are located in my territory — using all the knowledge I'd garnered in combination with thoughts of Raener, I pull from the scant energy, create my pýlē, and... cross my fingers.

My feet settle on cushiony, icy-cold grass — the air where I've landed much cooler than in my territory. So cold, in fact, that my nipples harden and bumps rise on every inch of my skin. The sensation, though, is not bothersome. Just... different. In the least, it quells my still-heated skin from the moment with Blaze.

After the initial shock in climate difference and the blinding light of a high sun, I am able to focus on the surrounding area. On first inspection, it appears I've traveled into a miniature village of some sort. A quiet, empty one. Or so it appears.

This village sits atop one of a seemingly indefinite amount of other tall mountains: waves in a sea of them, just like Raener had described.

I turn in a slow circle until my eyes land on something recognizable — at least where Raener's stories are concerned. To my delight, a set of natural steps leads a path up the steep portion of this mountain. In the distance above me, a large structure — made of tree timber and terra, from the looks of it — stands tall above everything else.

Drawing in a slow breath, I fill my lungs with the crisp, cool air. On the exhale, my breath forms an intriguing, yet beautiful, puffy cloud. With my sight set on the bibliothēkē, I begin my ascent, deciding that experiencing the new topography and climate trumps my desire to create another pýlē just to pop myself inside the structure.

That, and although I know Raener has begun to spread news of my and Seala's existence, I fear showing up inside a building unexpected might cause an unwanted stir.

The walk doesn't take as long as I expect, because about halfway up, someone descending catches my attention. In a panic, I consider using a pýlē to travel back to the bottom, but the vortex, in and of itself, would give me away since every queen's pýlē takes on the color of her essence. Plus, a randomly appearing and disappearing basílissa might raise some concern as it stands.

White hair — so much like the surrounding white mountain tops — and almost equally as fair skin tells me Raener is who descends. So, instead, my mind whirls with what I'm supposed to do next, now that he is in front of me and we're alone.

He doesn't appear displeased to see me. He never does. But the occasional over-the-shoulder glance and quickened steps are evidence of his anxiousness. Our eyes lock, and he picks up the pace until he's on the same step as me yet still as far away as he can stand without tumbling down the mountainside. "Basílissa," he greets on a choppy breath. "Is everything okay?" His black eyes search mine for the answers before I can voice a response.

Not wanting to alarm him in any way, I simply say, "Yes." Though, if my opinion matters, that answer is not entirely accurate. His initial concern does transform, though, proving my answer was somewhat helpful in assuaging any preemptive concerns.

His gaze narrows. "You've traveled to a different queen's territory without a déō doúlos at your side?" he asks.

"I was under the impression I could travel throughout Ceteris as I please — with or without a déō doúlos's company."

"Have you witnessed any other queen do such a thing?" he inquires, already knowing the answer.

No.

The answer is *no*.

However, my response is contradictory. Chin lifted, I defend, "Brion taught me that if a queen should need her paidagōgós or mesítēs — if there is something important — she can seek them out without a déō doúlos at her side."

Raener's eyes flash, the bright-white sky reflecting even in the dark black of his pupils. "Yes. My apologies, Basílissa." He pauses, considering the situation for a moment. "The dwellings at the bottom of this hill are isolated study huts. Shall we?" he asks, motioning to where I came. I nod regally, and the faintest of side-smiles ticks up the edge of his lips. "Your inquiry is safe out here." Raener spreads his arms to indicate the entirety of the mountains. "What important item of business brings you to the bibliothēkē today?"

For the journey down, I at least attempt to casually convince him that the real reason why I'm here isn't because I want — need — him but rather because of a nightmare. To accomplish that, I bring up the very topic. His expression immediately changes to one of wary interest, proving that my attempt works.

Upon further elaborating, I discover that the topic of my nightmares are not new to him. He explains that Kallias had voiced his concern. Which, in turn, verifies my assumption that Kallias is, indeed, aware. When I elaborate the scenes and experiences therein, including how the lógos speaks to me, Raener's brows come together.

"This is worrisome, indeed. We are looking into it for you, but unfortunately I do not yet have an answer to provide."

When we're inside the hut, he gestures toward a mat and I sit down, bend my legs to the side, and adjust my bow so nothing gets damaged. Raener sits in front of me, as paidagōgói tend to do; he is the only paidagōgós, though, that makes my body catch fire when this close. Memories from the one and only time he and I hav—

"Truth is," he says, "I'm glad you've come here. I have some information to share with you. Before you were instructed to stay at the tower throughout your pregnancy, had Brion gotten to the lesson where a prophecy is mentioned?" he inquires.

"No... that does not sound familiar."

Raener swallows hard, his black eyes meeting mine. "There is a prophecy involving a mortal. The prophecy has been in existence since the paidagōgói Fell. It was one of the first revelations we'd ever received. Since then, there has never been a reason to dwell on it. A historic lesson that has had no sign of truth for so long it has become nothing more than a fable. A story. Something — if we were to have children — we would paint for them. A myth of hope. Wanting. A future residents of Ceteris could never truly receive. But one we all ache for."

My eyelashes flutter as I try to control my blinks of disbelief. "This realm... is beautiful. Everything in it is everything I know and love. How could they possibly want anything different? Anything more... or less?"

Raener's eyebrows curve inward in a look of sympathy. Instead of answering me in a sympathetic way, though, he reverts to his teacher intonation. "This mortal," he begins, "is prophesied to be an intermediary who lends to The Fallen's one and only chance at redemption prior to the final *Krisis*. When The Maker serves the final sentences."

Redemption. The one and only time I've heard of this is during the feed with Kallias. The man was attempting to repent so he could still return to Elysium one day.

"That... that can't be right," I stutter. "Surely I would know if somehow that was possible."

Raener swallows hard. "Not you," he delivers. "Seala."

"But... she's not mortal, right?" My head shakes in disbelief.

"As far as we know, that's right. But you are. You... Basílissa... are the intermediary they speak of.

178

Your job, your purpose — as it relates to the prophecy directly — is complete. The rest is in Seala's hands. Right now, unfortunately, we don't know anything more. Perhaps, though, those nightmares you are having are revelatory in nature."

An involuntary shudder courses through me. If that's the case — if somehow I am looking into the future of Ceteris — the result isn't good.

The weight of this news about my daughter presses down on me, too. "Is Seala in danger? What does this mean for her safety?" I ask with a low voice, the words catching in my throat.

Raener shakes his head, uncertain of the answer. "Considering the nature of what she's predicted to be able to accomplish, I'd say she's the safest of us all. But to assure that is the case, and to aid in making certain the prophecy is fulfilled, we should no longer keep neither yours nor Seala's identities secret. As soon as she is grown enough to travel on her own, we must assimilate her to the rest of the realm. To the queens, paidagōgói... every being... every territory."

A shaky breath rattles my chest. "Thank you for trusting me to be the first you share all this with." I incline my head toward him in respect. "She is already quickly becoming more and more independent."

Raener bends forward, bringing his head close to the ground between us. "Anything for my queen," he whispers. At that, he clears his throat, catching the mistake quickly. His eyes lift and pierce mine from under his long, black lashes, the white-silver hair falling messy over his brows as he waits for me to release him from the subservience.

"About that..." my words trail as I give him yet another nod, indicating he can straighten again.

Instead of sitting upright, though, he stands and holds out his hand to help me up but reneges almost instantly, curving his fingers into his palm. "Would you like to go for a walk?" he inquires.

My eyes widen and, no doubt, light up. "Yes. Do you think Amrita would mind?" I ask, pushing up off the ground without his assistance.

"As long as we stay within the paidagōgós canton, she won't even know... unless she were to make an unlikely trip here; however, visits are quite rare."

"How did you know it was me who'd arrived?" I ask as he leads us out of the hut and back into the chilly air.

"Each paidagōgós is assigned a specific territory. They can work within other territories, but just like the mesítēs, we can sense things about our assigned territory — and the queen who reigns there. I sensed the unique essence-energy within your travel pýlē right away."

Raener leads me to a winding trail at the edge of the study huts. The path curves around and down to the bottom of the mountain, I presume; from up here, you can't see the bottom through the hazy clouds that fill all the gaps between every mound.

"Speaking of travel pýlēs... I have never seen you travel. How do you get here? Surely you don't walk."

"Oh no, that would take many many astral rounds — and a raft — to do. Paidagōgói are only permitted to travel to and from here and their personal dwellings."

Due to the narrow track, in order to walk beside me, Raener must stay in close proximity. For a moment, when the breeze blows just right, it mimics the light brush of his hand, which in turn brings all the memories of when that hand could actually brush mine without consequence.

180

Which, also in turn, reminds me of the other reason I traveled here. "Raener..." I start. Beside me, new movement catches my attention and I look sideways in time to catch him rub the back of his neck and roll his shoulders before dropping his hand again.

Confronted with the complexity of how to proceed with the topic, we continue down the winding path in silence for a long while, instead. Longer than I've ever traveled by foot. So long, in fact, that my body feels the strain. There's a slight ache in my feet and a tension in my calves and thighs.

The thought causes me to examine Raener's legs. I now realize why all The Fallen have such defined muscles and builds — must be all the walking and working in which they participate. My own body, on the other hand, proves I don't do any of those things. Lifting a finger, I poke my belly and glance at Raener's stomach, which most certainly would not depress inward should someone — namely me — poke there.

Taking it one step further, I take hold of my hip, really grabbing so it fills my hand.

"Basílissa..." Raener groans. "Please stop touching yourself."

Having been lost in my personal explorations, the sound of his voice shocks me to attention, and I drop my hand. With a nervous chuckle, I poke the side of my butt. "I like this grabby stuff," I explain.

Raener chokes on a chuckle of his own that he'd apparently been holding back. "Yes... so does the majority of Ceteris. Or... they would if given the opportunity to grab it." His breath between sentences stretched longer than usual as the comment reminds us both of his lack of opportunity. An opportunity I hope to

181

change with this visit. "Most queens have… grabby stuff… since they're not as physically active as huiói."

Raener turns off the path onto a grassy flat area similar to the flat spot that consisted of the huts above us — this one, much smaller in size. And in the center of this flatland stands a large tree — a beautiful one unlike any I've seen in my territory. The foliage falls downward from the tall branches, veiling the trunk of the tree. Raener leads me toward it, pushes his hand through the flowing, viney leaves, and spreads it open like one might push aside the cloth of a hut's entrance.

I slip past him and find myself in an open cave of sorts. A tree cave. Surrounded by hanging branches and leaves rather than stone. "This… is amazing." I spin in a slow circle, taking it all in.

Raener walks to the trunk and leans against it, watching as I study everything. Closing my eyes, I breathe in the earthy and fragrant aroma.

"This is where I come to fast and perform personal studies. Rumor has it, this very tree is said to ward against evil — as long as you're in the confines of its branches and leaves."

Eyes still closed, I follow the energy that pulsates within the tree's roots, down deep into the terra. In comparison, this land has significantly more energy than my territory, which I find equal parts curious and frustrating. Sitara had indicated that the land's energy was depleting.

But here it seems plentiful.

Here, it could—

A gasp hitches in my throat as a new plan sparks in my mind.

Unaware of my internal revelation, Raener continues explaining more about the tree's mythology.

As he does so, I calm my expression, turn around, and begin walking toward him. When I stop mere inches away, he doesn't flinch but he does pause his speech and swallow hard. Black eyes blinking down at me, his next breaths quicken.

"Raener..." I restart what I'd tried to speak about when we'd first begun descending the mountain. "I can't fathom this existence without you as my déō doúlos."

In my peripheral vision, I catch his fingers tapping the side of his thighs. "Basílissa," he starts. "You can... and you will." The words come out quietly and lacking all the confidence a statement like that should have.

"Adrestia," I correct on a breath as I lean forward and bring my lips just a hairbreadth away from his.

"Please..." Raener begs on an equally breathy whisper. "Don't torture me like this."

"Torturing you is not the entirety of my intentions." To help me keep this close and balanced without touching him, I place my hands against the trunk on either side of his head for support. "But not trying... not attempting every angle... is slowly torturing me."

So close to my heaving chest, his own rises and falls, the panic inside him bubbling to the surface.

"What are you so scared of?" I ask on my next breath, dropping my gaze to his lips and back up again. "The pain?"

Raener tilts his face to the side and brings his nose close to my shoulder. Keeping the breath of separation, he inhales and drags his nose in an invisible line up the side of my neck, using every bit of space he can without making contact before whispering against my ear. "Because, Basílissa, were I to be sent to The Void, I would never see you again. Being removed from an existence with you would ruin me. The physical pain I

183

can handle… the pain of a broken heart and a lost existence without you, I cannot." He rests his head back against the trunk again, and his black eyes lock on mine.

Before fear or second guessing can overcome me, I close the distance between our mouths.

CHAPTER TWENTY-ONE

Similar to how I was able to heal a caged Kirian while the hélkō concurrently punished him, the effect works now with Raener as I send the smallest bit of healing energy from my personal reserves into the kiss.

Having gone so long without touching, the desperate emotional and physical connection overrides any potential consequence, and he melts into me, snaking his tongue out to taste and savor the short moment. But just as fast, the temporarily absent shock returns and, unable to escape otherwise with our positioning, he pushes me away. The hélkō uses the break in my healing connection to strike the hand he'd pushed me with instantaneously.

His wild, wide gaze darts over mine, hand coming to his mouth, and he slowly drags his thumb across his bottom lip as his mind works through every single implication of what just happened.

After an agonizingly long time he finally uses words: "No," he says, shaking his head. "Too dangerous." Even still, his eyes travel to my mouth and down farther, his gaze slipping between my thighs before flicking down to between his own. "Also, it takes a functioning cock to complete a binding," he analyzes, more to himself than to me. "And even when I could touch her, that vital part was... nonexistent."

Okay, yeah, definitely talking to himself. Maybe he's been spending too much time out here, away from other beings. Amused, I step forward and dip my head down to bring his unfocused gaze back to me. "Time," I state simply. His gaze focuses and attention returns to me. "Your cock needs more time. Hard to… get hard… when the hélkō is ravishing your body instead of a female."

"No… you see, that's the dangerous part. Manual healing of that sort will undoubtedly drain you. Kallias and Oryn are not around to accompany you to the mortal realm to feed right now if your energy should get too low."

I step forward again, and Raener takes a step back to match. "I will not let my energy get too low. You see… I've been planning this. In fact, breaking to feed, and attempting to return and finish, wouldn't work anyway. For the binding to be successful… for it to complete… there would need to be no break in the process."

Again I step forward, backing Raener into the tree. When I get close, his eyes close to escape the temptation. The risk. "Y-you… you should stop," he stutters.

"You are usually pretty intent on stopping me yourself. Why aren't you doing that right now?"

"Because, you've backed me into a corner I don't want to get out of," he whispers.

I brush the back of my hand against his. He inhales deeply and runs his fingertips along my knuckles. This time, I test a different method… one I wasn't so sure would work until just moments ago. Using the knowledge I'd garnered about how the land heals and sustains the existence of all the males in Ceteris, I channel the energy here, instead of my own, simply using myself as an intermediary to reroute its course — to heal him sooner and in a larger quantity than the land and I would do each on our own. And… to do so without using as much of my own energy. To accomplish this, I combine the two, much like creating a travel pýlē, my personal energy gives the remaining energy its directive.

When the hélkō doesn't strike, Raener slumps against the tree, slips his fingers between mine and lifts my hand to his mouth. Only then does he open his eyes again. Those black depths lock onto mine, and he brushes his lips along the sensitive underside of my wrist.

"There's nothing in the bibliothēkē that indicates this is possible," he says very seriously.

"Is all information found within the codices and scrolls strictly from things predetermined," I ask, dropping my gaze to where he now snakes his tongue out to trace my skin.

Keeping the flow of energy is not at all difficult, and with these isolated, small touches, it uses such a sparse amount it makes me wish I had thought to do this before. Not that he would've gotten close enough to allow me before, though.

Raener's head shakes in response to my question as he presses his lips against the sensitive spot, moving slow to the center of my palm, one small kiss at a time.

"Then let's make our own rule." I close my eyes and revel in the graze of his mouth.

A quiet, rumbling groan vibrates from his chest and delivers a similar vibration through every inch of my body. "I don't know what I like better" — Raener drags his thumb over the back of my hand — "touching you, or being the recipient of your response to me touching you." The words are said with the hint of amusement, but that lighthearted repartee drops with his next comment: "Adrestia, wanting you hurts. I never knew a soul could ache. For the entirety of my existence, these scrolls and codices have been my passion, the true energy that feeds me. The moment my eyes landed on you, my soul disconnected from everything else and attached itself to you. When you and Oryn bound, and I lost that ability to feel you, a piece of my soul shattered. Gone forever."

My pulse falters at the words. Shock disconnects me from my attempt to keep the healing line open, and I step away from him quickly. "Wait... Oryn... Oryn didn't become a déō doúlos that night," I mumble, confused, verbalizing the new detail I had recently learned and comparing it to Raener's words now.

Raener's head shakes. "Yes, he did... I was there."

"Oryn explained to me recently that it was the próskairos bond I accepted, not a déō doúlos bond."

Raener's eyes widen. "If that is the case, why could I no longer touch you as soon as the connection was made?" he asks aloud but, again, mostly to himself.

"I was already technically bound to a huiós. Already technically a queen," I state, unsure if my outward thoughts are helpful or only serve to make things more confusing. "If your assumption is that you could touch me because I was unbound and partially mortal, you shouldn't have been able to touch me to begin with."

Raener lets go of my hand while we discuss this new bit of information, but not without a longing glance — and one more kiss to the palm — first. As soon as we're separated, I let my energy rest. Raener looks past me toward the tree's curtain, contemplative. "A próskairos... Yes... That makes perfect sense," he whispers. If anyone can figure it out, it's certainly Raener or one of the other paidagōgói. Based on the cumulative transformation of his features, it appears he's already doing just that. First, his eyes clear as he blinks out the contemplative daze. Then, his raven eyebrows lift high, disappearing into the messy white hair at his forehead, and suddenly flatten as his eyes flash into a menacing squint. "That fucker!" The ensuing laugh and shake of his head does not at all match the preceding show of rage.

Once his animated brows return to normal, he sighs deeply and those bottomless, black eyes lock with mine. "Ceteris has an incredible number of safeguards for queens. None of which we've ever had to utilize — or if we had, on a much smaller scale. The use of próskairoi, for instance. But by default, the nature of this land, and the caste system, is designed with the basílissas' best interests in mind. In light of our newest revelation about your importance — your unique role — I imagine these rules were in place mostly for *you* all along. For the day that you would join us and set Ceteris on the course of its en—sorry, I went down a rabbit hole there for a moment." Raener clears his throat and reverts to the primary topic instead. "Basically, due to your desperate need for a travel companion upon arrival, and the fact that you are part mortal, it makes sense now that it triggered my ability to touch you. Essentially, I was in the running to become a próskairos — a temporary. To help. Like Oryn... to make sure you survived at all costs."

"But... you couldn't... function." My own eyebrows curve inward. "Raener, I would have fucked you on sight if it were possible."

Raener's mouth lifts in a half grin, his dark eyes twinkling in amusement. But the smile is soon replaced with his serious teacher face. "That... we get to blame the grigori for." Raising a single eyebrow, I cross my arms over my chest. He lets out a quiet chuckle before continuing, "Okay, fine. He's actually not at fault at all. I just like blaming him for anything possible. It's... no

189

one in particular's fault really. Just a lack of understanding of the last-resort rules. In short, you're right, given more time, you and I could have become bound."

A wide grin lifts my cheeks... but Raener's expression does not match mine. His chest moves up and down around a deep sigh. My smile drops. "But this is good, yes?" I ask, confused.

Raener shrugs. "A queen can only have one próskairos. You have chosen yours."

My back straightens and I lift my chin. "I did no such thing! I thought I was bin—"

"The hélkō doesn't lie, Basílissa. You and Oryn did not feel deeply for each other at the time of the bond; you used each other. You both had needs, and those needs formed your bond. Yet, you two connected in a way strong enough to start a déō doúlos bond; the color of his eyes proves as much. A regular próskairos's eyes will remain black."

I swallow hard and break my eye contact with him, my cheeks feeling hot despite the cool breeze filtering through the veil of leaves.

Raener's fingers touch the side of my face for the faintest of moments before he draws them away, clasping his fingers in a hard grip to counteract the sting of the hélkō. I allow his unspoken intention to guide my gaze back to his. "You do care deeply about him. Maybe you didn't fully in that moment. But you do now. I don't doubt that, nor does he. I also know for a certainty you don't regret being with him, even now, knowing it meant I would no longer be able to." His lips quirk up and a glint sparks in his eyes. "I'm going to give him hell about stealing you from me, though."

A small smile graces my own lips. I love that Raener is trying to make me feel better about the situation, but even this revelation doesn't provide the answer I so desperately want: how to ensure Raener becomes mine. How to be able to feel his skin against my own. To taste him. To hear the beat of his heart when my head rests against his chest.

My own thoughts seem to mimic his. He clears his throat and deepens his voice to reflect the seriousness of the topic: "This is why you mustn't risk your existence to try binding with me. We might have fun trying... for a time... but you will tire out. The act will not be sustainable. Because, no matter how long you push, I will always remain an ineligible huiós."

I hear him. I hear every word. He's right about Oryn: I do care deeply for my mesítēs and próskairos. I do not at all regret binding with him, even for the reasons we did so. The conversation Oryn and I had at the beach flits into my thoughts, though, and I whisper my own personal revelation aloud, "So, what if I turn my current próskairos into a déō doúlos?" When the question is out there, hanging in the air between us, my focus climbs back up to his eyes. Raener stares back at me, unblinking. His gaze begins to unfocus and refocus in quick succession in a similar way the Watcher's eyes do when they're communicating with each other.

"Who—who are you talking to?"

"I just told Oryn to get his ass over here. Tartarus... I'll give it a shot... or expire trying."

191

CHAPTER TWENTY-TWO

"**R**eally?!" I squeak, removing my bow and quiver with lightning speed and placing them against the base of the tree. My over-eager response comes off a bit too enthusiastic, similar to how my daughter might sound when he offers to tell her a story, but it cannot be contained.

Raener takes a deep breath and lets it out as his gaze trails over my face. "Yeah… really."

A widespread grin spreads across my face. Raener chuckles at my ever-blossoming excitement. Just as he lifts his hand to push aside the curl that had dropped in front of my eyes on account of his warm exhale, the spark of a travel pýlē fills the tree-leaf cave, drawing my attention away from the moment and over my shoulder, instead.

Despite how long I've been in Ceteris, this is the only instance I've witnessed anyone other than a queen travel. Instead of having a color, Oryn's pýlē is colorless like the air; it moves around him similar in appearance to the puffs of each breath-cloud that emits from our mouths.

"Adelphós, wh—" Oryn's words are cut short once his pýlē cloud dissipates and he sees the entirety of the scene. Based on the widening of his eyes, soon followed by the crossing of his arms over his chest, and the very Oryn-like narrowed gaze, Raener hadn't warned him of my attendance.

Nevertheless, he quickly reneges the attitude and bows his head and torso in reverence. "Basílissa."

"Próskairos," I address him by this newest title with an uptick of my lips while stepping to the side and turning to form a half circle between the three of us.

One of Raener's ever-expressive eyebrows rises, and he crosses his own arms, silently berating his best friend and Fallen brother for keeping the delivery of this news at a distance.

Oryn deflates. "I'm... sorry... I should have told you sooner."

Raener doesn't let him wallow in guilt, however. "You can grovel later," he says. "Adrestia and I need you to do something for us."

Oryn straightens. "Of course. Anything."

Unsure where this is headed, my head swivels back and forth from guy to guy as I eagerly follow the conversation.

"Fuck our woman here. But this time... mean it."

"I—" Oryn's voice catches in his throat. "I meant it the first time... And the sec—"

"You know what I mean, Brother," Raener states.

Oryn's dark-green eyes flash to me. "Basílissa? Is this what you want?"

The answer to that question isn't a simple *yes*. I mean... it is... but it's far from simple. By saying "yes," I want to mean it. I want to be certain I desire for him to become my déō doúlos — not to have him do so just because I need him to in order to claim Raener.

I don't want to use him again.

The delay in my response gives both men a false impression of my refusal, their expressions change — flickers of disappointment alighting in their gazes. "No... that's not... I mean... yes. Sorry..." I take a deep breath and try again. "Please don't take my hesitancy to mean that I am saying 'no.'" I direct my attention to Oryn and turn the same question on him. "How about you? Is this what you want?"

Oryn steps up to me and slips his hand under the back of my hair. "Yes," he answers, much easier than I am able to.

In his confident gaze, I find my own confidence. My head nods seemingly of its own accord, heart speaking on behalf of the words my mouth won't deliver.

Unfortunately, that's not enough for Oryn. "Adrestia... I need to hear you say it."

The answer isn't simple, but one thing is: I thought of him as my déō doúlos from the very beginning — from the moment he took my arm and showed me Ceteris. Not all love starts the same way, and sometimes it blindsides you. But no matter how it begins, the effect is the same. The recipient of that love will forever stay that way, regardless what circumstances bring you together, nor what might later tear you apart.

I press my forehead against his and close my eyes. "The ache I felt upon learning that you aren't already my déō doúlos was enough proof." I open my eyes and lock my gaze with his. "I need and want you as more than a próskairos."

Oryn nods. "Does this mean you will take Kohbi as your new temporary?"

The word *temporary* pierces my heart, because I refuse to ever think Raener as anything of the sort. Something about my expression has Oryn's eyebrows pinching together.

Raener takes that moment to remind us of his presence with the placement of his hand on Oryn's shoulder. "Adrestia seems to think that should a próskairos position open up, I may be eligible. With… a bit of effort."

Oryn's hand drops from the back of my neck and he takes a step back, his green eyes searching mine, a sadness darkening them. I match his backward step with a forward one of my own. "Oryn… I did not lie just now. Whether or not it works, I still want you as my déō doúlos. Completing our binding would happen either way." My earlier confidence fortifies. It's true. "But… that doesn't take away the fact that I want both of you… fiercely."

Oryn nods, the tension that had sprung up in his muscles, easing a bit. "Explain," he insists.

Raener inclines his head toward me, and I take a deep, calming breath before beginning. Instead of beckoning verbally, I take a couple steps backward and curve my finger at Raener, commanding him to follow.

Once Raener is between Oryn and me, we lock eyes, and I step in so close to him that the minute space separating us almost gives the impression we're touching anyway.

Just like I had done earlier, I pull a bit of energy from the land at our feet, mingle it with my own, and lean forward to trace the shape of his lips with my tongue.

When I open my eyes, Oryn's craning his neck around Raener's shoulder, looking wide-eyed at our mouths. A breathy chuckle leaves me and I break the connection, careful not to touch him any longer.

"No… it's too big of a risk." Oryn states after blinking the disbelief away.

"That's what I said," Raener sighs. "You think that's going to stop her from trying?"

"Our Little Rule Breaker? Not a chance."

"Right… so… we humor her?"

195

The two men speak about me as though I'm not standing right here. Regardless, I continue to let them do so anyway. When they're done, Oryn's gaze meets mine. "Give me your plan, and we'll go from there."

I side-step Raener, jump into Oryn's arms, and wrap my legs around his waist, giving him a big kiss… this time trying to hold back the child-like squeal of delight. From there, I explain how I envision it working and what will be required of each of them.

With every word, Oryn's arms move one at a time from around my waist until both hands are scooped under my butt. By the end of my explanation, his cock is rock hard, jutting out and bouncing under me.

Raener leans back against the trunk of the tree, a dark heat hazing his usually clear and astute eyes.

"You know," Oryn says, "this sounds like a pretty solid plan."

"You seem surprised." I laugh, pressing my nose against his.

"With you? Always," he responds, brushing his lips against mine.

"Got anywhere to be?" I ask, so accustomed to him being pulled in a number of different directions.

"Right here," he answers.

I wiggle a bit in his arms and he eases me back onto the ground, a hint of disappointment in having to do so evident in the small downward turn of his mouth. I take his hand in mine and lead him over to Raener. Raener straightens and claps his hands together. "So… mesítēs… shall we begin?" Raener uses the title with a haughty leer.

"You are already enjoying this, Paidagōgós." Oryn raises an eyebrow.

"You stole the love of my existence from me, Adelphós... now you get to fix what you broke." His voice drops. "Or at least try."

Their eyes meet, a deep bond and friendship that has lasted an existence thick between them. "Anything, Adelphós. Your happiness is important to me."

Raener bows his head to his former superior and gives him a soft smile of thanks.

Hopes are high, but the uncertainty still floats between the three of us. Even so, Oryn turns to me and lifts my hand to his mouth to place a light kiss on my knuckles. The kiss is anything but chaste. His eyes look upward from his downturned head and that dangerous dimple appears in his cheek as he gives me an equally dangerous smile. He looks at Raener and jerks his head to the side and Raener steps away from the tree trunk.

With my hand still in his, Oryn spins me around, wrapping both our arms in front of my stomach. He then takes my other hand in his and lifts them both, placing each above my head onto the trunk of the tree. Only then does he unwind our fingers and drag his hands down my arms, over my shoulders, and down my back before finding a new home at the grabby parts of my hips. "Taking you from behind," he whispers, moving my hair to the side and draping it over my shoulder, "is my favorite." The end of the statement is met with the sudden plunge of his cock.

My back arches, my pelvis tilts, my body instantly responding to take him as deep as possible. Oryn pulls out until only the tip of his shaft teases my opening and enters me again. Taking me, owning me, making sure whatever this binding requires, he will ensure it happens.

Bark splinters under my nails as I dig for a handhold. With each thrust, my body inches closer to the trunk until my entire front is pressed against it. The bark abrades my stomach, breasts, and upper thighs.

As hoped, the swirl and spark of a forming bond eddies around us, proving that gentleness and reverence are not needed for two beings to become one — that there can be a power shift and the bond will form all the same.

Because right now, in this moment, Oryn is dropping all of his control... all of his subservience... and he's giving it to me. Both physically and emotionally. By taking me hard, fast, and with an unbridled desperation, he's proving to both the bond and me that he belongs. That he is worthy of the title déō doúlos.

One of Oryn's hands leaves my hip and grips into my hair, instead, pulling all of it into a full fist and tugging my head back. His lips drag along the shape of my ear as he slips in a bit slower. "Start converting Raener now... while your energy is heightened..." The instruction comes out between pants of effort. "It is in this moment... that you are at your strongest..."

I nod and open my eyes, them having been previously closed while I was lost in Oryn's sudden turn of dominance — a dominance I've craved since Falling.

My gaze immediately finds Raener. His hand fists his cock nice and slow, black gaze touching everywhere on my body his fingers can't. "Come here, Adelphós," Oryn grunts, moving inside me, sheathing himself completely.

Raener steps forward, still stroking, still consuming me with his gaze, and his free hand traces a line from my temple to my chin. As soon as his finger makes contact I tense, overwhelmed with having to focus on healing while so consumed with the binding between Oryn and me. But my need to protect Raener — my desperation to make this work — has my energy pulling from the land with little effort. Just a bit of energy. Just enough to cover the light touch.

When he manages that successfully, he allows all his fingers to join in, splaying them over my cheek. I press my face against his touch, hungry and aching for it.

Oryn starts a much slower grind, his fingers from one hand digging into my hip and his fingers from the other hand twisting in my hair.

Raener's thumb brushes against my bottom lip, eyes following the movement, and he steps forward again. Knowing what is coming, I pull just a bit more energy from the land. When it mingles with my own, now fed in part through my binding with Oryn, I brush Raener's hand with the healing power. Before kissing me, though, he dips his thumb between my lips and I follow the motion, sucking the pad and curling my tongue around the tip.

Oryn's fingers dig into my skin, and Raener's head falls back with a quiet groan. But only for a moment. Because in the next, he's a step closer to test the power play between the hélkō and my abilities. His mouth brushes gently at first, with caution, then he drags the top of his lip against the bottom of mine, parting me for the entrance of his tongue in the next step.

Every progressive move, the strain becomes more difficult. I become acutely aware that one of us is going to get hurt at some point before the bond is complete. Possibly both of us. The question is… in the end, will the pain be worth the risk? And from what type of pain, exactly, will we have to suffer?

As if *pain* is a being in and of itself, scoffing at us, challenging us in this moment, Oryn bends his knees slightly and thrusts upward, causing a zing of pain to ricochet through my body. My insides silently scream "bring it," as my body does just that, shaking and exploding from within.

Raener's tongue slips inside and tangles with mine while Oryn gives me one last, hard upward thrust, shuddering. Oryn's warm breath hits my ear as he slips out of me and the press of his body releases its pressure of mine against the trunk: "I'll be right outside," he says as he slips out of me. "When you're ready, and if there is a need, we will feed."

CHAPTER TWENTY-THREE

For a few moments, Raener and I simply stand there, inches from each other, breathing heavy, heartbeats manic. His Adam's apple bobs and his dark gaze drifts from my mouth up to my eyes.

"Ready?" I ask in a whisper.

Instead of using words to answer, Raener gently places the tip of his finger inside the hollow part between my clavicles. Ready to counteract the punishment on account of his rebellion, I reach deep into the terra, gather enough energy to last us for a time, and wrap it around us.

When the act goes unpunished, he draws a line downward between my breasts. With each successful inch, he goes farther, past my belly button, and straight down to between my thighs. From there, without preamble, he dips his finger inside me and draws it upward once before dipping inside again, this time with two fingers. With a forward push, he moves inside me, pressing me back against the tree.

"Damn, you're beautiful," he groans. "Especially when your cheeks burn red, and your body shines from exertion."

My eyes open again and I give him a devilish smile, angling my hips forward to bury his fingers inside me as deeply as possible. His other hand leaves his cock, and moves to the side of my neck instead, fingers wrapping around under my hair to draw my head toward his.

He rests our foreheads together and slips his fingers out of me, choosing to rub circles over where I throb and ache for him and work me back up to another peak of pleasure. My gaze trails down to his cock. At a glance, it does seem bigger than usual. Then again, my hopeful mind may be playing tricks on me.

Raener catches me checking, and he sighs, drawing his fingers up toward his mouth. "Even if this doesn't work," he hums around his fingers, "I will dream about it again and again for the rest of my existence."

I angle my head and brush my lips against his, "It'll work."

His eyes find his cock and one of his shoulders ticks up in a small shrug.

My thoughts reel with what to do. We'd gotten this far. The sexual strain is certainly there. He feels it churning in his insides just as surely as I do. The healing is working. But... there's no significant change. At least, if there is, it isn't enough for us to bind physically in that way.

Raener's eyes dart up to the underneath of the tree and he separates us for a moment. His mouth pulls up into a smirk as he holds up both hands and wiggles his fingers. "Well, I've got these... and I could always fuck you with a branch or something."

My eyes spring wide, and I squeeze my thighs together. Raener laughs and steps up to me again, leaning forward to whisper in my ear, "I was kidding, spread those legs again," he insists, bringing his hands to my inner thighs.

They open easily, and he drops to his knees to dip his head between. "Even if it doesn't work... I'm at least going to make this memorable..." he explains between swoops of his tongue and gentle nips of his teeth. "If I am headed to The Void… I'm going out between your thighs in one way or another."

The admonition makes me chuckle, but my chuckle is quickly replaced by a squeak as he lifts me up. Worried I'll fall, my hands immediately go to his head as a grip for support and my heels dig into his back. But he keeps me against the tree for added balance. In a small panic, I pull more energy and blend it with my own since our bodies are now touching in a number of ways. The fact that he has enough trust in me to move and touch freely, knowing I will do everything in my ability to keep him from getting hurt, quite possibly turns me on even more. It certainly adds a heightened dynamic to the experience.

His teeth nip just under my belly button, him unable to dip his head between my thighs while I'm pressed up against his neck like this. His black eyes reach up toward my face. "There's a branch above you," he says. I slowly tilt my head back, and sure enough, there is. "Grab hold, and hang on."

With the support of the trunk at my back, the sturdy branch I'm now gripping, and Raener's strong hands and arms holding me up at the thighs, he's able to dip his head down to lick and suck me to orgasm. My eyes slam shut, thighs and arms quivering, both from exertion and pleasure.

Raener's tongue dips lower and slips inside with a twist before lapping back upward. A moan escapes my lips, and he hums against me.

The hum turns into a hiss, and his hands slip. My eyes shoot open and immediately fall to the evidence of the hélkō's presence on his inner forearm. Having been too consumed with the heady bliss of his warm mouth, I wasn't quick enough to react by sending the healing power into his body like I had planned and been executing all along. Instead, my body, mind, soul, and energy acts impulsively and pulls hard between us, resulting in an odd sensation I have never felt before.

The ensuing sensation is most certainly one I'm quite familiar with; the hélkō slashes me. A cough and gasp of surprise hitches in my throat, emitting as a small whine. I rush to redirect everything, to pull more energy from the terra, to mix it with mine, and to push it between us. Only then, do I realize the oddity — or coincidence — of where the hélkō had attacked me. My eyes seek out the throbbing wound on my forearm. Placed exactly as Raener's had been.

Raener fixes his grip, but instead of supporting me under the thighs, his hands move up to my waist. "Let go of the branch," he says.

As soon as I do, he slowly descends to his knees so I can plant my feet solidly on the ground. Once I'm secure, he scoots away from me, falling to his butt and creating distance between us. I instantly drop to my knees and scurry over to him. Scanning his entire body with my eyes. "A-are you okay?"

Raener's gaze shifts to where the hélkō had struck his forearm, and he rubs the now healed and invisible cut. His focus scans my entire body just as I had done to him a moment ago. When he sees the cut on my own arm, he impulsively grabs my wrist and twists my arm so the inner forearm is visible.

The hélkō attacks ruthlessly since I had let my healing focus drop when he'd moved away, and he promptly drops my hand.

Instead of looking upset or disappointed, his black eyes dart down to his cock, back up to my eyes, and his head tilts to the side. "I could swear my cock…

tightened... or something... did you just do something different with your powers?" he asks.

My eyes widen. "Yes... instead of healing you, I stole your punishment. But only very quickly while gathering my senses and organizing the route of power again. It was an accident; I didn't even know taking someone else's punishment was possible."

Raener lets out a heavy sigh and rubs his hand down his face with a groan. He shakes his head, silently pleading with me, eyebrows drawing inward.

Piecing together what conclusion he'd come to takes me a few heartbeats longer than it had taken him, but before long I realize what this insinuates and why Raener is now pleading with me.

In order for this to work, in this unusual scenario, someone has to take the punishment on behalf of the huiós who is trying to get away with the loophole. "Raener!" I gasp excitedly.

"Adrestia..." he warns. "No way."

A huge grin lights up across my face, and I stand up and rush to the waterfall of leaves, peek my head out, and warn Oryn what's about to happen. That if the hélkō brings me to the brink like it had before I'll need to feed immediately.

Oryn's eyes are calculative and concerned, but he nods. "I'm coming in to watch, though. I don't want to risk even the short distance of separation by being out here."

With that, the two of us join Raener inside again.

Oryn grins down at him and slaps him on the back. "You're a real boy now!" he says.

Raener glares up at him, unamused. "You're going to let her follow through with this?"

Oryn drops into a squat and the humor in his voice drops, too. "Yes, Adelphós. If anyone is cut out for handling this, it's Adrestia... and you."

"What has she done to you, man?"

"Same thing she's about to do to you, Brother."

One of Raener's eyebrows rise.

When Oryn stands, I take his place, sitting beside Raener. "Remember when you punished me with the hélkō? You had no problem drawing essence that time." I drop my voice for the next bit, "And I certainly had no problem being the recipient."

"This isn't a gentle warning like what I set the hélkō to do to my students," he insists. But the dark heat in his eyes contradicts the argument.

I respond with a shrug. "If your cock gets hard, that sensation alone will likely counteract the pain of the hélkō... and from there it won't take long."

Not too far away, Oryn chuckles. Raener looks over his shoulder. "With that tight pussy around your cock for the first time, I'll be surprised if it takes any amount of time at all."

"Well, for the sake of making sure the hélkō doesn't take her from us completely, I hope that's the case."

My eyes light up, squinting at the corners. "So... is that a *yes*?"

Raener blows a raspberry from his lips. "Yeah." He tries to look unimpressed, angry, worried... but the heat, excitement, and longing is there, too.

With the bit of terra-energy I had already collected, I place my hand at the center of his chest, direct him onto his back, and straddle him. "I'll use up the rest of this energy concoction I made then start stealing your punishment once it wears out. There's not much, so we

206

won't be able to play for long. I figure being on top of you like this, we can take immediate action as soon as your cock hardens enough."

Raener nods, the back of his head rubbing against the ground. I hover above him, and his hands come to each of my hips, his thumbs tracing light lines along the creases where my thighs meet my center.

Apparently Oryn isn't patient enough to just watch, though. He steps toward us, falls to his knees, and his mouth comes to my nipple. As his tongue flicks and teeth pinch, I take one of Raener's hands in mine and direct his palm up my stomach to my other breast. I move to his other hand and direct his fingers inside me.

Oryn's lips move from my nipple up to my neck and my lips, and he takes my mouth hot and hard. When his tongue thrusts between my lips, I press Raener's fingers firmer inside me.

"Adelphós," Raener's address is firm but mixed with a groan. "If you don't stop toying with what's mine right now, you're going to pay once we're finished."

Oryn chuckles against my mouth, his feathering breaths tickling my lips, but he obeys his best friend's request and steps away again.

I lean down and forward, bringing my mouth to Raener's. His hand moves from my breast around to my back and down, fingers tracing the long, knotted scar that marks my spine from the base of my skull to the base of my tailbone.

"The healing energy is about to deplete," I whisper against his mouth.

Raener swallows hard, slipping his fingers out from inside me and sliding them through my folds.

I don't know for certain when the hélkō is going to start, so I am unable to redirect it until it strikes him first.

And since the hélkō punishes in waves, it'll be that way the entire time we're attempting to bind: he'll feel the sting for a brief moment before my powers catch the punishment and latch on.

The first strike hits his hip, and I focus my powers on the mark, just as I had done at the tree. Sure enough, the punishment redirects, slashing my hip instead. Deep and unforgiving. I immediately double over, my hand clasping over the wound, fingers splaying over the weeping essence. My gaze drifts to Raener's hip. His mark is still there because I didn't counter it with the healing energy, but the cut is not as deep since it rerouted and my body took the brunt.

Dropping my gaze farther, Raener's cock is slightly lifted, the shape filling out. My eyes clash with his. "It's working," I pant, trying to speak over the pain.

Raener's head nods and he drags his fingers up to my nipples. The next time the hélkō attacks, closer in succession due to our constant contact, Raener twists my nipple between his thumb and finger. My head falls back, legs trembling, core aching, and the newest cut on my upper thigh burning relentlessly.

Again the hélkō strikes, and Raener slips his thumb into my mouth as he had done before. He depresses his thumb against my tongue as I'm sliced from armpit to waist. I wail around his thumb, eyes watering.

He drags it down my body again, bringing it to the apex of my thighs once more, the pad warm and wet from having just been in my mouth. The hélkō only gives me a few heartbeats recovery. In that time, I let my gaze drop to between our bodies, just as Raener's free hand comes to my waist. After a few priming circles, he lifts that hand to join the other on the opposite side of my hip and he eases my center down to take in his erect cock.

I'd been so consumed by the pain, so lost in keeping that connection open, I hadn't realized he was ready. But Raener did. My opening stretches as he spreads me with his thick girth. He doesn't slam into me; instead, he lowers my body inch by inch, eyes closed, chest moving up and down as he revels in the sensation of being sheathed for the first time.

Once my body is pressed firmly against his, Raener shudders and groans, his fingertips digging into my hips.

The hélkō strikes us harsh and unforgiving. Raener jerks beneath me, the tip of his cock striking a nerve deep inside. Together, the two of us ride the pain-pleasure combination. I rise, and when I fall against him, he plunges upward. A zing shoots down my back where the hélkō had attacked me on more than one occasion before, and his thrust causes an opposing zing of pleasure to zoom up my spine; the two clash about mid-back resulting in a fiery fusion.

Heat consumes me and wraps around us. The ground seems to come alive, rumbling under my knees. Hairs lift on every inch of my skin. When I open my eyes to witness the cocoon of the binding process, I am shocked to see Raener's hair sticking up everywhere.

His eyes widen and he slings his arms around my waist and yanks me to the side, rolling us out from beneath the viney tree-cave. "Oryn!" he yells. He uncouples us and pulls me off the edge of the incline that had led to the tree, dropping us several feet down and landing with a crunch onto a different part of the path below. Oryn appears, throwing his body over both mine and Raener...

...then, a loud pop and fizzle...

...and everything goes black.

CHAPTER TWENTY-FOUR

When my eyes flutter open, Raener is staring down at me, his brows netted together in the middle. He blinks rapidly a few times and lets out a big exhale. "Thank Belíar, you're okay. Get up, hurry." The relief in his features is quickly replaced with urgency.

I promptly move from my back into a sitting position and look around; at first inspection it appears we are still in the tree cave, just as we had been before I lost consciousness.

But… that can't be right. Something happened; Raener had rolled us out from under the tree. "What happened?" I ask as he helps me stand.

"In a moment," he whispers, handing me my bow and quiver. "Do you need to feed?"

That is a great question. I focus inward and give myself a quick assessment. "No. I… feel great," I whisper back, unsure why we're whispering to begin with.

My rational thought and memory of the moments before everything went black returns in small pieces. The memory of why I am here and what we were doing slams into me as I put on my quiver and adjust my bow over my shoulder. I spin around and take his cheeks between my hands to study his eye color, pinching him so firmly that his lips contort.

Still a bottomless black.

My lips curve downward and shoulders slump as I loosen my grip. But at that moment, a shimmer of light filters through the leaves and a dark, almost black, amber flickers in their depths. The frown quickly converts into a huge smile, and I jump into his arms, wrapping my legs around him.

His nose meets my neck and he inhales deeply, slipping his hands beneath my weapon and squeezing me so tight I fear the air in my lungs will be pushed out completely. He pats the side of my hip, indicating for me to stand.

"Okay," he whispers again, "We... have a problem." Fully attentive now, I straighten and give him a firm nod, trying to ignore how my insides twist with a mix of excitement and apprehension. "Amrita is pissed."

"Oh... she felt the borrowed energy?" I ask, pulling out the háptomai arrow — the one reserved for touch. I take his palm in mine, give him a quick slice, and wipe the shaft along the seeping essence.

Raener watches in amazement as the arrow glows, anxiously feeding on his new oikía power.

He then shakes his head and presses his lips together. It's difficult to discern if this expression is from worry, anger, or amusement. My confusion ends when his chest does a quick jerky heave as he tries to contain an outburst of laughter. "No. The energy in this part of the land belongs to the paidagōgói. Um... you... harnessed her powers."

"I did what?!" Raener clasps his uncut hand over my mouth to muffle the exclamation.

"What do you remember from right before you fell unconscious?"

My eyes drift to between his legs, and I step forward, reaching down to wrap my fingers around his hard cock. Raener groans and grips my wrist to remove my hand. "Well, I remember that part." I grin.

I put my playfulness on hold, letting the grin drop, since he is clearly trying to be serious. I go on to explain the power that swirled around us — the electricity — and how he slung us out of the tree cave.

"You... you struck my favorite tree with lightning."

"I did what?!" Raener has to cover my mouth again. "Why are we whispering?" I mumble into his palm as I return the arrow to my quiver. When he lets go, I finish my next thought: "I didn't mean to create lightning. But I had been envisioning the way you'd explained how our touches are like lightning in a storm. I'd channeled your power — touch — and electrified it."

Raener's lips turn up into a half-grin, but instead of responding to my lightning reference, he goes straight to why we are whispering. "Amrita is standing on the other side of those leaves, down the path a ways, while Oryn pretends to still be a mesítēs and tells her what to do — or not do."

"And... we're somehow safe in here?"

Raener smiles again. "Apparently the rumors are true after all; this tree wards against evil." Again his smile drops, though, as he switches to the seriousness of the situation once more. "Lightning doesn't just strike without Amrita knowing. Usually, lightning doesn't strike without her having something to do with it. In the mortal realm, every thunder and lightning storm is usually the direct result of her anger and wrath over something undoubtedly related to her pride being hurt. Which is often. That, or she'll churn a storm just to piss the mortals off and make them emotionally break."

"What should I do?" I ask my paidagōgós with a quiet voice.

"You're in her territory, so your punishment will be at her discretion."

"Correction, I am in the paidagōgói's territory, which just so happens to be located within Superbia. Does she assume you are still a paidagōgós?" Presented with a potential conflict, I immediately go into problem-solving mode.

Raener's eyes widen at this question, and he staggers a bit on the spot. I reach my hands out, cupping his shoulders to steady him. His eyes unfocus and fall to the ground. "I'm not a paidagōgós any more," he breathes.

With everything going on, my question must've only just now made him realize the loss. I let go of his shoulders and step back, dropping my hands to my sides. "I'm sorry... I... I didn't think to check about how you felt about th—"

Raener hushes me with a gentle kiss. "No, I just... there just hasn't been enough time for me to process the change yet is all. You're worth it." I blink at him and nod. "To answer your question, yes," he continues, "she will probably think I am still a paidagōgós."

"Okay... then... we use that to our advantage," I decide. Raener raises an eyebrow. I dart another glance at his still-hard cock. "But... um... for this to work, you need to control *that*."

Raener shoots a glance down at the appendage in question, and he swats at it. "Fuck! The damn thing has a mind of its own. It's like the head has an eye, and if you're anywhere within sight, it feels the need to point at you as though to say, 'Right there, Raener, that female right there, see her? Go!' Tartarus, if it was physically possible to curve around my body, you could probably

213

be standing behind me talking and it'd try to figure out a way to make sure I know you're near. Also… it hurts."

His dramatics make me chuckle as I cycle through ideas of how to get out of our current predicament. The only solution I can come up with, however, will require him to tame his cock and act as a paidagōgós who is here simply teaching the new queen.

"Think about Seala," I suggest. "Or… Brax." That addition is included with the upward tick of my lips.

Raener reels back, eyes wide. "Well… yes… those should do the trick." He nods resolutely and takes a deep breath, turning away from me to begin the process.

Meanwhile, I detail what I meant by using his prior paidagōgós position: "You said the time has come to begin spreading news of Seala and me, correct? Of the prophecy. Well, you can start there and further explain that my powers are unlike those of the other queens — that they are of a set which can play off of all the powers of Ceteris as a whole. And as my assigned paidagōgós, you believe it is of the utmost importance I take my lessons here, in a controlled environment."

Raener spins around, his cock soft once more. "Do you think that is true?" he gasps. "I… tempter's bane, you make me feel like the dumbest paidagōgós in all of Ceteris. That thought had not even crossed my mind."

"Well… no… I was making that part up. But come to think of it…"

"Come to think of it… you may very well be right. Empiricism — the senses — interplays with almost everything." He waves his hand. "Forget about that for right now; we really need to get out of here. Something feels off… I… I can't quite put my finger on it." Swaying slightly, Raener steps to the curtain of leaves, opens it, and gestures me through.

214

Shoulders back, chin out, and a deep inhale and exhale, I leave the safety of the tree cave.

Amrita might be a senior queen — as they all are where I am concerned — but it's all about impressions and perceptions here. Who will intimidate the other first.

The answer to that question is most certainly Amrita. As soon as the tree is behind me and we are down the curvy path a ways, there she stands, regal and beautiful. The prominent angular slash of her eyes makes her appear even more fierce and utterly terrifying. The uniqueness of her features reminds me of Kohbi, and I recall that he came from this territory.

I move my bow from my shoulder, take out the háptomai arrow, and hold the two at my side loosely. A warning.

When her eyes look down her nose at my power object, I finger the fletching and push my newly garnered, albeit diluted, power of touch into it. The arrow glows, and Amrita's hand moves to a spot at her hip to grip her own power object.

The ornate handle of what appears to be some sort of three-edged hand blade glows a bright blue.

"Basílissas..." Oryn steps between us. "Watch yourselves. Ceteris has enough problems below the surface right now as it stands, we do not need an internal war to begin after an existence of peace between the queens."

Amrita tilts her chin back farther. "She is breaking the rules and must be punished."

The faintest of smiles ticks up on Oryn's face at the reference of me breaking the rules but he quickly straightens it.

Raener comes to our aid: "She has done nothing of the sort, Basílissa." He drops to his knees and genuflects at her feet. Amrita snaps her fingers and he rises. "I am certain you heard news of her arrival in Ceteris and have come to the conclusion that she is not like the other queens. That she is different. It is for that very reason we have taken extra precautions to ensure she receives the best education possible... in such a short timeframe." With the last part, he drops his voice, whispering it menacingly.

Amrita's eyes widen a bit and she steps closer to her attending déō doúlos, the knuckles of her object hand brushing against him.

"Seems I remember a time when yah, too, did nah understand all tha rules, Basílissa Amrita." This statement does not come from Raener nor Oryn, but rather from behind Amrita and her déō doúlos. I recognize the unique accent of a previous wanderer — and my déō doúlos — right away. Kallias has decided to join us.

Amrita does not turn around to see our approaching visitor. Rather, her déō doúlos protects her back, stepping between her and Kallias.

Amrita turns her head just enough to bring one of her ears closer to the impending conversation behind her, all while keeping a wary side-eye on me. My gaze travels around her, and I lean to the side to make sure my déō doúlos isn't in any danger in his interactions.

When I do, the two men are engaged in an embrace, clapping each other on the back. Once they're done reuniting, Kallias steps past Amrita, faces her, takes a knee, and bows his head. "Basílissa," he susurrates.

"Ah, hello there, old friend. Traveling still, I see?" Amrita lifts her free hand and gestures toward the rolling hills and mountains.

"When a need arises, yes, I suppose so," Kallias responds, eyes still to the ground.

"Stand up," I command through clenched teeth. Oryn and Raener may have a need to pretend they are not mine, but Kallias does not, and I refuse to feed into this apparent notion she may have that her and Kallias are anything more than friendly.

From my point of view here, staring down at the back of his head, even being friends is too much.

Amrita quirks an eyebrow as Kallias does exactly what I demand. He then turns around and bows his head, lifts my hand, and places a light kiss along my knuckles, raising his gaze to mine, a sinfully wide smile pulling across his handsome face. "My queen," he says with the tone of a whisper but using a pitch loud enough that Amrita will undoubtedly hear him.

"As I was saying," Raener clears his throat, continuing what Kallias's arrival had cut short. "This requires some visits to the paidagōgói's village."

While Kallias takes a stance at my side, Oryn supports Raener: "Yes, and this is not a request, but a requirement." One of these astral rounds, if he is not careful, all this pretending may catch up with him.

Amrita grips the handle of her dagger harder, and the sky darkens. Everyone's heads tilt back, eyes moving toward the sky. Everyone's except for mine and Amrita's.

Having guessed at the need for my touch arrow, considering that was the power which drew her attention here to begin with, I now decide against it and quickly make a switch, swapping for the arrow bound with essence from my daimónion. Akouó: the power of hearing.

The swap is so fast, Amrita scarcely has time to react. React she does, though. The sky crackles with a different type of lightning: the type that webs across the sky, interconnecting the clouds.

Amrita lifts her object, but my arrow is faster than her throwing speed, and the tip strikes the metal blade, knocking the dagger out of her hand before she releases.

My intention is not to cause harm but to make sure there is an understanding between us. All the same, it is not my arrow that stops her; the eerie silence that follows does.

The rumbling of thunder, far-off sluice of rain hitting treetops, and crackle of an intense lightning storm brews above us. All the elements are still there, but the sound of her concoction is now utterly silenced. A dangerous ringing takes its place.

Her eyes search sky, seeking proof that her storm still continues to form. As soon as they do, I release the shield, churn the audio into one, big fusion of noise, and crash it down on her all at once.

Amrita and her déō doúlos fall to the ground, hands over their ears, essence seeping between their fingers.

I step up to her, bend down, pick up my arrow, and return it to my quiver, not even bothering to make eye contact.

Amrita crawls forward, stumbling on hands and knees toward Kallias's feet where her dagger had bounced to after she dropped it. On her hands and knees at the feet of my déō doúlos... as she should be. As soon as she picks it up, her and her déō doúlos form a vortex of blue and leave, taking the storm with them.

Her dark-blue eyes, like a midnight tempest, so dark they can nearly be mistaken for black, find mine between the swirls of her energy, and I realize in that moment I've either done something really smart...

...or something incredibly stupid.

My BINDING WITH RAENER had counteracted the pull of energy it took to take his pain as my own, but pulling that stunt for Amrita is a different story.

Once the last of her pýlē remnants disappear, I stagger on the spot. All three men catch me together. Their hands, a web of safety. Kallias's eyes widen as they find Raener's touch is no longer harmful, but time is too short to discuss it. "Raener," I breathe, reaching for my próskairos.

"I cannot, Basílissa. Your déō doúloi are here and available for you; I am only a back up."

Unable to argue or figure out yet another way to break the rules, I simply nod and take Kallias's outstretched hand, instead. "Take us back t' tha territory first," Kallias says, a hint of caution in his voice. "Se—"

"Ah..." Before Kallias can finish, Raener cuts in, swaying a bit. He blinks rapidly, holds up a finger, clears his throat, squeezes his eye shut tight, and shakes his head. "Something is wrong. I... I feel like I need to get to Seala."

I flit a glance between Kallias and Raener. Kallias gapes as he takes in my new próskairos's unusual state. "When I left her, she was feeling weak. That's why I came here," he explains.

"She needs to feed," Raener breathes low, hand over his chest.

Oryn swallows thickly, inspecting Raener and me. A realization of some sort occurs to him, and his features morph, much like Kallias's had, into a stunned expression. He steps to Raener, placing a hand on his shoulder. "Brother, somehow through Adrestia, the protective instincts you have gained on account of the próskairos bond must extend to Seala. Go to her. Crete a pýlē just like your paidagōgós one, but instead think of Seala as your destination. The pýlē will not steer you wrong."

An existence spent mediating in situations like this aids in forming his choice of words and delivery. Calm. Certain. Informative.

Raener takes a deep breath and nods firmly, working immediately thereafter to create a travel pýlē.

The entire situation is so bizarre and confusing. The synapses in my mind aren't quite firing as fast as they might under circumstances where a fight with the hélkō, a battle with a queen, a binding — make that two — and the depletion of my own energy aren't in play.

It isn't until Raener has disappeared that I piece together my daughter is unwell, and I need to get to her, too.

In a sudden panic and rush, I grab both Kallias and Oryn's hands and create a pýlē faster than ever before. At least I have that going for me considering the knee-jerk reaction was to just stand and gape. "Where is she?" I ask.

"Blaze," is Kallias's quick response.

The three of us land inside Blaze's dwelling in an instant. Raener, Blaze, and Brax are all bent over Seala. "Fawn," Blaze whispers, tapping her cheeks with his fingers.

My daughter, her very build suddenly drastically changed, lies listless on the floor, marks from the hélkō scattered over her body. My fists ball at my sides, red

220

blurs my vision, a sadness and the weight of a thousand rocks of guilt consuming me.

I had left her.

I left my daughter.

This is my fault.

"You didn't know tonight would bring with it another growth spurt," Oryn says, looking down at me as I crumble to her side. I simply blink up at him with pressed lips and curved eyebrows.

Raener places his hand on her shoulder, and I grip her fingers while also reaching back for Kallias.

"Oryn, place your hand on my shoulder. Brax and Blaze, back away."

Brax and Blaze step back hurriedly, separating themselves as far as possible without leaving. My mind reels with where to take her — with what scene might be the most appropriate and filling for our daughter. I look at Raener and say, "You choose. You are her próskairos."

Raener swallows hard but he does not turn down the responsibility. He closes his eyes, and when he gives me the cue, I create a new vortex, pulling so deeply from beneath the terra that I worry it has taken too long before the small amount of energy finally reaches us, commingles with my own, and the pýlē forms, large and vibrant around us. As the air whips around the whole building to accommodate the many participants, I fear Brax will be trapped and sucked through. "Brax! Leave!!!!" I scream over the raucous noise.

I can only hope my message got to him in time, because in the next instant Oryn, Kallias, Raener, Seala, and I are in the mortal realm…

…in a church.

221

CHAPTER TWENTY-FIVE

Everyone's eyes grow large. The first of us to snap out of shocked stupor is Raener.

He chokes out the mix between a laugh and the cough he'd conjured in an attempt to cover it up. "Well, this is certainly not where I expected my first accompanying feed would be," he states, studiously scanning the building while never once removing his hand from Seala.

Kallias comes to my side, Oryn on the other, and I reach over my shoulder into my quiver to remove an arrow. The two of them study the room, seeking out our influencing possibilities, I presume. The congregation is somewhat slim considering the amount of available seating, but there are still plenty of attendees.

As soon as the fletching touches my fingertips and I draw it out of the quiver all the way, a weakness overcomes me — an unfamiliar sensation that overrides my weakness from being drained. My fingers tingle, and the arrow falls with an eerie echo onto the marble floor. My vision pulsates, and my chest and lungs tighten.

"Get her out of here!" Raener hollers.

Kallias and Oryn usher me toward the ornate double doors. As the three of us leave, a woman slips in, ghosting right through us. Her wide, vacant stare catches on mine as we both look over our shoulders and our eyes meet an instant before the door closes. A chill skirts over every inch of my exposed skin.

As soon as we are removed from the interior of the building, I gasp in a lungful of air. My awareness returns, soon followed by a debilitating forlornness and fear like none other. "Seala!" I choke, turning and sprinting back toward the church doors.

Hands catch me in motion, pulling me back before I can enter. "Shhh, shhh," Oryn hushes, bringing my head to his chest. "There's nothing we can do. Raener has to help her from here. This church is warded. It is holy. Our kind are not permitted inside."

"Oryn, I must go to them. Something is terribly wrong."

Something is terribly, terribly wrong.

Both men deny me with the shake of their heads.

"Do not make me do something unkind. Don't make me take action against you." My voice is calm, but the igniting rage inside me is not.

Oryn's features become studious and somewhat forgiving as he takes me by the shoulders and looks into my eyes. He swallows hard and peers back over his shoulder near the church's entrance just as the door flies open and Raener comes rushing partway out.

"Scratch what I said about getting her out of here. The place is compromised. Wards are down now. You have to come. All of you. There's a situation."

The three of us rush inside and find Seala standing in the middle of the aisle, arms outstretched upward. An incredible influx of curiosities hit us all at once. First, she'd grown. Quickly, and suddenly. If it weren't for her still being dressed in the cloth Brax insists she wear at all times — now at about knee length, the material not as loose — we may not have even recognized her right away.

Our gazes simultaneously move from her to the stage ahead. The woman who had passed me on the way in stands similarly, facing Seala, arms up and outward.

Her irises are glowing red, face tilted toward the ceiling, body shaking. I immediately pull an arrow, nock, aim, and draw.

"Ma, no!" Seala yells, somehow sensing my intention without so much as a glance behind.

I don't strike the woman down, but I don't disarm my bow either. Instead, I close the remaining distance to Seala and stand next to her, bow very much still at the ready. A mix of murmurings and melodic-like conversation fills the room as the congregation becomes riveted on the stage.

Raener, Oryn, and Kallias form a semi-circle at our sides, unable to do anything but watch. Oryn leans toward my ear, his voice dropping into a deep, ominous pitch. "She has been possessed by a daimónion."

"I thought you said this building is warded against evil."

"That's because it was when we got here."

I absorb every single thing in the large room. Every person, every seat, every pattern in the marble, and let them explain the things I do not yet know. "This woman," I realize, "is the leader of this church. Or, she *was* before her possession. I mean she still is; however, she now has a sidekick."

Beside me, Seala recites something, mumbling under her breath.

I flash a look at Raener and jerk my head so he'll come closer. "Weave me a tale," I whisper so as not to bother Seala. Whatever she is doing seems to be feeding her, and at the very present moment there doesn't appear to be a risk of danger where she is concerned. Though, I have a feeling that will be changing quite soon.

"Your daught—"

"Our daughter."

"Our daughter feeds by influencing… good."

An odd, sensation blooms and expands in my chest. "Well, that might be problematic should we ever decide to feed together," I whisper back.

Raener nods and continues, "Don't put your bow down, Adrestia, because right now she is acting as the woman's will — as a mental light while the woman fights a horrific battle."

I flick my attention to the woman in question. "She doesn't look as though she's fighting much. Aside from her red eyes and the tremble vibrating her limbs, she appears to be…" I search my mind for the word I had learned not too long ago. "Praying."

"Our biggest battles are always the internal ones. Hidden. Festering and bleeding from within."

A shiver courses through me, and I readjust my aching fingers, making certain I still have a good hold on my bow and arrow.

Raener explains, "Humans seldom recover from daimónion possessions. Their wills are no match for that type of evil."

"I… I don't know how much longer I am going to last without feeding," I breathe out, finding it increasingly difficult to stand.

Seala's focus does not waver, but her voice and pitch does as she stops her recitations and addresses me. "Ma, Rae Rae, Papa K, and O… listen… we need to take the daimónion out of her body. She is strong. She wants him gone. She speaks to me. Begs. We… we have to help. I'm not sure how much longer I can keep her reassured. Every second that goes by, her resolve weakens. It is through her, a leader, an influencer here on Earth that this daimónion is converting others to Belíar's side."

I turn to my former paidagōgós, and our eyes meet. "Create a pýlē, Basílissa. You must draw him out in that way. Speak to him. Distract him. Seduce him."

My head shakes. "I... I don't have enough energy to create a pýlē. Creating a pýlē means I must use the remnants of my round-trip reserves for returning to Ceteris. And if... if I return there, I will not have enough to come back for the feed."

My thoughts are so conflicted on the matter. Seala is not being harmed. She is safe at our side. She is fed. Strong. I... on the other hand... am not.

"There is no other way, unless Seala lets the woman go and we allow the daimónion to continue his job here."

Oryn cuts in, "Raener, we do not know the consequence of her playing a role in stopping Belíar's efforts here on Earth. The queens are required to support his efforts, not put a stop to them. Her disobedience could be detrimental."

Kallias adds to the conversation: "Yes, but even Belíar does nah want tha daimónia convertin' vessels. It does nah count when tha human does nah have a choice."

"Be that as it may, he is converting others in the process," I point out, indicating the small congregation with the tilt of my head. My mind follows one trail after another, and an idea sparks. "I will do the daimónion's bidding — convert the congregation myself. One by one, we will influence each member, feeding concurrently, while also giving the daimónion no reason to stay here. Once the congregation is influenced, I shall create and hold a travel pýlē, seduce him out of the woman's body. After that, I take him back to Ceteris with me and strike him down there." Before letting the guys answer I lean toward my daughter. "Can you hold her a bit longer?" I ask.

Seala swallows hard, arms trembling. "Yes, I think so."

"Will it be easier if you touch her? Place your hands on her shoulders? Rest your forehead against hers?" I ask, sending a similar, silent question toward Raener. Raener nods his approval.

"I can try," Seala says.

Raener immediately takes over, guides her to the front of the room, and she does exactly as suggested while he keeps a close eye on her and the daimónion's behavior.

The congregation watches as the woman simply appears to be speaking in tongues. Oh, she is definitely speaking *glossolalia*. Albeit, this time the words are from the daimónion... from Belíar.

I immediately turn to a man in the congregation, one who had been pining over the female church leader for quite some time, and I pierce him with Kallias's arrow.

The rush of energy is instantaneous.

From there, Kallias and Oryn help me weed out the sinners from the saints, which is surprisingly easy to do here in this particular church. Having heard a number of Raener-told stories about such places, I assumed the attendees would be unlikely candidates for proper feeds.

That is not the case, though. In fact, the building is ripe with energy for the taking. Mostly because, from what I can tell, many of the people who are praying do so without attaching any meaning or purpose to the prayer. No heart. Just words. A script. A habit. One that, at some point long ago, lost meaning.

Or… they are simply pretending. Here at the behest of someone else.

Should the leader not be possessed, perhaps these people would be more of a spirit to refuse my influence. However, with her consumed by the daimónion, the very air is impressionable.

Arrow after arrow we pierce their moral safety nets. Weasel into their minds. Make promises. Paint experiences. Ruin expectations. There comes a point where I cannot hold the energy in its entirety. Nor can my déō doúloi.

One by one, the congregation leaves the building, no longer desiring to be there. Their will… their resolve… challenged by mine and my déō doúloi.

And it is with that extra energy that I decide to finally create the pýlē. Wisps of energy hover in the air, silvery and light. I return the arrow to my quiver, return my bow to my shoulder, and hold my hands out to pull the extra energy into a tunnel.

The vortex becomes so large, so powerful, I fear containing it will soon be impossible. From the middle of the room, my eyes fall to the possessed woman and I speak with a low, seductive voice, encouraging the daimónion to come out and play. Influencing him to feed on something bigger… better.

Through her eyes, his flash red — a lick of flame burning the woman from within. Having learned through conversations with Kirian that in addition to the energy of a queen, her essence is also desirable — if not more so — I reach into my quiver, pull out an arrow, and use its sharp tip to score the palm of my hand before returning it.

Raising my arms up in the air, palms out, I give the daimónion an offer he should not be able to refuse: all of my energy, all of my essence, available for the taking.

Like me, my daughter will not stop until this ends. And I wouldn't dare ask, nor expect, such a thing. While Seala fights for the woman, I feign fighting for the daimónion, promising him the sinful energy collected from the congregation as a tribute.

Again, the woman's eyes flash red, and again I speak to him. Her eyes leak human tears, but her expression is one of anger and rebellion. Her soul weeps from the inside, begging to be free from his wrath, while he controls the rest.

My energy is too much, too tempting... so much more than the single vessel he has borrowed can accomplish. "Come to me," I whisper. "They are ours. Your job is done here. Let us feed together."

The woman screams manically as the daimónion steps out of her body. Legs, haunches. Horns, instead of hair. Yet, nothing more than an apparition here in this realm, much like my déō doúloi and me.

Him leaving her body isn't what was painful, but rather, his residence within. The consumption of her mind, thoughts, and actions. The persuasive and continuous influence of his dark brush against her thoughts.

He steps forward and she collapses to the ground, overcome. Tears stream down her face and her body trembles. Seala collapses with the woman, draping over her in the only type of embrace she can achieve in this realm. Covering the woman like a blanket.

The daimónion moves into a crouch, his long, lithe tongue snaking out as he covets the essence now dripping down my forearm in a stream of silver sustenance.

"Seala," I speak low, cautious. "Take your fathers back to Ceteris, Love. Travel like Raener has described in his stories, and how he will teach you to do now. Listen to him; he will not lead you astray."

Seala lifts her head from the woman's shoulder and gives me a quick nod before standing and reaching her hands out for Kallias and Oryn.

I study the two of them, take a deep breath, and return my attention to the daimónion. Without looking back again, I address them. "Get her as far away from the forest as possible and call for Blaze and Kirian as soon as you hit terra. Be quick."

Movement in my periphery proves they've heard me. I am able to meet them with a final glance as soon as they are behind the daimónion, each holding one of Seala's hands while Raener rests his atop her shoulder and whispers instructions in her ear.

Seala's pýlē forms... a beautiful, white one... and the daimónion takes in a deep breath, his nostrils flaring at the crisp, rich scent of her energy. To counteract the temptation, I step all the way forward, nearly brushing my chest against his.

I have never been this close to a daimónion other than Kirian. Pulse pounding, throat tightening, I drag an essence-covered finger along the daimónion's mouth. "Adrestia, no!" Raener yells. But it's too late. Two things happen concurrently: Seala pops them to Ceteris, and the daimónion's fangs descend and latch onto my neck.

With a deep breath and calming thoughts of my own daimónion just to help ease the panic, I close my eyes and imagine that pile in the forest Blaze had taken me to... the one I very much intend on making sure this daimónion will now reside, feeding the terra beneath, once I'm done expiring him.

I gather all the remaining energy and use myself as an intermediary, delivering it from the congregation directly into the daimónion through the essence he now consumes.

When the pýlē has just barely enough energy remaining to complete the travel, I release the connection, and deliver us out of there — daimónion still very much attached to my neck, hands gripping my head, claws digging into my scalp.

CHAPTER TWENTY-SIX

The daimónion and I fall onto the forest floor in a tangle of limbs and essence. As soon as my pýlē disappears, I reach up, grab one of his horns, and yank him off me before he's able to recover from the unexpected journey.

Traveling always leaves us dazed for a blink or two, but it appears daimónia take longer to adjust. Thankfully, this works in my favor, since I don't exactly have strength or speed to assist with my goal.

The rapid slinging of his body off mine results in a nasty tear along my neck from his fangs. On instinct, I cup my hand over the gaping wound and pull it back to check for essence loss. My fingertips are saturated. I shuffle away from the beast, hobbling on my knees and one hand as the other hand tries to stop the flow of essence for long enough that the energy inside me can close it up.

The dizziness that overcomes me when I attempt to stand, though, is certainly not reassuring the process will be as quick as it tends to be for smaller wounds.

Seeking support, I stumble toward the nearest tree and lean my shoulder against it, making sure to position myself in a way that keeps the daimónion in my sight.

As I gather my senses, the daimónion shakes his head side to side rapidly while rolling over onto his feet.

His red eyes lift and bore directly into me, underbelly heaving and shoulders rippling as he adjusts into a crouch.

A booming roar precedes the disappearance of his body before he lunges, though. Instead of one daimónion, two now grapple and roll over the terra. Black essence sprays every which way, the glint of fangs and claws sparking every so often.

Kirian's matted and essence-coated hair is what clues me in to whom my travel companion's competition is.

Not only had I brought this daimónion back into Ceteris, I had brought him here with an incredible amount of energy and power. Kirian is strong and he has not only the strength of a daimónion but the will and determination of a huiós. But even so, he's no match for a daimónion who holds the amount of energy this one does at present.

The essence pouring from my neck seeps through my fingers in steady spurts with every rhythmic pound of my pulse. Coming to terms that my efforts to heal are all for naught in this moment, I reach for the geúomai arrow and nock my bow.

The two daimónia are a blur, though. If the shot misses, Kirian could expire from my hit. Another fact of concern is that if Kirian gets the upper hand and kills him before I can immobilize the daimónion myself, the energy I had forced into its form before traveling will disappear. It will no longer be able to replenish our land's energy veins.

The rogue daimónion has to expire by my hand. But, more importantly, I need to make sure my arrowhead doesn't pierce the wrong beast.

Unsure what else to do, I blink away the blur of pain and disorientation and get as close to them as possible, hoping to prove as a distraction yet again and, in turn, ensuring the two separate long enough for me to make the shot.

"Stand down, Adrestia." A male's voice punches through my concentration. The voice is familiar but my fuzzy mind is unable to figure out which of my men are addressing me.

In response, I shake my head and step forward again. "The... the energy." I cough and sputter, trying to swallow around the essence coating my throat. Bow still prepped, I aim at the ground near the fighting beasts and loose. The arrow lands with a thunk into the terra exactly where I had aimed.

It takes a moment — a slash here, a growl there — but the two stop, their heads turning first toward the arrow, then snapping up to me. I'd purposefully used the arrow magicked with Brax's olfactory powers, hoping that maybe a gust of wind, or the agitation of the terra from their grappling would stir up the scent of my essence. Based on the way both daimónia now stare directly at me, I'd take a wild guess that it worked.

Quickly, while they are still and before their instincts kick in, I pull another arrow from the quiver, set my aim, and release. My arrow lands between the rogue daimónion's horns with perfect precision. His body jerks and shakes beneath Kirian until there is no body there at all. Ash and energy melt into the ground, giving my land in this area a much-needed boost.

Relieved, I sling my bow over my shoulder and fall to the ground, scooting backward to the tree that had supported me before. With gentle fingers, I feel for the wound on my neck again, easily finding the raw and gaping gash. I lean my head back against the trunk and close my eyes.

"Adrestia!" that same man's voice yells, encouraging my eyes to reopen. My response comes delayed, the warning missed. The daimónion I didn't shoot lunges for me.

Kirian's blue-green eyes turn red mid-jump. His claws strike across my face, and I fly sideways away from the tree, both my bow and quiver sliding off on impact.

He gnashes his teeth and his head dips low, tongue snaking out to taste the wound. But then his body goes limp, falling onto me with every bit of his weight. In the next instant, Blaze's face is nearly nose to nose with mine. "Basílissa," he breathes, his fingers running across various areas of my face, eyes darting with each movement. When I try to respond to him, I can't speak. All I can do is stare, unblinking.

"Fuck!" he yells, scanning over his shoulders in every direction before his gaze alights on me again. "I... I'm not your próskairos, Adrestia. You need to get up. I can't help you." His warm hands meet mine and he lifts me up partway before bending into a crouch and situating himself to scoop me into his arms.

My próskairos isn't coming because he's helping our daughter...

Blaze stands and rushes us out of the forest. With every step he takes, my body heals painfully slow. Unfortunately, I still can't seem to speak, not without choking and coughing. Each time I try to, it only serves to panic him more, so eventually I stop trying altogether.

It doesn't take long before I'm placed on a pallet and left by myself while Blaze goes in search for one of my déō doúloi.

:get up:

A voice I hadn't heard in quite some time filters into my pain-induced haze.

:now:

Impatient. Frustrated. Enraged.

:come to me:

Moments ago I had been unable to move. But now, that tug, that insistent pull of the hélkō, presses into my belly and yanks. My back arches off the reed pallet, bending to its will. To Belíar's will.

The next pull removes me from the pallet entirely, and I stumble on hands and knees across the dirt floor.

Pushing up with as much effort as possible, I manage to make it to my feet and stagger outside, following the pull. Knowing that if I don't, the punishment will mess with my body's attempt to heal. It'll hurt me more, and I'm in no state to heal wounds on top of the wounds that already exist.

Obeying the demand, the hélkō leads me back into the forest. Back to where Kirian and I had been just moments before. Signs of a scuffle are still there, but what's worse is that Kirian is not. A pool of silvery-black essence muddies the ground instead.

Lurching forward, I follow the line of his essence deeper into the woods, straight into the familiar nightmare from previous sleepless nights. Hands covered in essence, exhaustion pulling on me as I run deeper, engaging my muscles and stamina as much as I can.

:come to me:

The voice whispers, reassuring, persuading.

The ground rumbles beneath my feet. However, this time when the abyss slits the terra, I fall, tumbling into the never-ending blackness.

* * *

WHEN I OPEN MY EYES, I'm not in the mortal realm as I tend to be when I become drained. Instead, I am in my dwelling, with my oikía surrounding me, heads down, morose.

The first to notice my eyes open is Blaze, because his black gaze had been riveted on me already. As soon as my wakeful state registers, though, he snaps his fingers and my daimónion comes to his side and pops him out of the chamber with not even so much as an extra glance in my direction.

The room becomes alive: Kallias, Brax, Oryn, and Raener all close in on me.

"Seala?" I ask, testing out my voice.

"Good," Raener answers over a hard swallow and a not-so-subtle glance at Brax.

I shoot up into a sitting position, not much caring for that vague answer. Oryn's hand comes to my shoulder to steady me as my eyes lock on Brax. Brax's eyes find mine easily and his shoulders droop. "Where is she?!" I screech, wriggling out of Oryn's firmer press.

A noise, a barely muffled hiccup meets my ears. I pull on my hearing sense. Seala is here, in her room... and she's crying. I sling my legs over the edge of the pallet.

Raener's hand halts me; he places it on my thigh and squeezes lightly. Our binding comes rushing back, and his touch is the only thing that keeps me still. A touch I had yearned for, but that we've scarcely been able to enjoy yet. "She... won't stop crying. And... and she won't let us in."

I jump to my feet and rush to the door to her room, knocking lightly and as calmly as possible.

"Go away!" She screeches.

"Seala," I coo. "Open the door." For the first time in her existence, I wonder why the hell we put up such a thing to begin with, but with a glance over my shoulder at the men surrounding my pallet I remember why.

Seala doesn't answer, though. Instead, she only cries harder. I spin on my heel and face Brax, hands on my hips. "Break in," I state, clenching my teeth together. "You're a giant. Break her damn door down."

Brax's eyes widen and he shakes his head slowly. "No... I... I want to respect her..."

"Y-you want to respect her?!"

"Seala!" I yell again. "Open this door or else Da is breaking it down."

Seala's wail turns to a sniffle. "I'm an abomination, Ma. Just like Da said I would be."

I seek out Brax with a narrowed glare, hands still on my hips. "You!"

"I didn't say that to her. I... I would never," he stutters out.

"I can hear you!" Seala screeches through the door. "I... I heard you talking to Rae Rae about it before."

Brax presses his ear up to the door. "You are not an abomination," he says softly but still in that booming giant voice.

"I am." The tears and sniffles come again.

"Why?" he asks. "Why would you believe this?"

Everything goes silent — her sniffles stop — aside from a small sigh, she says no more. Trying extra hard not to make a peep. Pure obstinance.

Brax's patience morphs into a grigori-sized anger, and he slams his fist against the stone, cracking it from ceiling to floor. Seala hiccups and her wailing returns. "Do not make me force myself in there," Brax says with a low and threatening voice.

Again, silence.

Just when his patience is beginning to wane once more, her door creaks open and she stomps past us, hands on her hips, and turns to face the group.

Slowly... she unfurls... wings. Large. Beautiful. Pure white. Not blackened by soot from Tartarus.

Brax sways on the spot but manages to catch himself on the wall before tumbling over.

All of Seala's defiance crumbles; her bottom lip wobbles and her reddened eyes well with a familiar liquid.

"No... Seala..." Brax reaches out for her. "You... I just wasn't expecting..."

The room swirls white and silver...

...and Seala disappears.

CHAPTER TWENTY-SEVEN

Brax

Seala disappears. She creates a travel pýlē unlike one I have ever seen and disappears. I had thought it scared me when she wouldn't come out of her room. But not knowing where she is now worries me more.

Adrestia stands still beside me, staring at the spot, her breasts moving with every heavy breath.

"I... I didn't mean to upset her," I choke.

"We have to find her," Adrestia whispers. "She... she could be anywhere. What if she goes into the forest? What if she tries to travel to the mortal realm without a companion?"

"I will help," I offer.

Adrestia's eyes dart up to mine. "Everyone will," she says, placing her small hand on my clenched fist. "Kallias, check the beach. Oryn, find Kirian and Blaze and have them scour the woods, then act as an intermediary between search parties. Raener, search the village and question the huiói. Brax and I will travel to the edges of the territory and search there."

All the men begin to leave her dwelling right away — probably feeling just as unsettled as me. Adrestia catches Raener before he leaves, though. "Can... can you feel her?" she asks, and my eyebrows come together in the middle.

Raener looks up at me and down at Adrestia again before shaking his head. "Not right now."

240

"What do you mean by this?" I demand, a growl forming in my voice. "Paidagōgós, if you ever *feel* my daughter I will tear off your head!"

Raener swallows hard, and again my eyebrows move inward even deeper. When I look at Adrestia, she seems just as confused.

"Before we start looking for her, can you explain to me what... what happened?" she asks.

Raener nods and begins right away. "I have somehow become her próskairos by proxy—"

"You have what?!" My hand shoots out to the paidagōgós's neck, and I lift him in the air. He doesn't even flail, though, which makes me all the more angry.

"Brax," Adrestia's calm and sweet voice hums to me, "release him and let him explain so we can go look for our daughter." I do as she requests, but not nicely. He falls on his ass on the dirt floor.

Raener glares up at me as he stands and dusts himself off. "Sorry, Basílissa, I should have chosen my words more carefully and done some precursory explaining. My physical bond is with you only. However, the empathic bond you and I share extends to Seala. If she is in danger of losing too much energy, I will sense her need to feed. Nothing more, though."

Everything Raener says only adds to my confusion. "You are not a próskairos," I say simply.

He responds by stepping to Adrestia, twisting one of her curls around his finger, leaning forward, and giving her a kiss on the cheek. My eyes widen impossibly large. "You... you can touch her?"

"Yes, Grigori," he states. "She's broken the rules again. Now, I am her próskairos — not paidagōgós."

"When will you stop breaking the rules, Adrestia?" I huff and glare down at her.

"Never," is her certain answer.

"Will you be able to travel to me if you learn of her whereabouts?" Adrestia asks.

"No, but I can find one of your déō doúloi and relay the information to him; he can deliver it to you."

"Okay, that works. Thank you."

Adrestia lets go of my hand and steps even closer to him. He brings their foreheads together and she closes her eyes, taking a deep breath.

"We will find her," he promises. She nods, accepting his words for truth, and breaks away before taking my hand again. "Ready?" she asks me.

I squeeze her hand lightly and nod. She transports us to the dwelling entrance and from there journeys to the very edge of the woods, beyond the watchtower.

Together we call for our daughter, watching the border rather than the woods, since we know Blaze and Kirian will get help from the sikárioi to search everywhere trees grow.

After looking along that side of the border for quite some time and not finding anything, she delivers us to another side. And again another. We spend a good part of the astral round searching our assigned areas, our hope becoming more and more bleak the longer we go without finding her or hearing from someone who has.

The entire time, guilt eats me up on the inside. I love my daughter. I didn't mean to… to make it seem like she'd frightened me or that I was upset with her transformation. I am not. Confused, yes. But she is beautiful and amazing. She is not a beast. She is not a Nephilim. She is not a grigori, like me.

When there is no more area for us to search, Adrestia brings us to Oryn's location, first asking him for an update. Like us, no one else had any luck either.

Adrestia tilts her head to the side, eyes going unfocused at a spot in the distance as she considers something.

Mind made up, her attention turns to Oryn, and she says, "You swore that Sitara is trustworthy. Do you believe she would be trustworthy enough to help us find our daughter?"

CHAPTER TWENTY-EIGHT

Adrestia

Oryn blinks and swallows hard, but when he delivers his answer he does so with squared shoulders and a sharp nod. "Yes."

Brax looks down his nose at my mesítēs-turned-déō doúlos — yet another item of news to which Brax is not quite privy. Then again, as far as Brax is concerned, Oryn had been my déō doúlos ever since the night of my welcome gathering. Poor Brax; he's been thrown for a loop a number of times today. I'm not sure how many more surprises he'll be able to handle before flying off the edge.

Either way, those updates and more detailed explanations will need to wait until later. Right now, I have a queen to visit and a daughter to find. "Take me to her," I command, weaving my fingers between Brax's and placing my other hand on Oryn's shoulder.

Since I have never learned of nor traveled to Sitara's territory, I don't want to waste time by guessing and getting it wrong. Every inch the sun descends in the sky, our daughter remains missing longer; for all we know, she could be hurt or lost. A heaviness settles in my stomach at the thought. For this reason, I leave the task of choosing our destination to Oryn.

Even despite the tremendous amount of energy the daimónion and I had brought back from the mortal realm, when I reach deep into the terra to create my pýlē, it still

244

cannot be accessed at the surface like it had been when I first arrived. For a fleeting moment, I wonder how the woodland creatures and huiói are even surviving, considering they depend on the land to do so.

To accomplish the task of traveling right now, it even takes an extra amount of my personal stores to access enough energy and create a pýlē significant in size to bring Brax, Oryn, and me to our destination.

For the first time, I fear what the implications of these conditions might mean in the long term. I worry that while traveling to and from territories — or, worse to and from the mortal realm — we will not be able to make the round trip.

It is not the case this astral round, though, thank goodness. The three of us land in a bountiful garden with ease. Out of curiosity, the first thing I do is check the localized energy. Like in Superbia, the energy here in Acedia is more bountiful. This discovery makes me equal parts angry and sad. I am not a capable queen, I realize; my distaste for influencing is clearly negatively impacting my territory.

When my attention finally focuses on everything else around us, an equally bountiful number of males stand, gaping. It's not me they're gaping at, though. All eyes are on Brax.

Grigori are not supposed to travel, because they are not supposed to be déō doúloi.

When the initial shock wears off, though, their eyes lower to me — filled with curiosity and surprise. My guess is they had heard of a new queen, but seeing her in the flesh is entirely different.

However, their gazes quickly morph again once they land on Oryn. Apathetic. Unimpressed. A couple even look like they might harm him. My eyes travel to

245

Oryn, and his meet mine as he gives a nervous chuckle and lifts his shoulder. "Oikías do not take it lightly when a member leaves," he whispers in explanation as Sitara parts the crowd and dismisses everyone with the snap of her fingers.

"Oh! I love visitors!" An enormous grin spreads across her beautiful face. She approaches me directly — not Brax, not Oryn, but me — and bows her head, hunching her shoulders in a deeper genuflection than the most basic one, displaying a higher form of respect than what a basílissa would typically bestow to another.

Again my eyes travel to Oryn; he gives me a soft, encouraging smile. "Thank you for approving of my unexpected arrival," I state, drawing her attention back up to my face. I offer a similar form of respect, though not as deeply as she did.

"Come," Sitara says, turning around and gesturing over her shoulder. We all fall in line as she takes us into her dwelling — yet another show of respect and trust.

When every being in my party is situated, she clears out the room, even dismissing all of her déō doúloi.

This trust is not for me, I quickly realize, but rather on account of Oryn being in attendance; she trusts him just as much as I do. It is through Oryn that this meeting is acceptable. Safe.

As much as I would like to sit her down and ask her a million questions — about being a basílissa, about males, about how to help my territory — the specific reason we're here is far more important than my insatiable curiosities.

Without further ado, I cut straight to the chase. "You can feel emotions and were able to sense my daughter during the gathering," I begin with a reminder

246

to us both. Sitara nods once and patiently waits for me to continue. "She is missing; we cannot find her. I would like your help."

At this Sitara's dark eyebrows lift, and her indigo eyes widen. "Of course, I am happy to help. What do you have in mind?"

A pent-up breath releases from my lungs, but I work carefully to measure its escape — slow and calm through my nose, so Sitara doesn't witness just how relieved I am about her agreement. "Travel with us to my territory; I feel confident that she would not travel beyond. But, she has hidden herself well; perhaps you will be able to sense her emotions and that will bring us closer to finding her?"

Sitara's hands come to her lap and she twirls her ring — her power object — as she contemplates. Her eyes meet Oryn's, however briefly, and I am reminded again that she once valued and appreciated his advice. Much like I do now. Oryn keeps his expressions carefully controlled, though, the tension of helping two queens that have both worked his cock at some point no doubt coiling up in his muscles, if the hardness of his shoulders is any indicator.

A response comes shortly after in the form of her standing and calling for a couple of her déō doúloi.

When they arrive, Oryn bends to my ear and states, "Love and hate. The two most powerful emotions. Every being usually falls somewhere between the two at any given moment over a wide range of reasons."

Without another word, Sitara creates a pýlē.

Brax, Oryn, and I stand quickly and I follow Sitara's lead, creating a pýlē of my own. The mix of our combined energies fills her dwelling with a treacherous squall. In a blink, the six of us arrive in my village's communal area.

"To begin, take me to the areas you think she would most likely be," Sitara directs.

Of course, we have already searched those places but not knowing what other approach to take, I defer to her request. "Seala has a fondness for the paidagōgói's dwellings, the beach, and the watchtower."

Sitara closes her eyes, and she takes in a deep breath before opening them again. "We shall go in order, starting at the watchtower, moving onto the paidagōgói's dwellings, and ending at the beach."

Again she closes her eyes, this time to pull energy and create a pýlē.

The pýlē doesn't form. Instead, she gapes, mouth parting in a silent gasp. She hadn't anticipated the depth of access. I lift my chin and straighten my shoulders, daring her to challenge my competence. But she surprises me once more; Sitara's lips tilt up in a small smile and she places her hand on my shoulder. "You know, it has been quite some time since I have taken a stroll. Shall we?"

Beside me, Oryn chokes over a strangled cough-laugh. To which Sitara responds by hurling an unamused glare in his direction and following it up with the roll of her eyes. She scoops her arm around mine and pulls me away from him, bending to whisper in my ear. "I tend to avoid most forms of physical exertion." She pauses, and her lips quirk at the side. "Most forms. Walking being one of them. That stated, I know how worried you are about your daughter, and I cannot bear the idea of not helping appease that worry."

From the village, it doesn't take long to get to the watchtower. During the walk, Sitara remains quiet and contemplative, eyes tracking the area. Though, it is evident she's not tracking via sight only. Something else guides her, something more intuitive; her eyes simply track out of habit.

While she focuses on emotions, I concentrate on my own oikía powers. With Brax and Oryn being the closest in proximity at the present time, the taste and smell senses are strongest. As though Sitara can perceive what I'm doing, she clears her throat and says, "May I offer a suggestion? A tip between queens?"

"Yes, of course," I respond easily.

"When your powers get stronger, you'll be able to taste and smell the hint of salt in something even so small as a teardrop."

I come to a stop. "How do you know about her tears?" I ask, pressing my lips into a thin line.

"She is here, not close, but somewhere nearby. The wind carries with it her sadness. She… she is not happy with herself. Something has greatly upset and concerned her. That type of sadness, or self-loathing, is most commonly present in mortals. Or… at least beings who are part mortal or have been at some point in the universe's history." Sitara dares a glance up at my giant.

Brax has never cried, but now I can't help but wonder if he could. Though, I admit, I hope there never comes a time when he's driven to such an emotional reaction.

With that friendly council, though, I close my eyes and wait for the breeze to blow yet again. I do not sense Seala's sadness, nor can I yet taste the salt of a tear. But, in the least, the breeze might tell me in which direction she hides.

When the back of my hair ruffles, my curiosity is appeased; the breeze comes from the edge of the territory where the beach is. I turn around and head that direction, and the group follows with no questions asked. En route, Kallias and Blaze join us, having had no luck on their ends as well.

No one bothers to inquire about Sitara's presence either, because she is a queen and doing so might be considered an insult, or because I am walking arm-in-arm with her and that immediately lessens their concern.

On foot, the trip to the beach does take quite a while. During that time, she decides to bring up the topic of my land's energy. Part of me is thankful that she is the one to bring it up — the prideful part of me, the one that would have been ashamed to bring it up of my own accord. As a basílissa, I am responsible for this area, and I am failing.

"As you know from my unexpected visit not too long ago, all of Ceteris is well aware of a depreciation in realm-wide energy. During that visit, I witnessed firsthand the significant difference in your territory's reserves versus that of the rest of Ceteris. Even then, there was a sign of the energy here waning to dire levels. Despite that, I did not expect it to get this bad so fast."

There are several things I want to say, questions I would like to ask, ways I might try to defend myself and my territory, but my tongue refuses anything more than a simple hum of understanding.

When it is evident I am not going to provide an elaborated response, Sitara continues, "The Seven has been filling these lands since Ceteris came into existence. This portion of the realm has always been limited. Do not blame yourself."

"When I got here, the veins were full," I state simply — most certainly blaming myself.

"When you got here, the veins directly beneath your village were full. The accessibility did not extend outward much beyond that. There is a small area of trees, huts, and water. The rest is desert land, is it not?" she asks.

"Hills and ravines, but otherwise, yes, mostly deserted areas. Your land, on the other hand, seems quite fecund," I mention.

"It is, but not like it used to be. You just haven't yet experienced how a land that is truly full appears beneath the surface. The Seven and our territories have time; we have enough reserves to sustain us for quite a while. But they, too, are waning. Each astral round, no matter how much influencing we accomplish, the usable energy lessens."

"Do The Seven truly believe my daughter and I have something to do with that?"

"Well, Basílissa, can you blame them? Seven Queens — Seven Sins for all of our existence and in the codices. An eighth shows up, this eighth queen somehow bears a child, and at the same time the land ceases to hold the energy we feed it?"

"No... I do not blame them. But I also cannot influence enough to replenish my land *and* theirs. Nor can I consume enough energy to *take* from my land and theirs. I agree something is terribly amiss, but Seala has nothing to do with this anomaly."

Sitara nods. "Unfortunately, your word is not good enough." She doesn't mean this as an attack, nor to dampen my spirits. It is a simple and profound fact. "The way our realm is run, the queens meddle with very little outside of their immediate territories. They do not bother with what the paidagōgói, the mesítēs, et cetera, are responsible for. That means you and Seala. All the same,

251

with the directions things are taking, they will be forced to bother. Eventually, you will be required to interact with them and suffer the consequences of not having the proof you will need to ensure the safety of your oikía."

"If the basílissas don't usually go out of their way to engage with the others, why did you?"

Sitara looks at Oryn and back at me again. "We had a similar... interest." She steals a glance at her déō doúlos — the one specializing in love. "My research quickly revealed with which queen Oryn intended to commit."

"Thank you for releasing him," I whisper with a smile and the slight downward tilt of my head.

"You're welcome." She returns a smile of her own, but the smile quickly disappears and her gaze drops to her ring which now glows an odd mix of black and deep brown. "Your daughter is in that cave just around the bend... and she is not alone."

CHAPTER TWENTY-NINE

Trying to keep my voice calm, authoritative, and regal like a queen, not like that of a mother who is about to crumble into pieces any minute, I call for my déō doúlos who knows the most about this area. "Kallias, please search the cave." Alongside that knowledge, his heightened sight is also a beneficial addition inside the dark cavern.

Kallias runs ahead and promptly disappears around the corner. I'm convinced the salty water runs through Seala's veins sometimes, so it comes as no great surprise that she is here — aside from the fact that I know Kallias had already scoured this spot and came up empty-handed.

Brax's hand finds mine and squeezes. Or at least I thought that was the order of events, but I soon realize it was actually my own hand that had initiated the squeeze. Around his finger, my knuckles are white. He was squeezing me back in return, giving personality to the anxiousness we both share.

Having been in this particular cave before, I know it isn't big enough to contain all of us.

"You all will need to stay out here." Before hurrying off to join Kallias, I place my hand on Sitara's shoulder. "Thank you. You are welcome to stay, but if you have more important things to tend to, you may leave."

She nods and takes a step back to return to her déō doúloi's sides, but she doesn't create a travel pýlē.

Not wanting to waste anymore time with formalities, I turn and take my leave, walking briskly down the hill and around the corner. Brax's heavy-footed steps follow me but stop at the opening when I continue inside.

The oikía power bond between Kallias and me strengthens as soon as the cave's black walls surround us. Pulling on Oryn's hearing power, I focus on the farthest end of the cavern. Kallias's accented lilt and the sound of faint sniffles meet my ears. Both noises serve to relieve me substantially. But Sitara had indicated that Seala was not alone in here, even before Kallias entered.

I remove my bow and quiver and hold them up to my chest, step into the water, and wade as quietly as possible toward the back. The rock Kallias and I had bonded on comes into view and I continue around it to where the water becomes deeper. Just beyond, the ground slowly rises until I am once again on solid ground, and I quickly return my quiver to my shoulders and nock an arrow, pulling on my power of sight as guidance.

The contrasting white of Seala's new wings is the first thing I see, shortly followed by the dark contrast of Kallias's coloring as he squats near her, arm over her upper shoulders. The two of them argue quietly, their focus on a bundle of something on the ground.

When I take another step closer, the item on the ground takes shape and is not a bundle nor an item at all, but a being. A huiós.

I return the arrow to my quiver, bring my bow hand down to my side, and approach my daughter, opposite Kallias. He removes his arm so mine can replace it.

My gaze travels over the huiós who lies curled in a ball, but my words are reserved for Seala. "Are you okay?"

Her glistening green-gold eyes turn to mine and she blinks, releasing a couple of tears. When she takes a deep inhale and exhale, on the exhale she breaks, her forehead falling to my shoulder. "He... he... needs help... Ma... and I... I cannot... help... him."

With a hushed tone, I shush her, pressing the side of her face against me and rocking slightly.

Kallias slips his hands under the huiós's arms and pulls him away. The huiós let's out a very unhuiós-like, bone-chilling growl, but apparently doesn't have enough energy to fight against the movement. Kallias uncurls the man and studies him intently from head to feet.

When the scrutiny is temporarily over, he approaches my side and brings his mouth to my ear. "I have nah seen anythin' like this before. Most of him appears t' be huiós, but his hands an' feet have claws like a daimónion. That is nah tha strangest part, though. His skin is decayin' kinda like a putrefaction, but... different. Like it is part of him. It is nah healin' nor is he fully putrefyin'."

"We have to help him, Ma," Seala insists, wiggling out of my arms and crawling toward the huiós's claw-tipped feet.

I reach out to pull her back but Kallias stops me. "He can nah harm her in tha current state," he explains.

Trusting my déō doúlos, I crawl beside Seala, instead, and place my hands atop the huiós's abdomen. "Would you like me to try healing him?" I ask.

She nods and sits on her butt, drawing her knees up in a way that adjusts and protects her wings. Kallias joins us, taking a protective stance near the huiós's head.

255

There is an unfortunate predicament with my idea to heal him for my daughter's sake, though: if the land is not healing him on its own, my efforts may not do any good.

Nevertheless, I decide to at least try. Envisioning below the water and rock, below the dirt and pools of water, I seek out the healing energy. Instead, something quite odd occurs; an energy higher up draws my attention instead. Somewhere nestled in a spot closer to the surface that I had missed? My thoughts and focus travels back upward. When I reach the surface again, though, my search comes up empty.

I sense the energy.

It *is* here.

Somewhere.

But where?

Brows coming together, I open my eyes and peruse the crevices within this cavern. The energy… it is visible around us — those flickering iridescent blue and green ball-like creatures Kallias and I had found in here before. Unseen by everyone else but us because of our shared oikía power.

"The specks of light," I whisper. Kallias's golden-brown eyes meet mine. "They are comprised of pure energy." My gaze drops back down to the huiós before lifting again and studying the speck-covered cave. "That must be why he came here. His provisions are incredibly low; he was seeking energy."

Instead of taking steps to borrow energy, much like I did when healing Kirian and Raener, I pull from the balls of light. One by one they wink out, falling, shriveled to the ground as I collect the source of their existence.

With each loss, my spirit breaks a little. I do everything possible to harvest just enough needed to give the huiós a boost. He coughs and sputters, his raspy voice now able to form words once again.

If anything, we can speak with him — determine what is going on, work out a solution. "What happened to you?" I ask.

The man tries focusing on me, eye color flickering back and forth between the red of a daimónion and the black of a huiós — a transition far more terrifying to witness than the ocean-blue and red combination Kirian's go through on occasion. "I... I don't... know..." the huiós tries. "I... slowly became... weak... The hélkō... punished me... when I... could... not... perform... my duties."

My eyes dart to Kallias. "Is he a resident of my territory?" I ask.

Kallias studies the man closely. "Yes, he was one of tha reed bed workers."

"If the hélkō punished him on account of being disobedient, why wasn't he sent to the cages?" I press. "Huiói who break the law of the land and resist, do they not get caged or is that only reserved for newly Fallen?"

Kallias nods. "Yah, that is usually tha case."

"A voice—" The man chokes, coughs, and his body shakes violently. Seala squeals and bursts into a new wave of tears, moving onto her knees and scurrying closer to his side. The huiós's black eyes meet her watery gaze as she places each of her hands on his shoulders. The two engage in a silent conversation; he blinks a couple times and she nods, sniffling.

Kallias and I share an uncomfortable glance. Refraining from stepping in is difficult when our daughter's safety is uncertain. We inch closer, ready. Just in case. But for what?

Seala drops her forehead to him, closes her eyes, and speaks quietly — so quietly even I cannot hear her with my power. She is able to seclude herself from the powers around her — to shield herself from them. This knowledge brings with it a clarity as to why we were unable to find her earlier. She was shielding herself from our efforts.

The man closes his eyes and goes limp. With my hands still on his torso, I can feel his remaining existence, but it is just a mere speck.

Seala lifts her head, moves into a squat, and scoops one arm under his knees, and the other under his shoulders. "We must hurry." She lifts the man with the strength of a grigori. There is no struggle, no strain; she merely turns around and walks down the rock, through the water. Kallias and I are shocked into stillness for a time. But when she quickly approaches the mouth of the cave, we jump up, rush forward, and run into the water. The weight and volume presses against us like water tends to do, slowing our attempt.

It takes a bit of extra effort, but we manage to catch up with her at the mouth of the cave. She steps around the corner and carries the huiós to a spot on the shore. More of my men have now joined the awaiting party; Oryn, Raener, Brax, Kirian, Blaze, and Sitara and her déō doúloi part as Seala walks through them, fully focused on a task to which none of us are privy.

There is nothing more to do but watch as she distances herself from us, stops at a point that pleases her, and turns toward the water. She expands her beautiful, large wings and gives them two big shakes. Millions of little water droplets descend to the sand at her feet, making copious little darkened dots appear in contrast to the red clay.

Head back, eyes pointed toward the waning blue sky, and mouth moving in a quiet recitation, she tilts her wings, bends them at the joint, and flaps a few times. Her feet leave the ground, but she lands right away, wavering a bit. Brax steps forward now, her struggles calling to the da and protector in him. But I quickly reach my hand out and wrap my fingers around his.

Seala looks over her shoulder at us, and I give her an encouraging nod. I have no idea what I am agreeing to, nor what I am encouraging, but I know it's good and right. That whatever she is driven to do, she knows better than any of us.

Like the doe in the woods, I realize with the glisten of tears in my eyes, Seala is intuitively driven to perform this task. Whatever it might be.

Again she extends her wings, lifting them higher this time, and brings them down with a powerful thrust, lifting her feet once more off the ground. She makes it higher the second attempt, but still finds herself back on the ground, balancing the huiós in her arms precariously.

Then comes the jutted chin and squared shoulders. A posture I have taken on many occasions when balancing that fine line between patience and impatience — that line I refuse to be stuck walking.

On her third try, she shoots up into the air. Her wings lift from this ascended position and she concurrently creates a powerful vortex. The pýlē wraps around her and the huiós, and the two of them disappear mid-flight. Her pýlē closes with a pop, leaving the group of us gaping up at a clear, Seala-less sky.

CHAPTER THIRTY

I f it weren't for the position of the sun, now well below the horizon, I would not know how long we have been standing here gaping at the point in the sky where she disappeared. Collectively, though, none of us have a desperate need to search for her again. We all intuitively know she is not here on Ceteris. Not with a pýlē like that. Not with the way she had left.

When our legs and hearts become weary with the wait, we all find spots on the hillside. None of us — Sitara and her déō doúloi included — intend on leaving. Not until Seala returns.

In the meantime, I contemplate the incredible changes that have occurred in the course of the last astral round. One significance that stands out among the rest is how Seala is suddenly no longer a small girl. Clearly, a growth spurt had taken her when I had disappeared to visit Blaze and Raener. She emerged a young woman. With breasts…

…and wings.

As a result, the transformation must've drained her substantially. Having slept by my side, rather than on her own pallet, since the day she was born, our constant contact ensured she was always full of energy; I never noticed a difference in levels dropping with each growth spurt.

Then again, maybe this transformation required my absence. I have become of a mind that down here in Ceteris, everything happens for a reason. Watching as she so easily, so naturally, molds into this new role, rather than being ridden with guilt over my absence during this pinnacle change, I am instead filled with pride.

My attention moves from guy to guy. Our oikía. Our family unit. And I'm exceedingly grateful for each of them.

After many, many sun positions, I finally address the topic that I know is weighing the heaviest between us all. "That huiós," I begin, "he appeared to be in a partial transition from huiós, daimónion, and putrefying — a horrible limbo between the three. The transition clearly took a toll on him, and the energy in this territory is not available enough to counteract the process — to keep him strong during the full transition. A transition in which outcome, in and of itself, is not quite clear."

Every being remains silent: my former paidagōgós and mesítēs, and even Sitara and her déō doúloi.

"Blaze?"

"Yes, Basílissa?" he responds, straightening his shoulders from where he'd been hunched over sharpening one of his arrows.

"Give me an update of the state of our forests and daimónia activity, please."

Blaze's eyes flash a glance at Sitara and back to me. When I answer his silent question with a nod, he begins. "Rogue daimónia sightings have increased significantly. The sikárioi are killing a hundred or more every astral round, yet still they come."

I am listening, but my focus is on Sitara, watching for any unusual reaction or response. She most certainly has a response to this, but it is not unusual. Her eyebrows rise.

"Sitara?" I ask, my voice as honeyed as I can make it. "Have something to say?"

"I cannot speak for the rest of The Seven, but Acedia has not had trouble with the daimónia population. Never mind that there aren't many residing in Acedia to begin with."

"Well, yes, I suppose not. This is the rebel territory after all. It is not surprising that a good portion of the population here, both past and present, challenge — and lose against — the hélkō. And the mere fact that most of them, aside from newly Fallen, traveled far and wide from other territories just to get here proves their strong will and determination. Traits required for the daimónion transition."

"Do not misunderstand, Basílissa," she states, narrowing a glare at me. "I didn't mean to sound as though I assumed you were driving the huiói in your territory into rebellion. I was simply stating an observance. And while I cannot speak for the other queens, I feel certain they are also not plagued by an overabundance of daimónia."

I am only silent on this topic for a moment while her words set in. "Daimónia feed on energy from lesser beasts, do they not? Perhaps our problem is simply that. They have tapped out their usual sources and now drain my land of energy by pulling so deep and so far it has created a ripple effect. We take care of the daimónia infestation, and our problem is solved."

"Yes, that is certainly something worth looking into," Sitara agrees.

Blaze snorts, and Sitara immediately gives him a displeased glare, seeing as all the other guys had remained silent, respecting the discussion between queens. Blaze's definition of respect varies according to

262

his mood… which also greatly varies. He doesn't bother to request a spot in the discussion; rather, he just dives in: "Basílissas," he starts with a huff, "it is not that simple. The sikárioi have been working from sunup to sundown every astral round to 'take care' of this so-called infestation. You're talking about the growth of a species over the course of Ceteris's entire existence. This territory was designed to hold the majority of the daimónia population. It's not them that are outnumbered, we are — the huiói who live here. If it weren't for the pathetic excuse of a boundary line, they'd be hunting us, not the other way around."

Sitara does not look surprised by Blaze's rant. But my lack of knowledge on the topic proves just how much I still don't know. Which enrages me. My fingertips tingle, a ringing peals in my ears, a pungent scent singes the fine hairs in my nose.

Brax's large hand drops to rest on my knee, the Watcher in him being the first to sense unbalanced power roiling inside. His touch immediately grounds me.

Even Blaze picks up on something, and his eyes bolt to mine, eyebrows curving downward. "We all know, though," he continues slowly, "that daimónia do not require much energy at all. They thirst for it, but to survive, a minimal amount is actually required."

No, I did not know that, but Blaze at least worded it in a way to save me from any further embarrassment. Even still, my teeth grind together, and I move my gaze out toward the water, focusing on the black waves until I'm ready to speak again.

Choosing words that will at least make it sound like I know what in Tartarus I am talking about, I eventually state: "Regardless, with the population as abundant as it is, the energy balance was bound to tip one day. Even if something else is at play here, we start with a major cull. The ones who have gone rogue already, yes, of course. But drastic times call for drastic measures; I want traps set up in several areas. Have the sikárioi work together to lure them out and take care of as many more as possible in that way."

Blaze swallows hard but he does not challenge me, no doubt carrying the weight of how his first slip made me feel. Instead, he gives me a sharp nod. "Consider it done."

Only a moment of silence passes when Sitara speaks up again. "May I be of service, Basílissa?" she asks. Everyone reacts one way or another to that. Oryn, however, finds it the most difficult to hide his surprise; he shifts, drawing his knees up higher than before.

Sure, Sitara had helped me when called directly upon to find Seala, but for a basílissa to offer services to another queen? Even in my short time here I know that is unheard of. Not to mention, she's the damn Queen of Sloth. The laziest queen of them all.

As if she can read all our minds, she rolls her eyes, pointedly looking at Oryn. "I did not mean me directly. But my sikárioi and Watchers—"

Sitara is unable to finish the explanation when the sky lights up above us. We are all instantly on our feet as the clouds churn and twist into a white and silver tunnel. Seala shoots out of there and plummets toward the ground.

Brax has never moved so fast. He stomps forward, his big giant footsteps tremendously helpful in closing the distance. He holds his arms out, catching her in a tangle of body, limbs, and wings.

He can't cradle her like one might think a being would be cradled, due to her wings, but he somehow manages to work around them as he draws her to his chest and dips his forehead to hers. His shoulders heave and his fingers grip her so hard I fear it might actually hurt her.

The two of them share some words that the rest of us don't bother to pry to hear, and he places her on her feet. Seala takes a deep breath and folds her wings flat against her body.

I turn to Sitara, and bow my head. "Thank you for your help and for your offer of further assistance. I understand there will come a time when you will likely want me to repay you. Feel free to visit when you are ready. But for now, I must ask you to leave. We would like to reunite with our daughter."

Sitara inclines her head. "You're quite welcome. Consider repaying me with friendship. I love my men, but it has been a long existence with The Seven, and I fear I do not fit in with them as I should."

This response comes as a surprise, but also a relief. Some deep, internal part of me craves the companionship she offers.

She does not wait for an answer from me, though. With the snap of her fingers, her déō doúloi bracket her and the three of them create a pýlē — with quite a bit of effort — and leave.

SEALA KNOWS WHAT IS COMING next. None of us will rest until we understand what went on and what that might mean — if anything — for her well-being. She walks over, stands in front of all of us, and attempts to sit with her new wings. First she squats, lifting them in the air behind her, then she adjusts her legs into a cross-legged position and spreads out her wings comfortably behind.

265

The flicker of a memory presents itself in my mind's eye — of sitting that same way once upon a time.

"He has been delivered," she says simply. Her eyes widen and the young girl comes out again as she leans forward and grasps Raener's hands. He had scooted closer to her, and the two now sit knee to knee. "I met him, Raener! I met The Maker! Elysium is more beautiful than even your stories describe."

A chorus of gasps soon follow as we all gape at this news. Raener had spoken of redemption for The Fallen, but hearing of it actually happening firsthand is nothing short of amazing.

Raener speaks up, feeding on her excitement and thirst for knowledge. "The original decree was that The Fallen were not eligible for redemption. Their misdeeds angered The Maker so much he promised their existence and their end would be either here in Ceteris or in Tartarus. That there was even a chance at redemption was a secret held tight and through riddles, only to be revealed on His time. You, my dear" — he reaches out and cups her cheek — "are our only hope."

All our ensuing questions are silenced when she lifts her hand and cuts the rest of us off as we all open our mouths to eagerly inquire at the same time. "Please," she says. "I cannot speak more of my travels."

We all share glances. She may have had a growth spurt into young womanhood, but something about her first delivery transformed her even more.

When I stand, she follows the motion. The two of us face each other, and I wrap my arms around her neck. The guys all gape at us, but it is Blaze that speaks up, opening his mouth when the rest cannot. "She looked like you when she was born and every day since as she grew, but now the two of you are nearly identical, aside from your eye color."

I cannot see the two of us side by side, but our eyes meet at the exact level. Of body, she is done growing. But of heart and mind, I have a feeling the both of us still have a long way to go.

CHAPTER THIRTY-ONE

This astral round has both rushed and crawled by, each bit of excitement increasing the speed with which the sun moves in the sky. But even now that Seala is safe, and we have all retired, my body and mind are torpid as though several astral rounds have passed opposed to just the one.

Brax followed her into her room immediately on our arrival and hasn't left since, the two of them speaking in hushed tones. There are tears and grumblings, too. When Brax finally emerges, the deep grooves in his features make him appear even more exhausted than me.

He comes to my pallet side and drops to his knees. "Basílissa," he says, "sleep with me in the tower tonight?"

I sit up straight and place my hand on his cheek, marveling at the size difference for a moment before responding. "Yes, of course." My attention turns to my oikía. All of whom, except for Kirian, are in here, too.

"One of us should be present, since Brax cannot take you for a feed should a need arise," Oryn states.

Brax grumbles and stares at Oryn pointedly. "No, Mesítēs. It has been too long since I have buried myself inside her, and I will wait no more. The rest of you are not invited."

When Brax returns his attention to me, I give him a playful pout. Out of all my men, he is the only one who has not had me to himself since Seala was born. Which is saying something since she's a woman now. Wow... time sure flies. And... so does she.

Belíar, I am tired.

But not too tired that I can't take a grigori cock.

I sling my feet over the side of the raised pallet and stand, wrapping my arms around his head and pressing his face between my breasts. Brax groans, tilts his head to the side, and takes my nipple into his mouth. But not for long, though. He drags his teeth over the hardened peak, drops his hands to each of my thighs just below my ass, and picks me up. I twist my legs around him, digging my heels into his back since he's too wide for me to be able to hook my ankles. No matter, his strength offers enough support.

Once he has returned to his full height, I look over my shoulder at the others. "We will be fine. Please stay here with Seala; I know she doesn't need to be watched at all times any more, but I would feel more relaxed knowing she has some support here. She has had a long, exciting day. Someone hand me my bow and quiver... and that herb from Kohbi and Xanth?"

Kallias collects everything, dropping the vial into my quiver's pocket, and situates my power object on my shoulders and back, working around a giant who refuses to put me back down now that I am secure in his arms.

When everything is in order, I press my nose against Brax's. "Steal me away," I whisper. He creates a pýlē and we land outside between my dwelling guards. "Oh, you're getting better at that!"

"Yes, Basílissa, I have been practicing."

"Of course you have." I close my eyes and reach deep into the terra to take us to the tower, but the energy doesn't come. Not at all. A rock drops and settles in my stomach. "We are stuck here," I breathe, each breath quickly becoming more and more ragged than the one before.

Brax slides me down his body until my toes touch the ground. "We can walk," he says.

"We have no choice," I respond, taking his hand. "Tomorrow, this will be addressed. Tonight, though? Tonight is reserved for you and me."

* * *

"ON YOUR KNEES, Grigori," I demand. Brax immediately does as he is told, the corner of his mouth lifting in a pleased grin. There is something incredibly empowering about bringing a giant to heel. A Watcher. The muscle of Ceteris. Technically I can bring every male to heel, but having them fuck me out of their own passions — their own primal, rough needs — I generally much prefer that.

Except for with my giant, I decide. With him, I want this control. I want his deep, raspy voice to beg me to let him inside.

With that in mind, I drag his taller-than-average stool to between him and the window, press it against the stone, and climb atop. With my upper back to the open night sky, and the bottom of the oval-shaped window supporting my lower back, I sling my legs over each of his shoulders, grab the back of his head, and draw him to between my thighs.

Brax growls and dips his tongue inside me before dragging it out and looping around and through every aching, wet fold and bundle of nerves. Back arching against the stone windowsill, my head tilts into the evening on the other side. When his hands come to the

270

top of my thighs, I pry them off and shoo them away. "No hands," I say around a moan.

He swipes his tongue from where my ass touches the stool and upward before pulling back with a grin. "Is that not what I am doing? Basílissa, I do not have to touch you with my hands to make you cum." To prove his point he dips his head again and flicks me with the tip of his tongue, hands out at the side palms on display. "You do not smell like you want me to stop touching you," he says, inhaling deeply.

That's when I realize just how terrible I am at this commandeering stuff. Apparently, Brax has already figured it out and is now mocking me in a way as he drags the edge of his teeth along the most sensitive part between my legs and takes a nip.

To which I respond with an intentional score by the hélkō, right along his inner thigh, near his balls. Brax hisses, but instead of jerking away from me, his mouth suctions onto my clit and he drives me to orgasm immediately.

Chest heaving, hands gripping the back of his head, I shudder around him, completely and utterly under the control of his mouth. "You play dirty," I breathe.

He chuckles and wiggles out from under my legs, hands still up, an accomplished look on his face. Bending to my ear, he purrs, "You do not tell a Watcher what to do, Basílissa. I may have been careful before, but now that I know you can take my cock so easily, things have changed. Try bossing around one of your other admirers. Like Raener; he is the obedient type."

At that I snort-laugh. "None of my déō doúloi are 'the obedient' type. Rule breakers. The lot of you."

"You like it that way."

I groan and throw my head back, "You are not wrong."

Brax slides his hand to the back of my head, encouraging me to look at him again. When I do, he drags his lips across mine, and whispers, "How do you want to be fucked, my queen?"

"Hard... and from behind," I answer eagerly.

"Turn around and place your hands on the window edge," he states drawing back and fisting his cock nice and slow.

Okay, yeah, I need to practice telling my men what to do a bit more. But not right now... because grigori cock.

I adjust on the stool, moving my knees to the seat part and turning around. The entire village, blanketed in black, lies in a massive expanse ahead and below.

Brax presses against my opening, inching inside a little just to lubricate himself before thrusting in the rest of the way. My body lurches forward, and my elbows fall to the window's edge, the rough stone creating pock marks in my skin. His fingers dig into my hips as he thrusts inside me again with a grunt.

He slips one of his hands around and lays it flat against the bottom of my stomach below my abdomen. When he slides in again, slow this time, he bends forward to bring his mouth to my ear. "Curve your lower back inward, your pelvis back" — he presses down in example — "or else this will hurt."

"Why is it going to hu—"

Brax slams inside me and all the stars in the sky triple. The mix between a yelp and a moan peals from my lips. My entire body clenches around him. Again his hand presses inward, and again he slams inside, causing those same stars to burst. "Oh, fuck," I pant.

Brax groans. "You like that, hmm?"

"Mmm," is my response.

Now that I know what to do to help him gain the deeper access he needs, his large hand moves down from my stomach to stoke the flame between my thighs. When he slides back partway, I engage my hips the way he taught, and he thrusts inside me, adjusting his legs to press his upper thighs against the back of mine, sealing us shut. Filling me completely.

Instead of pulling out, he stays like that, grinding and circling slow against me, every bit of his width and length buried and touching all of my insides at once. With the mix of his finger rubbing slow, deliberate circles against my clit, the two together build something powerful inside me, drawing out my power, calling to each sense.

Brax groans. "Breathe, Adrestia. Breathe," he says. A rush of breath leaves my lungs and my panting returns.

The building resumes. "Brax," I beg with a whine, the tables turned. He doesn't wait for me to beg more, though. Hearing his name tumble from my tongue undoes my giant. He pulls out slightly and pounds back into me over and over again until both of us are shaking together, his cock throbbing, and my inner walls encouraging it to continue until he can no more.

His arm loops around my waist, holding me up, and his head comes to my upper back, cheek pressed between my shoulder blades.

"You know how I would like you next?"

"How?" he rumbles.

"With Raener. You two need to learn to work together."

273

Brax roars with laughter, slings me up, spins us around, places me on the reeds, and crashes our mouths together.

CHAPTER THIRTY-TWO

Brax and I both wake up earlier than we normally would, the weight of the condition our territory is in following us into slumber and settling there, poking and prodding the crevices of our dreams.

On waking, we both begin to gear up, Brax straps on his sword, and I situate my bow and quiver. When we're ready, he steps behind me, removes the vial from my quiver pocket, returns to my front, opens the vial, and places a bit of the powder on the tip of his finger.

I open my mouth, lift my tongue, and he swipes the powder beneath, ending the process with the drag of his lips against mine. A kiss filled with the remnants of heat from last night, but also with a quiet dread.

We scarcely look at each other, knowing that this astral round is bound to be a challenge. After all, for the first time in Ceteris's history, a territory is deplete of energy. A territory I am responsible for. A territory that sustains my oikía and the village huiói.

This reminder brings me out of the quiet mental thoughts immediately. I rush up to Brax just as he's getting ready to open the watchtower door. My hand covers his over the handle, and our eyes meet. Tired. Weak. Despite the sleep we got last night.

"H-how are you feeling?" I ask.

He takes in a deep breath and lets it out. "Not myself," is his response. "It is a feeling I have not ever experienced. Now I know how you must feel as your energy begins to drain."

My heart constricts and dread washes over and through me. "How long do I have to fix this?" I ask.

Brax shakes his head and lifts a shoulder.

With a painful, tight swallow, I let go of his hand so he can finish opening the door.

The two of us circle down the watchtower's staircase in silence. If my men begin to lose energy, I can help them, but only until my own energy wanes. And if that happens, we will all be in trouble.

No one needed to be told to meet at the start of this astral round, the morose blanket that covers the land sets its own command. Every male with whom I have ever interacted waits for my appearance at the village center.

While they wait, Seala has them congregated, her sweet words and embellished stories of Elysium giving everyone a new hope. A new motivation. A new drive and determination. A fight for survival.

When Brax and I approach, a dozen or more heads turn in my direction. Oryn, Kallias, Raener, Kirian, Blaze, Kohbi, and Xanth step forward and join my side, creating a semi-circle that faces the rest of my village.

I don't even have to hold my hand up to silence the crowd. They're already silent. My territory huiói know that bowing is not a thing I demand, but they each take a knee anyway, even despite the exhaustion etched in every single one of their faces.

When they have all returned to their original standing or sitting positions, only then do I begin my address. "I need to better understand what this depletion means for the territory as a whole. How far it extends. How grossly the beings within my boundaries are affected. And any other type of information that can be gleaned." The crowd murmurs in understanding and agreement. "To make this simple, you study and search wherever you are each most comfortable doing so, everyone can meet back here to report findings at sunset. Create a fire, we'll spend some time together as a village, and my oikía and I will discuss further action at that time."

The village huiói all move straight into action, breaking into groups of friends and acquaintances and spreading out in every direction possible.

"Seala!" I raise my voice over the din of conversation as each group plans and discusses their individual courses of action. She approaches, and my eyes catch on how her wings outline the shape of her body. A body she still wears that same cloth on. It's much more form fitting and shorter now, but it suits her... and it appeases Brax. The rest of my oikía have grown to appreciate it, as well, since she's far more *formed* than even I am at this point. "Would you be willing to join my group?" I inquire. "We are still unsure of your role where the land's energy is concerned. I would like to see if today's search reveals anything."

Seala straightens her shoulders and nods, and I continue, now directing my instruction to the remaining huiói around me. "I want to check as many hiding spots as possible. Caves, jetties, undersides of cliffs, unused huts — things of that sort." Each being specializes in the land in a different way, so I know between all of us, they likely know about a good number of hidden locations.

Not to mention, they had likely recently been in or near them during our search for Seala. "I know by not separating, and since we can't travel, this could take a long time, several astral rounds even, but..." my words trail as a rock lodges in my throat. *But I don't want any of you out of my sight while your energy is depleting,* is

277

what I was about to say, but I can't seem to deliver those words.

A warm hand grips my shoulder and squeezes. "Where do you want to start?" Raener asks.

"Near water. Kallias and I found some energy-creatures in the cave down by the bowl. The huiós had sensed the small amount of energy and was drawn there. Unfortunately, he had no way of accessing it."

"Caves line tha shore, but there are only a couple large 'nough t' serve as a hidin' spot. We will go straight t' those. They are nah too far. Just beyond where huiói go to rest," Kallias offers.

I remember the spot he is referring to quite vividly; it is where I met him. "Perfect. Let's get started."

* * *

FINDING SIGNS OF DOUR TIMES does not take long. We don't even make it to the first cave. Kallias had led the way to the rest area, and there, within the dome-shaped shelter, more than one huiós in similar states to the one we had found in the cave are huddled together, seeking warmth, or energy… or both.

Oryn lets out a pained breath. "Ah, the rest area is one of the more energy-rich locations — designed for the purpose of replenishing huiói after particularly grueling tasks or long stretches of work. The land as a whole feeds them, but this area provides an extra boost."

"So, it makes complete sense that they would come here."

Seala is already kneeling at one of the huiói, speaking to him in a hushed tone. As I step inside the shelter to join her, the scent of rot, decay, and putrefying

278

essence hits me hard. My hand instantly moves to cover my nose and mouth and my stomach churns.

Brax remains outside so as not to take up too much room inside, but with a glance over my shoulder, I can tell by the way he scrunches his nose and curls his lips that he, too, caught a whiff.

"Kirian? Blaze?" I request the two males who know most about daimónia, and they promptly join my side. The three of us squat around one of the huiós Seala is not speaking with. "What are we looking at here? What has happened to him?"

"I have never seen anything like this," Blaze reveals. "He appears to be a hybrid of some sort, like Kirian... but worse. Different."

Kirian, the half-breed daimónion himself, speaks up. "The hélkō... the putrefaction process... stopped as soon as I began to take on the daimónion form," he explains. "As far as I am aware, daimónia are not punished by the hélkō. Their punishments come in the form of starvation or at the mercy of a sikários."

Starvation. Yes... it makes sense considering how some go rogue, attempt to cross the boundary, or are easily drawn to pýlēs.

Blaze follows up Kirian's comment with, "It's almost as though the hélkō is attacking, but" — he shakes his head and runs a hand through his hair — "initializing yet not finalizing the actual putrefaction. Like he's in a constant state of punishment minus the relief of being sent to The Void."

"If anyone can call it a relief," I mumble under my breath, eyebrows curving inward as I take in the sight.

"Would you not?" This comes from Xanth, who now joins our little circle. "Especially after experiencing pain the likes of what they've had to endure at this point?" Oryn clears his throat behind us, and Xanth bows his head. "Sorry, Basílissa, I have overstepped."

What I want to do is narrow a glare over my shoulder at Oryn, because it's possible *he* is the one who overstepped. But I choose not to, because they understand how this works way better than me. Plus, I know he's just trying to keep the peace. He was a mesítēs for a long, long time, after all.

Instead, I nod to accept Xanth's apology. "You are right. There was a time where the hélkō dragged me to the border between here and The Void. I would be lying if I said I didn't consider the relief disappearing altogether might bring."

Xanth drops his voice and says, "I did not know. My apologies, Basílissa."

"This is where your prior assessment is lacking. Even despite the pain, I am glad the hélkō did not win. That it did not take me. I would suffer all over again for an existence here with my oikía."

"They — we — are lucky to have you as our queen," Xanth whispers.

"Well now, that is subjective." My gaze drops to the suffering huiós at our feet. The rock that had settled in my stomach tosses, collecting mass as it does.

What do I do?

I want to scream that question so loud the entire realm hears me. But I don't, because I'm supposed to know what to do to protect my land and the beings therein.

"Ma," Seala says, barely a whisper amid the oppressive silence that had cloaked the shelter. I stand and go to her, kneeling at her side, careful not to step on her wings. Her head turns toward me, eyes glassy and red. There has never been a sadness so deeply etched in her beautiful face. "He will not go to Elysium," she explains with a shaky breath. "He does not want to."

My attention turns to the huiós, and I tilt my head, taking him in. His eyes are riveted on me, but he does not speak. "He spoke to you?" I ask my daughter.

"Not with words," she says. "Their intentions are just as loud."

"Help me understand."

She seems to consider this for a moment, giving me the impression that like us, there are unseen things restricting her. Things that, should she disobey, would trigger consequences. "There are three requirements for them to be delivered into Elysium," she starts. "They must be close to expiration. They must have never been stricken by the hélkō in their existence here on Ceteris. And" — she blinks several times, trying to hold back her tears — "they must *want* deliverance."

Again my focus returns to the huiós. His eyes are still locked on me, but he is otherwise inanimate. Then… he blinks. An ice-cold tingle races down my spine. Seala is right, their silent desires are louder than words.

I stand, nock an arrow, and aim it at the huiós, straight between his eyes. "No!" Seala screeches, but one of my men holds her back before she can work around her wings to stand.

"If you cannot deliver him, I must," I say simply, my voice steady despite the bob in my throat. We're opposites, her and me. Good and evil. I may have not always been this way, but circumstances and environment change beings.

The arrow hits with a sickening squelch. The putrefaction process kicks into gear and he disappears into the hungry and desperate land. A faint smile appears on his face in the blink before he is gone forever.

CHAPTER THIRTY-THREE

Morose and heartbroken, Seala moves on to the next huiós and she gives us the news that he has chosen a similar fate. Again, I snuff the small bit of remaining existence from him.

One of the group does choose to carry on his existence elsewhere. Seala picks him up, carries him to an open space outside of the shelter, and in an instant she is gone, the huiós-hybrid with her.

Tired and defeated already, I turn to my group. For the briefest moments, I consider asking them why. Why would a huiós choose to go to Elysium? Then again, why would they choose to be sent to The Void? But upon further contemplation, those answers are not lost on me.

There was once a time when The Fallen were rebellious enough to not care much for living in Elysium anyway. Their very choice and behaviors sent them here. For that reason alone, why would they want to return?

The answer therein is actually even more simple: a change of heart.

"Most huiói would be hard pressed to be eligible. To have served their entire existence here untouched by the hélkō?" Blaze scoffs. "The Maker has not made it easy."

"The Maker does not make anything easy," Brax returns. I alternate glances between each of the men surrounding me. I have seen most of them get struck by the hélkō with my own eyes. Men who are perfectly good and worthy of *choice* — at least in my opinion.

But that seems to be the thing about worthiness...
its definition varies just as much as the multi-faceted
meanings of pain. Every being is bound to have a unique
take on the topic.

With a deep sigh, I state, "Well, each of the huiós-
hybrids I expired provided the land here with just a taste
of energy. If we find more, that is one way to help get the
territory huiói a scant amount of energy at least."

Even as the words are delivered, I know the small
amount this task will provide is not enough. Nowhere
near it. Something bigger needs to be done.

Just before my pregnancy had begun to show, when
I was still taking lessons with Brion, we had broached
the topic of mass-influence: the way a queen influences
a mortal influencer and that single influence creates a
trickle effect of subsequent sins. Thus, a trickle of energy
being fed to the land.

The experience in the church with Seala served to
provide a large energy push, as did the subsequent
takedown of the daimónion withholding the extra
energy, but it concentrated in the forest. Even so, it is
depleting rapidly.

This moment is not the first I had considered how
to accomplish such a thing. However, it is the moment I
am choosing to try. Over the course of my residence,
over my many feeds, I have been watching, searching for
the right person to influence, and with the present state
of Earth right now, I think I have just the person figured
out.

I approach Oryn for the task. Not because this
influence will have anything to do with taste, but because
he would be the most likely to stop me should I be
making a terrible decision. "Join me on a feed? We have
just enough energy here for me to create a pýlē now.

Perhaps I can secure a strong enough influence to aid our efforts here for a time."

Oryn nods. Everyone else hears, too, so I don't bother to repeat myself. Oryn and I separate from the group, far enough to protect Kirian and Brax. I gather what little bit of energy I am able and deliver us to the unsuspecting victim I have in mind.

* * *

WHEN I HAD FIRST FALLEN, this would have been a scene I avoided at all costs. But the time for taking chances is nigh. Where there's sin, there's sustenance... alas, here I am. This time, corporate crime is the cause.

Over the past few mortal years, their realm has become quite... unideal. The overall morality here has been helpful to the queens of Ceteris at least, but a new challenge has arisen. Where there's sin, there is also a large number of mortals trying to counter that sin. A balance that is as old as time itself. No matter the definition of time.

Nevertheless, something big happened. Well, something small to the mortal eye, but with a bit of influence, I intend to use this one small 'thing' to tip the scale in our favor.

The interesting point is... the world would have turned out this way anyhow. But, as to how I've chosen to play a role, is by victimizing one particular individual.

Power is funny. Those who hold it are often transient Makers. Temporally speaking, of course. Attuning that power often comes at a cost... a cost that usually affects other people — the ones without power.

In this scene, a power-hungry, smart, blasé woman is one of the reasons the mortal world becomes a wasteland even before The Maker commences the official end. Influence from The Seven does not aid, nor change that. Their influence simply plays a role in determining who rises and who falls.

But in what manner things go down… that's where I come in. On one hand, this mortal woman can continue under the guidelines her agency has presented. On the other, she can rewrite the rules and take matters into her own hands. Mass genocide — "all for the greater good."

Honestly? The mass genocide promises more innocent souls to be returned to The Maker. For the humans, it is a "blessing in disguise," as they like to say. Taken before their time at the cost of someone else's bad behavior.

I'd been taught that the greater the sin, the greater the feed… but the greater the sin actually means how far that sin reaches. In this case… it'll reach on into the millions.

For that reason, and as expected, Oryn stops me before I follow through.

The shock on his face is more than evident. "What are you doing?" he asks, trying to keep calm, but his concern is clear. Not that I can blame him, what with me going from weeping during my first big influence, to being ready and willing to do something on such a grand scale.

During my pregnancy, we'd been keeping it simple. Attaining enough energy to feed my déō doúloi, supply the land our quota, and keep me healthy. All the while, I would people watch and memory feed — studying the way they think so that should a need ever arise we could make a statement.

"Belíar is so energy hungry, he seldom thinks of the consequence. And the other queens, from what I can

285

tell so far, aren't much better. All this influencing we do — all in an effort to balance the scales in Belíar's favor — is being stolen from us, putting our land and our lovers at a great risk."

Oryn is patient with my explanation up until this point, but at that last revelation, he can no longer keep quiet. "Basílissa, we don't know that he's the culprit."

"The Seven... I can sense them becoming anxious. Before long, they'll start visiting other territories — ours primarily — in search of extra energy reserves. In search of the reason. The Seven are not welcome here... not now that Seala is performing duties for The Maker directly. Belíar is definitely up to this declivity. The increase in rogue daimónia... whatever is going on to the huiói we found today..."

"You've been planning this... but you choose to only bring this all up to me now?"

"When, Oryn? When else was I supposed to bring it up?" I lash out, stepping closer to the woman who is absorbed in something electronic. Again he stops me, wrapping his hand around my wrist.

But the words I said sink in, his hand drops, and he takes a couple steps backward. The motion is enough to make me stop as well. After the shock of my frustration settles, he steps forward again and brings his hands to my cheeks — a motion that is so very Oryn. "You should have confided in me," he whispers, caressing my cheeks with his thumbs — something that is also very Oryn, and that tends to calm me down very quickly.

This time is no different, although my thoughts and words remain the same. I press my lips together and breathe deeply in and out through my nose. Oryn's dark-green eyes search mine, trying to read my thoughts. "Tell me more about your plan here," he suggests.

"Had you not previously been a mesités, would you question me so?"

Oryn's nostrils flare and he bites back what I imagine he'd really like to say, going with a simple, "Likely not. But, I was a mesités for a long time. Therefore, I still feel bound by that duty."

"Maybe one of these astral rounds you'll be the slave of one, rather than two," I grind out, pointing out the tie to being a mesítēs that he still seems so bent on befriending more so than his queen.

Oryn is unable to keep his patience with my nagging. "That's the plan, Adrestia." His voice is raised — a tone I've only ever heard him take with other men. Never with me. "The habit is not an easy one to drop. Be patient with me, please."

I step forward, pressing into him, and he melts into me. So easily.

We may have first bound as a means to an end, but I am his cock's biggest weakness… and we both know that. Which is exactly why he often avoids me, seeking out work instead. Thankfully, this avoidance has lessened since our binding became official-official.

I reach between us and grasp him, clenching my fist around his shaft. "Fuck," he hums, letting his head fall back.

"Ideally, yes," is my response.

Oryn straightens and looks me in the eyes. "Don't do this," he says, returning to the topic of this underhanded influence.

I release an angry growl and let go, turning my back on him once more. As frustrated as I am, I still don't want to challenge his knowledge by refusing him an answer to the question he'd asked, so I lean against the woman's desk and face him.

He still stands there, head back again as he mumbles something to the ceiling. "What the hell are you doing?" I ask.

"Talking it down, Adrestia. What the hell do you think I'm doing?"

Ohh, he's in a mood.

I kinda like it.

"Okay. Well, to answer your question earlier, my plan is to teach Belíar a lesson. Break some rules... without really breaking them, of course." That softens him right up, and he finally meets my gaze again. "By influencing her to take the mass-genocide approach, we're getting a lot of energy over time. Belíar will be pleased. Our territory will be fed. It will also serve to insure a significant quantity of souls return to Elysium rather than be sent to Tartarus. Might take a few visits — a few influences to really push her over the edge — but each time we'll get fed, and when the sin moves into action, Belíar will take a major loss in his army numbers."

Oryn stands there blinking repeatedly. He even tries to say something but fails. When he does finally get his focus back, he starts with, "Have you mentioned this to anyone else?"

"No, of course not." I cross my arms.

"The... the other queens will start visiting the victims — using their fear and desperation to survive to influence them. In a world-changing, life-threatening situation like you're talking about, humans will attach to sin like leeches: raids, trespassing, stealing, rape, things of that sort. But you... you want to influence their murder?"

"I want to save them, Oryn! Save us! Isn't that what this is all about? What happens after their mortal existence? That's the ultimate goal, right? Or have I just completely misunderstood?"

"No... no, you seem to understand quite well." Usually I'm pretty good at reading him. But right now I can't tell if he's horrified or impressed. Both maybe?

"So, Mesités" — I bow at the waist — "do you need to stop me? What does your other master demand?"

Oryn presses his lips together and exhales sharply. "My other master is a selfish bastard. The more energy, the better."

"Let the games begin," I say with a crooked grin.

CHAPTER THIRTY-FOUR

The feed is so simple — so easy — that it hardly feels like I did anything at all. In fact, when Oryn and I return to Ceteris, there is no proof the act provided my land with any sustenance whatsoever. No energy. Not yet at least.

I take a moment to explain to the awaiting huiói that the type of feed I did should send a steady trickle of energy to the land over the course of many moon-cycles.

In the meantime, I will need to do a number of smaller feeds. Well, regular feeds. That, or finish off many more daimónia. Whichever, we will require enough to sustain us all for a short while until the steady trickle begins to come through.

To accomplish this part of the plan, I turn to Blaze and Kirian. "We will need energy from the rogues that the sikárioi slaughter. During your next hunt, keep them alive? On the brink of expiring? Then call for me, and I will finish them all myself. Kirian, keep an eye out for anything amiss. Anything that needs looking into. Be careful, though. Please do not venture past the daimónia boundary too far."

Kirian, eager to keep busy, doesn't wait. He bounds away in an instant.

Blaze gives a sharp nod and says, "Consider it done, Basílissa."

I place my hand on his shoulder and squeeze. I miss him. And when he covers my hand with his — a gesture he is usually hard pressed to do — it proves to me he feels the same. The two of us share a knowing look —

an understanding that says if things were different, he wouldn't be just a sikários anymore, no matter how much he teases me against such a thing.

That eventually, he would have given in to my suggestions and come-ons. But now, my oikía is filled. Four déō doúlos, and one próskairos. Everyone is aware that Raener is meant for an official oikía position. The one reserved for touch. And both Blaze and I know that I wouldn't risk having Raener lose that position even if he may never become a full déō doúlos.

It has been said that a queen can take a próskairos and turn him into a déō doúlos, but we are yet uncertain if Raener is eligible for such a transition. If there's a loophole. A rule to bend or break.

Gazes lingering, he bows his head slightly, recognizing the war in my mind. The wish and desire to grow my oikía beyond five. Our hands drop, and everyone resumes walking, moving on to the next place in search of more huiós-hybrids.

The astral round is a long one, filled with essence and energy. Seala stays busy, but not as busy as she would like. As for me, on the other hand, when she can't take a huiós, that means more energy for us, so there are times in which I am at odds with how to feel about her delivering them to The Maker. There is a deep sense of protection for my land and my oikía embedded within me now.

To make matters even more challenging, each delivery provides her energy and sustenance. Energy that does not come from Ceteris. Nor does it mingle with our energy. It is upon this discovery that we come to realize she is most certainly not the culprit for the localized loss of energy.

Amid everything going on, this is certainly a welcome and relieving discovery. If The Seven come, they will have nothing against my daughter. That, and I imagine once their territories learn of what Seala can offer them, they very well might have a rebellion on their hands should the queens refuse their subjects that choice.

Much to Seala's dismay, however, she is just one being, amid millions. As of right now, she can only deliver one at a time. An issue I imagine she will soon figure out a way to work around.

With a deep, cleansing inhale and exhale, I call a close to the astral round. This round has been long, and we are all weary. "Again at sunrise," I command. "Oryn, please see to it that updates are collected from the village huiói and come to me with news before I retire for the night? Brax, touch base with The Watchers, see if they have any information to share?"

"Of course, Basílissa," Oryn and Brax say. They immediately leave to retire. Kohbi and Xanth follow suit.

"Raener? Join Kallias and me tonight?"

Raener's eyebrow rises. "Oh, so you give me the most challenging directive of them all," he quips.

"Now you know, it's only challenging if you struggle."

Kallias takes my hand in his and squeezes. I look up, expecting to see his bright, contagious smile, but instead there is a deep-rooted weariness there, etched all over his features. Not only that, but his skin is pallid, lips ashy.

I turn to him and take both of his hands in mine. "You are weak," I choke out over a difficult swallow.

"I am afraid so," he says.

I look around to those who still remain. We are all a bit tired, and most certainly in need of more energy, but not like Kallias.

Fear and apprehension wash over me, but I do not want to show him this worry. "Time to retire; we all need the rest."

Raener and I look at each other. What plans I had for him and me will have to wait. Surprise, surprise. That's okay, though, of any coupling, the two of us are accustomed to that by now. Seems fate — or whatever one might call it — likes to keep us apart whenever possible.

Everyone returns to the dwelling before separating to do their assignments or retire themselves.

Seala retires to her room.

Kallias, Raener, and I retire to my chamber, and I lie between them, resting my head on Kallias's now sticky and clammy chest. He has not spoken much other than to grunt and offer the occasional, attempted smile at my request. Anything, so that I will know he is going to be okay.

Sleep doesn't come easy, because the truth is, I don't know that he is going to be okay. The Fallen do not get sick like mortals. Their primary adversary is the hélkō, and this is not that.

"What is happening in your mind?" I try to ask.

"Very little," he coughs out. Hearing his voice appeases me for a time. I fall into a semi-relaxed daze as I listen close to each breath he takes and each heartbeat.

Raener lies beside me, curving his body against mine. Making sure our skin touches in as many places as possible. Before long, he is fast asleep and I am still listening to Kallias's essence and energy, willing it to speak to me — to tell me what is wrong and how to fix it.

Even though I know.

It can't possibly be coincidental that huiós-hybrids are popping up left and right, and now my only huiós déō doúlos has fallen ill. Whatever external force is making this happen, has chosen Kallias as one of its victims.

My teeth grind together and nostrils flare as I palm his chest right above his heart. It's early on, but we've yet to see a huiós-hybrid survive.

"Sleep," his deep voice penetrates my thoughts, and I jerk my head back to look into his orange-hued eyes. Even in the golden orange, my silver mark weaves within like the glint of bright sun rays. "Ya will find a loophole. Ya always do. But ya can nah if you do nah have tha energy t' do so." Every word he makes is an effort.

For the first time, I am convinced that there isn't a loophole.

Not for this.

* * *

The air is heavy and oppressive. Something has shifted — something unseen yet felt in every inch of sinew throughout my corded body, with every pump of my legs, and within every muscle that contracts and loosens.

Darkness seeps into the forest and twists inside of me as if we are one entity.

The boundary nears. I skid to a halt.

:yessss:

The voice — the same one that taps at my mind without cease on a regular occurrence — speaks now, louder. Clearer. Its words wrap around an invisible tongue and pierce my awareness with a hiss of pleasure.

:come to me:

Come to me, come to me. That is almost all it ever says. This time, though, the tone is different. It is as though the delivery comes from a cave. From an earthy vestibule that both projects and protects sound. Transforms it. Morphs it. Manipulates it.

I shake my head, trying desperately to sling the sound away. But it comes with a physical pull, too. My body yanks forward. I drop to the ground on hands and feet, bracing myself, refusing to move another step closer to the boundary.

A roar pierces my mind and I lift into a squat, slamming my hands over my ears.

Then, a cacophony of howls and roars respond in kind, filling the forest.

* * *

WHEN I WAKE UP from this nightmare, there's no mistaking what — who — I am channeling in these visions that have been plaguing me.

Tired — in more ways than one — and desperate for answers, I turn over to face Raener, and I whisper his name.

His eyes open easily to my call, and he gives me a lazy smile. "Being woken up by you saying my name while you're pressed against me might be my new favorite thing," he whispers, leaning forward and giving me a soft kiss. "Something is bothering you, though." He lifts his hand and presses his thumb between my eyebrows, rubbing out the tension there.

"Yes. There is something I must do," I explain quietly. "Please... stay here with Kallias. If he gets wors—" My throat closes around the word, cutting the finality of it short.

"I will find you," Raener understands what I am asking and finishes for me.

"Thank you," I say with a leaden sigh, giving him one more kiss before wiggling out from between both men.

Raener sits up and takes a more guard-like position, moving to a chair at Kallias's side as opposed to remaining on the pallet. Bow and quiver secured over my shoulders, I give him a grateful nod and smile through the wisp of my forming travel pýlē just before I move on to the entrance of my dwelling.

CHAPTER THIRTY-FIVE

Blaze

My eyes are blurry and bow hand is weak. When I had checked on the other sikárioi earlier this astral round, they were in similar states.

There may soon come a time when the daimónia we are meant to overpower will overpower us instead. I have never been more thankful for the boundary than in this moon-cycle. Many are crossing the line, but many are still keeping to their side.

Whatever type of influence Adrestia had done is working, but as soon as the land receives that leak of energy it webs outward in an attempt to feed everything all at once. Each being hardly gets any helpful amount before that little bit wanes.

I know it'll help once each drop begins to build on the others, but until then, things will be a challenge. More than a challenge, really. A matter of existence. We will lose more and more huiói to the lacking energy the longer it takes for Adrestia's efforts to go into motion in a significant amount.

A rustle in the woods over my right shoulder jolts me from my half-sleep daze and I whip around, chiding myself for a poor response time.

Thankfully, it's just the half-breed daimónion, Kirian, coming to update me on his search findings. I assess the sky to check the position of the moon; he is early. I drop my bow hand and lean against the tree, waiting for him to reveal himself.

When he does, Kirian is positioned low, creeping through the forest on all fours. A chill tracks along my spine as his red eyes glow and look straight through me with each footfall.

Fuck.

I nock an arrow and move around the tree for cover, slowly tracking back to a different tree to throw him off.

Please do not make me kill you, Beast. I fear Adrestia would never forgive me. I very well may never forgive myself.

Kirian moves right past me with slow strides, feet and hands scarcely making a sound on the terra. He is, by far, the scariest daimónion in all of Ceteris. The others are simply beasts without minds. But add in the mind and smarts of a huiós and the oikía powers of a déō doúlos. He is a weapon. A weapon no one knows how to use just yet.

And, right now, that weapon appears to be targeting something. Kirian is lost to the realm around him; his beast has taken over, and he has an intent that I am determined to figure out. So… I track behind him.

When he gets to the boundary, he stops. Adrestia has warned him against this. Maybe the huiós inside still has a say after all.

His head flicks from side to side, compensating for the lack of having animal-like ears in shape. Whatever sound he hears, it is unpleasant to him; his horned head shakes side to side, huiós hair moving along with it. But his body has a different opinion and bounds forward. His claws gouge the earth as something within him wars with the unseen pull.

Another silent moment passes and he clamps his hands over his ears.

Eyebrows drawn inward, I search the woods for whatever set him off.

I jolt on the spot, my feet nearly making air at the suddenness of the hundreds of daimónia that now fill the area on both sides of the boundary. None of them see me, though, all guided by something intrinsic.

This... this is not good.

I may have been on the brink of sleep moments ago, but I'm wide awake now, searching for a way out. Adrenaline pumps through me, giving me a different kind of energy — the survival kind.

I need to get away from here and find Adrestia immediately.

CHAPTER THIRTY-SIX

Adrestia

Someone is advancing toward me from a distance. The crunch of leaves and clatter of arrows reveals who the visitor is before his arrival, though. Usually when Blaze walks around — or runs, in this case — he tries harder to be silent. A whisper on the wind. Not this time.

Additionally, the unmistakable woodsy male musk associated with him is interlaced with fear. That fear coats the back of my throat and causes my fingers to tingle and shake. My oikía powers are all battling for top spot as something unseen triggers them.

Kirian is who I am in search of, but my heightened senses seem to be honing in on Blaze right now, instead, so I trust that instinct and switch targets.

That fear, that anxiousness, flowing out of Blaze and traveling throughout the forest causes my own to spike; I want to run, to sprint through the woods, seeking him out, but he has taught me well. Plus, the oppression that was thick in the air in my dream is near stifling now, adding to my concern. I creep through its invisible fog, ópsis arrow nocked and drawn, scanning from right to left as I guide myself cautiously through the woods.

I spot Blaze well before he spots me. In fact, he doesn't spot me at all; he is on a mission, and his mission is to leave the woods, not run around within them.

I've never seen him move so fast, nor ignore so much of his surroundings. I screech to a halt and loose the arrow, aiming several yards ahead of his sightline. The arrow embeds itself into the terra at his feet and he stumbles forward rolling into a ball of man on the forest floor.

He is back on his feet in an instant, though, body circling, chest heaving, focus wild. When his black eyes finally find me he grabs my arrow, rushes forward, returns the arrow to my quiver, and takes me by the shoulders. We both try to get out our thoughts at the same time, each of us saying something about daimónia.

When he takes a recovery breath, I state, "My nightmares, Blaze. I… I think I am in Kirian's head. Partially. Like a blended dream. But… but this last one, none of it was me."

"The daimónia are gathering," he says around a heaving breath. There are hundreds of them… possibly thousands."

My heart stutters and drops. "Kirian?"

"He's there, too. H-he was trying to stop the pull."

"The hélkō?"

Blaze shakes his head. "No. This… this was something else."

"Belíar," I whisper.

"Maybe." Blaze's hands drop from my shoulders.

"We advance tonight."

Blaze gives me a sharp nod, but neither of us move, unsure what step to take first.

How am I going to gather an entire village if I can't use my energy to travel from area to area and deliver the commands? "The watchtower alarm," I answer myself aloud. "Gather the sikárioi, have them get started right away. Instruct them to bring the daimónia down to mere inches of their existences, but make sure they do not finish them off."

Understanding, Blaze gives me another nod. But he doesn't run off right away. His hand reaches out and comes to my cheek. Blaze has this unusual talent for knowing when my confidence levels are low — when I am frightened or worried. "You've been training for this. Both with Brion and with me. The mental and physical knowledge of how to lead. Do not underestimate yourself. And, regardless what any other being thinks, do not hesitate to break the rules." His lips quirk up at the side.

My face presses into his cupped palm, I take a deep breath with closed eyes, open them, and give him a sharp nod. When my eyes open, though, his have dropped to my mouth. They now flick back up to my eyes and down to my mouth again. He leans in and gives me a cautious kiss. His eyes squeeze shut tight and he swallows hard as he drops his hand and steps back.

That's when I realize it is not me he's trying to reassure. That it's himself. That kiss was a kiss reserved for the potential of loss. A just-in-case, goodbye kiss.

Blaze turns on his heel and runs off before I can say anything. There's no time for me to stand here and dwell on it any longer either. I take the opposite direction and make my way as quickly as possible to the watchtower.

Before my arrival to Ceteris, apparently The Watchers worked in shifts; however, ever since Brax and I became bound, Brax had made the decision to take on the main Watcher role permanently, unless otherwise pulled away for something imperative. Like the birth of his baby... or forming a search party. Only in those, and similar, instances does he call on another guard to sit in the tower. Mostly, so that I know exactly where he will be if ever needed, but also so I have a safe place to stay outside of my dwelling.

Be that as it may, I cannot enter the tower on my own. That ability is reserved for The Watchers.

To get his attention, I have to either instruct one of my dwelling guards to let him know I am coming, or take the same approach Blaze would during our nightly excursions: shoot an arrow inside or near the window.

Setting my position a good bit away from the tower so I have the arcing height to my advantage, I draw my bow and arrow, aim, and shoot. When I'm confident with the result, I shoulder my bow and run the rest of the way to the door. By the time I get there, Brax is at the tower's base waiting, arrow held out for me to collect.

Once I return the arrow to my quiver, he rubs a big hand over his eye and bends to my level. "Basílissa... let me guess... Raener couldn't get the job done and you've come to get a better servicing."

I give him a half laugh. "Hardly."

He must recognize the urgency in my tone, because his blurry eyes clear, and he straightens. "What is wrong?"

I explain what I had not yet told anyone about Kallias: he is in the process of converting into one of those huiós-hybrids.

Brax's eyes widen and he swallows hard.

"That is not all, I am afraid," I rush out. "Blaze has found a heavy concentration of daimónia gathering toward the far edge of our territory. Our guess is that they are planning an attack of some sort. Why else would they gather like that?" The question is directed more toward myself under a breath. "We need to take action. Now. Can you use the watchtower's alarm to gather the village huiói?"

"Yes. It is not something we have done for a very, very long time; my only worry is that the huiói will not

303

recognize the sound for what it is. That they will dismiss it as a new Fallen."

"Well, we won't know until we try. Sound the alarm, Brax. Be quick."

He turns away and rushes up the stairs, taking them several at a time with his giant legs.

There is no sense in me standing around waiting for him to return. I run straight to the village center, and wait there instead. Not too terribly long ago, I had instructed several assigned leaders to make sure that everybody met at sunrise to commence our next steps, anyway. The alarm may come as a surprise; however, the gathering and the task at hand should not.

The blare is loud and clear, echoing throughout the land as I reroute toward my dwelling to check on Kallias and discuss responsibilities and roles with Raener.

Raener is not alone with Kallias inside the chamber when I enter; Seala has joined them and sits at Kallias's side, speaking to him in hushed tones. Every muscle and tendon inside me locks into place. I do not want to tell her to stop talking to Papa K if she is speaking with him casually. But, knowing now what drives her, I do not want her there, because I refuse to lose one of my males. I refuse to lose any huiói in my territory; I intend to do everything in my power to make sure that doesn't happen.

But Kallias? One of my oikía? Belíar be damned to his own existence in The Void; one of my oikía will not be taken from me. "Seala… What are you doing?" I ask with as calm of a tone as possible.

"He is expiring, Ma."

"No." My hands clench at my sides. "You may speak to him, Seala. But you may not take him from me." Again my voice is calm, despite the rest of me being anything but. "You will not take him from me. Do you understand? That is a command from your mother and basílissa."

Seala turns a sympathetic glance in my direction. "Ma…"

I shake my head. "Seala…"

"Listen to me," she says. "Just like you have no choice in the requirement to influence mortals, I have no choice in the requirement to return eligible huiói to The Maker. No choice, Ma."

Chest heaving and nails biting into my palms, I narrow my focus on my daughter's eyes. "Are you telling me Kallias has never once been stricken by the hélkō? Are you telling me he is eligible? Is that what you are saying?"

Her green-gold eyes turn glassy. "He is one of the good ones, Ma," her voice trembles.

I tried to keep calm. I did. But the next words that come out of my mouth are not calm. They are boiling, scathing, and loud. "I know he is one of the good ones! But he is mine, and you will not take him from me!" I screech.

Raener had been standing by watching as his former practice of being a paidagōgós would insist. Learning. Understanding. But he approaches me now, spins me around, wraps one arm around my waist and presses the opposite hand over my head, pulling me against him.

"Shhh," he hushes. When I am unable to calm down, when the tremors in my body refuse to stop and the tears come, Raener lets me go, only to cup my face with his hands in order to force my attention to his face. "Adrestia."

I blink rapidly to clear my vision and my hands come to his wrists, both to feel grounded and to tear them away from me should the need arise.

"The alarms are done and your territory huiói are awaiting your leadership," he explains calmly. "By going out there and taking that next step, you will be one moment closer to learning more about what plagues Kallias. About how to make sure it doesn't happen to anyone else. To any more of our oikía. You'll be one step closer to returning here to be by his side."

My hands tighten around Raener's wrists. He drags his fingers lightly down my cheeks, collecting every tear. His touch leaves a trail of cathartic numbness in its wake. His dark eyes never once leave mine. When I loosen my hands, his fingers drop to my chest and he clasps his palms over my left breast; a pulsating warmth spreads there, and my heart instantly lightens.

Touch. He is using his próskairos-earned oikía power to ease my heartbreak. Again I blink at him. "Stay here... with Kallias? Take his pain away?" Raener nods and lets me go, returning to Seala's side. I walk up to join them once more before leaving, trace my fingers along Kallias's forehead and over his strong jawline, and bend down to brush my lips against his. A single tear drips from the corner of my eye, travels down my nose, and lands on his mouth as I pull away. "Raener, do not let her take him; I forbid it."

CHAPTER THIRTY-SEVEN

Raener was right; every being called upon is waiting in the village center, the crowd overflowing to between the huts and beyond. Oryn and Brax join my side immediately. I gesture to Brax to bend down to my level and he does so. "Deliver some instructions for me, will you?" Of the three of us, he is by far the loudest on account of his size.

Oryn whistles and someone in the crowd whistles back — a process I had forgotten experiencing the day I arrived and first approached Kirian's cage.

Mentally swatting the memory away, I provide Brax with the necessary details: "We will all walk together to the edge of the territory. Advance slowly, I do not want them wearing out before we get there. When we do arrive, no one will attack until my order, unless it is in self defense."

Brax rises to his full height, cups his hands around his mouth, and delivers the instructions to a now ready and waiting crowd. As he does, Oryn's shoulder brushes against mine and he leans toward my ear. "Brax filled me in on the state of Kallias." I glance at Oryn, pressing my lips together and taking a hard swallow. He doesn't know that Seala sits at Kallias's side, threatening to take him from us forever.

Right now, all Oryn knows is that this affliction might take him from us forever anyway: a trip to the Void or a trip to Elysium. Which is worse? Both are about equal to me at this point. Both strip him from my side too soon. "Yeah. If there is anything that can be done—"

"You'll figure out a way," he finishes my statement.

"Or expire trying," I use the same saying Raener had when we were binding. Because it's the truth. When it comes to this love, this connection we all share, if there is a way, I will do whatever it takes. "To start, though, our territory needs an energy boost. There's no way he'll survive if the land can't aid in healing him. That much I do know. Anything beyond is uncertain."

Oryn gives me a soft smile just as Brax is finishing the delivery of my demands and every being around us has begun to spread out.

The journey is long and arduous. None of the huiói seem to mind, already accustomed to traveling by foot. Plus, many of them journeyed much farther to get here. As for me, on the other hand, I am not used to it; every muscle and joint in my body aches. In turn, my energy reserves attempt to counter the ache and heal, forcing me to stamp down the effort; I cannot become drained when not enough terra energy is available to help me make a trip to the mortal realm.

Brax and Oryn can sense the strain and Brax keeps on insisting he carry me. A queen. Being carried by a grigori. I will not make my subjects toil, while I am carried to battle.

About three-fourths of the way — and about two astral rounds — to our destination, the sikárioi I had instructed Blaze to gather join us. Blaze included.

He may not be a direct line in my oikía, but when he steps beside me and joins the march, I feel one more being complete than I had before.

He takes my hand in his and weaves our fingers together, as he has been inclined to do on occasion beginning soon after our secretive meetings. The act alone gives me enough strength to press forward

"Their numbers are growing," he states. "Your front line will be at the first wave before the sun rises."

I look up at Brax and clear my throat to get his attention. "Catch up to the front, and make sure they stop as planned? On your call they may attack. When at all possible, remind them that they are instructed to not kill — debilitate, but leave the kill shot for me. Also, make sure no one harms Kirian."

None of us have heard from nor seen my daimónion since Blaze caught him lost in the persuasion of the lógos and initiated into the ever-growing group of rogues. We can only assume at this point that he remains among them.

Brax bounds off, his long legs making triple the distance than any other type of being could.

"I have delivered this same news to the sikárioi," Blaze reveals. "Though, they aren't very happy about it." When I whip my head toward him, he gives me a smile and a wink. "The land might feed us, but we quite enjoy the killing part."

"Maybe one of these astral rounds I'll be able to make it up to them," I offer.

Blaze shoots me an appalled glare, to which I respond with an eye roll. "Not like that. Besides, like you, the other sikárioi probably aren't into queens."

"Oh, they're into queens."

"So, I've just managed to want the one, sole, sikários who prefers solitude?"

Blaze hesitates with a quip, but when decided, he responds with, "Precisely."

To which I simply squeeze his hand. He squeezes me back. Blaze is possibly the most confusing male I have ever met. Either way, I quite like him — déō doúlos, próskairos, or nothing at all, I shall keep him anyway. In Kallias's words: *The hélkō can ultimately choose yah oikía, but it can nah choose who ya decide t' love an' want.*

With Brax gone from my opposite side, Oryn now walks in line with me. I turn my attention to him, the thought of Kallias bringing with it a reminder of what is to come. "Mesítēs," I address him as such depending on the purpose of my need. That way he knows under which guise I am requesting advice, even though his mesítēs days are now in the past.

"Yes, Basílissa," he returns the formality with a side-grin.

"I know we are so-called immortal" — I scoff at that, considering we are hardly immortal where the hélkō and Belíar are concerned — "but, should we rest and begin again at sunrise? We have been walking for nearly two astral rounds. I fear for my subjects' well-being."

Oryn thinks thoroughly on this for a time, no doubt playing out many scenarios in his mind before coming to a conclusion.

And his conclusion is not what mine would have been, which is exactly why I sought his advice in the first place. "No. We are losing energy not only from exertion, but also from time. The longer we wait, the weaker we will become."

"Thank you," I respond. "Perhaps with this first wave," I address this part to both Oryn and Blaze, "I can expire enough to give our army the energy needed to continue. Maybe after that, we can afford rest — send the front line to the back after each wave?"

Blaze grunts and nods. "Yes, that is a good idea."

My voice and confidence drops, and I direct my next question to him, "Can we win this?" I ask.

Blaze pulls to a halt and turns toward me. "Yes." That's all he says, though. It's the look he gives me, the same look I remember from the night he introduced me to that doe; she was not afraid because it was in her nature to birth the foal. The look Blaze gives me now implores that as a born — well, Fallen — leader, I should not second-guess my decisions.

"Okay," I reply.

He still doesn't let us walk, though. The two of us stand there with a million more things we'd like to say. He chews on the inside of his lip and his eyes dart between mine.

"D...did you..." He can't get the question out, but I know exactly what he is asking. But why? Why now? A simmer of anger bubbles up inside me. Rage and disappointment. "Yes. Raener is my próskairos now. His oikía power is touch — a diluted version."

Blaze blinks rapidly before clearing his throat, nodding, and turning us back to fall in line, pulling me into a short jog to catch up.

I want to ask Blaze a dozen more questions.

I want to reach out to Kallias and continue the conversation we'd started on the beach about the intricacies of growing an oikía — update him on Raener's new position and inquire as to what — if anything — I can do to further expand.

But that option is not available.

I consider asking Oryn, but decide against it, choosing instead to focus on the present.

"Should I attempt to catch up with the front line?" I ask next. "How far behind are we after they battle the first wave?"

"About an eighth of an astral round; however, based on how the huiói in front of us have slowed, I would guess that the first wave is already upon us. You wouldn't have time to catch up anyway," Blaze answers.

I search around for my grigori so he can place me on his shoulders and I can look ahead, but his absence reminds me that I had sent him to the front. Best we can do is walk. Walk for several more sun positions until we are met with enfeebled daimónia.

Considering I did not deliver news to the front line to fall back after their attack, and for the next in line to press forward, I can only hope they do this naturally.

I soon recall that earlier Blaze was able to let the other sikárioi know to not expire the daimónia, and realize that he, like the other huiói who hold unique positions, must be able to communicate inwardly with the other sikárioi.

So, I turn to him with a request to relay these new specifics. He, indeed, is able to deliver the news to the sikárioi on the front line, who I am told will, in turn, pass on the information.

I let out a weighted exhale; not only is my body weary, but so is my mind. The responsibilities of a basílissa require a lot of thinking, and time is not exactly on our side for me to mull and contemplate at a leisurely pace.

Perhaps it is due to all the thinking, but although the entire journey seemed to creep by, these next few sun positions fly. Before long, the huiói in front of us are splitting in various sections, working their way through, over, and around almost-expired daimónia.

As soon as I come toe… to shoulder… with one, a new vigor fills me. In this moment, I finally feel useful — not just a queen sitting back and being witness to the declension of her territory, not sitting back and learning while the rest of the realm carries on, pulling the bulk of the weight.

It doesn't take more than a single inhale and exhale for me to whip out an arrow and finish off the first struggling daimónion. Perhaps I am showing him a kindness. Whether or not they even have a conscience, or whether or not they feel fear or sense pain is questionable. Even so, I can't imagine lying on the cold, hard ground having your essence gurgle out of your slit neck can be any sort of comfortable.

When I loose and stare at him as he putrefies and becomes one with the terra, it isn't a daimónion I choose to see, though. Instead, I envisage Belíar in the deep, red depths of his eyes. "Come to me," I mock, using Belíar's favored words under my breath.

CHAPTER THIRTY-EIGHT

Similar moments are replayed over and over again for nearly an additional astral round. Yet, so focused on the task at hand, I scarcely pay any mind to the position of the sun except to notice when it rises and sets. Move forward, collect energy. Move forward, collect energy. Again and again.

Blaze stays by my side, watching my back and front and keeping a keen eye on every single daimónion I prepare to shoot, in the off chance one should spring up at the last moment, driven by the scent and sight of a basílissa.

On and on this trend continues, until I can no longer pull my bowstring back because my fingers are cracked and coated in essence.

Desiring nothing much more throughout the experience than to make sure my territory huiói regain their strength, I let my own energy drop until I simply cannot afford to do so anymore.

With shaky fingers, I return my arrow to the quiver, chest heaving, eyes wild, and drop my bow hand.

Blaze's arm brushes against mine as he stands similarly, having been unwilling to be more than just a couple feet from my side. We had finally worked our way through the entire territory of huiói. Those of us who had started the journey in the far back are finally on the front line. The multitude of troops has slimmed, as each grouping stays back and sets up camps in the more energy-prolific areas after each wave.

Brax had rejoined us, unwilling to stay behind when I was still marching ahead.

There is a welcome stretch of what appears to be a section of forest that is free and clear of daimónia. I was not remiss to notice that the amount of kills had increased with each wave, though.

Needing a bit of a break myself, but not wanting to stop the forward movement, I instruct Brax to press on with the remaining huiói while I stay back with Blaze and Oryn to feed and make a plan moving forward. "Now that there is enough energy out here, I will simply travel to catch up," I explain to him when he doesn't seem overly thrilled with the idea. He grunts and stomps off, and I shoot Oryn a silent plea. Oryn shakes his head, amused, and jogs after my giant to do what he does best. Mediate.

Brax is worn, and seeing as he cannot travel with me, nor help heal me in any capacity at this point, it bothers him that he is of little to no use at my direct side in this moment. Of course, he is of every use by my side just by simply being here. But when we're in the middle of a daimónia killing spree, each being must split up according to his strength. And his, of course, is being a Watcher. Staying with the front lines and giving them a heads-up as they encroach on the next wave.

Blaze, on the other hand, knows the most about this particular wave of daimónia, because come to find out, it is the area he'd caught Kirian in a few astral rounds prior.

"So, like the paidagōgói and mesítēs, you are able to use a pýlē to travel to different sections where sikárioi hunt?" I ask, piecing together yet another thing I did not realize at first, but have since surmised.

Blaze turns to me and takes in a deep, steadying breath. "Yes."

My eyebrows come together in the middle as I study his features. He... "You haven't been allowing the land to heal you." I finish the statement with a firm press of my lips and a narrowed glare.

Blaze steps forward once and lifts his hand to my face. "I am not feeding until my basílissa does."

"Blaze... There is plenty here for you. Heal."

His fingers skim over my cheek and down to my jawline, black gaze following. I dip my head to snag the attention of his focus again. Blaze's eyes are always black, but there's something different about them now. They're... darker somehow, his pupils dilated, leaving only a hint of the iridescent black ring of his irises visible.

Again he steps forward, but there's nowhere for him to go, because I am standing here; his body presses against mine, and those obscure eyes drop to my mouth.

"The haímaboúlomai," I whisper. Blaze's blood desire emits from him in waves, calling to my own. His eyes watch as my mouth forms the words, and his tongue snakes out to wet his lips. All of which causes a chain reaction in me. Once the worry and confusion fades, I realize that his fingers and chest are not the only body parts touching me. His cock is, too. My focus falls to the point of contact between us and back up to his face again.

Blaze drags his thumb along my bottom lip. "Adrestia..." It is as though part of his mind tries to engage in normal conversation, but the other part challenges that effort.

"Blaze..." I respond.

"Why the fuck is my cock hard?" he says in a breathless whisper.

"Because," my own voice drops as I slip my tongue out to taste the pad of his thumb, "as I have been trying to convince you for moon-cycles now, you're supposed to fuck me. Female-male anatomy, that's how it works... sometimes."

Blaze groans and his head falls back and eyes close. He removes his thumb from my mouth, but doesn't take his hand away. Instead, he straightens and leans down, brushing his lips lightly against mine.

My eyes close and every inch of me wakes up, despite the all-consuming weakness from a lack of energy.

However, something contradictory happens within the chambers of my heart. I palm his chest and push him away, uncoupling our mouths. "This isn't right," I say, rolling my eyes and grumbling out the words. "You haven't wanted this. Not ever." Yes, I know I tease him, but that is how we work. I tease, he says "no."

Blaze covers my hand with his and wraps his fingers around mine before eating up the small bit of space between us. Again his mouth alights on mine, tongue swooping deep inside before his teeth drag down, taking my bottom lip with them. "I lied," he mumbles against my mouth.

My eyes flick up to his. "Look at me, Blaze." He does. "You're not thinking clearly."

"Mmm," he hums, slipping his bottom lip behind his teeth before releasing it with a pop. "You're right... I'm not thinking clearly." He delivers these words slow and contemplatively. "But, see, that is just the problem; I am always in my own head. Stuck there." He lifts his free hand and palms the side of his head. "But when I am with you, you pull me out. You drag me into yours. Being with you is like being perpetually consumed by the haímaboúlomai. You are addictive, just like the blood desire is."

317

Again he shifts against me. My body vibrates everywhere we touch. His engorged shaft presses against my lower belly. Dampness forms between my thighs, so contradictory to the ache in my heart. My gaze falls and I swallow hard. "Blaze…" In an effort to be the queen I've been taught to be, to not show weakness, I lift my attention again and steady my focus on him. His eyes drill into mine, waiting.

Regal, strong, brave… I still drop my voice to the barest of whispers, "There is no confusion for me. We tease, but I have always wanted you. To me, this isn't a silly game of chase. This isn't hubbub, where I close my eyes, shake, and hope for the best. I want you, but I'll not even risk taking you inside me if by some miraculous chance something works out and you are placed into a permanent spot in my oikía without a des—"

Blaze cuts the words off with the crash of his mouth against mine. His hands slip to my shoulders and he removes my bow and quiver before removing his, too. The way he tosses each item to the side carefully, not carelessly, proves to me that he is still somewhat of a sane mind, and it serves to relax me a bit.

Lips moving against mine, tongues crossing like the blades of swords, he lays me down right there on the leaf-littered ground and slips inside me with one long, thorough stroke.

Hearing that I want him, mixed with the fact that his cock is hard to begin with, was all the permission he needed. Enough to fulfill his part of the bond in deciding for himself.

A long, heady moan pushes out of me with that stroke, mixed with the whispering of his name on my tongue as I grab his ass in the palms of my hands and squeeze while simultaneously pulling him into me deeper, harder. But Blaze is already in deep... in more ways than one. He's already working my insides, both at my core and in my heart.

He props one of his elbows on the ground beside my head, and the fingers of his other hand wrap around the back of my neck. He moves inside me again, eyes alternating half-lidded glances from my eyes to my mouth and back again.

Again he strokes my body from the inside. He opens his mouth slightly to say something; instead, his eyes close and he takes in a deep breath, sliding out and back in with measured intent, slow and deliberate.

He brings his lips to mine again, and this time he does speak: "I can't ever find the right words to say to you. You... scare me, Adrestia. I could get lost in you." As if to make his point, he buries himself inside me just right, making sure there's no more room left. My neck arches as a deep-bellied groan leaves my lips. He presses down on my chin with his thumb, rerouting my attention back to his face. An orgasm builds within me, and having his color-changing eyes pierce mine with so much aching need, it forges higher, stronger, threatening to burst. Pinned beneath him, my entire body heaves with each breath.

Again he drops his mouth to mine, "If I get lost in you, Adrestia, what if I never find myself again?" How does he stay so controlled, so intentional with each thrust, each word, each graze of his fingers?

If he's expecting a thoughtful answer, there's no way I can provide. The only words that float through my mind in this moment are, "Well, I suppose we're about to find out," because in the next, my insides are clenching and making a statement of their own around his cock.

Blaze grunts and quavers inside me, unable to keep hard and focused when my body tightens around him so fiercely, so desperately, and with so much command.

When we're both done, he stills, eyes wide, and rolls off, falling onto his back. I immediately prop up on my side, place one of my hands on his chest, and let out a breathy, "You still with me? Or do we need to find a search party?"

Blaze's eyes meet mine, and the corner of his mouth ticks up. I blink a couple times. Did—I shoot up into a sitting position and hover over him, studying his eyes. When we were binding I had most certainly noted they had begun to change, but...

"What?" he asks, his voice just this shy of panicked.

I shake my head. "Nothing, I just th—" Nope... there it goes again. I reel back, scooting away from him, just as he also shoots up, grasping the sides of his head.

Something heavy, dark, and pressing fills my mind, as though a grigori-sized rock was placed in there and now takes up every crevice of space.

Oryn's voice penetrates the sensation, but barely. "Adrestia?" His hand comes to my shoulder. He'd been nearby and had likely witnessed what just happened between Blaze and me.

"Blaze," I choke out. "Is... is he okay?"

"One of the other sikárioi is helping him now."

"It hurts, Oryn. My... my head. It's heavy... dense. Full. I... I don't know how to expl—"

"Drea! No!" Kirian screams, swiping his arm out in an attempt to catch me before I am gone forever. But it's too late. Thank goodness.

320

"Drea," he says my name with the mixture of a cry and a scream. I squeeze my eyes shut as wind and blackness wraps around me — as hundreds of other Fallen plummet through the abyss.

Then, just as he is about to be nothing more than a spec above, just as I am taking my final glance and am about to let the tears flow to blur the rest of my vision, he jumps.

"No!" I wail, the tears coming for an entirely different reason now.

"Adrestia!" Kirian's deep voice, filled with so much panic and pain, screeches through my mind.

"Adrestia! Adrestia... Adrestia..." With every panicked yell, his voice morphs.

My eyes snap open and lungs pull in air.

"Adrestia!" My name falls from Oryn's tongue upon returning, my shoulders shaking violently. "Adrestia!"

I blink rapidly, drop my hands from where they'd been gripping my head, and will myself to concentrate.

When Oryn finally comes into focus, something moves in my periphery, and in the next instant, Oryn is being pushed to the side by a stumbling and fearful Blaze.

Blaze falls to his knees in front of me, matching my own positioning, and he grabs my shoulders. "Basílissa," he urges, trying to do what Oryn could not. Trying to call me back into the present and out of the memory of a now incredibly vivid and clear past.

He moves his hands from my shoulders to cup my face. "Are you with me? Come back. Come back before it takes you forever."

The concept of being taken forever slams down on me, bringing with it the reminder that I am trying to save one of my déō doúlos. I take in several choppy breaths and hard swallows, focusing with every bit of my effort on Blaze. "Wh-what what is going on? What happened?" What I really want to say is "Where's Kirian — I need to talk to Kirian," but my mind isn't quite there yet.

It is getting there rapidly, though, and with the pieces and thoughts all forming and transposing into real memories, a frustrated sadness is attached.

"Look at me. I need you to look at me," Blaze continues. "I need to know you are here. Right here. In Ceteris. Fighting a battle against rogue daimónia."

Something about those words brings me all the way back to the surface. I blink once more, eyes clearing, and give him a sharp nod, bringing my own hands up to his face in similar motion.

Every line of muscle in his shoulders droops and loosens; he nearly falls backward in relief.

"Talk to me," I whisper, watching his eyes flicker over and over again from red-brown to black.

He nods, head moving under the cupping of my hands. "The sixth sense," he states. "We are bound. My oikía power is the sixth sense. Our... our minds can see and intermingle with the other side of the veils."

I... I didn't even know there was a sixth sense. No clue. When Blaze had thrusted inside of me, how our binding would translate was a mystery. I had wondered if he would take on the sense of touch, leaving Raener with a borrowed version, or if the binding wouldn't work at all and he would be punished or sent to The Void.

My focus seeks out Oryn who now sits on the ground, hands between his knees as he looks back and forth between Blaze and me.

Blaze continues to speak, quickly, as if we're running out of some unknown time, "I have always been able to sense the daimónia. Always. The signs have been there."

As it had been doing all along, that vision, that memory of Kirian still pokes at me, maturing by the heartbeat. "Did you see the vision I had?" I ask.

"Yes, but I have a feeling your version came with more than just the vision."

I give a sharp nod. "Yes. I need to see Kirian…" I pause for a moment, pressing my lips together before continuing again. "And give him a hug… and a kick to the cock."

Blaze's eyebrow rises, and I shrug. "I remember everything. Why I'm here… Why I am different."

CHAPTER THIRTY-NINE

Oryn still listens, but he also watches: wary, concerned, frightened? I drop one of my hands from Blaze and reach out for my former mesítēs.

He scoots to me and takes my hand. "Raener explained to me what you had proposed in Superbia — about how your oikía powers have the ability to interplay with those of the other basílissas. There is one queen, though, that I was unable to connect your powers with. Until now."

I know in an instant who he is talking about. Vialla, the Basílissa of Vanagloria. Dark magic. "You seem concerned. Should I be, too?"

Oryn takes in a deep breath. "There are good reasons why The Maker placed a veil over each realm. Some of the realms are better left untouched. Out of sight, out of mind. The sixth sense isn't only for tapping into Elysium. In fact, I would place a bet that you still can't quite do that in its entirety. Tartarus… and possibly even The Void, though, yes."

"The Void? But I thought The Void is technically… nothing."

"You thought right, but there is still an in-between. A passage of delivery. My guess is that's why you were able to access the memory about Kirian and you. You pulled all the details from that moment when you were Falling — those moments falling through the veil between Elysium and Tartarus."

"Yes," I whisper. "I think you are right." My mind replays all the details again. Each time, a new rage and frustration slams into me. I remember a lot. Everything that went through my thoughts in those moments. Bits and pieces of my previous existence with Kirian, yes, but mostly why I was Falling, and the fact that Kirian...

I drop my other hand from Blaze and let go of Oryn's hand. Instead, I ball them into fists in my lap before pushing off the ground and spinning in a slow circle, throwing all my senses out at once, seeking out one daimónion in a forest of many.

I can sense his mind, feel him fighting a mental battle. I can also tell that he has attained the memories — the same ones, but from his perspective. And he, too, is looking for me. When I turn to look down at Blaze, he has already stood and is holding out my power object items. "Kirian and I are connected via your sixth sense," I reveal, shrugging into the quiver and situating the bow onto my shoulder.

Blaze nods. "Yes... that is due to the fact that he is a daimónion. I have been able to sense him since he transformed." He pauses for only a heartbeat before continuing, "Kirian is not the only daimónion I sense right now, though."

So wrapped up in memories of Kirian, I had dropped anything else out of my awareness. I tap into my bond with Blaze, so I can "see" what he sees.

The next, large — and final — wave of daimónia.

No longer in need of a feed, due to our binding, I reach out for Oryn and Blaze. They immediately take each of my hands, and I create a travel pýlē, popping us up to the still-advancing final line of our small, but powerful, army.

The energy levels are sufficiently filled, but certainly not in an amount to last an existence — even if we defeat this unexpected army of rogue daimónia. This problem isn't going away soon, nor easily. Possibly not ever.

Our pýlē travel ends at Brax's side, since he was the most displeased about our separation. "I can see them," he updates me immediately. "Mere dots right now, but the front of our group will reach them soon."

Blaze shakes his head and slaps his temple repeatedly. "Fuck, it's uncomfortable… Rogue daimónia are not the only beings present in their numbers." I snap my attention to him while still taking steps forward. "I…" he squeezes his eyes shut then quickly opens them. "I can't make sense of their essence-energy."

Brax eyes Blaze and does a double take, coming to a halt on the spot, nearly causing a crash of moving huiói. "Sikários…" he says low, menacing, dropping into a defensive pose.

"Brax?" I question, standing between them. Oryn takes my side.

Brax notices the two of us protecting Blaze, and he gets out of the defensive pose. "Why are his eyes red? Why do I feel powers in him?"

"He is part of our oikía now," I state simply. "Sixth sense. He has a direct connection with the veils."

"Red eyes… like a daimónion?" Brax lifts an eyebrow.

"Well, brownish-red. But, yes, similar to a daimónion, I suppose."

Brax bends and squints at Blaze. Blaze rolls those brown-red eyes. "You better not be a daimónion. One in her oikía is enough, Sikários. I will kill you myself."

Blaze straightens his shoulder and lifts his chin at my giant. "Grigori… you'd have to catch me first," Blaze teases.

Brax turns to me, "Stop the rule breaking," he states.

"Never." I smile up at him.

He grumbles and huffs as he turns back toward the advancing huiói. "Weapons ready," he rumbles over his shoulder. "Time to fight."

My mind reverts back to what we had been talking about before Brax's outburst and cycles through a few things before landing on the memory of my binding with Kallias. "After Kallias and I bound, his oikía power revealed something we could not see without it. Our binding, the initiation of our oikía power, must've opened a new connection," I explain. "Keep astute, and keep me informed on anything different or new."

"Yes, Basílissa," Blaze replies.

I flash him a side-grin. "I could get used to you speaking to me all proper like that."

Blaze grins and brings one hand to the back of his neck, while twisting the fingers of his other hand with mine.

"Are you going to need to fuck after we kill this next wave?" I ask out of the side of my mouth.

He shrugs. "I think I would like to fuck at every given opportunity."

I get a giddy sort of pleasure at hearing this. "You know, I should refuse you like you did for so long with me. Make you suffer through the pangs of physical want."

He raises an eyebrow. "You would never." He runs his hand over his chest. "Not sure you have that sort of discipline."

I snort-huff at that. "Absence makes the heart —
and cock — grow fonder, Sikários." I wink at him, and
he groans.

Ahead of us, the clang of weapons and growl of
daimónia echo through the forest. Blaze and I release our
hands and ready our bows. Brax pulls his sword from its
sheath. Oryn wields his dagger. Various ticks and
swishes of huiói readying their weapons resound.

Up until this point, I had only been finishing off the
daimónia — ending what other huiói had started. But
now, we will charge at our own wave. Full on. And these
particular daimónia have a lot of energy. Not just within
their veins, but throughout their motivations and actions
also — a driven energy. They are not tired or weary.

Arrow nocked and string tight, I address my
sikários: "This is where the main concentration was,
correct? Where you saw Kirian?"

"Yes," he responds, searching the woods, his
sightline following that of the tip of his arrow.

"Do you have any additional reads on that
unfamiliar presence?"

Again he answers with a "yes," but this one is
delivered with a simple nod. "Whatever it — they? —
are, is more powerful than the other daimónia. Not as
copious, but… their presence is strong."

"Are my huiói in great danger where this
unexpected strength is concerned?" I ask.

"Possibly, yes."

"Okay… I want us up at the front. Call for the other
sikárioi as well, even if they are still healing and resting.
Have them travel here right away; I do not want my
inexperienced huiói in over their heads."

Blaze grunts an agreement. These communications
within certain circles of positions is a silent thing, and

Blaze is particularly good at doing it without drawing attention to the process. In fact, he continues to scan the forest while, I assume, also giving a mental call to the others.

Not wanting to bother Blaze, I address Oryn now. "Before, when we first started this journey — this clean up — I was unable to seek out Sitara's assistance, there was not enough energy to travel to her, nor to send any of my déō doúloi to Acedia on my behalf. She had offered her help, but I was unable to access it."

Oryn sheaths his dagger. "We can go, but I cannot travel there on my own anymore. As you know, I no longer have the mesítēs privileges I once had. To deliver her a message, you will need to do so yourself, but I am happy to attend."

I look around, pull on my powers to listen, scent the air for anything amiss other than what is obvious. There is definitely something off — something different here with this last wave, with this area. My body tingles with apprehension. Oryn watches and listens to all those subtle cues and says, "If we go now, we should get back in time, but that timeline is short. Make your decision, Basílissa," he nudges.

I distance myself and hold my hand out, to make sure any approaching or passing huiói know not to get close, and I take Oryn's hand in my other as I create a pýlē.

* * *

WE LAND IN SITARA'S GARDEN, and I am only able to appreciate its beauty for a heartbeat before I am knocked into the present and purpose of being here.

When I move to step forward, Oryn stops me. "We wait here. She will have sensed your arrival. Do not stroll through another queen's territory, whenever possible. Out of respect, you wait to be received."

Trusting Oryn's directive, I do as suggested. But my body tingles with anticipation — hands fidget at my side, feet adjust from one to the other. Sitara only leaves us waiting for less time than it would take me to form another pýlē, but in my eagerness, the waiting seems so much longer.

"Basílissa Adrestia," Sitara beams at me, approaching and wrapping me in a hug. But when she pulls back, her ring glows and she assesses it. "You are troubled."

"Very."

"Is it your daughter again?" she asks, placing her hand over her chest.

"No, it is the territory; I believe we have found the source of our troubles."

She raises an eyebrow. "I shall send my Watchers and sikárioi right away. What else can I do for you?"

I give her a small grimace. "Basílissa" — I bow my head — "I do not wish to put you in danger, but I believe you should be in attendance. There is much to be gleaned from what is yet to come."

She thinks about this for a time, yet ultimately nods in agreement. "Yes, I think you are right. When and where should I meet you?"

"Now. At the northeast quadrant of my territory."

Her chest expands and contracts on a heavy breath.

"Be prepared for battle," I state. From there, I do not wait for her response, itching to get back. She has agreed, there is no further need of discussion. I take a retreating step and leave in an instant with Oryn by my side.

CHAPTER FORTY

When Oryn and I return, the gathering of daimónia have converged. My eyes immediately fall on the presence Blaze had been picking up. I know because I sense them now, too.

Huiós-hybrids just like the ones we had stumbled on before. Almost. These, however, are not on the brink of losing their existence except for where our weapons are concerned. These ones are very much animated.

Blaze sets his sights on one and shoots immediately; the arrow barely affects the creature.

"Oh fuck," Blaze gasps, quickly nocking another arrow and shooting. Again, his efforts are nearly ineffective.

The huiós-hybrid he shot — twice — forges ahead, lifts one of my village huiói with a single-arm grip, squeezes his hand around the huiós's neck, and it pops off. Just like that. My hand comes to my mouth.

We're far enough back, arrows able to travel quite the distance, that there is no immediate risk to those of us in this circle, but I turn to Blaze and state, "Tell them to fall back."

"You want to retreat?"

"No. No. They need to back off though."

Blaze nods and delivers the command to the front. Our group immediately begins to recede. The hybrids do not advance on them; they stay within the area we had encroached. Seems they are somehow prevented from crossing an unseen boundary.

The air sparks, and a withheld breath escapes my lungs, my tension seeping away minutely.

But this time, it is not a queen.

Seala pops beside us, a lax Kallias cradled in her arms, Raener present. All that tension returns and amplifies. "Seala. You must go. It... it is too dangerous here." A new fear consumes me. I had been afraid for my huiói... but my daughter? No. She cannot stay.

"Da!" she hollers for Brax and he whips around, eyes instantly wide, head shaking side to side.

"Get out of here!" he bellows.

"No," she says, holding Kallias out toward him. Brax presses his lips together but relieves her of Kallias nonetheless. "Ma." Arms free, she turns to me and takes my hand in hers. "He is expiring, Ma. He will not survive. He will not accept my offer, because he refuses to leave you."

"Is he still communicating with you?" I inquire, glancing at the back of my giant as he walks ahead, Kallias cradled in his arms.

Seala shakes her head. "No. He is beyond that. This is why I brought him here; I knew you would want to see him once more."

"Brax!" My entire body gives out and Blaze catches me as I tumble to the ground, screaming out my giant's name. All of my attending oikía stop as Brax places Kallias between us.

"Seala," I choke out, unable to give Kallias my full attention while she is here and in danger. "You have brought him to me, now you must go."

"I am needed here," she states, standing. "There are huiói to deliver."

I gape up at her, a mix of sadness and terror roiling inside me. "Those of my fighting huiói?" I press my lips together. "We have not yet lost any... not until just a moment ago before I insisted they fall back. And that one is gone... there was no hope for him." The image of his head rolling across the terra flicks into my mind.

Seala takes a step back, and another. "Yes, if I can get to your huiói in time, I will help them. But I am not here for your huiói. Mostly, I am here for the hybrids."

"Seala. Listen to me." I stand to approach her. My eye catches on Sitara, who had apparently shown up while I was so distracted by the arrival of my daughter and expiring déō doúlos.

Sitara's eyes are horrified upon alighting on Kallias. But I cannot address her right now. Focusing on my daughter, I continue, "If you even get near a hybrid, it will expire you; you will not be able to deliver any huiói in need, because you will not exist." Sharing those words twists my heart. I immediately have to put the visual of my existence without Seala out of my thoughts, lest I not be able to function at all.

Seala shakes her head, still so obstinate, lips pressed into a straight line. "I do not know how it will work, all I know is that it will. That this is my calling, and no matter what, I will be given the tools or talents needed to accomplish that for which I am destined."

Brax is squatting low beside Kallias with the others. I meet his gaze over my shoulder, and he stands to join us. "Then you'll not accomplish this calling on your own. Your da will help you. But do not think for one moment he will refrain from expiring a hybrid that should prove a threat. Raener will be in attendance at your side as well."

Brax crosses his arms, imposing. Raener takes my hand in his and lightly drags his thumb over my knuckles, deriving a pleasant, calming warmth.

334

Seala knows there is no stopping this new plan. She simply nods, spins on her heels, and walks away. I reach up, wrap my fingers around Brax's forearm, and simultaneously squeeze Raener's hand. "Protect our daughter." I direct the request to both of them.

"With my existence," Brax states. His arms uncross and he bends down so we are face to face, his clear-blue eyes challenging mine. "You be safe," he begs. "I love you and do not want to come back from helping Seala to be less the woman I love."

I sweep an appreciative regard over my gathered déō doúloi. "I have the best help. And, now, Seala does, too." I take his cheeks in my palms and rub his nose with mine. He tilts his head to the side and kisses me gently. "I love you, too," I whisper.

Raener squeezes my hand tight and lifts it to his mouth to place a small kiss there before letting go. The two run after Seala who now heads in the direction that is guarded by daimónia and hybrids.

I squeeze my eyes closed. Upon opening them, I decide I will not worry myself with her nor Brax. Not yet. Right now, I need to see to Kallias, speak with Sitara, and plan with Blaze.

Sitara does not complain when I choose Kallias over her. She simply finds a spot for her and her attending déō doúloi to wait.

I sit down at Kallias's side and take his hand in mine, eyes tracking over him from his long, twisted hair, to his strong legs. That beautiful skin tone of his is now ashen, much more like the color of the hybrid Blaze had just tried to shoot.

Kallias's eyes are closed, and his chest no longer moves with each breath. I look up at Oryn with watery vision, begging for all the answers. Blaze is who speaks up, though: "I sense him, Adrestia. He is not yet gone to us." My eyebrows curve inward as I look back down at him.

Oryn speaks up now, in response to my silent inquiry a moment ago. "You will know when you lose a déō doúlos. It will cripple you for a time."

Blaze takes my hand and places it on Kallias's chest, covering it with his. Through our hands, he shares the power between us that has not yet been tapped into. "Close your eyes, Basílissa," he instructs. In doing so, I am able to see the image in Blaze's mind: a black, wispy force of some sort floats within Kallias. "His soul," Blaze explains. "That presence I felt earlier, it comes from the hybrids. Unlike the daimónia, these hybrids still have their souls. This is why Seala is here. Right now, Kallias's soul is anxious. Something is changing, manipulating. A conversion; he is almost through with the process. Soon, he will be one of them — one of the hybrids. When that happens, we will not allow him to be near you. In fact, I would feel much better if we drag him to the boundary ahead and leave him with the other hybrids."

My mind and heart reel in confusion. If he becomes a hybrid, I won't physically lose him, but he will still be gone to me all the same. However, I also can't risk the existence of every being around me by leaving him to transform right here. Blaze is right. "Both Kallias and Kirian are to not be touched. I wish to keep my huiói safe, but I will snuff out an offending huiós's existence by my own hand if this order is disobeyed. Mistakes will not be tolerated on this count either." I exchange glances with those who are listening. "Make sure every being is made aware."

No one argues my demands. Together, Oryn and Blaze pick Kallias up to make the journey to the boundary. Before they step away, I whisper all my love for him in his ear and place a kiss on his forehead.

They leave and I turn to Sitara. She waits for me to approach; when I do, her déō doúloi genuflect. I clear my throat and shoot a hesitant glance at their queen. "The loss of a déō doúlos is not something that happens often; my own déō doúloi wish to give their sympathies."

"Thank you," I whisper. "Please stand. I have not yet lost my déō doúlos, but I appreciate the show of respect and kindness."

Sitara must keep her oikía on a tight leash, one that demands none of her déō doúloi speak to another queen. My lips quirk to the side. The men rise, give me a curt nod, and step back to her.

"Thank you for coming to my aid. I see that while I was taking care of a couple things your sikárioi and Watchers acclimated." I now recognize several unfamiliar faces amid the many huiói I had been traveling alongside for the past couple astral rounds.

"Happy to help," she responds.

"Mind if I pull you aside?" I inquire, mostly of her, but the question is also directed to her déō doúloi out of respect. They may be quiet, but I know they have their opinions.

She looks to each and receives a response that is not heard nor seen by me. "Yes, absolutely," she decides.

I lead us to a quiet copse of trees nearby, far enough away from earshot yet visible to both our oikías. "There is a new type of being. A hybrid — the mix between a putrefying huiós and a daimónion. One of my sikárioi attempted to take one down, yet after two shots with the bow, the beast was unaffected."

Sitara raises a single, black eyebrow. After a few more moments of contemplation, she asks, "May I offer a suggestion?"

"Yes, of course. Please do."

"In my limited experience fighting" — she chuckles at this, and I can't help but smile — "it is my understanding that, as with everything in this realm, if a task cannot be completed by a huiós, it is the responsibility of a basílissa — as she would be the only remaining option."

"This makes perfect, logical sense," I respond. "Did you know that when expired by our hand, the daimónia provide energy to the land?"

Sitara huffs, "Huh. No, I did not. You will be hard pressed to find a queen who spends time in the woods wielding a weapon, though."

"Even Kainda? Surely she knows."

"Now *that* is entirely possible. In fact, I'd wager a guess that she would be quite helpful moving forward."

"Can she be trusted?" At this point, I don't know in what way the queens would prove a risk anyway, seeing as we all work and exist within the realm of our individual responsibilities and nothing more. There is not much of a competition between queens, I have noticed. Each is too busy handling her own to bother with the others.

"None of the queens can be trusted, Adrestia," Sitara laughs. "Even I cannot be trusted."

"Ah, I see. Okay, well consider yourself not trusted by me. Just so long as you take down the creatures and not my huiói, there is no harm in a little assistance, I suppose."

Sitara's mouth quirks up in a smile. "You have a deal, Basílissa. So… I must fight today?"

"Yes, you must. Help me cull these hybrids?"

She twirls the power object on her finger. "I will do my best."

"Thank you." I bow my head with a chuckle. When I lift my gaze, it dawns on me that she is without a weapon. Well, not in the fighting sense. Not like the sikárioi. Not like me. Her power object is a piece of jewelry. "Please do not take offense... but you do not carry a weapon of the sort that can pierce a creature. How will you defend against them?"

A wry smirk lifts her lips. "You said they are part huiói, did you not?"

"I did."

Her face turns somber. "You, a part mortal, know better than most how crippling emotions can be. So crippling, in fact, that the strongest of them can convert into physical pain. I can bring these hybrids to their knees — make them beg to be set free from the chains of their emotions. You, Basílissa, can pierce them with your fancy arrow and finish the job."

A pleased grin spreads across my face.

"Adrestia!" This comes from Blaze, who has now returned with Oryn. Sitara and I both turn to face him. "I... I saw Kirian."

My eyes flare wide, and I step toward him, gaze tearing through the grouping of huiói into the direction of the invisible boundary. "Is... is he okay?" I ask, unable to see anything through the obstructions of troops and trees.

"His eyes keep flashing red, blue, red, blue. He's fighting — hard."

My heart does a manic flip. "He's been out here for at least two astral rounds, and still he fights against whatever is trying to control him?"

"Do you blame him? He has something pretty incredible to fight for," Blaze responds.

Again, the memories of our fall come rushing back, and I want to kick that impossible male in the damn shins. "Bring me to him."

Blaze shakes his head. Not to deny me, but out of fear and concern.

"You said this set cannot cross the special boundary, right?" I defend. "Kirian is not like the others; we need to get him on this side. We need to pull him out of the grip that side has on him before it's too late. There's a chance he will see me, sense me, and will come when I call to him. But he'll need the assistance of all my senses to overpower whatever — whomever — it is he fights against."

Blaze gives me a sharp nod. "I asked Oryn to stay there and watch him."

"Thank you for that." I turn to Sitara. "Join us at the front?"

Sitara nods and doubles back to her déō doúloi. Blaze and I clasp hands, but this time he opens the pýlē. The type of pýlēs created by huiói who hold positions have a special type of energy that does not require the terra's reserves. However, they do have different restrictions, such as where and under what circumstances they can travel.

We are taken directly to the boundary; he pulls me back immediately as a huiós-hybrid lunges as though it had been waiting for our arrival. An invisible shield protects us as his teeth gnash a handbreadth from my face.

I flinch at first, but then peer into his red eyes and feel around inside there using Blaze's oikía power to do so. Blaze was right, the soul is there, yet it is different. Heavier. Dense. Thick. Oozing almost.

Kallias's soul was still light and airy. Black all the same, but thinner and... softer. "Where is Kallias?" I inquire.

Blaze nods to a spot several paces away. They must've had to drop him and run; he lies prostrate on the ground just on the other side of this odd boundary. I rush over and drop into a squat, but I don't dare reach out and touch him — I don't dare cross the boundary. Not with our lack of a solid plan just yet.

I do mentally reach for his soul, though. Right now, it hovers somewhere between light and dark. "The transition is almost complete," I whisper.

Blaze holds his hand out, and I accept it. He points just beyond Kallias to a spot in the distance. The number of hybrids and daimónia are scattered throughout the forest, much like the trees. Motionless. Waiting. Except these "trees" breathe.

Amid them, Kirian stands out starkly — his still-huiós skin tone and long hair. The fact that he isn't ashy like the huiós-hybrids relieves me substantially. He is still himself, for lack of comparison; he is still the half-breed daimónion I came to know and love. He just serves a different master right now.

Unlike the still-as-statues hybrids around him, he paces. His hands occasionally come up to the sides of his head and he slaps near his nubs frantically. Occasionally, he'll drop into a squat and squeeze his eyes shut tight. "Belíar... he must be exhausted," I breathe out

"I am beginning to think he never becomes weary," Blaze chuckles. "Remind me to never go head-to-head with him. Ever." For as serious as Blaze usually is, I love how he tries to lighten the mood now.

Oryn approaches my opposite side and I take his hand, too, looking over my shoulder to find Brax and Raener who are nearby with Seala... waiting.

Brax consoles her, his massive arm nearly burying her body beneath it. Raener scans anything and everything. Assessing. Learning. Figuring. Our eyes meet and I jerk my head, indicating for him and Brax to join us.

The five of us line up at the boundary. "We're missing a couple of our oikía," I state through clenched teeth. "Time to take back what is ours. Beginning with Kirian."

CHAPTER FORTY-ONE

I drop Oryn's hand and turn to Blaze. "Give me one of your arrows," I demand, holding my palm up.

Blaze doesn't complain, nor question; he removes an arrow from his quiver and hands it to me. Accepting the arrow, I grab his palm in my opposite hand and slice him open before placing the shaft in the center of his palm along the cut. "I know this one does not have your power inscribed, but I am claiming it as mine — claiming your sense — and I will need this arrow to accomplish the tasks that are to come."

Blaze gives me a firm nod and small smile. The arrow glows as the power sets in, and I make a mental promise that as soon as Kallias is at my side again, I will have him transcribe the sixth sense into this arrow.

Because somehow, even though I don't yet know how, he *will* be by my side again. Before we end our existences in The Void. Together. All of us.

Blaze's arrow nocks perfectly in my bow. I waste no time taking aim at my daimónion. The trick here is that I cannot actually pierce his flesh; he will perish instantly. My arrow tip must pierce his nub, since that part of him is not pumping with essence like the rest.

I use our intertwined auditory power to attempt soothing him from a distance through the power of speech — just enough to where he will, hopefully, stop pacing and hunching. To keep him still long enough for me to aim with less risk to his existence. "Brax... help me deliver my scent," I request of my giant. Together,

Brax and I focus on enticing Kirian — on pulling his attention toward us just long enough for me to make the shot. To strengthen our efforts, I attempt speaking to him using a mental connection like the lógos might.

:kirian:

The response is immediate. Kirian slings his head around and begins to spin in a circle, seeking out the sound of my voice. When his head tilts back, nose pointing somewhat upward, I can tell Brax's olfactory powers have worked. Kirian's spinning stops and he faces us, having caught the whiff of my essence on the light breeze.

:be still:

My daimónion does exactly as he is told, and I let the arrow go before I overanalyze and lose my element of instinct and self trust.

The arrow pierces straight through his nub, sticking out on either side, front to back.

The force of the hit pitches Kirian to his back. He sits up, shaking his head. The rapid-fire eye color changes, leaving his eyes that familiar ocean-blue.

"Oh shit," Blaze explicates. "You... you removed Belíar's influence on him. The hybrids no longer sense him as one of their own."

All the surrounding hybrids turn toward Kirian and several lunge synchronously.

Kirian rolls to the side, scarcely avoiding the attack of one in particular. He manages to make it to his feet, eyes meeting mine. Calculative. They scan us, passing over the hybrids that pace to and fro in front of our line but don't touch us.

:cross the line:

Kirian falls into a crouch and one of the hybrids sails over him, missing its mark. He takes in one deep breath and, on the exhale, charges forward.

He is fast. I have never seen him run like this, but it is almost as though he's an animated pýlē. In mere heartbeats, Kirian is stumbling into our side of the boundary, caught at the ankle by a hybrid. Brax bends down and takes him by the wrists, yanking him the rest of the way in. However, the hybrid stays attached.

"Basílissa!" Sitara yells from somewhere over my shoulder. "Let's test our idea while we have a chance!" By the time her comment is delivered, she is at my side.

Kirian brawls with the hybrid. Having seen what it did to the huiós, my entire body becomes so taut, my limbs shake from the strain.

Blaze steps next to me and brushes his shoulder against mine — a quiet reminder that I cannot shoot if I am tight. I take a deep breath and ready my bow with an arrow.

In my periphery, on my opposite side, the unmistakable glow of Sitara's ring expands and pulsates. She extends her hand and aims the face of her ring toward Kirian and the hybrid. "I... I..." She stutters, hand shaking. "I am going to have to hit both of them."

"If it will not expire my déō doúlos, you have my permission."

She gives a sharp nod and the ring emits a beam of emotional energy, clashing into the feuding creatures.

Both males fall to their backs in an instant. Shocked. Stunned. Something.

I pull the string back tight, aim, and shoot.

But, I miss.

Again, Blaze brushes against me. I'm too wrapped up in my head — afraid for my daimónion. Worried about what Sitara did to him. Worried that if this hybrid gets up first, Kirian won't be able to defend himself.

I pull another arrow and try again. Closing my eyes, I focus on the feel of everything: Blaze brushed up against me; The tickle of the fletching; The tautness of the line. When I open my eyes, aim, and loose, the hybrid stills instantly.

His energy does not effervesce into the ground as expected, though. He convulses and seizes. His back arches and a thick, black ooze seeps out of him. Instead of into the ground, though, it rises into the air. My eyes widen as his soul leaves his vessel. Seala rushes forward and falls to his side.

Oryn steps to my other side where Sitara had just stood, his focus locked on my reaction. "What… what is wrong?"

"Y-can you not see that?" I ask.

Oryn looks the scene over again. Seala's fingers ghost through the mire.

"I see it, too," Blaze says. "A result of the power we now hold?"

"None of you can see the soul leaving his body?" I ask louder this time, turning in a circle to take in all the heads that shake side to side.

When I return my attention to the huiós-hybrid, the soul crashes back down and his vessel jerks. Seala scoops him into her arms and flies away instantaneously. She… she forced his soul back inside…

Stunned, the group of us stare, mouths agape, at the now-empty spot. Movement finally pulls me from the momentary astonishment and my focus falls on Sitara, now kneeling beside Kirian, hands on his chest. One of her déō doúloi, has a grip on her shoulder as she pushes some sort of energy into my daimónion. Kirian shoots up into a sitting position with a gasp, and Sitara falls back onto her butt.

His eyes immediately find mine, and the two of us rush toward each other, falling into a tangle on the ground. He hovers over me and bends down for a kiss. His eyes flash. Not red... but with recognition.

Both of our features transform into frustration and impatience, and we quickly separate and stand, squaring off. "You were not supposed to follow me!" I yell, uncaring who sees my fit.

"You were not supposed to Fall!" he yells back.

The moment of my Fall rushes back to both of us in an instant. Before all the chaos of the realms today. The Maker had a plan. A plan that would ultimately bring most every being through the sufferings of mortal life and back to Him, exalted.

I know, because I was there when this plan was delivered — a spiritual head bobbing in the crowd of beings during that pinnacle moment when Elysium became divided.

This division happened because not every being was on board with His plan.

That... is where Kirian and I come into play. Partners in Elysium, but always at odds between what was right and wrong. Always at odds... about everything, really.

When The Maker expelled all the beings who had taken Belíar's side — those in agreement to an alternative plan — Kirian was part of that group.

The ground shook. The realm quaked. The Maker would no longer allow anyone against him to be there. Those on Belíar's side were consumed by an abyss — sent to Tartarus for an eternity.

I loved Kirian; I could not imagine my existence without him. Worse, I couldn't fathom him suffering for an eternity. *That* is what broke me more. So... I pushed him aside and took The Fall on his behalf.

I sacrificed myself, so he could remain safe and unharmed in Elysium. I was an angel, meant for life as a human. He was an angel meant to Fall.

My efforts and sacrifice were all for naught... because he jumped in after me.

I don't have the memories of our sufferings in Tartarus, but I know they happened. In the end, though, I know we suffered them together. And, I have a strong feeling we were quite pissed off at each other during that incredibly long existence in chains.

The anger and frustration resulting from these returned memories slams us both hard. But... our existence here does, too.

In an instant, we're in each other's arms engaged in a crushing kiss.

"Don't ever fucking try to save my existence again," he growls.

"Nice try. You couldn't stop me then, and you can't stop me now."

"You know what?" he says, stepping back from me. "It's a damn good thing you never became a true human. Those mortals wouldn't have been able to handle you."

"Yeah... good thing, I guess."

We both smile and burst into laughter. "Do you think this is what it was like with us in Elysium?" I ask.

"Probably." His face becomes somber. "When you Fell" — he shakes his head — "I couldn't... Drea... I couldn't handle it. It debilitated me. All I could do was stare down at you and... and I wanted to be gone from the realms forever without you there. I didn't know where Falling behind you would lead me — us. All I knew was that I wouldn't find out unless I tried. By not trying, I was guaranteed a permanent existence without you."

"I was so upset. So scared," I explain. "When you jumped in after me. So... angry." The thought has my body trembling with that phantom rage.

He closes the distance between us again and wraps his arms around me. I immediately bury my head into his chest. Even his hugs are different now. "Well... if it's any consolation, I guess I am glad we both did what we did," he whispers.

"Yeah." I squeeze him tighter, harder. But not for much longer, because two sparks happen around us concurrently, and we jolt apart.

Both Seala and Sitara enter the realm at the same time. As they become adjusted, I take a moment to look around me again. Brax, Oryn, and Raener all stare at us, equally as stunned with the reunion as they were with the disappearance of Seala and the hybrid.

Raener runs a hand through his hair and... laughs. "Too bad you all didn't get those memories back sooner. Sure would have answered a lot of our questions."

Oryn shakes his head in disbelief.

Brax... just looks utterly confused.

Sitara approaches me, having apparently left while Kirian and I were reuniting, in a sense. "I had to feed," she explains.

I turn to her and wrap my arms around her shoulders. "Thank you for helping him," I whisper.

She nods and hugs me back. "I like these," she says.

"What?"

"Your hugs, they are different from hugging a male. You are... softer."

Over several moon-cycles, I have hugged my daughter many times, so this is not an unfamiliar sensation, but Sitara is right. A chuckle leaves me as I break out of the hug and step back. "We have some hybrids to take down," I state, and she nods.

"Hold still, Beast!" Blaze growls, and my attention whirls to him. Blaze and Kirian are presently engaged in... something that looks oddly like a headlock. I tilt my head to the side and assess the situation. Blaze is attempting to pull his arrow from Kirian's nub while he flails wildly.

Brax is nearby, all the color drained from his face — a sign of fainting I have learned all too well.

Cupping my hand around the side of my mouth I yell, "Raener! Heads-up!"

Raener reacts instantly, stepping to the side as Brax goes tumbling down like a cut tree. A huge grin spreads across his face. When my attention returns to Blaze, he is smiling quite large, too.

"Never gets old," the two of them say in unison.

Raener takes it one step further by sitting on Brax's chest and... waiting... ever so patiently for him to regain consciousness.

"Thank goodness for that boundary," I chuckle, shaking my head side to side, reminding everyone that we're mere feet away from huiós-hybrids who are ready to attack.

"Your oikía is quite possibly the most entertaining oikía I have ever engaged with," Sitara laughs.

Oryn and Sitara share a quick look. She smiles and he nods. I am not sure the meaning exactly, but I don't feel any sense of threat from the exchange. It does remind me that she had to release him in order for what he and I now have to be possible. "Seems I owe you more than one 'thank you'," I mention.

She turns her attention away from Oryn back to me. "Now, for that" — she flicks a glance up and down Oryn's body — "yes, you do."

Oryn rolls his eyes and comes to my side, slipping his hand around my waist. "You gonna let another queen look at me like that?" he whispers in my ear.

"Yes," I whisper back. "So she can imagine all the things you're going to do to me... and not her." Oryn chuckles. "You're enjoying this. Being had by one queen, and coveted by another."

"Well, I'm definitely not complaining," he responds.

A raspy groan draws our attention back toward my sleeping giant. He peeks one eye open, followed by the next, before narrowing his gaze on Raener.

"How does it feel with my stones on your chest, Grigori?" Raener asks with a grin.

"Light," Brax quips back as he slings him off and Raener nearly goes flying. Brax pushes off the ground and a shiver of repulsion shakes through him as he swats at the spot on his chest where Raener was sitting. "Ugh, I've never felt so dirty in all my existence. I even reek of you!" His nose crunches upward and he gags. Like a real gag.

Despite knowing we're about to engage in quite the battle, everyone bursts into laughter. Even Seala. It's a nice moment amid the dour circumstances.

Alas, all nice moments must eventually come to an end. The laughter dies, all of my oikía missing the boisterous and contagious laugh and smile often provided by Kallias.

As if on cue, as if the thought is collective, we all turn toward his resting spot.

Empty.

My gaze sweeps between the trees, landing on every huiós-hybrid's face along the way. Each of my attending déō doúloi join in doing the same.

Kallias is nowhere to be seen.

My heart drops into my stomach with a dull thud and I stagger a little. Oryn had explained that I would know, without a doubt, if he has left me permanently, though.

And I don't know that for a certainty, so I can assume he is still out here, now a converted hybrid.

A whimper and sniffle comes from nearby and my attention turns to Seala. I approach her and wrap her in my arms. All my déō doúloi join us, each of her fathers finding some way to console, whether it be by a simple touch or whispered words.

"His soul does not want redemption, Ma," she cries. "It will go to The Void; we'll lose him forever."

A debilitating sadness pours over me. It is with a heavy heart that I have to admit my next thought aloud: "Down here, we don't get forever."

CHAPTER FORTY-TWO

"**B**ut in Elysium, he can," Seala hiccups. "And what of the rest of us? The rest of his oikía?" I dart a look at Kirian. "We cannot go to Elysium. None of us are eligible. Why would Kallias want to be the only one sent there to exist forever, leaving us as nothing more than a long-lost memory."

It is through my own words that I now understand why Kallias chose to stay — why we all would likely choose that same fate if presented the opportunity. Similar to why Kirian jumped into the abyss after me.

Raener wraps his arm around her, and I step back to let them have a moment. "You cannot save them all, and by giving them the ability to choose, you have given them an amazing gift. Kallias — like the rest of us — has spent an entire existence doing Belíar's bidding. We are given only one opportunity — that of a binding — to make our own choice. He chose your Ma. And now, since he was eligible, you have gifted him something very few huiói will ever be gifted. I can only imagine how hard it was for him to decline. But, I can also imagine how overwhelmed he felt having been given the choice at all. You are a great blessing to The Fallen here in Ceteris. So, on Kallias's behalf, since he cannot tell you himself... thank you."

I turn my head away, working my throat over a tight swallow and blinking to clear the blur of tears. Unable to stand there any longer, lest I be forced to grieve something I am not yet ready to grieve, I walk away and join Sitara's side instead. She waits for my shaky breaths to steady and the tears in my eyes to dry.

When ready, I state, "Well… our idea seems to have worked." She nods, and I continue, "But you had to feed after? Does it use too much of your energy to be able to help me with more than one at a time?"

"Oh, no. The energy drop was due to the counter-influence I performed on Kirian so he didn't have to suffer longer."

"What did you hit him with?"

Sitara winces. "Loss. Heartbreak."

My hand clasps over my own chest as I study Kirian; his eyes are locked on me as though he fears if he looks away he'll never see me again. I give him my best reassuring smile. He gives me one in return.

I realize in this moment that I really missed him. Us. The us *before* The Fall. But that was also the us that never fucked, and I like the "fucking us" quite a lot, too.

Sitara speaks up again, "I didn't want to risk it not working, so I used a bit… much. With each hit, I'll kick it down a notch, until I am using the bare minimum to get the job done."

"Okay, that sounds great. I have six arrows, so six shots before I have to collect. Sometimes, whoever is with me will grab them as I go, though, which will make the transition a bit quicker. When we start, I would like to try bypassing your part to see if a single hit from me works."

Sitara listens intently to these new details.

"Can your déō doúloi use their power similar to how you can? I am a little concerned with the sustainability of this plan. You and I will tire expiring them all out on our own. Plus, it'll take too long. We will need breaks, crossing the boundary over and over again in between."

Kirian, with his auditory power, overhears the conversation and approaches, head and torso bowed toward our guest queen. Sitara clears her throat, releasing him. He turns to address me. "While your new arrow was in my nub" — he rubs the nub in memory — "it cut me off from the lógos's influence. That is how I was able to break free. If I cross that boundary line, though, there is a chance I will be influenced again."

"I know you would like to fight with us but I understand your need to stay on this side of the boundary, and I am fine with that. Perhaps keep an eye out for any rogues we may have missed, or any hybrid coming in toward whatever is pulling them this direction?"

"There is an underground spring and cave system. It is there where you will find some answers," he reveals.

"Did you—"

"No, I fought the pull in that direction. But all these hybrids are being controlled from there. The lógos gets louder and stronger when in closer proximity to that spot. Do not let your energy get too low, Adrestia," he warns, knowing the lógos will address me when my energy wanes.

"Thank you." I place my hand on his shoulder, and he bends down to give me a quick kiss. "Be—"

"Be safe. Yes… I know," I whisper.

He lets out a breath and nods before leaving to rejoin my other déō doúloi.

I turn back to Sitara. "Let's go do a couple runs. I will tackle the first one solo, just on the other side of the boundary. Then… we reassess."

Sitara nods and we both return to the main group.

355

"Brax and Kirian, work together to deliver this message to the huiói awaiting orders. Brax's voice is quite loud enough, but with your influence, Kirian, it should reach every necessary being." The two men nod and await my instruction.

"As of right now, we no longer have use for the troops; they are no match for hybrids. Sitara and I will do a couple trial runs to test some theories and go from there. Kirian will stay out here and work side by side with the huiói to keep on the lookout for rogues and journeying hybrids. Brax and Raener are sticking with Seala. Oryn, and Blaze... I would like you both to be at my side or taking my back at all times."

Blaze claps his hands together. This is his element, fighting and gore. The excitement is evident in the spark of his eyes.

Everyone breaks apart to handle their assigned duties. While Brax and Kirian work together to deliver instructions to all remaining huiói, Sitara and I, along with our attending déō doúloi, approach the boundary in a section where there isn't an immediate threat, giving me enough room to step over, make the shot, and step back.

"Oryn, you take my back. Stay on this side of the boundary. Pull me out if I can't do it fast enough myself." Oryn nods. "Blaze, you're coming with me. To... I don't know.... slaughter something in the absolute worst-case scenario — if my hit misses its mark or something tries to attack me in the process. But do not stay in there; you leave when I leave, unless compromised. Make a kill shot once, but don't collect your arrow. This attempt is all about gauging what might work and what doesn't." Blaze nods in agreement.

When he had shot the hybrid earlier, I had wondered whether or not the ineffectiveness had anything to do with the barrier, so this plan will also double to resolve that open-ended question.

Without another word of unnecessary explanation, I ready my bow, select my target, step across the threshold, shoot, and step backward out of the barrier again as the arrow sails through the air.

Blaze takes the same approach, and our arrows hit separate hybrids. His target doesn't budge; the arrow pierces between his horns and he simply stands there unfazed. My target, on the other hand, drops to his knees but nothing more

Ready for round two, I set my bow and arrow, step forward again, shoot him a second time, and exit. At this shot, he collapses.

We all watch from a distance as his soul does the same thing Blaze and I witnessed a bit ago. Seala moves to run toward him, every intrinsic part of her being unable to resist, but Brax holds her back. "No, Seala. We need a plan first. You must let a few go while we figure everything out," he explains.

War wages in her green-gold eyes, but she ultimately nods and Brax lets her go. Seala, Blaze, and I watch the soul leave his body and ascend until it is simply no more — dispersed into the air. Invisible. Again, I traverse across the boundary, shoot, and step back. My target finally feeds the terra, body shaking and melting as his essence converts to energy and seeps into the ground.

"Three arrows per hybrid," I deliver the words on a groan. "Two, if Sitara handles the first part. That's still… that's still not a sustainable plan." I wrack my mind, digging in my exhausted information base.

It takes a couple moments, but a new idea strikes, triggered by something Kirian had said just a bit ago about my new arrow having cut him off from the lógos.

Three arrows remain, one of which is the newest arrow that Blaze had slipped back into my quiver during one of my conversations with Sitara.

I pull the arrow and hold both it and my bow down at my side. "I have used sound more than once to create somewhat of a bubble or shielding effect," I begin to convert this new idea verbally, "I wonder if perhaps the sixth-sense arrow can be shot into the middle of congregating hybrids with the hope that it cuts them off from Belíar's influence long enough for a single attack to get the job done. The daimónia are similarly connected to the lógos, but I have a feeling this boundary, and these hybrids, have garnered this unusual strength via means relating to the lógos directly. If this plan works, we will be able to take them down just like we did with the daimónia, and in groups."

"So, you create the shield, we attack within it, then you finish them off for the energy?" Blaze summarizes.

"Yes, exactly."

"How can I help with this new plan?" Sitara inquires.

I turn to my remaining déō doúloi and scan their weapons. Brax's sword is far too big. Similar to Oryn, Raener wields a small dagger. I hate to leave him without a weapon, should he need one, but he has Brax, and Brax is a weapon in and of himself.

So, I jog up to Raener, explain to him the new plan, and he gives it up easily. I return to my group and place the hilt in Sitara's hand.

"Two-part attack," I explain. "You hit them with your power so you're not having to approach each too closely. When they're down, you stab them with the dagger — between the horns or over the heart."

Sitara's eyes flare.

Blaze grins wide.

Oryn laughs.

Sitara raises an eyebrow at him right along with the lift of her chin. "Do you question my ability?" she asks her former próskairos. Oryn's laugh fades and he shakes his head emphatically. "Good," she says, stepping close to him and pressing the tip of the dagger to his throat.

Oryn's eyes find me, his eyebrows curving inward. "Oh ho ho… nope. You brought this on yourself," I state with a chuckle.

Sitara grins and steps back, studying the dagger in her hand. When I glance at her déō doúloi, they both look positively worry stricken. My déō doúloi are quite accustomed to my hands-on ways of dealing with things. But Sitara, despite seeming fine with the transition, clearly hasn't fought in this manner a single day in her existence.

"Blaze. Oryn." Both men turn their attention toward me. "When it comes to her safety and her existence, treat her as though she were me, and help her déō doúloi should they need help in keeping her from too much harm."

My men agree easily, and her déō doúloi appear to relax a bit at the thought.

"Do they have tongues?" I ask.

Sitara laughs. "Oh yes, and they are excellent at using them. When we're in Acedia. On my pallet."

"That's not what—never mind." I don't bother to ask any further. She shrugs with a smile.

I lift my bow and nock the arrow. "Time to try, shall we?"

Everyone lines up along the boundary. I scan the area, bow nocked at my side. This time I pick a group that is closer, since we will need to stay inside the boundary longer. A group of three. I tilt my head in that direction to make sure everyone is of a like mind.

Together, we all step forward once, trespassing over the threshold.

Blaze intuitively places his hand on my shoulder to aid in the use of this newly garnered power as I aim and shoot. The arrow lands in the terra between the hybrids and we all dash forward.

Sitara pushes her energy into one target, I nock another arrow and shoot a different one, and Oryn rushes forward and brings the third down by cutting him deep along the shin. Blaze aids in incapacitating Oryn's target by pinning the hybrid's hand into the terra with an arrow.

My target passes on to The Void instantly, his energy nourishing the land just moments after. Sitara bounds forward and stabs her target between the horns. I step to the third hybrid and finish him off. From there, we all naturally form a back-to-back ring, our bodies intuitively moving in a big circle as though we are one.

That attack took just long enough to draw the attention of several other hybrids. The plan worked beautifully, but we are now surrounded.

Not only did my arrow make them vulnerable like we wanted, it also formed a shield around us preventing the others from getting inside. When one tries to launch forward, his body bounds back.

The problem this poses, is that we can't quite get to them—

Wait.

I pull my third, and final, arrow. My lips curve into a frown as I look down and realize it is Kallias's. I had subconsciously avoided using it — symbolically keeping it close. Unwilling to let it fly free.

Thankfully, for this idea, I won't have to; I grip the shaft in a tight fist, close to the arrow, and I break away from our small circle to come nose-to-nose with one of the hybrids that attempts to reach us. Lifting my hand, I shove the arrow through the barrier and between his horns. When he drops, the arrow pulls out with a wet *squelch*.

I don't even have to explain what to do next. The group spreads out, everyone who is able to do so taking on a hybrid. As soon as this congregation is at our feet, I select the next area for us to move — the one where my other three arrows are waiting. Blaze and I quickly collect our nearby arrows and quiver them.

As soon as I pick up that sixth arrow, the shield drops. Before too much time passes, I nock it again and shoot before neighboring hybrids realize the opportunity.

We all run to the next area and perform the same motions all over.

This is how it goes — over and over again in this manner — for a long, long while.

At some point, we begin to see Seala, Brax, and Raener sprinting to and fro. It isn't until we've cleared a sizable area, though, that I am able to briefly witness Seala's efforts.

She's faster now — scooping a huiós, voyaging to wherever it is she travels, and coming back within mere heartbeats. Most of the huiói are not eligible, I surmise, so she is able to keep this pacing.

In an effort to make sure she accomplishes what she needs to accomplish, and to give these huiói the gift Raener had mentioned, I keep my personal kill shots to a minimum whenever possible. The rest of my team brings them to the brink for me to go back through on our way out, during the cleanup efforts.

.Seala, Brax, and Raener follow our path, making things as streamlined as possible.

When we arrive close to the spring Kirian had mentioned — as per Blaze's navigational skills — the truthfulness of Kirian's assessment is evident in the concentrated amount of opposition: the remaining hybrids saturate the area, assembling in one spot, as though there is some sort of thing creating and placing them there, in a shared location.

"Well," I whisper. "That's not the approach I would have taken personally."

This… is going to be easy.

As we had done too many times to count at this point, I aim my new arrow at a clear piece of terra near them and embed it in the ground there.

Again, we all rush ahead. There are more in this grouping, and my shield is bigger. But I am tired. We all are. And I don't intend on doing this again this astral round.

In this battle, we will finish the last of them.

We break the barrier, weapons everywhere all at once. Sitara's déō doúloi stand back a distance, making sure she has a constant influx of power generating. After the first couple tries, I gave them permission to use as much of my territory's energy as needed, if it was available; that way she wouldn't be using her own reserves and risking an energy drop.

The ones Oryn and Blaze take down, I leave for Seala to check-in with. I stick to killing in the moment only if I absolutely must. Mostly, to protect one of my group from being compromised while they are engaged with another.

One such instance, though, throws me. Sitara takes one down with her power object and is going in for the kill when the flash of long, knotted hair catches my eyes. A screech tears from my lungs, but my yell doesn't reach her in time. Her dagger pierces Kallias's head, and he collapses to the ground. Sitara falls backward hand covering her mouth, and I stumble forward.

"Keep fighting!" I yell at the rest of them, crawling on hands and knees toward him, tears streaming down my face and onto the ground. I scoop my hands under his arms, drag him toward the embedded sixth arrow, keeping us as close as possible to the source of protection, and lay his head in my lap.

Draping my hands over him, I rock us back and forth. A wail shreds out from my chest, and I heave to breathe. A tug pulls my center, and I wipe my eyes to look down at him. His soul, black, thick, and oozing, transudes from his chest and I feel it in my own vessel. His soul is being taken and... and... it feels like my own is. A deep-rooted ache twists around me, smothering every sense.

"Blaze!" I yell, but it comes out as nothing more than a hiccup. "No!" I scream, placing my hands above the apparition. My entire body shakes and my heart stutters with each bellowing cry. "Kallias. Kallias. Kallias." I say his name over and over again, gripping at the only remaining part of the man I love, trying so desperately to claw at his soul, to pull it back in. To clutch it and hold it against my chest.

Blaze slides along the ground at my side and he takes my hands in his. Our energy hums — speaks to us. With our hands together, my fingers catch on the soul. They actually catch. With wide eyes, I join Blaze in watching as we stop his soul from rising any higher — from disappearing into the sky.

An incantation hums and vibrates in my mind, words I have never heard before, but that are loud and clear now. I whisper the words, over and over, and his soul begins to settle back down until it is inside his body again.

My hands frantically move over every inch of him, aching to touch everywhere all at once — to make sure he is intact. His soul is here, but he is still physically debilitated. His body... is not functioning. Blaze steps back, stumbling, and he calls for Oryn. The two trade places. As soon as Oryn is by my side, I know exactly what must be done.

Pulling energy from the land, I use it and my own to heal Kallias — to restart his heart and weave together the wound in his head.

It takes a lot of effort, a lot of the energy for which we had worked so incredibly hard to replenish my land. But if I use my own, it will require a feed, and he will regress; I would be forced to do it all over again.

As a result, selfishly, I steal from my own land. Steal from it to bring one of my déō doúloi back to me.

Even in using this borrowed energy, though, it still drops my own to dire levels. Something I know Kirian warned against. Especially this close to the cave.

Only when I feel the first couple beats of Kallias's heart do I stop. Only then. Not before.

Unsurprisingly, that voice whispers in my ear.

:come to me:

It's so close. I whip around, convinced it was said right beside my head.

:come to me:

I do. I stand. Oryn tries to pull me down. Blaze's insistent yells try to redirect me. He can hear it, too. I know he can. Nevertheless, my body moves toward the cave of its own accord.

All they can do is follow me, because when they touch me, the hélkō punishes them.

When we enter into the cave, what we find within is absolutely nothing we could have expected.

A female — one I certainly don't recognize — sits in a circle of flickering light, eyes closed, mouth moving in an incantation. The same incantation I just used to save Kallias's life.

"Vialla," Sitara whispers.

Vialla, dark in skin tone, much like how I envisioned Kainda might be but slightly lighter. Only slightly. Dark enough that if it weren't for the circle of small flames surrounding her, she would be hidden in the dim cave. Her hair is long and black like Sitara's yet somewhat frizzy like mine, just not as curly.

Upon hearing her name, Vialla's eyes open, shining an enthralling light purple. Violet. Such a contrast to her overall darkness. Bright. Vibrant. Glowing almost.

She narrows a glare on our group and reaches a hand toward the back of her head.

"Get down!" Sitara yells.

We all drop to our stomachs just as Vialla throws a multi-pointed weapon at us and scarcely misses.

"Not... ready." A raspy voice echoes through the cave, sending chills down my spine. "Must... leave."

Vialla darts a glance over her shoulder toward a darkened corner as she stands.

A daimónion.

Or perhaps it's a hybrid.

Maybe a bit of everything all rolled into one.

Whatever the creature is, it steps out from the darkness, rivaling Brax in size, yet more like Raener in girth.

Vialla reaches her hand out, he takes it, and they back away into the dark corner. As they do so she waves her free hand and all the small fires poof out, shrouding us in utter blackness.

TO BE CONTINUED

ABOUT THE AUTHOR

Adell Ryan is a hubby/wife pseudonym. Adell writes unconventional love stories about fierce women and their numerous male suitors. Because let's be honest, we need more than one to satisfy our multi-dimensional needs. Right? Ryan simply puts up with Adell's crazy fantasies and toots her horn regularly. Occasionally he'll add in a shoulder pat, and a deep, sexy "Damn that's good stuff."

That southern boy (bless him) stole this northern girl's heart and they live together in the deep south, raising their three boys. When Adell isn't writing she's homeschooling — primarily working on dictation, making sure they say 'creek' instead of 'crick' and 'fire' instead of 'fer.' She also dabbles in photography and graphic design. Oh yeah, and reading. Every. Night. Much to Ryan's dismay. Sometimes she puts the steamy stuff down and gives him a quick kiss on the forehead though.

To be the *first* to know about new releases and exclusive behind-the-scenes stuff, join the fun in her Facebook Group: facebook.com/groups/authoradellryan/

You can also check out her website at https://www.adellryan.com and sign-up for her newsletter.

Still not enough? Find her at the listed social media platforms as well!:

| Goodreads | Instagram | Pinterest |
| BookBub | Twitter | Patreon |

Made in the USA
Coppell, TX
23 June 2020